To History teachers.
History was my favourite subject at
school – and has been ever since

TIME
AND TIME AGAIN

www.**transworldbooks**.co.uk

TIME
AND TIME AGAIN

Ben Elton

BANTAM PRESS

LONDON • TORONTO • SYDNEY • AUCKLAND • JOHANNESBURG

TRANSWORLD PUBLISHERS
61–63 Uxbridge Road, London W5 5SA
A Random House Group Company
www.rbooks.co.uk

First published in Great Britain
in 2014 by Bantam Press
an imprint of Transworld Publishers

A CIP catalogue record for this book
is available from the British Library.

ISBNs 9780593073568 (cased)
9780593073575 (tpb)

Addresses for Random House Group Ltd companies outside the UK
can be found at: www.randomhouse.co.uk
The Random House Group Ltd Reg. No. 954009

The Random House Group Limited supports The Forest Stewardship
Council® (FSC®), the leading international forest-certification organization.
All our titles that are printed on Greenpeace-approved FSC®-certified paper
carry the FSC logo. Our paper procurement policy can be found at
www.rbooks.co.uk/environment

Typeset in 11/14.5pt Sabon by Falcon Oast Graphic Art Ltd.
Printed and bound in Australia by
Griffin Press

2 4 6 8 10 9 7 5 3 1

MIX
Paper from
responsible sources
FSC® C016897
www.fsc.org

www.randomhouse.com.au
www.randomhouse.co.nz

Historical note

In 1687 Sir Isaac Newton published his *Principia*, a work generally acknowledged to be the most influential publication in the history of science. In the book, Newton described his three laws of motion and thus revolutionized human understanding of the physical universe.

Six years later in 1692 Newton suffered a nervous breakdown. The symptoms included insomnia, deep depression and debilitating paranoia. This crisis in Newton's life is known as his 'Black Year', a period during which even his closest friends and associates thought he had gone insane.

Newton eventually recovered his mental faculties but had seemingly lost all interest in science. He turned his attention instead to the study of alchemy and the search for hidden meanings in the Bible.

In 1696 he became a civil servant, taking an administrative job at the Royal Mint. The world's greatest physicist, mathematician and natural philosopher was to remain in this position until his death, thirty years later.

The cause of Newton's breakdown and his subsequent retirement from science was not known during his lifetime and remained a mystery thereafter.

Newton's Epitaph by Alexander Pope:

> *Nature and nature's laws lay hid in night;*
> *God said, 'Let Newton be' and all was light.*

1

IN CONSTANTINOPLE, on a bright, chill early morning in June
1914, Hugh Stanton, retired British army captain and professional adventurer, leant against the railings of the Galata Bridge
and stared into the waters below. There was a stiff breeze blowing
and the early light sparkling on the gun-metal river made the
choppy crests twinkle like stars.

Stanton half closed his eyes and forgot for a moment that this
was the mouth of the Bosphorus, ancient sewer of Byzantium, and
imagined instead a heavenly firmament. A faraway galaxy dotted
with infinite points of divine light. A gateway to an incandescent
oblivion.

Opening his eyes wide once more he saw the river for the
poisonous shit soup that it was and turned away. If he ever did
decide to kill himself a bullet would be quicker and a great deal
cleaner.

The morning traffic creaked and rattled across the newly
metalled bridge and Stanton found his eye focusing on a woman
in a burka on the opposite side. She had been bending low over
the sweets and pastries on display at a coffee stall and now she
turned away, a billowing black cloud followed by a small girl and
an even smaller boy, both clutching paper bags into which they
dipped sugar-coated fingers.

Stanton realized to his surprise that he was crying. Tears that
had been prickling behind his eyes for months were all of a
sudden glistening on his cheeks. Those children were so very like

his own. Different colouring and clothing, of course, but in scale and attitude they could have been his Tess and Bill. Even the way the little girl put her hand on her brother's shoulder to restrain him at the kerb, so proud of being the older and the wiser of the two. That was exactly what Tess would have done. Probably all big sisters were like that.

Angrily he wiped a sleeve across his cheek. He didn't believe in self-pity. Not under any circumstances.

Just then the peace of the morning was disturbed by the throaty roar of an engine as on to the bridge from the northern side skidded an overloaded, open-topped tourer. Stanton recognized the model, a Crossley 20/25. Cars were a passion for him and he knew every British type ever built. The occupants of this one were all young men, well-heeled hooligans on a spree, braying and hollering, clearly still drunk from the night before. *Feringi*. Foreigners bent on mischief, coming down from the Pera district where the Westerner was king.

Pedestrians scurried for the pavements as the car clattered across the bridge, the driver beeping his horn and shouting as if this busy public thoroughfare were his own private driveway. Stanton heard English voices, merry laughter laced with effortless contempt. They were embassy staff perhaps, or servicemen in mufti; the British had a lot of military in town, advising the sultan on how to drag his army and navy into the twentieth century. Or, more importantly, trying to stop His Munificence from seeking advice on such matters from the Germans.

The young Muslim family who had been occupying Stanton's attention were in the process of crossing the street when the car came into view, Mother concentrating on ensuring that the children avoided the various piles of horse dung that lay in their path. Now she swept up the boy with one arm and grabbed the girl with her other and began to hurry them towards the opposite side, a scurrying black flurry of burka and kids.

But then the little girl dropped her bag and, being only about seven and not quite as grown-up and mature as she liked to think,

2

pulled away from her mother to retrieve it. The mother turned back in panic and now the whole family stood in the path of the oncoming car.

The massive machine bore down on them. Nearly fourteen feet long and six wide, it seemed to completely fill the bridge. Almost a ton and a half of wood, glass, rubber, brass and steel, a monster, roaring and trumpeting as it approached its kill, the great shining black fender arches framing its huge goggling eyes. The thrusting tusks of its sprung-leaf suspension threatened to skewer any soft flesh and young bone that lay in its path. Black smoke billowed from its rear. Sparks spat from behind its grille. No dragon of ancient legend could have seemed more terrifying or more deadly.

The monster was still perhaps some fifteen yards away from the terrified mother trying to hang on to the squirming little boy while pulling at the girl, who was frozen with fear. Any car Stanton had ever driven would still have had ample time to brake. But this was a very different type of machine, with primitive steel and asbestos disc brakes fitted only to the rear wheels. What was more, the stunned-looking youth at the wheel was drunk, and the road was wet with morning mist and covered in slippery horse dung. Even if the driver did manage to hit the brake, the wheels would lock and the beast would surely skid wildly for tens of yards, taking the woman and her little children with it.

These thoughts occurred to Stanton all at once and only in the most fleeting and compressed form for his whole being was already in motion, his body accelerating away from the railing against which he had been leaning with all the energy of a man who by both instinct and training kept himself in a state of permanent physical readiness.

The young mother turned, her coal-black almond eyes staring out from the letterbox window of her face covering, wide with terror as Stanton, having covered most of the distance between them, launched himself into a long dive with arms spread wide. He hit them perhaps a half second before the car would have done, he and the little family passing in front of the oncoming machine with so little time to spare that the fender knocked Stanton's foot as it swept by. He felt himself turning in mid-air, the family still gathered in his arms, causing the whole group to spin almost full circle as they crashed down on to the stones together.

The monster bumped and skidded on its way, horn still tooting and its braying occupants shouting more merrily than ever, pleased if anything with the terror they had caused. It was time sleepy old 'Istanbul', as the locals still insisted on calling it, recognized that the pace of life in Turkey was changing. If they wanted to be a Western nation they'd better learn to act like one, and they could start by getting out of the way of traffic.

Stanton was lying on top of the woman. Her veil had been dislodged and his cheek lay against hers. He felt her hot breath gusting past his ear and her breast heaving against his body. The little boy was half caught between them and the girl stretched out alongside.

He got quickly to his feet. This was Ottoman Turkey after all and the woman was clearly highly orthodox. While he couldn't imagine even the most conservative of mullahs taking exception to the physical contact he had been forced to make, it was still an uncomfortable and threatening intimacy. He didn't want an irate husband getting the wrong end of the stick and reaching for the long curved knife so many of the locals wore openly on their belts.

He had a job to do, and currently his first duty was to leave no trace.

He helped the young mother to her feet as she stuttered her thanks. Or at least he presumed they were thanks. She was speaking Turkish, which he recognized but did not understand. However, the gratitude in her eyes as she readjusted her veil would have been clear in any language.

People were gathering round, babbling in a variety of languages. Besides Turkish, Stanton recognized Greek, French and Arabic, and there were certainly others. The Galata Bridge must have been the most cosmopolitan thoroughfare on earth. Babel itself could scarcely have been any more polyglot.

'I'm very sorry, uhm, madam,' Stanton began in English, not quite sure how to address the woman, 'but I don't speak—'

'She's saying thanks, although I'm sure you guessed that,' a voice said at his shoulder. Stanton turned to face a middle-aged man in the ubiquitous linen suit and straw boater of the European nabob. 'She says you saved her children's lives, and hers, which of course you did. Neat bit of work, I must say. You shot across the bridge like you had the bailiffs after you.'

A man in a uniform pushed his way through the crowd. Stanton thought he was probably a policeman but he may have been some sort of militia or even a postman. Turkish officials loved an extravagant uniform.

He felt someone take his hand and shake it.

Someone else slapped his back.

An old French gentleman seemed to be offering to stand him a drink, although by the look of the man's red and bulbous nose this was more by way of grabbing the excuse to have an early one himself.

This was all wrong. His duty was to pass through the city like a shadow and suddenly he was the epicentre of a crowd. He needed to get away.

But the young mother kept thanking him; holding up her crying children, her big dark eyes shining with gratitude, thanking him over and over again.

'You – my – babies,' she said in slow, faltering English.

Her meaning was clear. He had saved her babies, nothing in the world could be more important.

But he hadn't saved his own.

How could he have done? His family had never even been born.

2

IN CAMBRIDGESHIRE, in the early morning of Christmas Eve 2024, Hugh Stanton, retired British army captain and professional adventurer, was riding his motorbike through the frozen dawn.

There was thick mist on the ungravelled, icy road and the markings had long since faded from the potholed tarmac. If Stanton had deliberately sought out the most treacherous and deadly conditions in which to ride a powerful motorcycle at high speeds he would have struggled to find better.

Which suited him very well.

Death was the only prospect in life to which he was looking forward with any degree of enthusiasm.

It would be such a simple kill too. The road was empty, no other headlight beam illuminated the freezing darkness. There'd be no risk, no collateral damage. A clean hit. Not like on those awful desert operations he'd sweated through back in his army days, when there always seemed to be dead women and babies caught up in the tangled wreckage of exploded Toyotas.

This target was isolated and prone. Stanton had only to action the strike. One tiny turn in the direction of a tree. A little twist on the throttle for good measure, and oblivion.

Except . . .

What if there really was a hell?

Stanton was as close to being an atheist as prudence allowed but Cassie had been a Catholic. He therefore had to allow for the faint possibility that hell existed and, if it did, then self-murder would surely condemn him to it. Not that the idea of fire and brimstone bothered him much. An eternity of satanic torture might actually serve as a distraction from his own company, which he was beginning to find almost unbearable. The fear Hades held for Stanton was simply that if there was such a place then it was a certainty that Cassie and the children wouldn't be there.

Angels didn't go to hell.

The possibility of him spending eternity in a different place to his lost family was simply too terrible a thought for him to take a risk on, no matter how remote. Therefore, despite his longing for release, he kept his grip steady on the handlebar and his concentration firmly on the road as tree after tree shone briefly grey-bright through the misty dark, branches spread wide and welcoming. Like a lover's arms, promising peace.

Stanton flicked on his indicator. The Cambridge turn-off was approaching. He knew the road. He'd ridden it many times as a student, hurtling back from London in the small hours, a take-away meal clamped between his thighs, feeding himself through the open visor of his helmet.

Now he was returning, on his way to have breakfast with an old tutor, Professor Sally McCluskey, an eminent military historian who had been his favourite teacher as an undergraduate. More than just a favourite, in fact, McCluskey was one of the few people in Stanton's life whom he'd ever felt close to. A large, jolly woman with bloodshot cheeks and a poorly bleached moustache who liked nothing better than to hog the fire with a drink in her hand and revel in the glorious and bloody past. To McCluskey history was alive and vibrant, a thrilling cavalcade of heroes and villains, deathly plots and brave dreams. She had held weekly debates for her students in her cosy drawing room in Great Court, which she called her 'What ifs?' Long lazy afternoons during which she'd serve beer and crisps and challenge terrified but delighted undergraduates to imagine and justify alternative historical scenarios. Scenarios which, but for chance and luck, might easily have made up the content of her lectures.

Stanton could see her still, standing before the fire, wearing an ancient military greatcoat, which she used as a dressing gown, vast arse placed firmly and unashamedly between the flames and the students. Cheery glass in hand. Barking out her chosen 'What if'.

'Come on, you dozy swine!' she'd boom in a voice that had developed its tone on school hockey fields and been honed to rafter-rattling perfection over decades of coaching ladies' rowing teams on the river Cam. 'What if King George had accommodated the American colonists' demands and allowed them a handful of MPs at Westminster?'

The debate that followed would always be loud and lively and end invariably with McCluskey ignoring her students' efforts at a conclusion and barking out her own.

'Well, there'd have been no bloody War of Independence for a start, and the US would have developed along Canadian and Australian lines. The hamburger would never have been invented, there'd be no chewing gum dotting the pavements, and the world would never have heard of high school massacres. Can you credit it? *America*, lost for the sake of an extra dozen members in the House of Commons. *AMERICA!* The richest prize on the bloody planet. Gone, for want of a few paltry seats on the cross benches. George the bloody Third wasn't just mad, he was *completely tonto*! Bugger him, say I! Who cares if he did a bit of farming and was nice to children? He lost us America and he was an *arse*!'

What fun those long, semi-drunken Sunday afternoons had been. The debates always degenerated into loud, name-calling battles between the Marxists, who contended that much of history was inevitable, the result of preordained economic and material forces, and the romantics, who believed that history was made by individuals and that a single stomach ache or an undelivered love letter could have changed everything.

Professor McCluskey had been firmly in the romantics' camp.

'Men and women make history! Not balance sheets!' she'd shout at some cowering Dialectical Materialist. 'The great and the flawed. The evil and the honourable. Josephine married Bonaparte because her previous lover was threatening to throw her on the street! She *despised* the little Corsican corporal. Is it therefore any wonder that two days into their honeymoon he buggered off to conquer Italy, thus sealing Europe's fate for a generation? If that old town bike had put as much effort into servicing Boney's boner as she put into pleasuring her numerous other lovers he might have hung around screwing her instead of prancing off to screw an entire continent!'

In Stanton's view, Professor Sally McCluskey had really known how to teach history.

He'd kept in touch with her after graduating, maintaining a sporadic email correspondence from the various parts of the world in which he'd found himself, and when her note had arrived asking that he spend Christmas with her at his old college, he'd accepted. Since Cassie and the children's deaths he had cut himself off entirely from what few old friends he had, but he couldn't help being intrigued by the urgency of the professor's tone.

I beg you to come, she'd written. *We have matters to discuss of the utmost importance.*

He was skirting through the edges of the town now. Early workers were shivering at the bus stops, hunch-backed figures bent in supplication over their phones, each face an ash-grey ghost illuminated by the screen.

It had been fifteen years since Stanton had graduated and Cambridge, like all towns, had become a wind-blown shadow of its former self. Faded signs promised books, toys, pharmacists' and fresh market produce but the only things for sale behind those broken boarded windows were drugs and semiconscious girls. Shops were history, just like horse troughs and suits of armour. Nobody bought their stuff in the physical world any more.

Dawn was breaking as he approached the College. A pale monochrome light gently stirred the frost-crisp sleeping-bag cocoons pupating in the alcoves of the old familiar walls. Venerable stone edifices that had stood since the Tudors.

Graffiti-covered now but still deeply stirring to a man like Stanton, who loved the past. Those stones held within them the sonic echo of every footfall and every cry that had ever disturbed the racing molecules at their core. If Stanton had had an instrument sensitive enough he could have listened to the hammer blows on the very cold chisel that had shaped them.

There was a porter at the Great Gate just as there had been when Stanton first arrived in 2006 as an eighteen-year-old undergraduate. There, however, the similarity ended. Gone was the avuncular, strawberry-nosed Mr Pickwick figure in a bowler hat emerging from his cosy lodge. The porter who welcomed visitors to College in 2024 sat behind a thick screen of glass and wore a fluorescent yellow high-vis jacket, despite there being scant possibility of anybody bumping into him.

'Look at the camera,' the porter instructed, scarcely glancing up from the game he was playing. 'No fucking way, bro! That is fucked. That is fucking mental.'

Stanton didn't take offence at the tirade; the porter was just communicating with some third party on the phone on which he was playing his game. Undivided attention was a thing of the past; if you got annoyed about people talking to their phones while also dealing with you, your head would explode before lunch. Besides, if you were slightly famous, as Stanton was, it was a sort of blessing. If a person didn't look at you then they wouldn't ask to have a photo with you either.

The iris machine beeped, flashing up Stanton's identity, a barrier opened and he tried to hurry through.

He wasn't quick enough. His fierce blue eyes, lean, weathered, handsome features and close-cropped, sun-bleached hair were unmistakable, particularly to the sort of young man who stared all day at his phone.

'Oh my God, it's you, innit?' the porter said. 'It's Guts.'

'No,' Stanton replied. 'Not any more. Just Hugh.'

'Fuckin' hell! It is. It's Guts,' the porter insisted. 'Eh, man,' he went on, now speaking once more to the third party on his phone.

'You won't believe who's standing here. It's only Guts! Guts Stanton. Yeah! *I know!* Fucking mental!' The porter addressed himself once more to Stanton. 'I love your stuff, man. I can't believe it's you. This is amazing. Can I get a photo?'

Stanton wanted to say that he was in a bit of a hurry but he knew it would be more trouble than it was worth. The young man was already struggling out of his tiny cubicle and Stanton had plenty of experience of 'fans' whose adoration turned instantly to outrage and vociferous offence when they considered themselves dissed.

'Yeah. Fine. No worries. Happy to.'

The porter tried to throw an arm round Stanton's shoulder but Stanton was well over six feet tall and the porter's high-vis jacket made it hard for him to raise his arm. He had to settle for grasping Stanton round the waist, which was slightly uncomfortable for both of them. Then he reached out with his other hand and took the selfie.

'Nice one. Fucking mental,' the porter said, already thumbing at his phone to post the picture online. 'What're you going to have for breakfast then, Guts? Gonna dig up some worms on the quad? That'd do you for the day, wouldn't it? Plenty of protein to keep your core temperature up.'

'Yeah, probably,' Stanton replied.

He hated being famous. He hadn't asked to be a celebrity, although he knew very well that it had been his own fault nonetheless. And it had been fun for a while – and important in its own small way. Those little survival videos he'd begun posting on the net in an effort to kindle the spirit of adventure in disaffected young people were something he'd enjoyed doing and been proud of. Why should only posh kids get to experience the exhilaration of testing yourself in the wild? He'd wanted to lure a few gangstas out of the ghettos and on to the hills. But then he'd done some cross-promotion with some city charities and youth groups and it had got out of hand. He'd become an internet celebrity and been chucked out of the Regiment for blowing his anonymity. Like they weren't all scrabbling for publishing deals themselves.

Stanton walked through the arches of the magnificent old gate and into Great Court. That certainly hadn't changed. It was still 'great' by any standards: the chapel on his right and the fountain to his left. The same gravelled paths that had been trod by centuries of undergraduates. A non-stop stream of bright, optimistic young spirits that stretched back for five hundred years. Spirits for whom even sadness and sorrow were living, vibrant things, the stuff of poetry and song. Burning passion, impatient ambition, unrequited love. Not like the sorrows that come later.

Failure. Disillusionment. Regret.

He passed the entrance to the chapel and thought about the names on the memorial to the Great War inside. Sometimes, as a young student, he had sat alone in the darkening evening and read them. All those young men, cut down at their beginning. He'd felt so sad for them then. Now he envied them; they died at the high tide of life. When the sun was rising.

> *They shall grow not old, as we that are left grow old:*
> *Age shall not weary them, nor the years condemn.*

Lucky bastards.

3

'I WAS SO VERY sorry to hear about your terrible loss, Hugh,' Professor McCluskey said, pouring tea from the same china pot she had used during Stanton's student days, 'and I thought since neither of us has anyone to spend Christmas Eve with, we might as well spend it together.'

Stanton accepted the proffered steaming cup but declined to return the warm smile that accompanied it.

'I'm not really interested in Christmas, professor,' he replied. 'Christmas doesn't mean anything to me any more.'

'Christmas means the birth of our Saviour,' McCluskey remarked. 'That means something, surely.'

'The bastard never saved me.'

'Perhaps he hasn't finished with you yet.'

Stanton looked at his old professor long and hard. There were few people he respected more but there were limits.

'I really hope you didn't get me here to suggest I take comfort in religion,' he growled.

'Not in the slightest,' McCluskey replied. 'I don't think religion should *be* comfortable. That's where it all went wrong for the Anglicans, trying to be comfortable. Deep down people want fire and brimstone. They want a violent vengeful God who tells them what to do and smites them if they don't do it. That's why the Prophet Mohammed's doing so well these days. I've occasionally thought about switching myself. At least Allah's got a bit of fire in his belly. But you see I could never give up the turps.

Speaking of which, drop of brandy? You've had a chilly ride.'

It was scarcely eight thirty in the morning and Stanton was about to refuse but McCluskey didn't wait for a reply before reaching down for the bottle of cognac that was standing on the floor between her swollen ankles. She snorted at the large picture of a diseased liver that government statute required the bottle to display, then slopped a substantial shot into each teacup. 'Quite frankly, when it comes to comfort I'll take booze over faith every time.'

'I don't need booze. I've had plenty of booze. It doesn't help.'

'Still, since it's Christmas. Cheers!' The professor chinked her teacup against Stanton's and, having blown loudly on the surface of its contents, drank deep, sighing with satisfaction.

'All right, prof,' Stanton said, 'what's all this about? Your email said you needed to see me urgently. Why?'

'You've been in Scotland, haven't you?' McCluskey asked, ignoring Stanton's question. 'I spoke to your colonel.'

'How the hell does he know where I am? He chucked me out.'

'They keep tabs on you. Still think you might go blabbing about all your thrilling clandestine missions. You could make a lot of money.'

'I don't want to make a lot of money. I never did. They ought to know that. And anyway, even if the bastard does know where I am, what's he doing telling you? I thought the Regiment was supposed to be discreet.'

'Your colonel was a Trinity man. That sort of thing still counts for something even now.'

Hugh nodded. Of course it did. Even now. With the country torn apart by every kind of division society could produce, sectarian, religious, racial, sexual and financial, those ancient ties still bound. You had to be born to it to get it, and Stanton's mother had driven a bus. Cambridge on an army sponsorship had been the first time he'd become aware of the shadowy workings of the Old Boy network and it still took him by surprise.

'All right then, what do you want?' he asked. 'Why did you go looking for me?'

'Getting there, Hugh, getting there,' McCluskey replied with that touch of steel in the soft tone that had cowed so many generations of undergraduates. 'But I'd prefer to come at it in my own way and my own time.'

Stanton bit his lip. Some things never changed. McCluskey was still the professor and he was still the student. You never grew out of that relationship, no matter what happened in later life. McCluskey had taught students who went on to become cabinet ministers, ambassadors and in his case a decorated soldier and celebrity adventurer. But they'd all be eighteen again sitting on that ancient Queen Anne chair with those wild, bloodshot eyes drilling into them from beneath the great tangled eyebrows. McCluskey's Hedges they were called, now painted a quite ridiculous jet black. Stanton wondered why if she could be bothered to paint them she didn't also trim them a bit. He took a sip of his tea. Even through the taste of cognac he recognized the leaf McCluskey always served. English Breakfast infused with strawberry. He hadn't tasted it in fifteen years.

'I've been in the Highlands,' he conceded. 'Up in the remote north-west. In a tent on the hills above Loch Maree.'

'Chilly.'

'A bit.'

'Scourging and purging, eh?'

'I just thought some serious physical discomfort might be a distraction.'

'Which of course it wasn't.'

'No.'

'Bloody stupid idea.'

'I suppose so.'

'If you're going to mope about, you might as well do it with the heating on.'

'I suppose I was kind of hoping I might die of hunger or exposure.'

17

'Goodness gracious! Really? Then why don't you just shoot yourself?'

'I don't believe in suicide.'

'Ahh. In case there's an afterlife. I understand. So you thought if you pitted yourself against the elements, Mother Nature might do the job for you and dispatch you to oblivion without a stain on your conscience?'

'Yes, I suppose that's what I had in mind.'

'But unfortunately you're "Guts" Stanton. The man nothing can kill. Too much edible lichen on the rocks. Still some sea trout beneath the ice for you to impale with a sharpened biro. Enough twigs and heather to weave a life-preserving windbreak. We all loved your shows here at College, Hugh. *Terribly* proud. Undergrads are always asking about you. I tell them you used to catch rats with your bare hands during lectures and eat them raw.'

'I caught *one* rat,' Stanton replied, 'and I certainly didn't eat it. That probably *would* have killed me.'

'Well, you can't help your legend growing. *Guts Versus Guts*. Brilliant show. I downloaded all of it. Even paid for it. Well, it was for charity.'

Stanton winced. *Guts Versus Guts* had been a good enough *idea* for a title. None of this Man against the Wild stuff, that was just bullshit. In Stanton's experience Man was never *against* the Wild because the Wild didn't care if you lived or died. When man tested himself against Nature that was exactly what he was doing, testing *himself*. Which was why Stanton had given his little video hobby the title that he had. But it had been stupid to use his old army nickname. It was all very well for your mates to say you were one crazy, fearless motherfucker and name you 'Guts', but it was just showing off to use the name in the title of a webcast.

'Anyway,' McCluskey went on in something slightly less than her usual booming volume, 'just to say sorry and all that. About the accident. Commiserations . . . meant to write when I heard about it. Dreadful business.'

McCluskey was stirring extra sugar into her tea and looking very uncomfortable.

'Accident? I don't see it as an accident,' Stanton replied. 'It was murder.'

McCluskey looked up from her cup. 'Murder, Hugh? Really?'

'Well, what else would you call a mum and two kids getting wiped out in a hit and run? On a zebra crossing?'

'Well, yes, put like that—'

'As far as I'm concerned it was murder, and if I could I'd give each of them the death sentence and carry it out myself.'

'And I'd hold your coat,' McCluskey replied. 'But they never found them? All four got clean away?'

'Yeah. Back to whatever crack house or meth lab they came from.'

Stanton held out his mug. McCluskey splashed more brandy into it.

'So you've just cut yourself off then,' McCluskey asked, 'from your previous life?'

'I suppose so.'

'What about friends?'

'I never had a lot of friends. In my job it was easier.'

'Family then?'

Stanton eyed McCluskey with a hint of suspicion.

'Is there a point to this?'

'Just making conversation, Hugh.'

'I don't think you are. I think you want to know.'

'In that case,' McCluskey replied sternly, 'you might do me the courtesy of giving me an answer.'

Amazing, she'd turned the tables and put him on the back foot in half a second. He'd faced down bears in the wild but he couldn't face down McCluskey over a cup of tea. You didn't get to be the first female Master of Trinity without knowing how to run a conversation.

'I know your mother's dead,' she went on. 'Ciggies, wasn't it?'

'Lung cancer, yes.'

'Good for her. If you're going to get killed might as well get killed by something you love. And you're an only child, of course. Father still around?'

'Don't know. Don't care. Never knew him. Now come on, professor, what is—'

'And your wife's family?' McCluskey ploughed on, refusing to be drawn. 'Surely they'd be your family too now. United in grief and all that.'

Stanton shrugged, no point fighting it.

'Tact never was your strong point was it, professor? All right. Since you insist. No, I'm not close to Cassie's mum and dad. They're New Agers, hippies really. They never came to terms with their daughter marrying a soldier, particularly one from Special Forces, who they think are just terrorists in uniform. And the webcast thing pissed them off even more; thought I was encouraging yobbos to kill endangered species. They never liked me, and Cassie dying didn't change that. I haven't seen them since the funeral.'

'Excellent.'

'Excellent? Why excellent? Where's this going, prof?'

'All in good time, Hugh,' McCluskey replied. 'The weather's dreadful and we've got all day. So where have you been living in general? I know you haven't been home and you can't have spent three months on Loch Maree. Even you couldn't have survived the deep freeze we had last November.'

'Oh, I've been here and there,' Stanton replied. 'Guest houses, travel lodges. Bit of sleeping rough. I find moving on passes the time.'

'Passes the time until what?'

'Till I die, I suppose.'

'So you're just giving up?'

'What's to give up? The world's a mess, I've got no interest in it and I've got no interest in myself either.'

'And what would Cassie think about that?'

'Cassie isn't thinking about anything. She's dead.'

'You're a soldier, Hugh. Even if they did chuck you out. Good soldiers don't give up.'

Stanton smiled. That wasn't the sort of sentiment you heard a lot these days. Even in the army old-fashioned notions such as courage and honour were viewed with deep suspicion. Not 'inclusive' enough.

There was a knock at the door. Breakfast had arrived.

'There you go, Sally,' one of the caterers said as the professor signed for the food. 'Enjoy, Sal.'

Stanton had never heard McCluskey addressed by her first name before, let alone heard it reduced from Sally to Sal.

'Ah yes,' McCluskey remarked once the caterers had left. 'I'm Sal all right. There are no exceptions in the new cultural egalitarianism. But the funny thing is that no matter how many times everybody uses each other's first name, the rich still get richer and the poor still get poorer and nobody actually gives a damn about anyone. Ain't life grand?'

'Look, professor,' Stanton said, accepting a plate of fried breakfast, 'are you going to tell me why you asked me here or aren't you?'

'I'm going to try, Hugh, but when you've heard me out I think you'll concede that it's not a simple thing to explain.'

'Have a crack at it.'

McCluskey helped herself to some bacon and eggs, on top of which, to Stanton's disgust, she drizzled honey. 'I knew getting into this was going to be difficult,' she said through a mouth full of food. 'Let's start with this. If you could change *one* thing in history, if you had the opportunity to go back into the past, to one place and one time and change one thing, where would you go? What would you do?'

'Professor, you know bloody well I'd—'

'Hugh, *not* you personally. You can't go back to the street in Camden and stop your wife and children from stepping into the road. I want an *objective* not a subjective answer. This isn't about you and your private tragedy. It's about us and our *global* tragedy. About humanity.'

21

'Screw humanity. I don't give the whole stinking bunch of us more than a couple of generations and good riddance. The universe is better off without us.'

'But surely we're not irredeemable?' McCluskey suggested.

'Aren't we?'

'Of course not. No race that could produce Shakespeare and Mozart is irredeemable. We've just lost our way, that's all. But what if you could give us a chance to do better? Just one chance. One single move in the great game of history. What's your best shot? What would you consider to be the greatest mistake in world history and, more to the point, what single thing would you do to prevent it?'

'All human history has been a disaster,' Stanton insisted. 'If you want to fix it, go back a couple of hundred thousand years and shoot the first ape that tries to get up and walk on two feet.'

'Not good enough. I won't accept lazy apocalyptic cop-outs. I want a proper answer, argued from the facts.'

'Missing your students, prof?' Stanton asked. 'Can't survive the holiday without one of your "What ifs"?'

'If you like.'

'I don't much. I'm not really in the mood for games.'

'You're not in the mood for anything. You told me you were just passing the time till you die so clearly you don't have anything better to do. What's more, it's Christmas and it's minus ten outside. Why not indulge me? Eat your brekkie. Have another cognac and do a favour to a lonely old bitch who fancied a bit of company and knew you'd be free because you're even more lonely than she is.'

Stanton looked out of the window once more. There was a big storm brewing and even to a man who didn't care if he lived or died, Christmas Eve in a Travelodge was an unpleasant prospect. McCluskey's sitting room was warm and filled with lots of comforting-looking things, things that dated to a time before he or Cassie or the children had ever existed. Books, pictures, antiques. He closed his eyes and sipped his tea and cognac. It occurred to him that he was already slightly drunk. But it was a nice mellow sort of high, the first booze buzz he'd enjoyed since . . .

He shut the thought from his mind and focused on McCluskey.

'All right, professor,' he said, 'since it's Christmas.'

'Then game on!' McCluskey said, clapping her yellow, nicotine-stained hands together. 'Come on. Best shot. What is humanity's biggest mistake? Its worst disaster?'

As if on cue, there was an alarming rattle at the window and a squall of heavy hail crashed against the glass, threatening to smash it in. The two of them turned to watch as icy stones the size of marbles began bouncing off the pane, which fortunately had been reinforced against what was becoming a common occurrence.

'Well, there's your answer, I reckon,' Stanton said. 'Climate change. Got to be the big one, hasn't it? Earthquakes, tsunamis, droughts, floods, tornadoes, mini bloody ice ages. The Gulf Stream gets turned off and suddenly East Sussex is Northern Canada. A couple more years of failed harvests and the whole world will almost certainly starve.'

'Climate change is a *consequence*, Hugh,' McCluskey replied sternly. 'A consequence of global warming, which is *also* a consequence. A consequence of burning carbon, which among other things powers our cars. Would you uninvent cars?'

'Not me, prof, I'm a petrolhead, you know that. I reckon a perfectly tuned V8 engine's worth a couple of icebergs any time.'

'Central heating then? Refrigerated food? Incubators for the premature? Stair lifts for the infirm? We don't normally think of those things as *disasters*, do we? But they all contribute to global warming. Shall we uninvent them?'

Stanton felt a familiar sensation, one he hadn't felt since he was twenty-one, the sense of McCluskey running rings around him.

'Well, it's a matter of scale, isn't it?' he said, struggling to hold his own. 'Of course, there are lots of benefits, but the fact is that ever since the industrial revolution—'

'Would you call *that* a disaster?' McCluskey interrupted,

pouncing gleefully. 'Would you prevent it? That thing that brought health and plenty to untold billions? Cheap food, cheap clothes, cheap power. Levels of comfort delivered to entire *populations* that previously not even *kings* had enjoyed? Besides which, you couldn't prevent it even if you wanted to. The industrial revolution wasn't a single event, it was the result of any number of scientific and technological breakthroughs. No one thing began it, not even the Spinning Jenny, despite what was once taught in schools, and I'm only allowing you to change *one* thing. So, sorry, Hugh, no good, you'll have to try again.'

Stanton actually laughed. He hadn't laughed in over six months. It felt strange. But also liberating.

'Come on then, professor, out with it.'

'Out with what?'

'It's pretty obvious you've decided on your own answer. You're just waiting to shoot me down in flames a few times before you tell me what it is. Just like you did to us when we were students. I could say anything. The invention of gun powder. Splitting the atom. Taking small pox to the New World and bringing back syphilis. The Romans coming up with decent plumbing then ruining it by using lead pipes. And you'd tell me they were all wrong because you know where this is heading.'

McCluskey drained her teacup and splashed another shot of cognac into it.

'Well, you're right and you're wrong, Hugh,' she admitted. 'I do have the answer, but I certainly don't know where this is heading, no one on earth could know that. But I know where it *began*. In this very room, as a matter of fact. Possibly in these very chairs. Two hundred and ninety-seven years ago.'

Stanton did the mental arithmetic.

'1727?'

'1727 indeed.'

McCluskey pushed away her half-finished plate and put her Nike-clad feet up on a little padded footstool. Then, with stubby brown-stained fingers she filled an ancient tar-coated pipe with tobacco, which she appeared to keep loose in the pocket of her greatcoat.

'Don't mind if I smoke while you're still eating, do you? Illegal, of course, within fifty metres of a person or a building, but what's the point being Master of Trinity if you can't be master of your own sitting room?'

'I don't mind,' Stanton replied. 'I did two tours in the Mid East; everybody smoked, including me.'

'Well, I do think you need a pipe to tell a good story.'

'You're going to tell me a story?'

'I'm going to tell you the first half of one, Hugh. The second half hasn't been written yet.'

4

Two hundred and ninety-seven years before Stanton returned to his old university to visit the Master of Trinity, another ex-student, and one rather more eminent, had stood at the lodge door with the same intention.

The Master's Lodge had been quite new then, a relatively recent addition to the College, scarcely a century old. Not much older in fact than the ex-student himself, who was eighty-four, an immense age for the time. The old man had gout and a suspected kidney stone but he had nonetheless come all the way from the comfort of his niece's home in London, where he was spending his final years, in order to deliver a package of papers and a letter.

A letter to Professor McCluskey.

The old man had hoped to be discreet about his arrival at College but a hundred eyes had stared from leaded windows as he made his slow progress across the Great Court. Word, he knew, would be spreading like wildfire. After all, he was a very famous man and that fame had been established here in Cambridge, at Trinity. He was, without doubt, the College's most celebrated son, and in all probability would ever remain so.

It was he who had brought order to the universe.

The laws of motion. The movement of planets. The nature and substance of light. Optics, calculus, telescopics and, above all, gravity were all areas of understanding that the searchlight of the old man's mind had revealed to an astonished world. Small wonder then that crowds of young men in black gowns had thrown down their books and come scuttling from their various rooms and chambers anxious to catch a glimpse of a legend, to be for a moment close to the very epicentre of modern practical philosophy, long gowns flapping like wings as they scurried across the quad. A swarm of intellectual moths drawn to the blinding light of true genius.

But that light was fading now. Sir Isaac Newton's eyes were dimming. Pain racked his body and torment troubled his extra-ordinary mind. It was this torment that had led him to make the taxing journey back to Trinity. To deliver the letter and the package of notes into the care of Richard Bentley, the Master of the College.

Having entered the lodge, leaving the crowd of chattering students outside, Newton paused in the hallway while a servant took his coat. He glanced ruefully up at the long sweeping stair-way he knew he still had to climb.

The Master appeared at the top of the stairs, his arms thrown wide in salutation.

'Welcome, Sir Isaac! You do your alma mater and my house a great honour.'

Newton grunted and patted the ornate banister. 'It's every bit as ridiculous as word has it,' he said.

Richard Bentley winced. His decision to install a spectacular new staircase in the Trinity Master's Lodge had been a matter of considerable controversy.

'The cost has been much exaggerated,' Bentley replied primly.

'One can only hope so,' Newton muttered, putting an unsteady foot on the first step, 'or I doubt Trinity will be buying any actual books for a while.'

'Ha! There speaks His Majesty's Master of the Mint,' Bentley said, but rather too loudly and pretending to laugh. 'I hope you haven't come here in your official capacity, Sir Isaac. Am I to be audited?'

'I do not *audit*, Mr Bentley. I am not a *clerk*.'

'I was being merry, Sir Isaac.'

'Then I envy you that ability,' Newton said, puffing as he laboured up the last of the stairs. 'I am come not in any official capacity, Mr Bentley, but on an entirely personal matter. A matter, in fact, of the *utmost* privacy.'

'You intrigue me, sir.'

'*So* private that it will require the swearing of a solemn and binding oath of secrecy.'

'My goodness, how exciting.'

'It is. But not for us.'

Bentley helped the great man into his drawing room where wine was served, after which Newton instructed Bentley to dismiss all the servants and lock the doors.

'Now draw the curtains if you will, sir, and light a candle,' Newton said. 'For this thing which must remain in darkness should begin in darkness.'

Bentley couldn't help smiling at the old man's sense of drama. Newton was well over eighty, after all, and perhaps approaching the doddering senility of Shakespeare's seventh age.

When the room had been rendered suitably dark and mysterious, Newton produced a cross and made Bentley swear an oath upon it.

'Do you, Richard Bentley, on your honour as Master of Trinity College and before God as a Christian gentleman, swear that all that passes between us in this room will *remain* in this room and no word or hint of it shall ever be divulged to another soul, save to one person and that be in a letter to your successor?'

Bentley agreed.

'Kiss the cross and repeat your promise,' Newton demanded.

Again Bentley did as he was told, but this time the indulgent smile was replaced with just a hint of impatience. Newton might be universally acknowledged as the greatest mind in England and probably all the world but he, Bentley, had written the celebrated *Dissertation on the Epistles of Phalaris*, which was no small thing either.

'There, Mr Bentley,' Newton said. 'You are become a

Companion of the Order of Chronos. The first of their number! Unless you count me, which I suppose we should. So let us say the second of their number.'

Bentley gave a spacious wave as if to indicate that he was content to be number two. 'Chronos. God of Time?'

'The very same, Mr Bentley.'

Newton settled himself into the beautiful new Queen Anne winged chair on which he was sitting and took a sip of claret. 'You will recall,' he began, 'that many years ago, at the time when first we corresponded on theological matters, I had some disturbance of the mind?'

Bentley nodded uneasily. He was indeed aware. There could have been few members of Britain's intellectual establishment who hadn't known about the nervous breakdown Newton had suffered thirty years earlier at the height of his fame. Or the deranged and paranoiac letters he had written at the time to both friends and rivals, letters filled with wild accusations of conspiracy and betrayal. Or the dark talk of alchemy and the search for hidden messages in the Bible, which had led many to conclude that Newton's mind was gone for ever.

'The world believes I had a fit,' the old man went on. 'That my mind was crazed with madness.'

'You were over-worked, Sir Isaac,' Bentley said soothingly.

'They thought me mad, Bentley,' Newton snapped, 'and well I might have been, for what I'd discovered should have driven any-one to lunacy.'

'Discovered, Sir Isaac? But all the world knows what you discovered and you are rightly lionized for it.'

'The world knows only what I *published*, Mr Bentley.'

For the first time Bentley's supercilious manner deserted him.

'You mean,' he asked, 'there's more?'

The great philosopher was silent for a moment. The creases on his thin, lined face deepened a little and the heels of his shoes tapped on the parquet floor. He scratched absent-mindedly at that famous long, lean nose, then passed the hand beneath his wig to scratch his head.

'You remember how it was a year before my madness,' Newton began, 'when you delivered your little lecture . . . what was it called?'

'*A Confutation of Atheism*,' Bentley said. 'Though I venture "little" is too small a word. It was after all considered the most—'

'Yes, yes,' Newton interrupted. 'Whatever its size, in it you sought to show that my work *proved* the existence of God. That my great theory of planetary movement self-evidently required the hand of an *intelligent designer*, the architect of all things.'

'Yes I did, Sir Isaac. I treasure the letters of approval you sent to me at the time.'

'Well, I was grateful for your intervention. Some called me a heretic then. Many still do.'

'Well, I wouldn't put it as strongly as—'

'Don't mollycoddle me, Mr Bentley. A heretic is what they call me. But just because I question the theology of the Trinity doesn't mean I'm not a Christian man.'

'Sir Isaac, is this really the place to . . .' Bentley could see that Newton was about to go off on his infamous and downright dangerous hobbyhorse.

'The trinity is a mathematical impossibility!' Newton barked, slapping the little table on which his glass was standing and up-setting his wine. 'Three separate entities can*not* also be the same thing. Three peas cannot also be one pea! Any more than can a father, a son and a holy ghost. Such a thing defies logic. Besides which, it is idolatry, because if the Father and the Son are the same thing, then those images of a dying man we put upon our crucifixes are also images of his father, hence images of God. Hence idolatry, sir! And they call *me* blasphemous.'

Bentley was shifting uncomfortably in his seat. This wasn't the sort of conversation anybody wanted to have, even in private. Particularly a person like him, who owed his position to the monarch's patronage. It hadn't been many years since people had been burned in England for things like denying the Trinity.

'Uhm . . . is the question of the Trinity relevant to what you came here to discuss, Sir Isaac?' Bentley enquired gently.

'Since you ask, no, actually it isn't,' Newton admitted grumpily.

'Hmm. Well, perhaps we should return to this business of Chronos, of which you spoke. You mentioned unpublished discoveries, Sir Isaac? That would indeed be an extraordinary and exciting thing.'

Newton accepted another glass of wine to replace the one he'd spilled. It seemed to calm him, for when he spoke again he had regained his composure.

'You know that I've had more time for thinking than most men, Mr Bentley,' he said. 'I am a bachelor. I've been little in the company of women save for my nieces and I'm no hand at social intercourse. All of the effort people commonly expend in the cultivation of love and friendship I have been able to devote to my observing the workings of God's universe.'

'Of course, of course, Sir Isaac.'

'When first I wrote to you about atheism,' Newton went on, 'I let you know that I was happy that the world should come to understand the effect of gravity on planetary motion. I could see that my great idea which explained the movement and the shape of the cosmos was beautiful and allowed for a still fixed and ordered universe ordained by God.'

'Yes, yes.'

'But what if my mind had run further along the lines it had begun upon? What if there was an area of discovery I did *not* make public? Because instead of the eternal order of a divinely ordained planetary dance came the possibility of man-made chaos?'

'Chaos, Sir Isaac?'

'What if it wasn't merely *objects* that were affected by the power of gravity? Not just apples and planets?'

'I don't understand, sir. You have shown to the world so

brilliantly that gravity is the force that binds all things together and fixes their place and progress in the heavens. What else could gravity exert a force on?'

'Well, light, perhaps,' the old man said, glancing at a shaft of sunshine that had appeared through a gap in the curtains as if on cue. 'Perhaps it might bend light.'

'Could we then see round corners?' Bentley enquired, unable to conceal a smile.

'We might, sir, we might. And then there is something else again.'

'What else?'

'Chronos.'

'Time?'

'Yes, time, Master Bentley. What if gravity can bend time?'

Newton could not have known that the extraordinary idea that occurred to him in 1691 and which was to cause his mental breakdown the following year would lead directly to Hugh Stanton, a man born in 1989, saving the lives of a Muslim mother and her children in 1914. But what he could see, and see very clearly, was that there was nothing fixed or ordered about the future.

'Tell me, Mr Bentley,' Newton asked, staring at the dregs in his wine glass, which was empty once more, 'if God gave you the chance to change *one thing* in history, would you do it? And if so, *what would you change*?'

5

THE PROGRESS OF the day had done nothing to lighten the skies over Trinity College. If anything, the storm raging above Great Court was gathering force. A rare warm thermal current, lost and directionless in the climatic chaos that had torn it from its ancient course, had brought rain among the snow and hail. The icicles hanging from the fountain in the middle of the quad had turned to silvery waterfalls, a grey and grimacing stone overbite of drooling needle teeth.

In the Master's Lodge Professor McCluskey had been occupying her preferred position of hogging the fire while she told her story. Now she stumped across the room to the window and rubbed a spy hole in the condensation to look out.

'Blimey,' she muttered, peering into the violent and sodden gloom. 'Now *that* is blooming weather.'

'Never mind about the weather,' Stanton replied. 'Are you seriously telling me that Isaac Newton wrote you a letter?'

'Yes, he did,' McCluskey answered, throwing a triumphant fist into the air. 'Not me *personally*, of course. The letter he left with Richard Bentley was addressed to the Master of Trinity, New Year's Day, 2024. It was a sacred trust, to be handed down, unopened, from Master to Master until the appointed date. Imagine how surprised Bentley and old Isaac would have been if they'd known that three hundred years hence the recipient of the letter would be a woman! Now that *would* have shocked the crusty old buggers. Newton saw plenty standing on the shoulders

35

of those giants he talked about but I doubt he foresaw that the Master of Trinity would be a smokin' hot babe.'

McCluskey drew a pair of pendulous breasts in the film of water on the window, adding the curves of an hourglass figure on either side. 'Good story, eh?' she remarked, turning back towards the room. 'Perfect for Christmas, don't you think?'

'Yeah, and I think "story" is probably the operative word here. Are you seriously telling me that the Masters of Trinity have held in their possession a letter and a box of papers from *Isaac Newton* for three hundred years and kept it secret?'

'Of course,' McCluskey said with genuine surprise, 'just as I did after I took up my position, waiting for the appointed time. We are all Trinity men, even when we're women. We had been given a trust.'

'And not one of them, out of all those masters, even read it?'

McCluskey began clearing up the remains of the breakfast.

'It's possible, I suppose; took a peek and resealed it. But they would never have made what they saw public because to do so they'd also have to make public their betrayal. And since the information Newton left us is *extremely* time specific, there was nothing in it for them anyway. Finished?'

Stanton grabbed the last bit of bacon from his plate before handing it to her.

'Nothing in it for them beyond a document of incalculable historical value,' he said.

'This is Cambridge, Hugh. Documents of incalculable historical value are pretty common here; we don't get as excited about them as most people do. Newton sent lots of letters, many considerably pottier-sounding than the one I'm telling you about and most of them are gathering dust in the College library. People only ever want to see the *Principia* anyway. Just like they go to Rome and spend their entire holiday queuing to stand in a crowd and stare at the roof of the Sistine Chapel while the whole Ancient Empire lies scattered at their feet. Anyway, the point is the letter is genuine. I had it carbon-dated and the handwriting checked against known sources.'

'OK then, I'll buy it, professor,' Stanton said. 'So what did Newton say in his letter?'

'I'll read it if you like.'

McCluskey reached for the mantelpiece and took a creased and yellowing parchment from inside a Toby jug of William Gladstone. Then she dug a pair of thick, plastic reading glasses from the pocket of her greatcoat, blew a few strands of tobacco from the lenses and holding them before her face like *pince-nez* began to read.

'*To Whomsoever be Master of Trinity on New Year's Day 2024* . . . That's me!' she said, interrupting herself gleefully. 'Pretty cool, you have to admit. Newton wrote to me!'

'Yes, I get it, prof.'

'Just saying,' McCluskey replied sniffily before turning once more to the letter . . . '*Greetings! From three hundred years ago!*'

'Wow,' Stanton observed.

'Wow indeed,' McCluskey agreed. 'But it gets wowsier. *Sir, be you old? Be you with few earthly ties? If so, then the contents of this box belong to you. Otherwise I charge you find another who is without dependants and pass this box to him for it is his business and not yours* . . .' McCluskey paused to refresh herself with tea and cognac. 'Bit of luck I fitted the bill, eh? If I had a hubby and thirteen grandkids, I suppose I'd have been honour-bound to pass it on.'

'And would you have done?'

'Don't know. Fortunately I wasn't put to the test. I think Newton knew he was on pretty safe ground there. Most of us Oxbridge Death Eaters are married to the gig . . . anyway, he goes on. *Then, let you, or your designate, search about within the University for Professors and Fellows who are also with few ties. Find ye patriots and men of conscience. Find Classics scholars and those who have studied history, also mathematicians and Natural Philosophers. Men who have spent their lives in consideration of the Universe and its workings. And let them be old, their time remaining among earthly cares short. Find ye these companions even if you must include men of Oxford to do so.* Oxford, Hugh! Imagine that? From a Trinity man! You can see how seriously he was taking it.'

Hugh shrugged. He'd always found the supposed rivalry between the two 'elite' universities a boring and unconvincing affectation. As far as he was concerned, they were just two halves of the same grimly pleased-with-itself institution. The way they went on about hating each other was really just a way of reminding the rest of the world that no one else mattered.

McCluskey continued: '*When once assembled, ye band of venerable brothers shall, with due solemnity, convene a secret Order. And that Order shall ye name Chronos after he who was God of Time. Let ye Companions assemble in attire befitting your academic standing and the solemnity of the occasion. Feast you well so that you may be in good cheer. Open then the packages of papers which I do bequeath you and in the order I command.*

'*Act then according to your conscience as all good men of Trinity have ever done and I hope ever shall.*

'*Your servant,*

'*Isaac Newton.*'

McCluskey folded the parchment and put it back in the Toby jug. 'Interesting stuff, eh?'

'Well, if it's true it's bloody amazing,' Stanton replied. 'So what was in the papers?'

McCluskey smiled. 'You wish to join the Order of Chronos?'

Stanton shrugged. 'I presume you *want* me to join since you've brought me here and told me this much, and since I am a single man without dependants and therefore have clearly been picked to fit Isaac Newton's requirements.'

Picked to fit Isaac Newton's requirements?

He could hardly believe he was saying such a thing.

'Well,' McCluskey said, 'let me tell you. Last January I did as Isaac told me, I chose my companions. All donnish, dust-covered sad acts like me, with no life but College. And I convened the dinner. Did it just as Newton said, with "due solemnity": candles and prayers and some nice music and an excellent meal, and when we'd finished eating we opened his papers.'

'Quite a moment,' Stanton said.

'Yes. Quite a moment.'

McCluskey put down her glass and fetched from a corner of the room a wooden box about the size of a piece of cabin luggage, dark oak and bound with steel bands. She placed it on the footstool between herself and Stanton.

'The package of papers was in that?'

'Yes, it was. Newton's box, kept safe in the attic of this lodge for three hundred years.'

'A lot of papers then?'

'When you've heard what they describe I think you'll agree he was astonishingly concise.'

Setting her pipe once more between her teeth and reaching down over her vast bosom, Professor McCluskey lifted the lid and drew out a second yellowing parchment.

'The first thing we found was a question,' McCluskey said, handing the parchment to Stanton. 'A historical question, accompanied by a stern warning not to delve further into the papers until we'd answered it.'

Stanton looked down at the parchment. 'The same question you asked me.'

'Exactly. If we could revisit one moment from the past and change something, what would it be? Right up my street, eh? It's almost like the old boy knew I'd be the one to get his letter.'

'And did you come up with an answer?'

'Yes, we did. Pretty quickly, as a matter of fact.'

'And?'

McCluskey sucked her teeth for a minute. Stanton could see that she was absolutely revelling in the moment.

'Well, it has to be a date of *European* significance, doesn't it?' she said eventually. 'Or possibly American. Let's face it, for better or worse the last half dozen centuries on earth have been shaped by what we like to call Western civilization. Do you agree?'

'Yes, I suppose so.'

'Of course you do. I gave you a First, didn't I?'

'Two one.'

'At any rate you're not a complete idiot.' McCluskey reached under the tails of her greatcoat and rubbed at her huge buttocks, which were no doubt getting extremely hot, positioned as they were right in front of the fire. 'So tell me, Hugh. When did it all go wrong? When did Europe lose its way? When did its worst ideals triumph over its best? When did its wilful vanity and stupidity conspire together to destroy its beauty and its grace? When did it exchange its power and influence for decadence and decay? When, in short, did the most influential continent on the planet wilfully and without duress screw up on a scale unequalled in all history and in one insane moment go from hero to zero, from top dog to underdog? From undisputed heavyweight champion of the world to washed-up, penniless has-been, col-lapsed, bloodied and brain-dead in the middle of the ring having punched *itself* to death?'

The freezing rain outside was turning once more to hail. It came smacking at the windows in great flapping sheets, squall after dirty squall. There was lightning too, periodically illuminating the deep and gloomy clouds. Without a clock it would have been impossible to know what time it was. Or what season. Not that there were seasons any more.

'You're clearly talking about 1914,' Stanton answered quietly.

'I can't hear you, Hugh, the storm's too noisy.'

Hugh raised his voice, staring McCluskey in the face and giving his answer as if it was a challenge.

'1914 is the year Europe screwed up.'

'*Exactly*,' McCluskey exclaimed. 'History's greatest single mistake and the one that could most easily have been avoided was the Great War.'

Stanton took his dirty teacup back from where McCluskey had stacked it and having rinsed it out with a soda siphon helped him-self to another shot of cognac. It was Christmas after all.

40

'We-ell,' he said thoughtfully. 'Clearly it was an unprecedented world catastrophe, no arguing with that. But I'm not sure you can give it *exclusive* number-one status. There have been even worse bloodbaths since.'

'Exactly!' McCluskey cried out, doing a little dance on the rug. 'And every one of them *without exception* was made inevitable by what happened in 1914. That was the watershed, the fork in the road. The Great War bequeathed us the terrible twentieth century. Prior to that point the world was an increasingly peaceful place in which science and society were developing towards the common good.'

'You might feel differently about that if you were a Native American,' Stanton suggested, 'or an indigenous Australian. Or an African in the Belgian Congo—'

McCluskey actually stamped her foot in frustration.

'Oh come ON, Hugh! I'm not saying anything was or ever could be remotely *perfect*. Nor am I suggesting that historical readjustment could ever change human nature. Men will always take what isn't theirs, the strong will always exploit the weak – no amount of historical tinkering could ever stop that. What I am saying is that in the summer of 1914 the *general* tide of human brutishness appeared to be ebbing and an age of peace and international cooperation beginning. For goodness' sake, they were having so many International Exhibitions they were running out of cities to host them! In 1913 they'd had one in *Ghent*, for God's sake. A city that by 1915 would be pulverized into oblivion. This was the point at which European civilization, which had caused so much misery to itself and others, was just starting to *get things right*. Social Democracy was dawning; even the Tsar had his Duma. The vote was coming. Education, health, standards of living were all improving in leaps and bounds. The subject races of the great empires were setting up congresses and preparing themselves for self-determination. The flowering of arts and sciences in the capitals of Europe was more vibrant than at any time since the Renaissance. It was . . . *beautiful*.'

'Well, I don't know that I'd—'

But McCluskey was brooking no argument.

'Beautiful!' she insisted. 'And then – suicide. The insane, perverse, *wilful* self-destruction of a collective culture that had been *four thousand years* in the making, smashed *utterly* almost overnight. Never to rise again, and giving way in its stead to a genocidal global hotchpotch of half-baked fanaticism from both left and right. The Soviet Union corrupting Marx's great idea into a contagious global nightmare in which entire populations would be murderously enslaved. And the United States destined to take the worship of competition, consumption and excess to the current point of planetary extinction.'

Stanton stood up. It seemed the only way of getting a word in edgeways.

'Now hang on!' he said. 'You can't blame the Americans solely for the collapse of the environment.'

'Not any more we can't, but they started it. Who taught the peoples of the world to consume beyond their needs? Beyond even their *desires*? To consume simply for the *sake of consuming*. The world's greatest democracy, that's who! And look where *that's* got us. I tell you, the Great War ruined *everything*. The lights went out and the brakes came off. Just try to *imagine* what the world would be like now if it had never happened – if the great nations of Europe had continued on their journey to peace, prosperity and enlightenment; if those millions of Europe's best and finest young men, the most highly educated and *civilized* generation the world had ever known, had not died in the mud but had instead survived to shape the twentieth century.'

Stanton could see her point. All those names on the chapel wall just metres from where he sat and on every town memorial and village cross. What good might those young men have done had they lived? What evil might they have prevented? And in Germany? And Russia? Had their lost generations also survived, surely they would have stopped those morally bankrupt mediocrities who emerged from the rat holes and drove their nations towards absolute evil. Without the corrupting catalyst of industrial war, where might those countries have gone?

'You're right,' he said. 'Can't fault your argument. 1914 was the year of true catastrophe. So you answered Newton's question. You got to delve further into his papers. What did you find next?'

'What we found next was a sequence of four numbers.'

'Numbers?'

'Yes, numbers that were the end result of a lengthy and complex equation. Newton had written them on a slip of paper and sealed them in another envelope three centuries ago. And the sequence of those numbers was One Nine One Four.'

'1914?'

'1914 indeed.'

'Isaac Newton predicted the Great War?'

'Don't be ridiculous! How could he have done that? He wasn't a soothsayer! He was a mathematician, a man of science. He dealt in empirical evidence. He didn't arrive at those numbers via some Nostradamus-style mystical mumbo-jumbo. He did the maths.'

'I'm really not following, prof. Agreed, 1914 is a year of vast historical significance, but what's that got to do with maths?'

'All in good time, Hugh, all in good time,' McCluskey said, draining her teacup and stretching broadly. 'That's enough for now. I need a nap. Can't handle boozy brekkies like I used to.'

'But wait a minute on, you can't just—'

'I've told you everything I am qualified to tell, Hugh. Bigger brains than mine must take over from here. Don't worry, all will be explained after the service.'

She was already disappearing towards her bedroom.

'Wait a minute,' Stanton called after her. 'What service?'

'It's Christmas Eve, Hugh. Carols at King's, for God's sake. Even a bloody atheist like you can't miss that.'

6

'*Bayım bayım, durun!*'

Stanton heard a little girl's voice behind him and turned to see that the Muslim child he'd saved from the speeding car was running after him. Struggling with something. His bag.

He'd forgotten his bag.

His bag!

How could he have been so stupid?

He'd left the majority of his money and equipment in his room at his hotel but he still had with him a handgun and a small computer, water purifiers, antibiotics and a state-of-the-art field surgical kit. Items which, if lost, would take at least a hundred years to replace. And he'd walked away without them.

Sure, he was disorientated but it was still an unforgivable lapse.

Allowing emotion to cloud his judgement and losing contact with essential equipment was about as ill-disciplined and un-professional a mistake as a soldier on active service could make. In fact, he absolutely should never have intervened to save that family at all. Quite apart from the possible repercussions on history of saving a family who had been destined to die, he could quite easily have been killed himself by that careering car, thus ending his mission before it had even begun.

But when he turned round and looked into the big jet-black eyes of the little Turkish girl who was struggling up behind him with his bag, her broad smile framed between outsized loop ear-rings and cascades of coal-dark silken hair, Stanton was glad he'd let instinct be his guide. Somewhere in that big dusty city there was a father who would be spared the death in life that he himself was living.

The bag was quite heavy for a little girl to carry, although not as heavy as it looked, being made of Gore-tex disguised to appear like old leather and canvas. She held it up to him, grinning a big gap-toothed grin. He took it and turned away. He couldn't speak to her or even look at her for long. For all that she was olive-skinned and dark-eyed and her hair was shiny black, she reminded him too much of Tessa.

He made his way off the bridge. Leaving the broad modern thoroughfare behind him, he plunged at once into the matted tangle of ancient streets and alleyways on the south side of the Golden Horn.

Despite the disorientation and confusion he was feeling, Stanton could not help but be intoxicated by the magic of his situation. He was in Old Stamboul, fabled city on a hill. Ancient soul of Turkey. The gateway to the Orient where East met West and for twenty-six centuries the heartbeat of history had been heard in every wild cry and whispered intrigue. Where enchanting music played all down the ages as swords clashed and cannons roared and poets told their tales of love and death. Armies had come and armies had gone. First Christian, then Muslim, then back, and back again, but Stamboul had remained. Church had given way to mosque and mosque had given way to church then back to mosque. And through it all, the people of Stamboul had gone about their business just as they were doing now. Unaware of the fact that there had now arrived among them the strangest traveller in all the city's long history.

Stanton gave himself over to the romance of the moment. Kicking his way through the stinking piled-up rubbish. Tripping on erratic, uneven paving stones laid down when Suleiman the Magnificent was Sultan. Avoiding the mass of dogs that snarled and whimpered as they scavenged for food at the little bread and fruit stalls lining the tiny streets. He was lost almost at once within a labyrinthine warren of alleys and passages. Dark, shadowy flights of steps disappeared into tiny cracks between sagging buildings, up towards half-hidden doorways or down into stinking, dripping cellars. And sometimes, enchantingly, into fragrant sunken gardens. How Cassie would have loved to glimpse into those gardens.

Quite suddenly Stanton found that he couldn't recall her face.

He stopped dead in his tracks and was roundly cursed for it by a fierce bearded man in a keffiyeh who was driving two skinny, bleating goats with a stick. Stanton stood stock still, ignoring the man and his animals as he struggled to bring to mind the most precious memory he possessed.

It was the panic. He knew that. The sudden fear that she was fading, like some figure in a photograph in a time-travel movie. He struggled with his confusion, desperate to bring her face to mind but just making matters worse, like trying to remember a familiar word but chasing it further away by trying to retrieve it. He forced his brain to place her in a familiar situation. There she was! He'd found her. Picnicking on Primrose Hill when the children were tiny. Smiling up at his camera phone.

Bang!

'*Çekil yolumdan!*'

The alleyway was crowded and another passer-by in a hurry had cannoned into him, a big man in a bright blue turban, a flowing white tunic and loose pyjama-y trousers. A man with two pistols and a knife stuck in his belt. Stanton mumbled an apology and moved on.

One corner, then another. A darkened passage then a burst of light and a tinkling fountain in a walled square. Horse dung on his nostrils then delicate perfume. Tobacco, hashish, oranges, fried meat, rose water and dog piss. There were so many dogs.

He heard shouts and clattering and the squeal of metal on stone.

Just in time Stanton jumped to avoid a sweating carthorse as it skidded down the street in front of him. Stamboul was a city on a hill and the gradients of some of the alleyways were almost precipices. The foam-mouthed beast was struggling to restrain the heavily laden cart which theoretically it was pulling but in practice now threatened to push it down the steep hill. The drover cursed Stanton and pulled on the horse's reins. The man knew a *feringi* when he saw one, an obvious foreigner in his Norfolk jacket and moleskin britches. A man out of place and out of time.

Stanton felt exposed. Eyes peered out at him from deep within dark and barred recesses. Others flicked a glance through niqabs. A young soldier strode past, chest out, eyes front, but he too stole a glance at the foreign stranger. It felt to Stanton as if those eyes could see through him and knew his secret.

He needed to pull himself together. He'd already been nearly killed twice that morning, first by a car and just then by a horse. He might even have been killed by the man with the pistols in his belt. Life was clearly cheap in the old city and offence, once taken, was mortal.

He had to concentrate. Whatever his personal sorrows might be, he had a mission to accomplish and one he truly believed in. Cassie and the children were gone, evaporated like the morning mist on the Bosphorus, along with the century in which they'd lived. He couldn't save them but it was in his power to save *millions* of others. Young men who would very shortly be choking on mustard gas, hanging limp on barbed wire and vaporized by shells. Unless he changed their fate.

But to do that he needed to keep his head.

He decided he would drink some strong Turkish coffee, and found a cafe on a tiny square in the shadow of a mosque. Everything in Stamboul was in the shadow of a mosque. Or else jammed up against some decayed and rotting palace which in its days of glory had housed a prince or potentate with his eunuchs and his harem. Nowhere else on earth, Stanton thought, could current decay have lived so entirely within the shell of past glory.

It reminded him of London in 2024.

The little cafe had just two small tables and a counter but it was scrupulously clean and well ordered. There was a splendid hookah pipe on display in the window and neat little rows of pink and green sweetmeats lined up in a glass cabinet on the counter. Each table had a well-brushed, tasselled velvet cloth on it, a clean ashtray and a small bowl of salted almonds. Such calm and order amid the seemingly random chaos outside allowed Stanton his first moment of reflection since the Crossley 20/25 had thundered on to the Galata Bridge.

He was shown to a seat and brought coffee and bottled water. Whatever suspicion of *feringi* he had felt out in the street was not evident in the cafe. Business was always business, whatever age or town you were in.

Speaking in Turkish, the cafe owner pointed at the cakes and pastries. Stanton made an expansive gesture as if to say that he was happy to be served as the proprietor wished.

He was brought some marzipan and a kind of semolina doughnut in a sticky syrup, the first food he had eaten since dinner the evening before, a hundred and eleven years ago. It was a strange sort of breakfast but he was grateful for it. He laid a ten-lira note on the table and indicated that he didn't need change. The man smiled and returned to his coffee, newspaper and cigarette.

Prayers were being called in the mosque outside. Stanton could see the devout beginning to assemble in the little square outside the window, beyond the hookah pipe. Reaching into his pocket he pulled out his wallet. Slimmer now than he was used to, no plethora of plastic cards, no photo ID. Just some post-Edwardian Turkish currency.

And two printouts.

Letters which better than anything else could remind him of his duty and focus his resolve.

Cassie's last two emails.

The one asking for a divorce.

And then the final one. The one that had offered a glimmer of hope. The one she had written in reply to his pleas and his promises. The one he'd been rushing home to answer face to face.

If you can just change a little.
No, not even change. Just be yourself again. The man I married.
The father of our kids.
That man was every bit as passionate as you are. But not as angry.
Every bit as tough. But not as hard.
Every bit as cool. But not as cold.

Stanton swallowed his coffee and held out his cup for a refill.

He'd wanted so much to prove to her that he could be that man again. But four drugged-up hooligans had denied him the chance. Cassie had died thinking him unredeemed. Tess and Bill had died thinking that Mummy was leaving Daddy.

Because Daddy was a stupid selfish bastard who didn't deserve their love.

I never minded being married to a soldier. Because I knew you believed in what you were risking your life for. What you were taking lives for.

I never minded being married to an idiot whose idea of inspiring kids was to see how close he could get to death without actually dying.

Even when we had kids of our own and you still kept on doing what you did. Even though you weren't just risking leaving me without a husband but our children without a father, I still didn't mind.

Because that was the man I signed up for.

Just like you knew you married a girl who'd rather lie in bed and watch daytime TV than go hiking up a mountain in a storm.

A girl who didn't want to get her scuba ticket. Or go paragliding (or watch you doing it either).

We both knew who we were getting and we were fine with it.

But who's this new guy, Hugh?

I don't know him? Do you?

Really, Hugh? Seriously?

A security guard? A hired gun? A glorified minder?

You leave me and Tess and Bill at home to go off and be some billionaire's bitch? Would you really take a bullet for those people, Hugh?

Is that how little we mean to you?

She was right. It was crazy. Why had he done it?

Bitterness? Boredom? Pride?

All three. But pride was the big one of course. Stupid male pride. After they kicked him out of the army and the webcast thing went sour, he just hadn't known what to do with himself. Hanging around the house, fighting with Cassie, shouting at the kids. He'd felt . . . unmanned.

And there was the money. He'd never cared about it before and nor had Cassie. They'd always had enough, always got by. But then *Guts Versus Guts* made them briefly wealthy, or so it had seemed. Wealthy enough to make the down payment on a proper family house in a really nice area. There was a second baby on the way, they'd needed more room and he'd just *done* it. Without even telling her. She was angry at first, of course, but he knew she'd love it. That house had been the first real home they'd ever had. Before that it had been just short rentals and army housing.

He couldn't just let it go.

He couldn't tell Cassie and the kids that they had to pack their bags because he could no longer meet the payments on the mortgage. He was too . . . proud.

So we can't pay the mortgage! We'll move. We'll get something cheaper, or rent, or live in a tent! You're good at that. If you're bored, read a book. If you need a job, go and stack shelves at a supermarket! Wash cars if you love them so much. Sell hamburgers. Do you think we'd care? That Dad isn't a hero any more? Do you think you're a hero now? Maybe you imagined yourself rescuing terrified princesses from sex traders or saving stolen school kids from crazed warlords. You always were an overgrown

boy scout and we loved you for it. But the truth is you're just a
bodyguard to the most selfish people on earth.

She'd been right of course. When Stanton had been approached
by an old SAS comrade to join an international 'security'
company, there'd been a lot of righteous talk about protecting the
vulnerable from predators. Doing the tough jobs that the
authorities couldn't or wouldn't do. Fighting pirates, guarding
crusading education ministers from fundamentalist assault.

But when Cassie's emails had reached him he'd been leaning on
the rail of a superyacht in the Aegean. Suit, dark glasses, earpiece.
For all his big pay cheque, he was just another goon, riding shot-
gun for the Boss man. Working for the new master race in their
floating world. The twenty-first-century boat people, that ever-
growing flotilla of billionaires and trillionaires who had taken to
living at sea where they could be isolated and protected from the
rapid social breakdown their own activities had played a large
part in causing. Climate-change refugees in the truest sense of the
word.

I was proud of you when you risked your life on peacekeeping
missions, saving children who were just like your own.
   I was proud of you when you risked your life making your videos
to help inspire kids who weren't as fortunate as ours.
   But risking your life for media moguls? Oil tycoons? Real-estate
parasites? So they can fiddle about on their yachts while the rest
of the world burns?
   Forget it!
   Bill and Tess deserve a dad who cares more about them than
about dealing with his own stupid demons.
   If ever you bump into the guy you used to be, get him to give us
a call.

That last line had been the glimmer of hope. He hadn't called.
He'd run. Resigned his job that minute. Gone ashore and headed

for the nearest airport. He was going straight to London. To get down on his knees and promise to be the man Cassie wanted him to be. The father Tess and Bill needed.

But he never got the chance to make those promises, let alone keep them. They never even knew he was coming home . . .

Stanton drained his second coffee and poured himself a glass of water.

Then he heard a voice. An English voice.

'*Garçon!* Coffee and cognac, and be quick about it!'

His whole being froze.

He knew that voice.

7

THE MORNING RAIN and hail had long since turned again to snow as Stanton and McCluskey made their way across the Cam towards King's College chapel, which rose up before them through the icy mist cloaked in white.

'Did you ever *see* anything so fine?' McCluskey remarked as they paused for a moment on the King's Bridge. 'Doesn't it lift your soul just a little?'

'Sorry,' Stanton replied. 'Just makes me think how much Cassie would have loved it.'

'Ah yes.' McCluskey sighed. 'Such is the terrible irony of bereavement, turning every familiar joy to misery. Each smile a twisting knife. Each thing of beauty an added burden of pain.'

'Thanks.'

The service was indeed agonizingly beautiful. Like a second funeral. The many flickering candles. The swelling voices of the choir. The readings in the mighty poetry of the King James Bible, strangely moving even to a non-believer. The unbearable majesty of a ritual that had remained almost unchanged for three hundred Christmas Eves.

After the service McCluskey didn't take Stanton straight to the lodge at Trinity as he had expected but instead she put her arm in his and led him through the freezing wind across the quad to the Great Hall. Stanton noticed that quite a number of other members of the King's congregation were heading in the same direction, all venerable College figures, stooped with age, holding their various forms of fringed and tasselled hats to their heads while their gowns billowed in a gale that threatened to blow the frailer ones away.

Two porters were standing at the entrance to the Hall and others had taken up positions around the Great Court. They wore the traditional bowler hats (made somewhat ridiculous by the compulsory high-vis jackets) but something about their manner suggested to Stanton they weren't porters at all. Too focused, too likely looking. Stanton had briefed enough security details in his time to know one when he saw one.

Inside the five-hundred-year-old building, however, the peace and serenity of the fusty old College remained. In fact, it felt to Stanton almost as if he was attending a second Christmas Service. A string quartet was playing seasonal music and there was the same atmosphere of whispered reverence. Lines of chairs had been set out before a little lecture platform like pews set before an altar. And once more there were many candles, although these seemed only to increase the gloom, failing entirely to illuminate the beams of the great ceiling, which lowered above them deep in the shadows.

When McCluskey, who had been bustling about with a clip-board, had satisfied herself that everyone was present she led Stanton to the place reserved for him in the centre of the first row in front of the podium. Then she mounted the little platform and turned to address the room.

'Good evening, everyone, and a merry Christmas to you all,' she boomed. 'Each one of you knows the purpose of this gather-ing save for our newest and last Companion, Captain Hugh 'Guts' Stanton, late of the Special Air Service Regiment and renowned webcast celebrity. Captain, your fellow Chronations bid you most welcome.' There was polite applause, which Stanton did not acknowledge. He did not feel remotely that he had joined any order or that he was a companion to any of these people. 'Captain Stanton has been very patient with me,' McCluskey went on. 'I have told him scarcely half the story, so far being scarcely qualified to do so. I now call upon Amit Sengupta, Lucian Professor of Mathematics here at Cambridge and Newton's direct successor, to explain the matter further.'

Stanton knew of the corpulent Anglo-Indian academic who now rose from his chair and took the stage. Everybody in Britain knew Sengupta because besides being an eminent physicist he was also, as so many eminent physicists are, an appalling media tart. A man who appeared regularly on news and documentary shows commenting on any matters even remotely related to science and the cosmos. He was always introduced in the most breathless and epic terms as 'the man who has looked into the eye of God' or 'the man who has travelled in his mind to the edge of space and the beginning of time'. Sengupta himself, of course, always affected amused modesty at this sort of hyperbole, looking uncomfortable and claiming that he had in fact only journeyed back as far as fifteen seconds *after* the beginning of time and making it very clear that the first quarter minute of the life of the universe remained as much a mystery to him as it would to his driver or his cook. Professor Sengupta was also a hugely successful writer, having produced a work of 'popular' physics called *Time, Space and other Annoying Relatives*, which purported to explain relativity and quantum mechanics to 'the man in the pub' and of course didn't. In scientific circles it was said of Sengupta's book that it was easier to find a Higgs Boson particle without the assistance of a Hadron Collider than it was to find anyone who'd got past the third page.

The professor waddled up on to the stage like a seal taking possession of a rock. He wore a pinstripe suit beneath his gown and a yellow-spotted bow tie of the type favoured by professors who like to be thought of as a bit mad. On his head was his trademark Nehru hat, to which he had pinned a badge that said 'Science Rocks'. Sengupta opened his briefcase and made a great show of arranging certain papers on a small table before taking a quite deliberately long, slow sip of water. Finally he began.

'Newton's great leap of the imagination,' he said in his

pedantic-sounding, sing-song voice, which was half Calcutta lecture theatre and half London gentlemen's club, 'was to understand, *hundreds* of years before Einstein, that time is *relative*.' Here he paused for theatrical effect and also to dab rather primly at the water on his lips with the enormous, brightly coloured silk handkerchief he kept stuffed flamboyantly in the breast pocket of his suit. 'Time is not *straight* or *linear*. It does not progress in a regular and ordered fashion, and the reason for this is because it is affected by *gravity*. Yes! Just as are motion and mass and light, and indeed all the properties of the physical universe. It is, of course, generally believed that Einstein first proposed the idea of universal relativity but we in this room and we *alone* now know that in fact the first man in the world to make this leap of thought was our own Sir Isaac Newton. And we know also that Newton leapt further and with surer foot than Einstein ever did. For just as Newton showed the world that gravity explained the circular and elliptical courses of the *planets*, he also understood that *time* moved in a similar manner, twisting and ever turning, *shadowing* the expansion of the universe, bound by the gravitational pull of every atom contained therein. To put it plainly, Newton saw that time was *coiled*, and just as an understanding of gravity allowed him to track and map the course of planetary motion, it also enabled him to track the movement of *time*. And so *predict its course*.'

Here Sengupta paused briefly for another sip of water. He knew he had a sensational story and clearly did not intend to rush it.

'So what? I hear you asking yourselves,' he continued. 'Coiled or straight, time progresses and there is nothing we can do about it. Why in the blinking blazes was old Isaac getting his knickers in a twist? I will tell you why! Because gravitational pull is not *uniform*! Just as the planets deviate slightly from the perfect symmetry of their ancient courses, so it is with time. We must think of it not as a *perfect spiral* but more as a *disobliging Slinky* in which, once in a while, coils get crossed. Time will, on rare occasions, pass through the same set of dimensions *twice*. The coils of the Slinky touch only for a moment, within the most limited parameters, after which the spiral of time continues on its merry way. No harm done . . . But what, Newton asked himself in the tortured journeying of his fearful imaginings, if someone were *present* at that point in space–time when the coils of the Slinky touched? That person would exist at both the beginning and the end of a loop in time. And so now the spiral does *not* continue on its merry way. It turns *back* on itself. For simply by drawing breath, our intrepid time-*straddler* reboots the loop. All that had been in the past is now once more *yet to come*. History is unmade. The loop is *begun again*.'

Sengupta mopped his brow with his handkerchief and took yet another sip of water. The flickering of the candles cast a ghostly ripple across his face. The assembled Companions of Chronos leant forward on their walking sticks and Zimmer frames, hanging on the great physicist's every word.

'And Newton really *did his sums*,' Sengupta continued. 'It is scarcely possible to credit but this divine genius, working alone and without modern equipment, was able to tell us *when* and *where* time would next cross its own path. No wonder he went a bit loony. I think *I'd* be looking for secret codes in the Bible myself if I'd just written a map of time when everybody else was just starting to think about mapping Australia. Sir Isaac's conclusion was most specific. He calculated that the next closed loop in the space–time continuum would be one hundred and eleven years long, and that the point at which the beginning and the end would cross would occur at midnight on the thirty-first of May 2025 and at a quarter *past* midnight in the very early morning of the first of June 1914. I'm sure all of you can see the reason for the fifteen-minute time lag.'

Stanton couldn't see it, nor did he imagine that many other people in the room could either. Professor Sengupta had the self-satisfied habit common to many academics of pretending an intellectual equality with his audience in order to happily demonstrate his own superiority.

'It is, of course, because, as I have explained, gravity is not *even* or *symmetrical*. As each loop of space and time progresses, space and time are *gained*, just as in the case of leap years. And so although the two moments of departure and arrival are *simultaneous*, our time traveller will in effect arrive fifteen minutes *after* he leaves. And of course one hundred and eleven years *before*. Ha ha.'

Sengupta grinned broadly as if he'd made a great joke. There was a sycophantic murmur of forced mirth in reply, in which Sengupta allowed himself to bask for a moment before continuing.

'The contact of these two separate moments in time will be minimal and fleeting. It will last for less than a second in time, and the *spatial* juxtaposition will be, to employ Newton's own delightfully colourful phrase, "no bigger than a sentry box outside St James's Palace". Any person *standing* in that imaginary sentry box in 2025 would *also* be standing in it in 1914, *instantly* wiping out the previous reality and beginning the creation of an entirely new one. The whole one-hundred-and-eleven-year loop will be begun again. And the *location* where that notional sentry box will stand, the spatial coordinates where the twisted Slinky of space–time will cross itself, occurs in Istanbul.'

'Constantinople!' McCluskey shouted, unable to resist jumping up. 'In *Europe*! I mean, *come on*! Is that fate or what? The place is barely seven hundred miles from Sarajevo! Fifteen hundred from Berlin! Newton's coordinates could have dumped our man anywhere: the summit of Everest, the middle of the South China Sea—'

'The burning superheated core of the planet,' Sengupta interjected. 'Space–time is no respecter of physical mass.'

'Exactly,' McCluskey went on exultantly. 'Instead it's "Who's for a cup of Turkish coffee and a bit of belly dancing?" This is divine intervention, I tell you – it's got to be. God gives us one shot at changing history and puts it exactly where it's needed most.'

'Let us be clear, Professor McCluskey,' Sengupta said sternly, 'whatever may be your religious beliefs, this is *all about science*. Newton, as I say, did the maths. He places his junction in space and time in Istanbul and his coordinates are fantastically specific. The crucial point occurs in the cellar of an old residential palace in the dockland area of the city. Newton secretly arranged for the purchase of the building, endowing that a hospital be established in it and ordering that the cellar henceforth remain forever locked.'

'Bet *that* cost a pretty penny,' McCluskey observed excitedly. '*Now* we know what the sly old bugger was doing at the Royal Mint all those years.'

'Yes, well, be that as it may,' Sengupta said firmly, clearly irritated at McCluskey's constant interruptions. 'The great man's hope was that the cellar would still be locked in 2025, thus enabling a traveller from that time to enter the sentry box un-impeded. It was a long shot given the turbulence of history but in fact he nearly made it. It was only in the chaos that followed the Great War that Newton's hospital finally was closed. Thus in 1914 the cellar was still locked under the terms of Newton's endowment.'

'But the cellar's still there!' McCluskey cried out.

'Yes, yes, Professor McCluskey.' Sengupta positively snarled. 'I was coming to that. The palace above it fell into disrepair and has been redeveloped many times but the foundations remain—'

'And we've bought it!' McCluskey shouted, now jumping up and joining Sengupta on the stage. 'It belongs to us. It will be wait-ing for us on the thirty-first of May next year. Waiting for you, Hugh. Waiting for Captain "Guts" Stanton.' She pointed her stubby, nicotine-stained finger towards him. With all the talk of 1914 Stanton found himself thinking of the famous Lord Kitchener recruiting poster. Perhaps McCluskey was thinking of the same thing.

'Your country needs you, Hugh. The world needs you!'

8

'COME ON, CHOP CHOP. Christ, what a country! I said coffee and cognac. And breakfast. Got any eggs? Fresh, mind.'

He'd heard that voice before.

His head had been bowed, his eye focused on Cassie's emails. Now, quietly, he folded them away in his wallet and put it back in his pocket. Then, as much by instinct as intention, his right hand slid down beyond his pocket and dropped down into the bag at his feet, fingers closing round the handle of his little polymer machine pistol.

Although God knows he couldn't use it.

Discharging a weapon like that with its awesome and currently unimagined capabilities could scarcely fail to raise the interest of every intelligence agency in the city. And as any student of military history knew, there were more spies than dogs in pre-Great War Constantinople.

'I said coffee! And a drink! Dammit, what's the bloody Turkish for booze?'

It was a curious voice, very clipped with short vowels, but the tone took Stanton back to Sandhurst. To officer training and all those private-school boys with their effortless sense of entitlement.

'Lazy kaffir's probably on some carpet praying,' the voice went on. 'They never stop praying, do they? If they spent less time praying and more time *doing*, then the country wouldn't be such a bloody basket case, would it?'

But it wasn't just the tone he recognized. He'd heard this *specific* voice before.

How could that possibly be?

He gripped the weapon tighter.

And then he remembered. His fingers relaxed around his gun.

How stupid. How very stupid. Of course he'd heard the voice before. Not in another century but scarcely an hour ago.

It was the idiot from the Galata Bridge, the driver of the Crossley 20/25.

He turned and glanced. It was them all right, the men in the car. All five of them. Early twenties. Boaters, blazers, flannel bags. Swagger sticks and old school ties. Smart enough but with blood-shot eyes and sweaty, pasty faces. Still half drunk. Hooligans. Wealthy ones but hooligans nonetheless. You got them in any age, any class. Swap the boaters for hoodies and they could have come from the twenty-first century.

Quite suddenly Stanton felt a terrible anger rising within him.

These could have been the four bastards who wiped out his family. They very nearly *had* wiped out a family.

'I *said* coffee and cognac!' the young man repeated loudly and unpleasantly as he and his companions slumped themselves noisily around one of the little tables, scraping back their chairs, lounging about and generally making it clear that they owned the place.

One of the others spoke up from behind a street map.

'I'm sure it's around here somewhere,' he said. 'Hey, you!' the man barked at the cafe owner, who having disappeared into his kitchen was now emerging with a tray of cups and a coffee pot. 'House of Mahmut – where is it? Girls? Dancing? House of Sluts? Where – Mahmut – House?'

The owner merely shrugged and shook his head.

'Bloody idiot's got no idea what we're talking about,' the first man said, '*and* he's forgotten the brandy. Oi, you. I said coffee *and* cognac.'

The owner shook his head and turned away, which infuriated the Englishman, who banged the table in protest.

'Don't you bloody turn your back on me, you bloody dago! I said, where's the bloody brandy?'

Stanton rose to his feet and picked up his bag. He knew he had to leave because he really wanted to confront these men and that would be a very stupid thing to do. His first and only duty was to pass the time until his business in Sarajevo as quietly and with as little impact as possible. His whole mission depended on the key events he was tasked with influencing remaining unchanged from when they had first occurred in time. Confronting gangs of semi-drunk posh boys in Old Stamboul was *unlikely* to affect the diary plans of the Austrian royal house, but it might.

The movement brought him to the attention of the five men.

'You, sir,' the man who'd been at the wheel of the car and who was the most vocal of the group said, 'you don't look Turkish. English? Français? Deutsch? We want some brandy. Do you speak dago?'

He should have just said no and walked out.

'You're in Stamboul,' Stanton said quietly, 'so have a bit of respect. This is a Muslim establishment. Obviously they won't have brandy. It's morning, so go back to Pera and sleep it off. But don't try to drive or I'll take your keys.'

For a moment the five young men stared in astonishment.

The leader collected himself first. 'And you would be . . . ?'

Stanton still could have turned around and left but he didn't.

'I'm a British army officer and I'm telling you that you'll get no cognac here because alcohol is proscribed under Islam, as even imbeciles like you must know. So why don't you just clear out and go home – but I warn you, don't try to drive.'

Five jaws dropped open in front of him.

This was stupid and Stanton knew it. These men hadn't killed Cassie and he was crazy drawing attention to himself.

'I know who he is,' another member of the party shouted. 'He was on the bridge this morning. He's the chap who nearly made us crash.'

'So he is! Wish I'd damn well hit him now.'

'I'm the chap,' Stanton replied firmly, 'who saved you from being under arrest for the manslaughter of a mother and her young children.'

Now finally he did try to leave, taking a step towards the door as if he'd said his piece. But he was already in too deep. The five young men were having none of it.

'The wogs can't arrest Englishmen,' the leader said. 'Or weren't you aware of that?'

'Funny sort of army officer,' another remarked. 'What's your regiment?'

Stanton bit his lip. He knew from the research he'd done in Cambridge that Turkey had traded sovereignty for foreign investment. No British officer was going to rot in a gaol for knocking over a few locals and this comfortable arrangement would have been second nature to the British in the city.

'Who are you, damn you?' the leader of the group demanded. 'I haven't seen you before.'

'I don't think he's army at all. I've never seen him. Anybody seen him?'

Stanton was feeling stupid. Why had he said he was a soldier? The foreign groups clustered around the embassies and hotels of the Pera district must inevitably be small and insular; the five men facing him would expect to know all their comrades in the city.

'Who the hell are you?' the one who had been driving demanded once more. 'I asked you what's your regiment.'

Well, it couldn't be the Special Air Service. That would not come into existence for decades to come. Or perhaps now not at all.

'I'm just a territorial,' Stanton replied, belatedly trying to blend into the background from which he had irrevocably and so stupidly leapt. 'Not real army at all, I'm a tourist really.'

But he knew he didn't look like a tourist, or at least not the type of British tourist usually to be seen gently taking in the sights of

Old Stamboul. He was tall, tough and rugged-looking, dressed for action in his thick socks and boots, grey moleskin trousers and tweed. The five men were eyeing him with growing suspicion.

'Show me your papers,' the lead man demanded. 'I want to know exactly who you are and where you come from.'

Stanton was carrying identification papers in both English and German. The English ones were in his own name and established him as an Australian gold-miner and engineer, but he certainly didn't want to have this identity placed on any official record. He was supposed to be a shadow, making zero impact on the history through which he was passing.

'You have no authority here,' Stanton replied. 'I might just as well ask for your papers since it's you who are bringing the army into disrepute. But it's getting hot and I can't be bothered so if you'll excuse—'

'Guard the door, Tommy,' the leader instructed. 'I think we need to talk to this chap.'

One of the group went and stood in front of the door. The other four took a step towards Stanton.

His options were few and none of them were attractive. He could, of course, drop to one knee, whip the machine gun out from his bag and kill all five of them. He didn't judge that any of the men facing him were armed. Even if they were, he felt confident that he could dispatch them all before any one of them was able to haul out and cock the type of heavy, steel handgun they might be carrying. Stanton's own little Glock was so reliable, rapid and accurate in its fire that with his special training and the added element of surprise his accusers would not stand a chance.

But creating a blood bath in the middle of a densely crowded neighbourhood was scarcely the action of a shadow.

Could he bribe them? He had plenty of money. But he guessed that his interrogators would view such an offer with contempt. Any effort in that direction would no doubt only serve to confirm their clearly growing suspicion that he was some kind of dirty foreign spy.

But if they held him and searched him and discovered all the various astonishing things inside his bag the game was up anyway. The authorities would hold him for ever trying to work out who and what he was.

In the time it had taken for Stanton to think these thoughts his opponents had taken two steps more towards him. Two more and they'd be within arm's length. Stanton resolved that he would have to fight them hand to hand. The space was small and he was in a corner so they couldn't all come at him at once. There was a good chance that given his superior training he would be able to punch his way through to the door with his bag. The odds weren't bad; there were five of them, certainly, all fit young men and soldiers too. But they'd been up all night drinking and it was highly unlikely that they knew any of the hand-to-hand skills which to Stanton were second-nature. They'd all have boxed but according to strict Queensberry rules and Stanton didn't intend to follow any rules. Whatever the odds, this offered him a better chance of completing his mission than spraying the crowded room with bullets.

Stanton had just determined that his first move would be a left-hooked karate chop to the prominent Adam's apple of the group leader, and in fact his left arm was already in motion, when the owner of the cafe appeared once more.

'Stop this please,' he said softly. 'Prayers are completed in the mosque.'

'Oh, so you can speak a civilized language when it suits you, can you, Abdul?' the leader of the five said over his shoulder as he advanced the final step towards Stanton. 'Well, bully for you, but I'm not interested in your prayers or your damned mosque.' The man addressed Stanton once more. 'Now you show me your papers, my friend, or you're coming with us to the military police to explain why you're impersonating a British officer.'

'And in a moment my cafe will be full,' the Turkish owner went on, and something about his tone gave both Stanton and his opponent pause. 'Full of Muslims, sir, devout Muslims and also

Turkish patriots. Must I tell them that you have insulted me and my house with your crude observations and your demands for alcohol?'

The young Englishmen were astonished.

'Are you *threatening* us?' the leader asked.

'This is Stamboul, not Pera,' the owner went on. 'This part of the city does not belong to foreigners. It belongs to us. You should leave now.'

Clearly the young Englishmen were torn, their pride and arrogance baulked at being ordered about by mere natives, but they could see that outside the window beyond the hookah pipe the tiny, ancient square was already filling up as the mosque disgorged. And the crowd was not the kind of westernized Turk that lived in Pera, this was Old Stamboul. There were no linen suits, no fezes, no clean chins, and no women at all. Instead there were pyjama-y trousers, flowing robes and flowing beards. Already two or three of the worshippers were at the door of the little cafe. Fierce men with knives at their belts. Stanton saw a pistol, although it must have been fifty years old.

The five officers might have been arrogant and half drunk but they weren't completely beyond reason. This was still the age of Empire, the British had been spread very thinly and precariously across the globe for two centuries, and they knew they wouldn't be the first soldiers of the Crown to disappear into a resentful local crowd, never to be seen again. The shock of Gordon's fate at Khartoum had cast a shadow across the psyche of late Imperial Britain every bit as traumatic as the death of any fairy-tale princess had done a hundred years later.

'All right, we'll go,' the leader said. 'But you're coming with us,' he added, turning to Stanton. 'Guy, get his bag.'

Once more Stanton stiffened in readiness. They most certainly were not getting his bag.

Once more it was the cafe owner who diffused the situation.

'No,' he commanded. 'My friend did not insult the Prophet. He stays. You leave.'

Now the door of the cafe opened and the first thirsty customers came in from prayer. Within a moment the little space was packed with at least ten puzzled-looking men watching what was clearly some kind of stand-off between a group of *feringi*. The owner turned to the newcomers and spoke to them in Turkish. Whatever he said caused them to glare menacingly at the five now beleaguered Englishmen.

'You'd better not let me see you again,' the leader snarled in Stanton's face. Then, with what dignity he could, he led his comrades out into the square, where they were the object of many sullen stares.

Stanton turned to his saviour and thanked him.

'It is I who should thank you,' the owner replied. 'It is not so common for a foreigner crusader in our city to treat a Muslim as his equal.'

'You speak very good English,' Stanton observed.

'Only when I choose to. Please. Another coffee.'

9

AFTER SENGUPTA'S LECTURE Stanton and McCluskey made their way back across the quad from the Great Hall of Trinity to the Master's Lodge.

'You *seriously* believe that you can send me back to 1914?' Stanton said, having to raise his voice over the blizzard that was blasting into their faces. 'And from the point when that happens ... the previous one hundred and eleven years will never have existed?'

'They will be yours to remake.'

'But in the meantime you've wiped out the entire population of the world, killing *billions* of people.'

'You can't kill someone who hasn't been born,' McCluskey said. 'But we will all be born, born *again* and better! A population made up of the same organic components and DNA but radically *improved* by the massive injection of the blood which will no longer be spilled in Flanders fields and in all the wars and genocides that followed. We'll all be back, captain! Every one of us and more, but not as we are now, a species of sick and sickening spiritual degenerates waiting for extinction, but as humanity ought to be. As I believe God *intended* us to be, or else why would he have given us this second chance to get it right?'

They had arrived at the lodge. McCluskey opened the front door but Stanton paused on the doorstep, allowing the snow to blow into the hall.

'God?' Stanton replied. 'You really think God wants you to

71

remove the current entirety of the human race from the universe?'

'Why not?' McCluskey said, ushering him over the threshold and closing the door behind him. 'They just sit around staring at their phones, what difference will it make? Besides, think of the lives you'll *save*! Starting with the Battle of Mons, the Marne, then first Ypres, then Gallipoli, Loos, the Somme, Ypres again and then Ypres for a third time and on and on. You were a British soldier, weren't you? The men who died in those battles are your comrades, it's your *duty* to save them. And all the other tens of millions of anguished souls who died in misery in the benighted twentieth century! Do you really think you have a right to *fail* to prevent a catastrophe just because that catastrophe has *already happened*?' McCluskey didn't allow Stanton time to answer this convoluted point before pressing on. 'Isn't that dereliction of duty, captain? If I didn't know you better I might even call it cowardice.'

She turned and began to mount the famous staircase, the one on which Master Bentley had spent so much money three centuries before and which Isaac Newton had climbed on the day he had begun the business of Chronos.

'Now wait a minute,' Stanton said, striding after her. 'Cowardice? I notice that you bunch of superannuated old fossils have been careful to avoid including anybody who might still feel their life was worth living.'

'Exactly!' McCluskey shouted, clapping her hands with joy. 'Newton thought of everything. *And let them be old!* he said. He guessed that if history needed any necessary readjustment then only those with little to lose would have the courage, the foresight, the *soul* to attempt it. But the old and decrepit can't save the world. Only the young and strong can do that. Which is why we found you, Hugh! You will be the last Companion of Chronos. And it's Christmas! This calls for champagne.'

She went into the kitchen and grabbed a bottle from the fridge. Soon they were both back where they had been that morning, glasses in hand, Stanton sitting in the old Queen Anne chair, McCluskey, as ever, hogging the fire.

'All right,' Stanton said, smiling. 'Let's suppose for a minute that you're not all deluded lunatics and that there really is an opportunity for a person to step into 1914. What do you think me or whoever it is should *do* when they get there? And please don't say you want me to prevent the assassination at Sarajevo.'

'Why not? That's *exactly* what I want you to do.'

'Oh *come on*, professor! That is just *so* lame.'

'Isn't the Archduke's murder generally considered to be the spark that kicked the whole thing off?'

'Yes, the spark! That's the point. You know as well as I do that there were complex underlying—'

'Dear me, Hugh,' McCluskey interrupted. 'You're not going to tell me that the war was an economic inevitability, are you? I cannot *abide* a Marxist, you know that. Cheers.'

McCluskey drank deep at her champagne and then struggled to contain the belch that followed.

'You don't need to be a Marxist to believe that global wars do not depend exclusively for their beginnings on the life or death of a single man.'

'But this one did,' McCluskey replied, when once more she was master of her oesophagus. 'Although not Archduke Ferdinand, as it happens.'

'What?'

'His death was, as you say, just a spark, and one we must of course prevent from igniting the bonfire. But the underlying cause was down to another man altogether. A Germanic royal, but not Franz Ferdinand. You see, *the wrong one died*.'

'What wrong one? How could it possibly come down to one man, royal or not? What about the balance of power? The system of alliances . . .'

'Yes, yes and the naval arms race and Germany's economic miracle and the railway timetables and all the endless catalogue of "causes of the Great War" which every school kid used to know and are now almost forgotten.' McCluskey picked up an antique flintlock from the mantelpiece and took absent-minded aim at a painting on the wall, a serious-looking cleric from the time of Henry VIII. 'John Redman, first Master of Trinity,' she said, squinting along the barrel. 'There's every possibility he was staring down from that frame when Newton visited Bentley and set this whole business in motion. I like to think so, anyway.'

Stanton didn't want to talk about John Redman.

'Stick to the point, professor,' he said. 'What man caused the Great War?'

'Well, the Kaiser, *obviously*. Stupid, stupid Wilhelm, Queen Victoria's wayward grandson. Unstable, bitter, jealous, dangerously ambitious, nursing any number of private jealousies and grudges. He *wanted* war. Nobody else did. They were all just falling dominoes. The Austro-Hungarians? They were having enough trouble deciding which languages to speak in their own parliament.'

'But the Russians . . .' Stanton began.

'Can't speak about the Russians.' McCluskey laughed. 'You can only speak about the Tsar. Poor, timid, confused Nicholas. He'd *never* have fought Cousin Willy if he'd been given any other choice. But Willy didn't give him a choice; Willy kept ramping up the odds. And of course Nicholas was allied to the French. Did *they* want war? Ha! They'd spent forty years draping their statues in black and moaning about Alsace after the Prussians beat 'em the *last* time and never done a thing about it, and never *would* have done either if the Kaiser hadn't thrown a million men at them. So who's left that matters? Us and the Yanks. The Americans were *totally* isolationist. It was in their blood. They'd opted out of Europe on the *Mayflower* and didn't want back in. They never would have joined in at all if the Germans hadn't started sinking their ships and sending inflammatory telegrams to Mexico. Which brings us to the British. The global top dogs, the ones with it all to lose. *Totally* secure behind the guns of the Royal Navy. Financial centre of the planet and carrying the bulk of the world's trade in our ships, a global pre-eminence that depended *entirely* on peace. Do you think anybody in Whitehall wanted to blow all that? No, Hugh, the truth is undeniable, it was Germany's fault, more specifically the *Kaiser*'s fault. Everyone was *talking* about war, as nations always do, and no doubt there were plenty of romantic young men itching to lead a cavalry charge, as young men will, particularly young men who have yet to grasp the full significance of what the machine gun can do to a cavalry charge. But the only world leader who genuinely *wanted* war was the Kaiser. We know it now and they knew it then because if there was one thing on which everybody agreed in the summer of 1914, it was that if war came it would be between Germany and the rest of us.'

'Germany had its allies,' Stanton protested, feeling very much as if he was in a lecture theatre.

'Oh come on! The poxy old Austro-Hungarian and Ottoman empires? They weren't allies, they were liabilities. The *real* powers in the world, the ones with a *future* as well as a past, were Britain, France, Russia, Japan and America on *one* side and Germany on the other – except it wasn't even Germany. It was the *Kaiser*. Him and his Prussian war clique sitting in Potsdam singing hymns to war. The rest of Germany wanted to do business. They were the workshop of the world. If they'd waited another decade they could have *bought* France and no doubt Britain too in the end. Germany had the biggest social democratic party in the world, the Reichstag wanted peace. But the *Kaiser* wanted conquest. And he was still the boss. That crazy bastard with a chip on his disabled shoulder the size of the Brandenburg Gate was *itching* for a fight. That's why he *always* wore military uniform. Where is he in all the photographs? Just think of a picture of Kaiser Bill pre-war and where was he?'

Stanton knew the answer McCluskey was angling for and of course she was right.

'On manoeuvres,' he said.

'Exactly! Playing bloody soldiers. It's all he ever did. He led the most scientifically and industrially advanced nation on earth and all he wanted to do was stand in a field staring at a map with his crippled arm resting on his sword hilt. How did Edward the Seventh spend his time? Boozing, gambling and whoring in Paris. George the Fifth? Bloody *stamp collecting*. Tsar Nicholas? Pretending to be a minor country landowner and pottering about his garden with his bossy wife, who was clearly infatuated with a whore-mongering peasant lunatic. The French were dancing La Belle Epoque. The Americans wanted to wind up the drawbridge and forget Europe existed. And *who* was out on manoeuvres? Who wore a helmet with a spike on top to walk the dog? Who was rearming at the kind of rate that would have made Genghis Khan blush?'

'Kaiser Wilhelm,' Stanton conceded.

'Yes, Kaiser Wilhelm,' McCluskey shouted. 'The cause of the whole damn catastrophe. So that's the plan, Hugh. We swap one dead Germanic royal for another. You will go to Sarajevo and prevent the assassination of the heir to the Austro-Hungarian throne and then you will go to Berlin and kill the Kaiser.'

'In 1914?'

'In 1914.'

Outside the bells of Trinity Chapel chimed midnight. It was Christmas Day.

'Now, I know what you're thinking,' McCluskey continued.

'I'm thinking we must be out of our minds to be having this conversation.'

'Yes, but apart from that, you're thinking if the murder of an archduke caused as much trouble as it did, surely killing an emperor could make things even worse.'

'Well, that's certainly a fair point.'

'But not if *the right people get the blame*.'

'The right people?'

'Absolutely. You see, if the Kaiser is assassinated, the first thing people are going to ask themselves is who did it?'

'Well, of course.'

'And nobody is likely to suggest that the culprit was a time traveller who'd leapt across a closed loop within the space–time continuum.'

'No, I think that's fair.'

'The problem with the murder of Franz Ferdinand was that it was committed by a foreigner and hence had the instant potential to precipitate an international crisis. If the Kaiser were killed by a *German*, or at least if it appeared that way, then the crisis is German and German alone. If it turns out that the killer was also a Socialist, then you have a bun fight that is likely to consume Germany for a considerable time. Germany had the largest and by far the most sophisticated Socialist movement in Europe. As far as the German establishment was concerned, the Left was public enemy number one. If the Left can be shown to have killed the Emperor, there will be a brutal police crackdown and the Left, knowing themselves to be innocent, will fight back. Germany will descend into internal strife. Britain will refocus its attention on the Irish Question, which was tearing it apart at the time, not to mention the Suffragettes. Russia will continue its slow progress towards modern statehood. France will be overjoyed at Germany's self-imposed agonies, which will most certainly keep it occupied through 1914 and probably for years to come. And whatever the Germany that emerges afterwards, be it left-leaning or right, it will at least no longer be led by a psychopathic war-monger. Besides which, by then the increasing prosperity and economic interdependence of the European powers, coupled with democratic reform, both of which were already well under way across the country, will have made war impossible. No two modern capitalist democracies have ever gone to war. And do you know what is the best part of all about this plan? Those lovely Russian princesses will never be murdered! Do close your mouth, Hugh. It's gaping open and making you look like a fish.'

10

S TANTON TOOK A sip of his beer and ate a pretzel. He was sitting in the Orient Bar of the Hotel Pera Palace on the Grande Rue de Pera on the European side of the Golden Horn. After his near escape at the little cafe outside the mosque he had decided to risk no further encounters and had taken a horse cab straight back to his hotel.

He looked about him at the fashionable pre-lunch crowd and wished he still smoked. Absolutely everybody smoked in 1914. Free cigarettes were offered on the bar; for a few pennies he could have a cigar. There were cigarette adverts framed on the walls. One, for a brand called Moslem, featured a sinister-looking character in a fez, and another depicted a very self-satisfied Sultan figure in a huge turban with an Islamic crescent on it, surrounded by a group of scantily clad dancing girls. Stanton amused himself for a moment trying to imagine which group would be most offended in the twenty-first-century world from which he'd come: health campaigners, feminists or devout Muslims.

The barman had spotted where Stanton's eye had fallen.

'Turkish or Virginian, sir?' He pushed the beautiful inlaid box towards Stanton while simultaneously proffering a light.

They looked so nice, those neat lines of perfect little white sticks. He'd smoked twenty a day until quite recently and enjoyed every one of them; more on active service. Most of the guys did. Who cared if you might die in thirty years when you had every chance of dying tomorrow from a concealed bomb? Smoking had been a kind of two-finger salute to the enemy. *We're not scared of you. Look, we're killing ourselves anyway.*

Stanton almost took one. To smoke a Turkish-blend gasper in the Orient Bar at the Hotel Pera Palace in Old Constantinople when the Ottoman Empire was still tottering was about as romantic a thought as a man like Stanton could have.

'No thanks,' he said.

He'd given up after he got Cassie's letter.

She hadn't asked him to but he intended it as absolute proof of his commitment to being a better man. Cassie herself had smoked when they'd first been together but had given it up when she got pregnant. Ever since then he'd known she desperately wanted him to give up too. She'd never hassled him about it but of course he'd known. Particularly after Tessa started noticing all those adverts with the rotting lungs and diseased eyeballs.

'Just another beer, please,' he said. 'No, wait. Scotch. Laphroaig.' Normally he preferred richer, more soothing malts, but right now he wanted something challenging and aggressive. He bolted the smoky, peat-flavoured shot down in one. It reminded him of the lichen, boiled roots and charred stag he'd survived on during his weeks sheltering by Loch Maree.

And it reminded him of McCluskey.

She'd given him Laphroaig on Christmas morning five months before. A little miniature in the toe of the stocking he'd woken up to find at the end of his bed. There'd been a chocolate orange, too, and a keyring from the Trinity College souvenir shop.

Also a letter of identification stamped 'GR' in the name of Captain Hugh Stanton, giving his year of birth as 1878.

'Little Christmas present,' she'd said through the cigarette that was clamped between her teeth as she brought in a breakfast tray. 'They didn't have passports as such in those days. If you thought you might get into strife you carried a letter and photo ID from the Foreign Office telling Johnny Foreigner to damn well leave you alone. Pax Britannica. don't y' know. Happy days, eh? They did a good job photo-shopping your picture, didn't they? I think the moustache suits you. So rakish. You're going to break all the little Suffragettes' hearts. Anyway, tea, eggs, toast and a shed-load of swotting for you. It may be Christmas but you have to work.'

On the tray, alongside the breakfast, were two computers, a tablet and a laptop.

'The tablet's got an excellent German language program on it.'

'Actually I speak pretty good German. Did my first three years' service on the Rhine.'

'Duh! We *know* that, Hugh. It was one of the requirements. Every bit as important as your practical skills. But "pretty good" isn't good enough if you're going undercover. Also don't forget that early twentieth-century German was a bloody sight more for-mal than what the slappers you'll have met in the bars of Lower Saxony spoke. So get swotting. Of course it'd be great if you could learn Turkish and Serbian too but they're absolute *swines* of languages. All in all we think absolutely fluent German is better than a half-arsed smattering of all three. You speak French as well, don't you?'

'Just schoolboy. And a bit of Pashto and Urdu.'

'Oh well. German's the thing. Native languages of both the Archduke you're going to save and the Emperor you're going to pop off.'

McCluskey sat on the bed and took a toast soldier.

'So you're keeping this up then?' Stanton asked.

'Keeping what up?'

'This massive and highly elaborate joke that for some reason you have chosen to play on an ex-student.'

'Still finding it hard to believe that five months from now you're going to step into 1914?' McCluskey said, swallowing toast while pushing smoke out of her nostrils. Stanton wondered where she'd learnt to chew and inhale at the same time. It was a skill he'd noted among the tribesmen out in the hills but it was unusual in Cambridge professors.

'Well, just a bit perhaps,' he admitted, unscrewing the top from his little whisky miniature and breathing in the rich, dirt-flavoured aroma. 'I mean, you know, seeing as how the whole business is clearly insane.' He replaced the cap. 'Is it some kind of thing for rag week? Get Guts Stanton to imagine he's preparing for the ultimate mission and stick it on the net for a laugh, *Guts Versus History?*'

'Do you really imagine I'd punk you, Hugh?'

'Well, it would be a surprising thing to do, I'll admit. But not as surprising as sending me back in time.'

'All right,' McCluskey said, rolling herself another cigarette and dropping bits of tobacco on to Stanton's sheets. 'Here's the thing. Of course we don't *know* for sure that you're going to make a quantum leap in the space–time continuum, but what we do know for sure is that Sir Isaac Newton *believed* you could. And that Sir Amit Sengupta says the mathematics on which that belief was based are sound. That's it. That's all we know and all you know. Now it may be that it doesn't happen. But surely, Hugh, *surely* as the inheritors of Newton's legacy we have a duty to at least accept the possibility and act accordingly? Can't you see that?'

Stanton ate his egg but didn't reply.

'And why *not*, for God's sake? You've told me yourself you're just killing time till you can get yourself killed. Well, kill it with me. It can't be any worse than sitting on the shores of a Scottish loch or trying to get the internet in a budget motel. Live here in the Master's Lodge. Improve your German. Study 1914 with a passion and steep yourself in the fascinating and varied expertise of the Companions of Chronos. What else do you have to do? What would be any better fun? What remotely do you have to lose?'

Stanton smiled. She had him there of course.

'You certainly chose the right bloke,' he said eventually. 'No ties. No life. No future. Not many like me about.'

'And a resourceful adventurer, German-speaking, with a keen interest in history to boot! Blimey, Hugh, it's like Newton himself sent you.'

'All right, prof,' Stanton said, smiling. 'I'll go along with it, for the time being at least . . .'

'Woohoo!' McCluskey said, shaking her head gleefully and sending a shower of dandruff fluttering down to join the layer that was already dappling the shoulders of her greatcoat. 'All right if I pinch another toast soldier?'

McCluskey grabbed one without waiting for a reply, took a bite, then leant forward to dip the remaining end of it into Stanton's egg. Stanton managed to get his hand over the egg in time.

'You can have a bit of toast, prof,' he said, 'but double-dipping someone's egg is not acceptable. In fact it's revolting.'

'I can see you've never had a midnight feast in a school dorm. You get rid of all that squeamishness pretty sharpish. I've taken second chew on another girl's bubble gum a hundred times.'

'I didn't have the advantage of a private school education.'

'That chip you have on your shoulder is going to get a lot heavier in 1914, you know. Posh people really *did* run things then.'

'Whoever has the money runs things, prof. Always has done, always will.'

'Well, anyway, to business. The tablet's for your German. The main computer is bedtime reading. A snapshot of Europe on June the first 1914 with particular emphasis on Central Europe and the Balkans. Every single thing we know from the price of sausages in Budapest to the staff of the British embassy in Belgrade, from train timetables out of Waterloo to the tensions between the Kaiser and his English mother, who he blamed for giving him a withered arm. Hindsight is our trump card and you need to cram it all. As we get closer to blast-off you're going to be spending a lot of time in the History faculty. It'll be during term time so for God's sake don't go falling in love with some winsome undergraduate with a short skirt and a burning interest in Renaissance Italy. Because I'm damn certain they'll all fall in love with a devilishly dishy mature student like you.'

Stanton shot her a glance.

'One thing I know is that I'll never fall in love again.'

McCluskey shrugged. 'Can't imagine that's what your Cassie would have wanted.'

'I've told you before, she's dead, she doesn't get a vote.'

'You could at least allow yourself a shag or two. You'll be swatting totty off like flies.'

'Prof,' Stanton said, 'let's just stick to Chronos, eh?'

'Right you are,' she said heading for the door. 'First German tutorial at eleven thirty. Fortunately your teacher doesn't mind missing his Christmas lunch. Call if you need anything, fags or whatever.'

'I still don't smoke.'

'Bet you will in 1914.'

'If ever I find myself in 1914, prof, maybe I'll have one for you.'

11

S TANTON STUDIED GERMAN through Christmas week, New Year
and most of January, every morning, seven days a week. He
spent the afternoons in physical training and then had supper with
McCluskey either in the Master's Lodge or in a pub. Sometimes
they'd be joined by experts on various aspects of early-twentieth-
century life but usually they dined alone. During these suppers
McCluskey's conversation centred almost exclusively around the
parlous moral, cultural and environmental state of the planet.

In February, his language lessons were cut back to two hours a
day and Stanton began to focus more fully on a study of the spring
and summer of 1914. Various experts from among the
Companions of Chronos arrived daily at the Master's Lodge to
assist him in cramming everything he possibly could about the
diplomatic, political, military and cultural landscape of Europe in
the months leading up to the Great War. He also studied practical
matters, train and boat timetables, hotels and currency, plus
motor mechanics and even the rudiments of how to fly an early
aeroplane, subjects of which he already had a working knowledge.
And of course he practised with the various items of equipment
the Companions had designed for him to take with him: the
computer back-up, the weapons and ammunition, the medical kit,
and the various IDs, official letters, bills and currencies.

Time passed quickly. Winter turned to a surprisingly old-
fashioned spring and a rare period of clement weather made the
campus beautiful. Young female undergraduates seemed to

blossom like fresh flowers among the ancient stones, wafting about the place in their breeze-rippled summer dresses.

'Enjoy the view,' McCluskey said as she and Stanton crossed the quad one morning. 'Won't be any short skirts where you're going. Not till about 1926 anyway. Perhaps not even then. After all, it was the Great War that liberated the independent woman and there isn't going to be one this time.'

They were on their way through the town to West Road where the History faculty was situated.

'I brought sandwiches,' McCluskey said, tapping her vast handbag, 'so we'll have a working lunch.'

'I've often wondered what you keep in those handbags of yours. Looks like you could fit the kitchen sink in.'

McCluskey was a woman who never ventured out without a substantial handbag over her shoulder. She had a fine and varied selection, some of which appeared to be actual antiques.

'What a woman keeps in her handbag is one of the ancient secrets of our sex and were I to tell you I should have to have you castrated.'

'Well, don't then. Where are we going, by the way?'

'The Incident Room.'

'Incident Room?'

'Well, it's just a tutorial room in the History faculty really but our espionage bloke was with the Special Branch before he retired and he wants to call it the Incident Room, so who are we to argue? Today we are investigating a murder. The tragedy at Sarajevo. The killing that screwed the twentieth century.'

The Incident Room had been well named, for that was just what it had been turned into. An old-style police murder room. The walls were covered with maps and diagrams of Sarajevo and Belgrade and of the mountainous area between, with routes traced upon them and arrows pointing to significant locations. There were numerous photographs of buildings, streets and of weapons, all connected by strips of various coloured ribbons. And of course the main protagonists in the tragedy: the Archduke and Duchess themselves staring grimly out from the centre of the display; Gavrilo Princip, the killer, closest to them, as he had been at the moment of their deaths. Princip was surrounded by various other sallow-faced young men who had been his comrades on the fateful day. Then the soldiers, Serbian army officers at one end of the wall and Austrian at the other. The former who plotted the murder, and the latter who so spectacularly failed to prevent it.

'It's all on the computer you've been given,' a hawkish-looking old man remarked. He had a granite-hard Glaswegian accent and a great hooked nose that could have torn flesh from carrion. 'But Ah like things old school, stuck up on a wall where Ah can see 'em.'

'This is Commander Davies,' McCluskey explained. 'Late of the Scottish Special Branch. Now retired. Our chief strategist.'

'Happy Easter,' Stanton said, shaking his hand.

'Nothing very happy about it as far as Ah can see,' Davies snapped back. 'The country's buggered, the planet's buggered and Ah'm buggered. We'll get straight down t' business, shall we?'

'By all means.'

'Colonel Dragutin Dimitrijević,' Davies said, levelling a laser pointer at the central picture on the Serbian end of the display. 'As hard a bastard as ever drew breath. Known then and now as Apis. The man who organized the killing that started the Great War. Do y'know anything about the man?'

'He was the head of the Serbian Secret Service,' Stanton replied.

'Aye, he was, and also, as is the way with spies, its principal foe. As fervent a pan-Serbian nationalist as ever drew breath. Led a secret terrorist organization inside his own department called Unification Or Death. Better known to history as the Black Hand.'

Davies said the words with flinty relish, like some ancient laird cursing a rival clan.

'The Black Hand! Don't you love it?' McCluskey said, slapping her thigh. 'If you're going to organize a ring of assassins you might as well give it a blood-and-thunder name, eh? These days they'd probably have called it a Neutralization Operative Committee.'

Stanton studied the photograph on the wall marked 'Apis'. Black uniform, white gloves. Sabre. A chest full of medals, golden epaulettes on his shoulders, a plumed fez on his head. An imperial, kaiser-style moustache sitting heavily on cruel pursed lips. An arrogant, cold-eyed killer. Stanton knew the type, he'd met plenty, and the fact that some of them had been on his own side didn't make him like them any better.

'You want me to prevent the assassination by killing him?' Stanton asked. 'I mean, in our little game of *what if*, he's your target?'

'Well, he certainly held all the *cards*. And he certainly *deserved* a bullet. Terrible *terrrrible* man. *Murderrrrous* man.' Davies seemed to chew each word, rolling his r's with morbid pleasure. 'Y'd no want to meet him in a dark alley. But then y'd no want to meet any member of the Serrrrbian military in a dark alleyway. Not then and not now. Crazed fanatical bastards to a man. Friend Dimitrijević was a man of truly *savage* brutality. D'y ken how he earned his position as Serbia's Chief of Espionage?'

'Not really,' Stanton replied.

'By organizing and *perrrsonally* leading the brutal murder of his *own king*! How's that for audacity? You couldna' make it up. Friend Apis thought the monarch he served was too conciliatory to the Austrians so he decided to kill him and install a king that better suited his taste. I say kill, *butcher* would be a better word. Because in 1903, him and a gang of cronies, all crown officers, mind, who'd sworn an oath of loyalty, stormed the royal palace. They shot their way through the building, forced the king's guards to reveal where the royal couple were hiding, then shot King Alexander thirty times and Queen Draga eighteen. They then stripped the bullet-riddled corpses naked, slashed them up with their sabres and *threw them out of the palace window*.'

'They did things rough in those days,' McCluskey observed.

'Aye, they did, professor. They most certainly did. I don't think I've ever come across a more violent spy. Or, and here's the point, Captain Stanton, a cooler one. Because the very next day he installs a different king and makes himself Chief of Intelligence. He then proceeds to dominate espionage in Central Europe for the following decade, culminating in the Sarajevo assassination. I would say it's no exaggeration to say that in June 1914 this man was the most dangerous man in the world. The question is: should we kill him?'

'Well, *obviously*,' McCluskey said, digging in her handbag for a sandwich.

'Ah'm askin' your man here, professor. Not you.'

Stanton stared at the photograph of Apis for a full minute before replying.

'It seems to me,' he said finally, 'that if we try to kill this man, one of two things will happen. Either we bungle it or we succeed.'

McCluskey snorted loudly as if she'd expected better of Stanton but Davies nodded.

'Go on,' he said.

'If we bungle it, which I think is the more likely outcome, we'll have seriously spooked him.'

'Why would we bungle it?' McCluskey protested through a mouthful of tuna mayonnaise. 'I don't think you're giving yourself enough credit. You're Guts Stanton, remember!'

'Prof, this guy stormed a palace in 1903 and personally killed his own King and Queen. Yet he's still alive and pulling the strings in the *same* palace more than a decade later. Just how good a survivor do you think he'd have to be to manage that? Colonel Apis must have been the most tempting espionage target on the whole continent. Every other spy in the game would have dreamt of taking him out. But not one of them did. Colonel Dragutin Dimitrijević was second-guessing assassins before breakfast. So let's not make the mistake of thinking that just because we're coming at him from the future armed with a slightly better gun, Apis is suddenly going to present a soft target.'

'But that's the point, Hugh! We have *hindsight*,' McCluskey countered. 'We know many of his movements from historical documents; that gives us a massive advantage.'

'Exactly. So I get close enough to take a shot but for any number of reasons don't finish him off? What's he going to conclude? That a time-travelling assassin has used history books to trace him? No. He's going to presume his network has been infiltrated and therefore *all* of his plans are compromised. He will put the Black Hand in lock-down and clean it out root and branch. He'll cancel the Sarajevo plot without any doubt, put Princip and the whole team to sleep and bide his time before beginning entirely afresh.'

Davies grunted approvingly.

'Stanton is absolutely right,' he said. 'A failed attempt would be a disaster.'

'Well, nothing's foolproof, of course,' McCluskey grumbled. 'But if we succeed!'

'Yes. let's presume for a moment our killer succeeds,' Stanton went on. 'He goes back in time and manages to put a bullet into the heart of the most experienced and accomplished spy in Europe. What will the repercussions be? It certainly won't mean the end of the Black Hand organization, that's for sure. Martyred leaders cast long shadows. Apis had comrades, blood brothers, men as tough and as fanatically devoted to the Serbian cause as he was. Look at them, Antić . . . Dulić . . . Marinković and Popović.'

Stanton turned to the grainy photographs that surrounded Apis on the wall, all connected by strips of green fabric tape. Hard-eyed men with frozen stares. Each one of them could easily have been a murderer or a cop, and of course each one of them was both.

'What will these men do with their leader slain? One thing's for sure: they won't give up. In fact, they'll be yearning for revenge. So who will they blame? Again, not a hitman from the future. They will blame their mortal enemy, the Austro-Hungarian Secret Service, and they will react by attacking the Austro-Hungarians where it hurts most. By *killing one of their royals*. Archduke Franz Ferdinand, for example. So by taking out Apis we don't remove the threat to the Archduke at all. We merely place the planning of it in the hands of different people. People whose plans *we wouldn't know*. Killing Apis is, in fact, as bad as failing to kill him because it removes our single ace. We *know* what Apis did. We know he had the Archduke killed on the twenty-eighth of June 1914 and we know how he did it. If that day changes we'll be as much in the dark as the Austrians were at the time. The only certain way to prevent the murder of Franz Ferdinand is to stop the man who *actually* killed him from pulling the trigger and to do so at the last possible moment.'

For the first time Davies's hard, craggy face seemed almost to smile, his thin lips grimacing like a knife cut in a mouldy lemon.

'You chose y' man well, professor,' he said.

'Yes, well, I told you he was good,' McCluskey said, slightly huffily. 'You didn't believe me at the time.'

The brief shadow of a smile disappeared as Davies turned his hawkish countenance back to Stanton.

'*Verrrry* true. If I were honest with you, Captain Stanton—'

'Ex-captain,' Stanton corrected. 'The Regiment chucked me out.'

'*Exactly*. And when the Chronos Intelligence Committee assembled last spring I didn't relish the idea of entrusting the future of European civilization to a man who'd sacrificed a promising army career in favour of media celebrity.'

'Well, that's not quite how—'

'But it's a fool who won't admit when he's wrong. And I like your style, son, I really do. McCluskey was right, you're the man for the job. The first part of which is to get to Sarajevo two months from now and neutralize the man who killed the Archduke.'

'Gavrilo Princip,' Stanton said.

'Aye. Princip. The man who fired the first shot of the Great War.'

'Stupid, stupid bastard,' McCluskey muttered bitterly.

All three of them turned towards the photo on the wall. An absurdly youthful-looking lad of nineteen, his sad, slightly bewildered expression and deep-set, almost romantic eyes stared back at them from an image that had been reproduced millions of times in the last century.

Could it really be possible that Stanton would be looking into those *actual* eyes in eight weeks' time? He was almost beginning to believe that it could.

12

IN THE EARLY hours of the morning of 31 May 2025, Hugh Stanton left Trinity College Cambridge in a small motorcade which he was surprised to see was travelling with a police escort. The Companions of Chronos might have been past their prime but they clearly still counted some pretty influential people among their members.

'Best to be safe,' McCluskey said. 'Imagine, Isaac Newton arranges a time-precise rendezvous with history across a distance of three hundred years and we miss it because we're stuck in traffic. We've got cops in Turkey too. God knows how it's been arranged but I do know that some of our people are still pretty well connected with the Foreign Office.'

As the little column of cars and motorbikes drove out of the college gates, Stanton glanced out of the window and saw the motorcycle he had parked near the porter's lodge. He'd scarcely ridden it since arriving at Cambridge five months earlier. The alarm signal had probably bled the battery dry by now.

He didn't think it was even still insured. The reminders were no doubt among the rest of the many months of post that would be piled up on the inside of the front door of the house that he had never returned to.

He wondered now if he ever would.

They left Cambridge behind and headed for the motorway. McCluskey was the only Companion of Chronos who was travelling with him. The others had said their goodbyes at a farewell dinner on the previous evening during which many emotional and increasingly drunken speeches had been made in Stanton's honour. He himself had drunk moderately but declined to reply. It was all too weird. They treated him as some sort of messiah figure, a hero ready to cleanse and redeem the earth from wayward humanity. Stanton didn't feel that way at all, not least because he simply could not believe in what they all thought was going to happen in Istanbul that night.

'I know deep down you don't actually believe any of this, Hugh,' McCluskey remarked.

'Look, I'm prepared to accept that *something* might happen,' Stanton conceded. 'Newton obviously believed it and he was pretty much the cleverest man who ever lived. Perhaps I'll be vaporized by a thunderbolt. Or else gravitational pull will tear me in half or suck me up into a black hole.'

'But you don't believe you're about to embark on a journey to the past?'

'Well, come on, do you? The Great War started *a hundred and eleven years* ago this August. Do you really think we can stop it now?'

'All I know is that I pray we can.'

They both lapsed into silence but Stanton could see that evangelical zeal still shone in McCluskey's eyes. She really believed. They all believed, those crazy old men and women who called themselves Chronos; imagined that they were all going to be genetically reassembled, young and lusty once more in the sun-lit uplands of a Britain reborn.

'Time will tell, eh?' McCluskey said, almost under her breath.

'Yes,' Stanton agreed, 'so you keep telling me. Time will tell.'

They flew from Farnborough by private plane. Most of the equipment Stanton had been supplied with travelled with them. But the weaponry was already waiting in Turkey.

'Even we Chronations can't get a telescopic-sighted rifle through airport security,' McCluskey explained.

The flight took almost four hours, during which McCluskey ate everything that was offered and as ever drank considerably. Then she managed to get herself stuck in the tiny loo.

'You know, they had one of the most famous seasons ever at Drury Lane in 1914,' she said once the stewardess had freed her and she'd waddled somewhat shakily back to her seat. 'The Diaghilev Company came from Russia and just blew London away. They did ten operas and fourteen ballets through the spring and summer and nobody had ever seen anything like it. Or, in fact, ever would again. Sets and crowd scenes on a truly epic scale, impossible to do today, nobody could afford it. You really ought to try and see a couple, maybe even slip one in before you go to Sarajevo. You'll have a month to kill, after all. But I'd send a telegram ahead from Istanbul if I were you because it was a very hot ticket. You'll probably need to go on the list for returns.'

'I'll bear it in mind,' Stanton said.

'And *Pygmalion*'s just opened at His Majesty's. Imagine it! You can go to the very *first ever production* of *Pygmalion*. With Mrs Campbell as Eliza and Shaw himself directing! Isn't that almost too wonderful to imagine?' McCluskey had a faraway look in her eye. 'The London Theatre in 1914,' she whispered almost to herself, 'now that *is* a dream.'

Then she fell asleep and didn't wake up till they'd arrived in Istanbul.

They were driven to the Hotel Pera Palace on the Grande Rue de Pera where rooms were waiting for them. As the porters helped McCluskey out of the car she paused for a moment and looked up at the imposing building.

'They restored it a few years ago,' she said. 'Got it right back to its original glory. So in fact this is just how it'll look tomorrow whatever happens. Whether you're in 1914 or boring old 2025.'

'I'm sorry to say I really do think it'll be 2025,' Stanton said, 'because there's no such thing as time travel, as we'll be forced to accept at midnight. When you and I are feeling pretty stupid standing alone in a cellar in the old dockland quarter of Istanbul.'

'Well, if that's the case we'll just have to find a late bar to toast

Sir Isaac Newton and the fact that even geniuses can get it wrong.'

It was mid-afternoon and having checked in and deposited their bags in their rooms, Stanton and McCluskey returned to the lobby where they met up with members of a local security company who had been engaged to take them to the property the Companions of Chronos had recently purchased.

'I thought we should have a bit of a reconnoitre while there's still some light,' McCluskey said. 'Don't want to be stumbling around in the dark tonight with no idea where we're going.'

They were driven over the Galata Bridge and down into the old dock area of Stamboul. There they found a street filled with houses that had once been wealthy but were no longer so. They pulled up outside a derelict building that in its heyday must have been an impressive city mansion.

A security man stood at the front door ready to let them in.

'Just one guard,' McCluskey explained. 'Don't want to be ostentatious. There's nothing here worth stealing and it wouldn't do to draw attention to ourselves.'

They picked their way in the gathering gloom through the ruin, stepping over shattered glass and bits of broken furniture. Quite recently the place had been squatted and there was much graffiti on the walls. Since then only tramps and vandals had ventured in and now the place reeked of piss. Not a single window remained whole in its frame.

Guiding themselves by torchlight they found their way via a precipitous stairwell down to the cellar, a much larger space than they had expected, with arched vaults disappearing into the darkness.

'It extends beneath the next house,' McCluskey explained. 'It was a wine cellar when Newton's agents bought the place and they just locked and barred the door. The wine was still there when the hospital closed after the war. It will still be there when you arrive tonight. Revolting, of course, after two hundred years but you should try one for fun. I know I would. Not many people get the chance to taste wine laid down in the early eighteenth century.

Imagine that. Wine laid down more than a generation before Marie Antoinette was born.'

Stanton didn't reply but instead took out a satellite navigation device and, following it, found his way to a place about seven metres from the door they'd entered by, halfway between it and the deeper darkness of the wine vaults. Then, using the coordinates Sengupta had supplied, he took a piece of chalk and marked out the relevant surface area.

'Newton's sentry box,' he said.

'Yes,' McCluskey said. 'Bit bloody tight, better mark the centre.'

There was a broken chair nearby and in the torchlight Stanton took it and placed it carefully in position.

'So this is where you'll be standing at midnight,' McCluskey said. 'Just think how pleased old Isaac would be to know that his message got through and that somebody acted on it.'

Standing in the silent cellar in the light of just two torch beams it suddenly all seemed very real to Stanton. As if this place really could be the gateway to another universe.

McCluskey seemed to read his thoughts.

'It has to be true,' she said firmly. 'Mankind deserves a second chance. A better twentieth century than the one we were born into.'

'Well,' Stanton said, 'I don't agree we deserve it. But right now I truly do hope that we get it.'

13

HAVING COMPLETED THEIR reconnoitre, Stanton and McCluskey retraced their steps through the now darkened building and returned to the hotel. That evening they met at the Orient Bar then went through to supper in the restaurant. Once again McCluskey made the most of the food and wine, determined to enjoy what she referred to as her 'last supper'. Stanton, on the other hand, ate lightly and drank only water.

'I suppose on the off chance that Newton's right I should have my wits about me,' he remarked. 'Don't want to time-travel under the influence.'

After they'd eaten, Stanton left the professor to her coffee and cognac and went to his room to change. Looking at himself in the mirror he reflected that he would cut a fairly unusual figure in Istanbul that night, wearing the socks, knee britches and thorn-proof tweed of an early-twentieth-century man of action. But then Istanbul was a renowned party town so he doubted anyone would notice much. Next he checked his kit, which he was carrying in one large holdall bag, plus a smaller one with an emergency version of the same. He had guns and explosives, medical supplies, his computers, IDs, and a great deal of money in various currencies and government bonds. These last had all been expertly forged from originals taken from museums and bank archives.

At 10 p.m. he met McCluskey in the lobby and once more they took a limousine across the Galata Bridge. The streets by this time were full of evening revellers so their progress was slower, which was why they had allowed themselves plenty of time.

Stanton stared out of a car window and decided that nothing was going to happen that night. The twenty-first century was just too *real*, too solid. It was the weekend and the city was in a party mood. Music could be heard through the doorways of restaurants. There were smiling, laughing faces everywhere. It didn't seem possible that so much living, breathing, *tingling* life could suddenly cease to exist on the stroke of midnight.

Once more McCluskey seemed to read his thoughts. Perhaps they mirrored her own.

'The world looked solid and unchangeable in the summer of 1914 too,' she said. 'Never more so. People thought no world had ever been more secure or enduring. But it evaporated into thin air. It disappeared from the universe within a few short summers. Don't you think this one could vanish just as suddenly?'

'Their world was destroyed by hot lead, poison gas and high explosives,' Stanton replied.

'Gas. High explosives. Gravitational shifts in space and time,' McCluskey answered. 'All physical phenomena at a subatomic level. A single shell from a big gun in the Great War could vaporize any number of men. Literally reduce them to cellular level. Transform their matter and send them spinning across the universe. I suggest that your component parts are about to embark on a journey no more dramatic. Gravity is without doubt the most consistent force in the universe. Everything exerts it, everything is affected by it. Why should time be an exception?'

As they got closer to their destination the crowds began to thin. This was not a fashionable area. The shouting, smiling faces had disappeared and the noise of carefree youth and partying was ever more distant.

'Nice and quiet,' McCluskey muttered. 'Just how we like it.'

But it wasn't to be. As the car turned into their street they were confronted by throbbing trance music. The pavement outside the previously deserted building was pulsing with light.

'Oh fuck,' McCluskey said.

The single security man was standing outside in the street looking extremely sheepish.

'I'm sorry, professor,' he said. 'They just invaded. It's somebody's twenty-first birthday. There must be two hundred of them inside.'

'Oh Christ in a box,' McCluskey said. 'Flash rave. Pop-up party. Newton didn't think of that.'

'You want me to call the police?' the guard asked.

'No!' McCluskey said quickly. 'Absolutely not. No time. It'd take hours to shift this lot and there'd probably be a bloody riot if we tried. Come on, Hugh.'

They pushed their way through the stoned and loved-up party-goers who were milling around the front door and made their way into the house. It was completely transformed from the afternoon. There were strobing, flashing lights, pulsating music and dancing, kissing, *squirming* bodies everywhere.

'You see, Hugh,' McCluskey shouted, 'it's like I always said to those bloody Marxist dialectical materialists. History is about people. Coincidence and capricious chance. This bunch of pissed-up ravers may turn out to be the reason the Great War happens and Europe is destroyed. Because of a fucking *birthday party*! But not if we can help it. Come on.'

McCluskey pushed her way through the sweating throng. She was, as usual, carrying a large handbag. In fact, this particular item was more like a small holdall and she wasn't shy in swinging it about to get people to move out of the way. Stanton followed on as best he could, struggling with his own heavy bags.

Finding their way was difficult; the rooms and corridors had all been hung with painted sheets and murals and looked nothing like they had done that afternoon. At least there was light, supplied by a generator that seemed to have been placed in the back garden since the cables were running out of the windows.

'They've got it bloody well organized,' McCluskey shouted back over her shoulder. 'Can't believe they've set this up since we were here. If they were as creative and innovative getting themselves jobs they wouldn't all have to be bloody anarchists.'

Stanton could hardly hear her. There were speakers hung in every corner of the building and the DJ was not shy with the volume dial.

Eventually they found their way down into the cellar, descending the little stairwell towards the battered and broken door, still hanging on a single hinge. The same door that Newton's men had locked three centuries before.

Any hope that the rave might have confined itself to the upper part of the house was quickly extinguished. There was a separate and if anything even wilder party going on in the basement. A different DJ, naked but for a tiny pair of glittering shorts, was dancing crazily behind his decks.

'The guy upstairs was steady drum and bass,' McCluskey shouted, 'but this bloke is real old school Hi NRG trance. Fucking awful, if you ask me. All music was shit after the kids switched from spliff to E.'

Whatever drug it was that the revellers were on, they were certainly having a fantastic time. Bounding and leaping about and throwing shapes with absolute abandon.

'My place-marker's gone and the chalk's been danced off the floor,' Stanton shouted into McCluskey's ear. He pointed at the broken chair, which had been kicked into a shadowy corner of the cavernous room. 'We'll have to re-establish the coordinates.'

If any of the young Turkish party people found it strange that an old lady in a woolly cardigan and a man dressed vaguely like a character out of *King Solomon's Mines* were pushing their way among them staring intently at a satellite navigation device, then they did not let it show. This was a flash rave after all and there were no rules. People could act as they pleased. As if to demonstrate this very point, a young woman with a shaved and tattooed head leapt suddenly in between McCluskey and Stanton.

'Guts!' she shouted in heavily accented English. 'I love you, Guts!'

Then having paused momentarily to bare her breasts, she clasped Stanton by the head with both hands and kissed him.

Fortunately the music was too loud for anybody but Stanton and McCluskey to hear the girl, otherwise Stanton might well have been mobbed. These were young people after all, Stanton's web constituency. McCluskey grabbed the girl and pushed her away.

'Bugger off, you disgusting slapper,' she shouted. 'And put your tits away. What would your mother think?'

Stanton looked at his watch. 'Two minutes to midnight!' he shouted, before focusing once more on his sat nav. 'The place is just over here, where those two are making out.'

Stanton pointed at a position on the floor where a young couple were dancing cheek to cheek and groin to groin, locked in a passionate embrace, mouths gnawing at each other.

'Blimey!' McCluskey yelled. 'We've got to clear a space for the sentry box or else you'll be staying here and a couple of drunk, half-naked students are going to find themselves locked in a cellar in 1914.'

Stanton struggled with his bags and his sat nav among the cavorting bodies while McCluskey attempted to make room for him. Having tried tapping the passionate couple on the shoulder and got no reaction, she resorted to twerking them out of the way by backing her substantial bottom into them and pushing. 'Quick!' she shouted. 'Before they snog their way back.'

The DJ interrupted his music to shout excitedly in Turkish. There followed a great cheer from everyone in the cellar.

'Oh my God,' McCluskey said, looking at her watch. 'One minute. They're counting down to the birthday.'

Stanton was staring intently at his navigation guide, holding it in one hand while he fended off dancers with the other. Taking one final extra step, he threw a thumbs-up to McCluskey to indicate he was in position, and put his bags on the floor, one on either side of his feet.

'Don't move!' McCluskey shouted while pushing away the

star-struck and still topless girl who was attempting to steal another kiss. Stanton stood his ground as McCluskey circled him flailing her arms, spinning like a Whirling Dervish and shouting furiously at the bemused and amused crowd.

'Fuck off! Fuck off! Keep back! Clear a space! Fuck off!'

'Fuck off! Fuck off!' the smiling crowd chanted back merrily at the mad old lady.

'Twenty! Nineteen!' came the Turkish countdown as the DJ led the crowd through the last seconds of 31 May 2025.

The topless girl threw herself at Stanton once more, intent, it seemed, on the prize of kissing him on the stroke of midnight. Perhaps she was the birthday girl and had decided Stanton was her present. He pushed her away but she just came at him again, wilder now, arms wide and pupils contracted, reaching into the space McCluskey was trying to protect. Into Newton's sentry box.

She grabbed Stanton round the neck. She was strong and determined. He felt her lips on his; he smelt spearmint lip gloss.

Then the lips were gone, leaving only the gloss behind.

'I said *fuck off*!' McCluskey's voice bellowed. The girl's whole head jerked backwards and a fat, mottled, broken-veined, liver-spotted fist swung through the air and into her face. He saw the girl's shocked expression and the spurt of blood that leapt instantly from what may well have been a broken nose. Then suddenly McCluskey appeared in front of him, putting her own arms around his neck. Clasping him. Crushing him to her. Now it was McCluskey's lips against his; he could feel the bristle of her moustache as she spoke.

'I'm coming with you!' she shouted. 'Hold me tight!'

'Fourteen! Thirteen!' the crowd was chanting.

'You're crazy!' Stanton shouted into her face. 'Think of the Butterfly Effect! Every step will change history. The more disruption, the less chance we have.'

'I'll be careful. I won't flap my wings much. I just want to see the Diaghilev at Covent Garden.'

'Nine! Eight!' came the chant.

The bloodied girl appeared behind McCluskey, her hands reaching round and clawing at McCluskey's face, her nails digging into McCluskey's cheeks and eyes. Stanton felt himself spinning. McCluskey held him, the Turkish girl held McCluskey. The three of them toppled over together, cannoning into other dancers as they collapsed to the floor.

'Six! Five!'

Stanton was on his feet in an instant. His bags hadn't moved. They marked the spot. The two women were also struggling to their feet.

'Three!'

He had only to step between the bags to be back in position.

But as he did so he saw that McCluskey was trying to step into the very same position. Her face, illuminated in the flashing lights, seemed maniacal, evangelical. Her fists were up once more. One was holding her big leather bag. She was reaching back, ready to swing.

At him.

She wanted to go with him but if necessary it was clear she'd be prepared to go without him.

'Two!'

He stepped between his bags, bracing himself against McCluskey's expected blow. Then there was an explosion of glass around her head, backlit from the strobe in the corner like a throbbing halo of twinkling stars.

McCluskey dropped out of his vision, revealing behind her the topless party girl, blood falling from her chin on to her breasts, the neck of a broken champagne bottle in her hand.

'One! Happy birthday, Feyzah!' the DJ shouted. '*Mutlu yıllar!*'

14

THE DARKNESS WAS absolute.

Except for the lingering images of party lighting that still floated on his dazzled retinas.

The silence was oppressive.

Except for the echo of the trance music that was still ringing and thudding in his ears.

It occurred to Stanton that if he truly had departed the time in which he had been standing, then that fading echo and the floating blobs of lights before his eyes were the last remaining sights and sounds of a world and a century that had disappeared from history. All the voices of those hundred years, all the howls of pain and heartache. The babble and the roar. The whispers and the song. Gone. All gone.

And yet still an Ibiza-inspired club mix and light show remained from that universe. Captured briefly by his senses. Fading fast but still there for a second or two more at least. The sole sensual echoes of an entire century of restless human endeavour.

And the taste of spearmint lip gloss. That too remained. And with it the memory of a girl's lips on his.

Was he in another world?

Or perhaps simply in another part of space? Suspended somewhere and nowhere in some strange limbo, lost in a Newtonian loop.

But that was just stupid. He hadn't gone anywhere. He'd just blacked out. Or else the cops had raided the joint and unplugged the generator. That was why there was no sound. No light.

Except, then, where was everybody?

Stanton felt his fists clenched so tightly that the nails were in danger of puncturing his palms. That had never happened to him before. It seemed to help him focus.

He risked his voice.

'Hello? Professor?' he said. 'Professor McCluskey?'

No reply. The silence just got deeper as his ears grew accustomed to it.

He slowly unclenched his fists and found that his hands were trembling. With a conscious effort, he steadied them. He reached into the pocket of his jacket and took out his torch.

The moment of truth had arrived.

Turning it on and shining it in front of him, Stanton saw that one thing remained the same. The arch in the cellar wall that had been in the background of his vision as the girl's face had appeared behind McCluskey's falling body was still there. A shadowy brick alcove.

He was still in the same cellar he had been in a moment before.

But he was alone and, except for the torchlight, in absolute darkness.

His stomach tightened. He gulped, swallowing hard. He felt for a moment that he might almost be sick.

He shone the light about himself. The dust was thick every-where, centuries thick. The alcove that he'd last seen crowded with kissing, groping people was filled now with ancient-looking bottles.

On the floor nearby was a small wooden chair and table. Cobwebbed and somewhat rat-gnawed. That chair, no longer broken, was the same one he'd attempted to use as a marker ear-lier in the evening.

Earlier in the evening? *Had* it been earlier in the evening or had it been a hundred and eleven years in the future? Except if that was the case, then there was no future any more. He had come to make it.

Stanton was a brave man. He was the Guts and there was none steadier in a crisis, but he felt almost overwhelmed. He swayed a little on his feet, the darkness disorienting him.

'McCluskey!' he called out, although he knew already there would be no answer.

And there wasn't.

Then he did something he had never imagined would be his first action on the other side of whatever it was he had crossed. He reached into his pocket and pulled out his iPhone. Turning it on he wondered whether it would even work, and of course it did, as had his torch. They would both continue to work as long as their batteries, charged in another universe, held out, and after that he had equipment in his kit with which to recharge them. Thumbing the screen with shaking hand he went straight to photos and clicked on 'Family album'.

And there she was. There they were. Cassie and the children. Smiling in the blackness, casting their glow upwards, illuminating his face. Just as once they'd illuminated his life.

He felt a little stronger. If he had indeed arrived where he was beginning to think he *must* have arrived, then it wasn't the light and sound of some random rave party that was the last echo of the vanished century. It was the precious, priceless images of his loves that had survived. He carried them with him still. In his heart, of course, but also in what was the last iPhone left on earth. And the first.

He turned off the phone and put it back in his pocket.

It was time to begin whatever it was his destiny to begin. His mission. The work of Chronos.

Putting the torch between his teeth he bent forward, leaning down in order to pick up his two bags.

The torch beam arched downwards and he saw her. McCluskey. Unconscious at his feet.

Such had been her burning desire to accompany him into the

past that even as the concussion had consumed her she'd somehow managed to contract her body around his bags, thereby sneaking into Newton's sentry box.

Stanton stared down at her. Her chest was moving. She was alive.

He played the light across the length of her body, an alarming thought striking him that perhaps a limb or a hand or foot might have been left outside the area of the box, in which case he might be dealing with some kind of time-mutilated amputee.

To his relief she appeared to be all present and correct, her swollen, wool-clad calves bulging out of her brown brogue shoes, the fat blotchy hands each with all their stubby yellow fingers intact. She'd made it across space and time in one piece. That same ruthless instinct to win that had made her such a terror of the ladies' fours and eights on the Cam and which had enabled her to become the first female Master at Trinity had served her well. She'd squeezed herself into the sentry box and he was stuck with her.

Kneeling down he tried to assess the extent of her injuries. The wound on the back of her head wasn't bleeding much but he knew with concussions that that didn't necessarily mean anything. It was perfectly possible that the brain itself was bruised, in which case there'd be pressure building on the inside of her skull. Champagne bottles were made of very thick glass and serious damage might have been done. At any rate he needed to ice it as soon as possible to reduce the risk of the brain swelling.

Incredible.

He had stepped back in time in an effort to save tens of millions, yet now he was stuck with looking after one selfish old woman.

It occurred to him that he really ought to just finish her off. Suffocate the outrageous old harridan and stash her tweed-clad corpse deep in the shadows of the catacombs. Why not? She had absolutely no right to be there, she had compromised the very mission she'd claimed to care so much about. She was a liability, a dangerous liability.

She grunted a bit and some dribble slid out of the corner of her mouth.

He knew he couldn't kill her. He wasn't a murderer.

Besides, he *liked* the old girl and, deep down, despite himself, he was half glad of the company.

A thought occurred to him. That big handbag she was carrying. Big even by her standards . . . more like a small holdall.

He opened it and shone his torch inside. The first thing he saw was an envelope marked with the seal of the Foreign Office and stamped 'GR', just like the one Chronos had supplied to him that contained his 1914 identification. This had been no spontaneous act. The outrageous old woman had been planning it all along.

Of course she hadn't planned to arrive in 1914 knocked out cold. She hadn't planned on a topless Turkish party girl smashing her over the head with a champagne bottle. Another victory for the Romantics. History just doesn't have a plan.

And now it was time to get her out of that cellar.

Then what? Who knew what lay beyond it? Could it really be Istanbul in 1914? Constantinople? He still couldn't bring himself to believe that. It was just as likely that they'd find they were spinning through space inside a small, cellar-shaped asteroid.

He opened the smaller of his two bags and brought out his medical kit. He knew it contained some ammonium carbonate to use as smelling salts. It wasn't an ideal thing to do, to jerk a concussed person back to consciousness, but there didn't seem to be any other way of getting McCluskey on to her feet. He certainly couldn't carry her and the bags unnoticed through an occupied house.

The salts brought her round a little. Her eyes opened, her jaw dropped. He clamped his hand over her mouth.

'Do *exactly* as I say, professor,' he whispered sharply. 'Don't speak. *Do not speak*. Just act.'

She was very woozy and certainly not entirely in the moment but she seemed to understand the instructions, or at least she followed them.

Still with the torch between his teeth he hauled her to her feet, then, clasping the handles of all three bags in one hand, he put his free arm around McCluskey's waist and half dragged her towards the door. Once there, he leant her against the wall and felt in his pocket for the skeleton keys Chronos had supplied him with. They'd promised that these keys could open any lock on earth in 1914. Of course, as far as Stanton knew, this particular lock had last been turned in the early eighteenth century. The quarter-master of the Companions of Chronos had considered this possibility and supplied Stanton with a tiny aerosol can of silicone lubricant, which he now applied.

The key turned and the door opened inwards: fortunately, since a cupboard had been placed against it on the other side that Stanton was forced to move out of the way.

At once he was hit by the smell of disinfectant. And vanilla . . . which Stanton guessed indicated morphine. He was in a hospital.

McCluskey sensed it too.

'That's morphine,' she mumbled. 'We're in Newton's fucking hospital!'

'I *said* don't speak, OK!' Stanton hissed. 'If we are banged up in Istanbul as housebreakers we'll miss Sarajevo, you stupid woman.'

McCluskey's head lolled forward and she put a finger to her lip. It seemed she understood him but she was so shaky and distracted Stanton could not be sure how long that understanding would last.

For a moment he thought again about leaving her. It was just so ridiculous. He should be calmly taking stock, pausing for a moment to assimilate the mind-boggling conclusion that Newton had been right, that every single thing he had ever known was gone. Time had rebooted itself and the last one hundred and eleven years were once more in the future.

But he didn't leave her behind. He couldn't bring himself to do that, any more than he could bring himself to kill her. Instead he got her and the bags out through the door, closed and locked it behind him, then leant her against a wall while he repositioned the cupboard and ascended the steps.

They were the same steps. There could be no doubt about that, although in much better condition than they'd been forty-five minutes before. Perhaps it was a blessing that he had McCluskey to struggle with, stinking of cigarettes and wine and dinner. It was a pretty effective distraction from the millennial-scale strangeness of his situation.

At the top of the steps there was another door, also locked, but which sprang easily open on application of the skeleton keys. Moments later the two of them were on the ground floor of the building. Once more Stanton pressed his finger gently to McCluskey's lips.

'Shhh,' he breathed gently.

He heard music. Opera of some sort, scratchy and poorly amplified. Somebody was listening to a gramophone.

He shone his torch along the passageway.

There were nurses' capes on hooks on the walls. A wheelchair and also a bed trolley. Rooms led off the corridor on either side, from one of which a shaded light shone through a half-open door.

Stanton crept slowly past, one careful step at a time, supporting McCluskey and trying not to bang his bags. Glancing in, he saw a young nurse working at her desk. It was fortunate for him she was an opera fan.

It occurred to Stanton that he was looking at a living, breathing soul who had died many decades before he was born. Truly no human being in all time had experienced such a thing.

The young woman shifted in her seat. For some reason Stanton felt that he would have liked to get a proper look at her face, the first face from a new world. An old world. But the girl did not oblige him by turning round; her cheek remained firmly in her hand as she concentrated on her work. Stanton and McCluskey crept on.

The geography of the old mansion was, of course, completely different to that of the derelict tenement the two of them had barged through an hour before, but the orientation of the building was the same and Stanton knew the direction in which the street lay.

All was quiet as they made their way through the house. As the gramophone music faded behind them Stanton was aware of some moaning and the occasional restless cry from elsewhere in the building. But the ground floor seemed to be deserted apart from the nurse at her desk.

Moving as quickly as he dared, he found the front door.

He was in the process of laying his hand on the handle when it opened in front of him. Suddenly and shockingly he found himself face to face with a neatly bearded man in top hat and tails, who was clearly even more surprised than Stanton was.

The cold night air focused Stanton's thoughts.

'My mother seems much better,' he said in English. 'I think perhaps an overnight stay isn't required after all.'

Then he bundled McCluskey past the startled man, down the front steps and hurried off up the street.

He was a soldier in open country supporting a wounded comrade and with three bags to carry.

He needed to find a cab.

15

IT DIDN'T TAKE him long. The dockland residential area was no longer poor and run-down. It was utterly transformed from the dilapidated and neglected place he and McCluskey had arrived in an hour or so earlier.

In the very next street he saw a horse-drawn cab being paid off and bundled Professor McCluskey towards it. She staggered along beside him, Stanton suddenly acutely aware that her attire, which only an hour before had been the deeply conservative dress of an old-fashioned matron, was now positively indecent in as much as her skirt reached only to her knee.

'Pera!' he shouted to the driver, pushing McCluskey into the carriage as the previous occupants vacated it. 'Pera Palace Hotel. Grande Rue de Pera.'

He knew almost no Turkish but on the previous day he'd made some effort to learn how to pronounce place names.

The cabby would have known where to go anyway. There weren't too many hotels that catered for *feringi* in Constantinople and they were all clustered in the same small area of the European quarter.

Stanton sat back on the hard, leather-cushioned seat and tried to take stock. Not of the bigger picture, the shocking truth that he was in a horse-drawn hansom cab riding through Constantinople in 1914. That was such a vast and existentially strange notion that he was fearful to focus on it in case it drove him mad.

As might a proper understanding of his personal loss. That

too was hovering on the edge of his brittle emotional defences, like a hammer above an egg. Because if history really had been rebooted and a previous loop in time begun again, then Cassie and Tessa and Bill had never existed. Nor indeed ever *would* exist, because the very nature of his mission was calculated to change entirely the course of future generations. He couldn't dwell on that. A second bereavement was more than he could handle at present. Better simply to ignore those deeper thoughts and focus instead on negotiating each second as it came before moving on to the next.

That had been his rule when making *Guts Versus Guts*, in those happy days when he'd dropped himself gleefully into life-threatening situations for the sake of a thrill and a webcast. Never consider the bigger picture, because if you do you'll just give up. If you're hanging on a precipice, there's no point worrying that the precipice is in a desert five days from water. Just get out of the precipice, then worry about the water.

The cab had left the dock area and was rattling over the Galata Bridge back up through the streets of Pera, which were mostly empty and quiet, it being past midnight. It occurred to Stanton that he and McCluskey were making the exact same journey in reverse that they had made just a couple of hours before. The same journey, except in 1914.

Once more the thought threatened to overwhelm him. He forced himself to focus on the moment.

He took stock of McCluskey, who was slumped beside him. She'd slipped back into unconsciousness and there was blood on the leather upholstery behind her head. That Turkish party girl had hit her hard. It takes a lot of force to shatter a champagne bottle.

He needed to get her into bed and to ice that wound.

Which meant checking her into the hotel. Could she pass muster? Her cardigan and blouse were just about all right but there was no doubt that her skirt would draw serious attention. He doubted that any lady had ever entered the Hotel Pera Palace on the Grande Rue de Pera with her calves and ankles fully displayed. Elderly lady or not, it was indecent. If then McCluskey were found to have sustained a serious blow, questions would certainly be asked. Questions Stanton did not feel equipped to answer.

The head injury was easy to cover. McCluskey was wearing a silk scarf round her neck and Stanton simply knotted it round her head and under her chin. Coupled with her cardigan it was a look more suited to a breezy day on Brighton Pier than a top-class hotel at one in the morning but it would do.

The skirt was a trickier problem. There was a neatly folded rug attached to the door of the cab. He took it and with considerable difficulty was able to tie it round McCluskey's waist, using his own belt to secure it.

He almost didn't have time before the journey was over. Despite the fact that they were travelling at only the speed of a trotting horse, the journey from Newton's house to the hotel had taken considerably less time than had the one in the big Mercedes from the hotel to Newton's house.

As Stanton struggled with the belt buckle they were already drawing up outside the very hotel in which the two of them had dined a few hours before. Stanton pulled the belt tight around the blanket and did his best to conceal the whole arrangement beneath McCluskey's cardigan. Then he gave her another whiff of the ammonia which brought her partially back to the surface.

'When I say walk, *walk*,' he hissed. 'Don't say anything.'

Her eyes opened but she said nothing.

Glancing out of the window as the driver brought the cab to a halt, Stanton noted that McCluskey had been right. The façade was pretty much the same as it had been when they left it, only the line of black limos was missing.

The cabby leapt down to open the door and Stanton reached into the smaller of his two bags and produced the colour-coded envelope that he knew contained early-twentieth-century Turkish currency. Nodding towards the blanket, which he was clearly intent on taking, he gave the driver five times its value. The driver wasn't going to argue his luck and he helped Stanton manhandle McCluskey out of the cab.

Instantly porters appeared from the doorway of the hotel. Stanton flashed more currency and waved them away from McCluskey, pointing at his bags. He then supported her through the doors while a porter followed with the luggage.

Inside the building the reception desk was in a different place to where it had been when he had checked in that morning but he could see that the Orient Bar was still tucked into the corner of the great atrium, the same place it had been when he had his drink with McCluskey before what she called her 'last supper'.

Last supper? Yeah, right. The outrageous old cheat.

He approached the reception desk with McCluskey stumbling along beside him; it being so late the foyer was almost empty, which was fortunate. Only the porter following behind with the bags and the staff at the desk were present to witness the arrival of this strange check-in party.

'My mother has had a fall,' Stanton said loudly and authoritatively in English. 'I need adjoining rooms. Do you offer private bathrooms?'

'In our suites, sir,' the receptionist replied, also in English.

'Then I need a two-bedroom suite. The best you have. Also ice, I presume you still have some in your cellars? Have two buckets sent up at once.'

At first the receptionist seemed pretty dubious about the new arrivals. McCluskey with her blanket for a skirt looked far from being a society lady and Stanton was not dressed in anything remotely resembling evening wear. But they were carrying letters from the British Foreign Office requesting and requiring they be afforded due assistance, and when Stanton insisted that the manager be called while casually playing with a gold sovereign in the palm of his hand, a suite of rooms was secured. The British were, after all, internationally recognized as being pretty eccentric and impervious to the opinions of foreigners. Mad old English ladies supported by sons dressed for what looked like hillwalking were probably not such an uncommon sight in the best hotels in Europe at the time.

A porter accompanied them in the splendid lift to the seventh floor and carried their bags into the suite.

A fumbled tip, a mumbled thank-you and Stanton was alone in a gilt and crimson-velvet sitting room dripping with luxurious Edwardian excess.

Again, Stanton decided to focus on the moment. McCluskey was running a fever now and muttering incoherently. He got her into the bathroom and bathed the wound on her head. It was a pretty deep cut and being on the scalp had bled profusely. The back of her cardigan was soaked in matted blood.

He sat her on the toilet and checked her pupils and her respiratory passages.

'What's your name?' he said.

'Professor Sally McCluskey,' came the reply. It was slurred but clear enough.

'Where do you work?'

'Cambridge. I'm the Master of Trinity.'

He thought about asking her what year it was but decided to leave that; the answer could provoke a brainstorm even in someone who wasn't concussed. McCluskey was functioning mentally, and as long as the brain didn't swell inside the skull she'd probably get away with a nasty headache. Nothing he could do about that till the ice arrived.

Of course, he needed to get her into bed, which wasn't going to be an easy task. She was conscious but not physically able and she was pretty fat and old. He struggled with her clothes, wrestling with the tightly knotted brogues and thick woollen tights, terrified of toppling her off the toilet. Eventually he got her down to her vast bra and industrial-looking pants and decided to stop there.

It occurred to him to look further into her bag and he found himself whistling at the brazen deceit of the woman. She'd come *fully* prepared. There were three sets of underwear, a plain black ankle-length dress of late Edwardian design and a brushed cotton nightie, all tightly rolled and packed Girl Guide-style. There was also British and German paper money, plus what looked like treasury bonds. There were various pills and medicines and, to Stanton's surprise, a small handgun, a Ruger LCP Six Shot in pink polymer. He wouldn't have imagined she'd tote such a girly piece but, pink or not, he knew the make and it was lethal at close range. He cracked it open and emptied the chamber, pocketing the bullets. His old professor had done a pretty bad thing barging into his mission and she was also severely concussed. For the time being at least he decided he'd prefer to have such an unpredictable associate unarmed. There was much else besides in the bag, which seemed to be bigger on the inside as ladies' bags often were, but Stanton had no time to explore the limits of his old professor's audacious duplicity.

He wrestled her into her nightdress and with some effort carried her to bed in one of the rooms that adjoined the sitting room, just as the ice arrived. Using a towel and a pillowcase to make a pack, he laid her head against it and took further stock. As long as the ice contained the swelling, he reckoned she'd be all right. A blow like that against a person in their early seventies was a serious thing, but for all her unhealthy lifestyle McCluskey was a tough old war horse. With luck she'd pull through. Not that he ought to care, of course. She was a lying, cheating traitor who had deliberately put the entire mission in jeopardy for her own personal gratification. But he did care. He liked her and always had. Now that she had made the leap with him and they were together on the strangest adventure in all of human history, he hoped she'd get to see whatever stupid ballet it was she'd set her heart on.

Her breathing was easier now. He felt that she was more asleep than unconscious. Apart from anything else they had both been up now since 4 a.m. the previous morning. He glanced at the beautiful carriage clock that stood on the mantel above the fireplace: 2.15 a.m. Allowing for a two-hour time gain for Central Europe, that was more than twenty hours.

120

And a hundred and eleven years.

No wonder McCluskey needed some sleep.

When she woke she was going to be in for a shock. A shock that he knew he himself must now begin to assimilate. It was time to accept it. Newton had been right. It was the early hours of the morning on the first of June 1914.

Not one shred of his life existed any more.

Apart from McCluskey, which was little comfort.

He took out his smart phone, looking for a signal despite knowing full well there could be none. But who knew? Those techy guys in LA were so clever that perhaps they'd downloaded him an app that could facilitate calls across separate dimensions in space and time. But of course they hadn't, and there was an empty pie shape where that morning four black bars had been.

He pressed music and scrolled through his library. Perhaps he would listen to some tunes. He didn't. It was just too strange.

He went out on to the balcony and stood against the railing. The Pera district was on a hill and Stanton could see the whole of Istanbul and the waters of the Golden Horn stretched out below. Lights twinkled then dimmed as slowly the last remnants of the city he must now call Constantinople went to sleep.

If history were to run its course, within three months the city would be at war. Europe would have embarked on the bloodiest and most terrible conflict the world had ever known. Only he and McCluskey knew that and only he could do anything about it.

He felt very small.

He didn't feel like sleeping so he sat on the balcony looking at the city for most of the night, going back inside only to check on McCluskey and change the ice until it had all melted. At about five in the morning dawn began to glimmer on the distant horizon.

The dawn of his first day.

He decided to go for a walk. McCluskey seemed OK. The signs of fever that she had exhibited earlier had disappeared. She was sleeping easily and soundly as her body readjusted to the shock.

He dressed her wound, put water and a bowl of fruit on her bed-side table and wrote her a note, which he left on her pillow.

DON'T PANIC! Newton was right and it has happened as he said it would. You have suffered a concussion and must rest. Do NOT leave the room. There is fruit and water and a Mars Bar (which I found in your cardigan) on the bedside table. I will return by lunchtime. Your watch is set to the correct time and there is a clock on the mantelpiece. You are a very bad woman but I guess I'm stuck with you.
   Hugh

For the briefest second he almost added, *P.S. I'm on my mobile.*

Next he bundled up McCluskey's blood-stained jacket and scarf in preparation for disposal. He took up the smaller of his two bags and went out into the corridor locking his suite door behind him and hanging out the 'Do Not Disturb' sign. Then he headed for the lift.

He thought he would wander down to the Bosphorus and watch the sun rise from the Galata Bridge.

Within a few hours he would have saved the lives of a young Muslim family and narrowly avoided sabotaging his own mission by confronting a group of British officers in a cafe.

History had begun anew. The future was already changing.

16

THE ORIENT BAR was thick with cigarette and cigar smoke. Stanton breathed deeply. Inhaling was almost as good as having one yourself and didn't break any vows. He ordered a second Laphroaig, The drink measures served at the Pera Palace were generous but he didn't feel at all affected. His whole situation was so intoxicating that he wondered if mere alcohol would ever do it for him again.

Since returning from his eventful morning in the old town, he'd been back to the suite twice to check on McCluskey. She seemed to be coming good slowly and he didn't think she'd suffered any serious injury. Of course, in 2025 he'd have taken her straight round to casualty for an MRI scan but that not being an option the best he could do was draw the curtains tight, advise rest and hope she didn't have any delayed traumas. He guessed that it would be at least a couple of days before he could move her, which worried him considerably, since having exposed himself so recklessly to fellow members of the British community he was anxious to get out of town.

It turned out he'd underestimated the old professor's recuperative powers.

'Hugh! Order your old mother a Bloody Mary, won't you?'

McCluskey was standing at the door. She'd got up, got herself dressed, found the lift and made straight for the bar like a homing pigeon. And there she was, in her floor-length dress, making a passable impression of an Imperial English lady, her hair done up in a bun at the back to cover her wound. She looked pale but she'd put on some lipstick and a bit of blusher to help with that, and although her walk wasn't exactly steady, she was certainly on her feet.

'Jesus, prof,' Stanton said as McCluskey walked towards him, holding on to chairs for support, 'you were out cold for ten hours, you need to be in bed.'

'Hugh,' she replied, her eyes shining despite her weak condition, 'I'm seventy-two, I don't have a lot of time. I am embarking on the single greatest opportunity that any bonkers old historian has ever been granted and I am not going to spend the first day of it in bed.' Reaching out for the support of the bar she leant forward and hissed into his ear in a robust stage whisper, 'Hugh, Sweetlips. We are in nine – teen – four – *teen*!'

'Excuse me, sir,' the barman interrupted before Stanton could tell her to shut up, 'but I'm afraid ladies are not accepted at the bar. Madam is welcome to take a seat at a table.'

'Bloody Mary *s'il vous plaît, garçon*!' McCluskey said, turning her back on the man and tottering towards a table.

'Plain tomato juice,' Stanton corrected, 'and some water.'

He hurried over to join her.

'Professor, you have suffered a concussion.'

'Don't I know it,' McCluskey replied. 'My head feels like the council are digging it up and laying drains.' She reached into her handbag, the same vast container that she'd brought from the future and which Stanton now noted was antique and had clearly been chosen to pass muster in an earlier age. She pulled out a little blister-pack of Ibuprofen, popping four out of the foil.

'Prof, *please*,' Stanton hissed.

'Oh come on, Hugh, nobody's going to notice.'

'We don't know *what* people are going to notice, professor. Now shut up and listen to me.' Stanton paused in what he was saying while the waiter delivered McCluskey's tomato juice. If she noticed the absence of vodka she thought better than to complain about it.

'Cheers,' she said.

'Never mind cheers! What the hell are you doing here?'

'I've told you. I'm not hanging about in bed while—'

'I don't mean here in the bar. I mean *here* in 1914!'

'Ah, yes . . . bit naughty that. Sorry.'

'*Naughty*. What you've done,' Stanton went on, struggling to keep his voice low, 'is betray every principle you've been claiming to hold since the day you brought me into this business. For five months you've been talking about a world reborn and a second chance for humanity and saving all the millions of soldiers in Flanders' fields and the prisoners in Russian gulags and it turns out the whole thing's been just a cover for you to go and see *Pygmalion*.'

'No, Hugh! Really. I promise. It's always been about the mission . . . but when it came to the moment I couldn't resist—'

'Crap! You'd been planning it from the start: getting ID made for yourself, renting that bloody pantomime frock.'

'No! It was only in the last week or two. As time got near . . . I was thinking two could fit in a sentry box, so why not?'

'Why not? Why *not*? Christ Almighty, you could have ruined everything before it even began. You might just as easily have knocked me out of position as get yourself into it when you were fighting with that drugged-up Turkish girl.'

'God, *her*!' McCluskey said with a smile. 'I'd forgotten about her. Anyway, I didn't knock you out of position and we both made it through so no harm done, eh?'

'No harm done yet,' Stanton said. 'But the fact that I was able to get a bleeding, semi-conscious old woman in what was basically a mini skirt out of that cellar, across Constantinople and into a hotel without being arrested for indecent assault was a bloody miracle. I thought very seriously about just knocking you off and leaving you there. I *should* have left you there. I'm responsible for the fate of the entire British army. You should be disposable collateral.'

McCluskey's face fell.

'Disposable collateral? That's a bit harsh, Hugh . . . I know what I've done is wrong but . . . *1914*. I just couldn't resist.'

For the first time in all the years he'd known her McCluskey actually looked contrite.

'Now, look,' Stanton said. 'The truth is we have both been screwing up. Our most important duty is to leave no trace on history until we're in a position to change it and neither of us are doing very well.'

McCluskey's mood lightened immediately.

'Really?' she asked. 'How do you mean we've *both* screwed up? What have you been up to, my boy? Not been making a beast of yourself with the belly dancers in the bazaars, have you?'

'As it happens I prevented a terrible car accident. Saved a mum and her kids.'

'Ah,' McCluskey replied, avoiding his eye, clearly all too aware of the resonance of this in Stanton's own past life. 'Well, you had to do that, didn't you? Of course you did.'

'Yes, I did. But if that family now decides to take a holiday in Sarajevo and bump into someone who bumps into someone and somehow changes the course of the Archduke's day . . .'

'Pretty bloody long shot, Hugh.'

'All events are long shots until they occur. That's what chaos theory's about.'

Stanton decided he wouldn't share the details of the rest of his morning's adventures with McCluskey. He felt foolish enough about the near catastrophic confrontation in the cafe as it was.

'So you listen to me,' he went on, 'I want you to go back to your bed and lie down again. You've had a massive blow and need to rest as much as possible. We leave town tomorrow and I don't want you keeling over on me at the station with some kind of cerebral haemorrhage.'

McCluskey's face fell.

'Leave town? I was thinking we could have a day or two in Istanbul. Constantinople, Hugh, in the dying days of the Ottoman dynasty. Think of it! The mystery, the magic. We can't just walk away from that.'

'We can and we must.'

Stanton was uncomfortably aware that the young men he'd nearly had a punch-up with were soldiers. Officers who would, in the way of the British army of the period, have plenty of leisure time. Leisure time they might very well choose to spend right where they were sitting, in the bar of the Pera Palace Hotel.

'We have four weeks to get through till our appointment in Sarajevo,' he went on, 'and we need to draw as little attention and make as little impact as possible. So, my plan is to leave Constantinople in the morning and head to Britain, where we'll stand out least. What's more, spending four days on a train is as good a way as any to avoid leaving any footprints. Once in the UK we'll lie as low as possible for a fortnight till we make the trip back.'

McCluskey frowned. There was a pocket on her dress, from which to Stanton's astonishment she now drew rolling papers and a pinch of loose tobacco.

'Jesus,' Stanton hissed. 'You can't roll a fag *here*!'

'Why not? I'm an eccentric English lady. There's no law.'

'There's convention! We are trying not to draw attention to ourselves. We are on a *mission*.'

'But actually that's the point, isn't it, Hugh?' she said, reluctantly putting the tobacco back in her pocket. '*You're* on a mission. I'm not. You don't need me. In fact, let's be honest, a gouty old drunkard like yours truly would be a liability. Why not leave me here? I'll be fine. I've got a million quid in forged Imperial Bonds sewn into my knickers and quite frankly the minute this Nurofen kicks in I'm ready to party.'

'No, that's not going to happen,' Stanton said firmly. 'Not for another couple of months anyway. Not till I've done what *you* sent me to do. Every step either of us takes, every breath we draw, in some small way changes the future from the one we know, from the template we're *relying* on to guide our actions. The only changes we want to make are the ones we've *planned* on making in Sarajevo and Berlin. Now, granted, you staggering around Constantinople taking in the sights is *unlikely* to change anything significant. But to be honest, you're a loose cannon at the best of times. I don't know what you might say or what you might do, particularly half concussed and ordering vodka for lunch. So I'm afraid you're coming with me.'

'But—'

'And I am telling you *now* that until we've succeeded in preventing the most catastrophic war in all history, you are going to do *exactly* what I say. Because if you don't – and please listen *very* carefully to this, professor – I'll shoot you and dump you in the Bosphorus.'

17

THEY LEFT CONSTANTINOPLE the following day, first class to Paris on the *Orient Express*. McCluskey, of course, could scarcely contain her excitement, muttering in wonder at every-thing she encountered, from the newspapers she bought at the Sirkeci terminal bookstall to the luxurious appointments of her own private compartment. Stanton had decided that they should book their tickets separately. He was still extremely nervous about McCluskey, whose very presence was testimony to her lack of conscience and reliability. If she did do something that drew the eye of officialdom, he didn't want paperwork to exist that linked them together.

On the other hand, it was fun having her along. He couldn't help smiling when he joined her in her compartment as the train pulled out of the station. She was just so utterly thrilled.

'Oh Hugh, *Hugh*,' she said, leaning back into the soft leather as the great steam locomotive eased its way through the Imperial capital. 'How good is this? No, I'm serious. How *good* is this? Are we not living, right now, the most delicious dream on the planet? We are tourists in history! Everybody's favourite fantasy. And we have our own private compartments. Private *first-class apartment* on the *Orient Express*.'

'We're not tourists. We're on a mission—'

'I know, Hugh, I *know*. But we can't do anything about it now, can we? Not travelling through Europe on a train. You've got your wish. We're out of harm's way. No butterflies in here. Let's

129

enjoy it! Look at this *exquisite* porcelain basin – you pull the strap and it just drops down. How absolutely lovely. That is *quality*. Not even billionaires experienced that kind of quality in our time. Everything in this beautiful little carriage is made of brass and polished wood and porcelain and leather. Real beautiful things, not plastic and hydrocarbon. And look! The window opens! An opening window on a train – we can actually let in the fresh air.'

She pulled down the window and let out a whoop of pleasure.

Stanton laughed. She was right. It *was* a pretty fantastic prospect. During his months of training with Chronos he'd never allowed himself to dwell much on the possibility that it might actually happen, that he might find himself living in the past. But now he was. And not just any old past, but early-twentieth-century Europe. A time when the miracles of technology were still virile and exciting: steam engines and flying machines, not smart phones and cosmetic surgery. When there were still wildernesses left to explore and mountains left unclimbed.

'You're right, prof,' he said, speaking louder over the noise of the rattling train. 'It is pretty exciting.'

'And a girl can smoke!' she exclaimed delightedly. 'I can sit back in my own seat which I've bloody paid for and have a bloody fag without some PC jobsworth claiming I'm killing a child in the next county. Go on, have one! You used to smoke like a chimney when you were an undergrad. I can remember bumming one off you at the back of the chapel in about 2006.'

She leaned back and drew, happily, luxuriantly, on her cigarette. Not a hand-rolled one this time either, but factory-made. She'd been like a kid in a sweet shop at the hotel tobacconist's that morning, buying a dozen different, long-forgotten brands.

'Players' navy cut, untipped,' she said, coughing slightly, 'made in the days when we really *had* a navy. Think about that, Hugh. We are *living* in an age when the Royal Navy is twice as strong as the next two navies put together! *Pax Britannica!* Britain's back on top! Feels good, eh? And once you've put paid to the Kaiser, Britain's going to *stay* on top.'

'Prof, I'm warning you. Shut up.'

'Sorry! Sorry. You're right. Won't happen again, must keep shtum about the mission. But go *on* – have a fag!'

'Can't. I made a promise . . . to Cassie.'

'But, as you've pointed out before, she's not here. And anyway, surely she wouldn't mind one little ciggie.'

Stanton looked at the tempting display protruding from the archaic packaging. Untipped. Pure tobacco.

Maybe he would have just one.

Just to celebrate. Because it *did* feel good to be thundering through Turkey on the *Orient Express* off on the best Boy's Own Adventure in the universe. *Guts saves the British army and the world!* Even Biggles would have thought that was over-reaching himself. Why not have a fag to crown the moment? It didn't mean that Cassie didn't matter any more. But he was on active service, road rules, what the girls back home didn't know . . .

He reached forward.

Delighted, McCluskey held up the pack. There is no happier addict than one who persuades a reluctant friend to join them and validate their addiction.

'Good man!' she said. 'But just so you know, I am aware that you *are* right to be strict with me. I've been horribly selfish and irresponsible and I should be ashamed of myself. But it'll be all right. You'll get this job done. I know you will. You're the perfect man to do it! You are the Guts! That's why I chose you.'

Stanton paused, his fingers on the tip of a cigarette, about to pull it from the packet. But he withdrew his hand.

It was her last phrase that stopped him.

That's why I chose you.

McCluskey shrugged. 'Oh well, your loss. I admire your self-discipline. That Cassie must have been one hell of a girl.'

'She was,' Stanton said quietly.

They lapsed into silence, McCluskey smoking happily, smiling to herself as she browsed greedily over the lunch menu.

That's why I chose you.

Stanton found his mind returning to the previous morning on the Galata Bridge. To the cold damp stones he had picked himself up from. To the moment after he'd saved the mother and the girl and boy.

He'd saved that little family but he hadn't saved his own.

Now, he suddenly wondered, had it actually been infinitely worse? Had he been the *cause* of their deaths?

'Lobster!' he heard McCluskey exclaim. 'They are serving *fresh lobster*. On a train! God, I love this century.'

Stanton got up. Opening the inner door of the compartment, he glanced out into the corridor. McCluskey, salivating over the lunch menu, scarcely noticed.

'O – M – effing – G,' she said. 'They do a sweet soufflé for dessert. You can't cook a soufflé on a train, surely? Well, let me tell you, boy, I intend to find out.'

Stanton sat down once more and stared at McCluskey.

Could it be true?

Had he *really* been so used?

They had needed him. That shadowy collective known as Chronos had needed him. Or at any rate, a man just like him. Guts Stanton, celebrated survivalist. Adventurer. Man of proven resource and decisive action.

But they had needed him without ties.

That's why I chose you.

Stanton's mind ran back to Christmas Eve, when he'd first learned of Chronos. He thought about the weeks and months since. Running in his mind through conversations past and finding that seeds of doubt had been planted which had only now germinated and were showing on the surface of his conscience.

He should have guessed before. It was so obvious when you came to think about it.

Once more he got up and checked the corridor. This time McCluskey noticed.

'Bit fidgety, Hugh? Something on your mind?'

'A bit, yes.'

'Care to share?'

'Yes, I would, as a matter of fact. I was just wondering how you knew that there were four of them?'

'Sorry? Not following. Four of who?'

'The hit-and-run murderers. The ones in the car who wiped out my family. "All four got clean away." That's what you said. On Christmas Eve when we had that first breakfast. How did you know how many of them were in the stolen car?'

'Well . . . I don't know. Did I say that? I suppose I must have read about it somewhere. Why do you ask?'

'You didn't read it. It wasn't reported. Violent death's a bit too common where we come from to make the papers and there was nothing on the net. No details were ever published. But you knew how many were in the car. *"All four got clean away"* – that was what you said.'

'I don't know what I said, Hugh, and I have no idea what you're talking about. Now are you going to have a look at this menu? Because I want to order lunch.'

'Last spring.'

'What?'

'That was when Davies said you were choosing your agent. On that day when we were in his Incident Room. When he said that he approved of your choice. Your choice of *me*. He said that the committee had met "last spring". And you suggested me. *Last spring.*'

'Yes, last spring, last spring, what about last bloody spring?'

'My wife and children were killed in the late summer, professor.'

'What has your family got to do with it? I brought up your name because you're Guts bloody Stanton. You're an obvious choice.'

'Yes, a choice who would most certainly refuse the job if it meant consigning the only people he loved on earth to an existential oblivion. A man who in fact would have tried to stop you with everything in his power.'

133

'Hugh, please. Come on! What the hell are you insinuating?' She had put down the lunch menu. And her hand was on her bag.

'You needed a soldier. A special operative. A trained man. Someone who could adapt to and survive in any environment.'

'Yes, but—'

'And it would also help if that soldier had some understanding of the past and the people and events that created it. A history graduate would be good. Decent German was another pre-requisite, you said so yourself. That's already a pretty specific order. But when you add to that the requirement that this soldier has to be *desperate* and *alone*, without love, a man simply waiting for death, a man who would happily step away from the whole world and everyone in it because there was nothing and no one he cared about any more . . . What was it Newton said? *Let them be without ties.*'

McCluskey's hand was inside her bag now.

'You might wait a century for such a very specific type of man and still not find him. But Newton only gave you a year.'

'This is crazy!'

She was smiling, trying to laugh. But for Stanton that big, red, happy face that had always seemed so gleeful now looked sinister. As if a mask had fallen away. He had spent a lifetime reading fear and lies in the eyes of his adversaries and he read them in McCluskey now.

'You chose me, professor, and then you set about ensuring that I was without those inconvenient ties. I can't believe I didn't work it out before. It's so bloody obvious when you think about it. You murdered my wife and children.'

McCluskey pulled the gun from her bag and pointed it at him.

'I could try to bluster it out,' she said, 'but you wouldn't believe me. Because you're right. It *is* pretty obvious. I mean, what are the chances of finding a qualified man who didn't care whether he lived or died?'

'Pretty slim.'

'We took a view, Hugh. We had to save the world.'

134

'And if it had turned out that Newton was wrong? I'd just lose my family?'

'Collateral damage, Hugh. You know how things go.'

'Oh yes, professor. I know how things go.'

Stanton's eyes had narrowed to two slits, burning into McCluskey, who was squirming with anguish.

'Oh bugger! Bugger, bugger, *bugger*,' she said. 'This is just awful. There we were beginning to have fun and . . . now I suppose it's all spoiled. It is spoiled, isn't it . . . I suppose.'

Her eyes were pleading. But her gun was steady.

'You had my wife and kids murdered, professor.'

'Yes but *now*, Hugh, now they never actually existed . . . So it's OK . . . isn't it? To move on?'

'It doesn't look very OK, does it? With you pointing a gun at me.'

McCluskey thought for a moment.

'All right,' she said. 'I know you can never forgive me and I don't blame you, of course, but you have a job to do, Hugh. The most important job in history and that's what you need to focus on now. So here's what I suggest. Our first stop is Bucharest in about five or six hours, so we just sit here tight together till then and, when we arrive, you get out. I'd go myself but frankly it's easier to cover you with this little six shot if it's you that gets out of the carriage. Fortunately we have our own door, which is *such* a civilized design, don't you think? You go off and fulfil your mission and I just disappear. You'll never see me again, Hugh. And I won't flap my wings too much, I promise. Bit of dinner and the theatre is all I ask and quite frankly I'll be dead in half a decade anyway. You have the whole world before you. A world you will have saved. Don't spoil all that for a bit of revenge.'

'How do you mean, spoil it?'

'Well, you see, if you *won't* get out of the carriage, Hugh, I'll have to kill you. You do see that, don't you? So that you don't kill me. That's obvious.'

'But what about the mission? The most important mission in

history? If you kill me, the Great War will begin again in just ten weeks. Europe's great calamity, professor. The thing we came to stop.'

There was a film of tears over McCluskey's eyes now, although that may have been as a result of the smoke drifting up from the smouldering cigarette clamped between her teeth. She had both hands on her gun now, arms held out in classic firing position.

'I *know* it's wrong, Hugh. And I *do* care, I care so much. All those millions of young men. The Russian princesses murdered in that awful cellar with their poor jewels sewn in their knickers. The terrible dictators, the wars and the genocides and the starvation to come . . . but . . . I'm just a selfish old fool, you see, and I do so want to see the Diaghilev ballet.'

Stanton stared at her. He had always been proud of his ability to read people and yet it seemed he had never known this woman at all. So weak, so selfish. So . . . *appalling* a human being.

'I loved my wife and kids,' he said.

'Oh I *know*, Hugh, I *know*.'

He stood up. Her knuckles whitened on the trigger.

'*Please* don't make me do it, Hugh! Because I will. I really will. Just get off the train at Bucharest. It's easy, it's all good. I'll be gone, I promise.'

'Goodbye, professor.'

He reached forward towards the gun. She pulled the trigger.

The hammer clicked against the empty chamber. McCluskey stared at it for a moment in surprise.

She clicked again.

'Bugger,' she said.

'You didn't think I was going to leave a half-concussed lunatic like you with a loaded gun in her bag, did you?'

She was about to speak but Stanton reached forward and took hold of her by the neck. He pushed his thumb deep into her windpipe, preventing her from shouting out.

'You were actually going to kill me,' he said, 'and screw the twentieth century. I really didn't think you'd do that.'

McCluskey could only offer a choking grunt in reply.

He dragged her to her feet and swung her towards the outside door of the carriage. In the same movement, he reached through the open window with his free hand and, jamming his back against the frame, opened it from the outside. McCluskey's eyes widened in terror as the door swung open.

'You're scared!' Stanton shouted over the rattling of the train. 'Big bullying old Professor McCluskey's scared. Scared of dying. Christ, I really would have credited you with more balls. Shows what a blind idiot I am, eh?'

The train was travelling through rocky, low-lying foothills. Glancing out Stanton saw that there was a steep, sparsely vegetated scree slope below them. Nobody was going to survive hitting that at speed. McCluskey could see it too. He felt her windpipe convulsing as her body tried to retch with fear. He felt a sharp pain in his shins as she began kicking at them.

He dragged her face towards his own. Their eyes met for a moment.

There was so much he would have liked to say to her.

About how much he hated her. About how much he hoped there was a hell and that she would burn in it for eternity.

But what was the point? He just threw her out of the train.

He watched as her body span and bounced like a broken doll crashing a hundred metres down the slope.

Stanton stepped back inside, leaving the carriage door open.

He checked in McCluskey's coat and bag for anything suspicious or anachronistic. He took her gun, which had fallen from her hand, her modern medicines and her underwear. There seemed to be nothing else which she had brought with her from the twenty-first century. Pretty much all that was left in her bag was booze and tobacco. The authorities could draw from that whatever conclusion they wished.

Checking the corridor for the third and final time Stanton slipped out of the compartment and returned to his own.

He was now entirely alone in a new universe.

18

THE NEWS THAT an English lady travelling alone had somehow managed to fall from the train spread through the carriages while Stanton was having lunch in the dining car. Some passengers to the rear had spotted what had looked like a falling woman and alerted the guard. A search of the train revealed a first-class passenger to be missing and the door of her private compartment to be open.

Stanton had just ordered the lobster and the dessert soufflé.

Fuck her. Let her rot in hell.

If he could have the moment of killing her again, the moment where her eyes had met his in mute appeal, he'd gouge them from her skull with his fingers before tossing her out of the train.

That murdering bitch. That *evil* bitch.

He'd been on his way home. To make it right with Cassie. They could have had nine more months together. Nine months of happiness and love, before being evaporated, oblivious, into time and space along with the rest of humanity. They would have been stars together. Him, Cassie, Tessa and Bill, twinkling in the same firmament. Instead, because of McCluskey, they had never even existed and he was exiled in a different universe.

Why couldn't she have chosen someone else? The regiment was full of hard men. Resourceful men. More experienced assassins than him. MI6 was busting with bored wannabe heroes desperate to get into the field but stuck behind computers because they couldn't speak any African or Asian languages. Why not choose one of them? But of course any other guy would have far more dependants and emotional loyalties than he did. His life was unique in its isolation. No parents, no siblings, no kids by previous partnerships. A loner by circumstance and later by choice. All he had had in the whole world was his own tiny little family. They *were* his world.

And *so* easy to kill. Two little kids, clinging to their mum. How simple is that? Knock the lot off at once.

Any other guy McCluskey and her murderous crew of skeletons might have set up would have put two and two together at once ... *Hang on,* they'd have said to that lying witch, *you needed a man without ties and now all my loved ones, devoted friends and extended family have been knocked off separately over the last six months. Something fishy here.*

They'd have shot the disgusting old Gorgon where she stood. In her study, in front of her fire, cognac in hand.

But *his* whole life could be dispensed with in one simple car crash. God, McCluskey must have punched the air in joy when she settled on him. He was absolutely perfect.

'I'm sorry, Cassie,' he whispered to himself, as he pushed the soufflé away untasted. 'I'm sorry, Tessa and Bill. It was me those bastards wanted. But you paid the price.'

Stanton kept pretty much to his compartment for the rest of the journey to Paris, ignoring the bar carriage and the occasional efforts of other passengers to make conversation with the tall, handsome loner when he took his meals in the dining car. There was, of course, some consternation over McCluskey's death. The express made an unscheduled stop at Lüleburgaz where police joined the train. Everyone in first class was interviewed, including Stanton, but since he and McCluskey had been careful to book and board the train separately and he had not been seen entering her private compartment there was nothing to connect him. The lady had been elderly and travelling alone. An opened bottle of brandy had been found in her bag and it was concluded that she had suffered a terrible accident while trying to open the window under the influence of alcohol.

Nonetheless it had been a close-run thing. Another potentially disastrous action which could so easily have ruined everything. Stanton imagined how he would have felt if he'd had to watch the oncoming disaster of the Great War while awaiting trial for murder in a Turkish prison cell.

More than ever he needed urgently to hide out. He needed to find a place where he would do no harm and where no harm could be done to him for the twenty-seven days that must elapse before he could begin his mission. On the spur of the moment he decided he would return to the shore of Loch Maree in the most remote part of north Scotland, the place where he'd first received McCluskey's email and his mission had begun. He decided he'd travel there directly, *Orient Express* to Paris, boat train to London, sleeper to Inverness and pony and trap to Maree.

There was a comfort in the plan too. In the excitement of the last thirty-six hours, Stanton had been finally starting to readjust to his bereavement. He'd even been on the verge of taking up smoking again. But the revelation of McCluskey's brutal treachery had torn savagely at a wound that had begun to heal. He knew he missed Cassie and the kids as much as he had in the first moment of his loss, and to this deep sadness was added the furious guilt that in a way he had been the cause of their deaths.

Of all the places in the UK he could visit, he imagined that distant Loch Maree would be the most similar to its twenty-first-century state. He'd been there only a few months before, trying to come to terms with his bereavement; he would return there now and spend another week or two saying goodbye to what he'd lost.

He made only one small exception to his plan.

On arriving in London he made a detour between Victoria Station and Euston Station, when instead of going direct he took the underground to Camden Town.

He hadn't intended to do it but on arriving at Victoria off the boat train he'd been seized with a sudden and fervent desire to do what he had been planning to do when he had jumped ship in the Aegean, on the morning he had put Cassie's emails in his wallet, given up smoking, resigned his job and headed for an airport.

To go home.

It was the underground map that made him do it. A very different map to the one he was familiar with but nonetheless featuring stations he knew, including his own, Camden Town.

He could still do what he had done so many times before when arriving at some London station. Just hop on the tube and go home.

To the same street. To the *same* house.

It was still there, he knew that. Or more accurately, already there.

In St Marks Crescent, in Primrose Hill. A nineteenth-century street. The very bricks and mortar he had bought with Cassie during their brief period of wealth after the webcasts took off. The home they'd shared. It actually existed in this new world he was living in. There was no real connection, of course; he knew that. The house was over a century younger than the one he'd known and nothing that he had ever touched or loved existed in it. But it was *there*. His house, just the same, or at least the exterior would be the same because it had been protected under its Grade 2 listing.

In fact, he'd seen it. Cassie had bought a print of the street *circa* 1910 at Camden Lock Market and it had hung in their hall. That picture had only been taken four years ago.

There was no Victoria line and wouldn't be for fifty years but the District Line was there, which he took from Victoria to Charing Cross, where he picked up the Northern Line for Camden Town. *His* line, although they had called it the Hampstead Line then.

He counted off the stations: Tottenham Court Road, Goodge Street, Warren Street and Euston. Half closing his eyes and ignoring the unfamiliar rattling motion, he told himself for a moment that it was 2023 and his family were at home, looking forward to

his arrival. A week earlier such a fantasy would have tortured him
but somehow now he embraced it, allowing himself to love the
memory rather than grieve over it.

Mornington Crescent.

Camden Town.

He was home. His station. He was a North London boy.
Camden had been his station as a kid and it had been his station
when he became a father. The long escalator to the surface was in
the same place; he stood on it at the same angle. He could have
walked home blindfold.

Up Parkway, over the railway line and right just before the
canal.

He stood for a moment before turning into St Marks, looking
beyond the canal bridge, along Regent's Park Road to the church.
It had been there that Cassie and the children had died. Or would
die. Or now would never die. Depending on how you looked at it.

He turned into the crescent and walked along. The cobbles and
the flagstones were different but the curve and façade of the
houses were much the same as on all the many previous times he'd
walked that street. There were even a few cars parked outside, the
first trickle of a tidal wave that was to come. No need for parking
permits yet.

He stood outside his own house for a moment or two, wondering if there were children inside, a loving wife waiting for her
husband to come home. Almost certainly there was a family; it
was a family house. There would be servants too, no doubt; a
couple at least. That much had certainly changed.

He thought about waiting, eating an apple he had in his pocket
and seeing if he could catch a glimpse of them. That family who
were the distant predecessors of his own. But then he saw that
there was a policeman approaching on his beat. That *had*
changed: no friendly bobbies in his day, just endless sirens in
the night. The copper was eyeing him now with a somewhat
dubious expression, as well he might. Stanton was a tough-
looking man and he had two holdalls in his hand. What would

143

such a figure be doing standing staring at a prosperous dwelling?

If that policeman asked him what he had in his bags, he was in trouble. It was time to move on.

'Goodbye, Cassie,' he whispered under his breath. 'Goodbye, Tessa and Bill.'

And then he turned away.

19

FOR ALL HIS fearsome reputation as Europe's most brutal and dangerous spy chief, the man known as Apis had organized, or rather failed to organize, the most cack-handed cock-up of an assassination in history.

This was the conclusion that Stanton was reminded of again and again as he pondered the details of the event during the lonely hikes he took from his solitary camp in the Western Highlands through the hot, midge-infested June days of the fateful summer of 1914.

He considered it again while journeying across Europe on his way to Sarajevo and it still took his breath away. He lay in bed in his cosy sleeping compartment, staring into the glow of the only working computer on earth. It was simply stunning what an utter farce the single most influential assassination in history had really been. It had, in fact, only succeeded at all due to almost uncannily spectacular bad luck.

Pretty much everything had gone wrong. The assassins themselves were a pathetic bunch, ill armed and terminally indecisive. But for a wrong turn, a stalled motor engine and the luckiest two shots of the entire century, the spark that ignited the Great War would have never occurred at all.

Stanton knew that it was never wise to underestimate a mission, but as he stretched out under the thick cotton sheets (of a quality he had never experienced in the twenty-first century), he couldn't help concluding that for Guts Stanton, ex-Special Air Service

145

Regiment, foiling this bunch of muppets was going to be a piece of cake with a cherry on top.

For the first time since midnight on June the first, he began to relax.

The journey across Europe was delightful, bathed from start to finish in the bright glow of summer sunshine. The summer of 1914 was a glorious one, a fact that every history book Stanton had ever read on the period had made much of, equating the wonderful weather with a golden Imperial period for Europe that was about to come to a sudden and terrible end. Living through it as he now was, Stanton could certainly see the point. The whole continent seemed almost to sigh with a deep and comfortable contentment. No doubt it was different in the slums and factory sweatshops, but journeying through the countryside, past endless ripe fields, picture-postcard villages and little towns, Europe really did seem to be the sun-drenched idyll that romantically minded historians had always claimed it was. Pastoral, timeless and achingly beautiful.

Lying in the darkness of his sleeper car, soothed by the regular rattling rhythm of the train, Stanton felt an overwhelming surge of emotion that it had fallen to him to save this paradise from destruction.

He thought of the email printout in his wallet. The letter Cassie had written.

I was proud of you when you risked your life on peacekeeping missions, saving children who were just like your own.

He was back on course, fulfilling the promise he'd wanted to make to her, to be himself again. Even if she had died before she'd had the chance to hear it.

'This is for you and the kids, Cass,' he whispered as he drifted off to sleep.

In order to get to Bosnia and Herzegovina, Stanton had to cross the entirety of the two great Germanic central powers, Germany and Austria, with which (if history was allowed to take its course) Britain would shortly be at war. In only a matter of weeks the press on both sides of the conflict would be screaming hatred at each other but that June a British tourist could not have been a more welcome guest, and Stanton's papers were stamped and his person saluted at every border.

'Welcome, sir! Germany is honoured by your visit!'

What did they know? Nothing. Only Stanton knew. Only Stanton and a few psychopathic Serb nationalists knew that as the boats and trains of Europe steamed about, delivering happy tourists and welcome guests to their destinations, already hiding out in and around Sarajevo was a terrorist cell. Six Pan-Serbian nationalist assassins recruited by the Black Hand. These men, armed and let loose by the shadowy Apis, would shortly commit an act that would turn all this peace and comfortable good fellowship to bloody carnage within eight weeks.

Except this time they wouldn't. Stanton was thundering between Frankfurt and Munich on his journey across Europe to stop them.

He arrived in Sarajevo in the late afternoon on 27 June and checked at once into the central hotel that Thomas Cook's travel office had secured for him by telegram from London. He went for a walk about the town and dined in a small restaurant down by the river. It was a strange feeling, knowing that elsewhere in the city the two groups of would-be assassins had also arrived and were meeting up for the first time. Three had been recruited locally in Bosnia Herzegovina, and the other three, including the killer, Princip, had come from Belgrade. Stanton knew that, unlike his, their journey had been a pretty tortuous one lasting almost a month and involving numerous safehouses and codes, a multitude of agents and even a secret tunnel. Once again, as he chewed on his schnitzel and drank his beer, Stanton wondered how it could have been that Apis planned so much of the plot so carefully and yet had left its execution up to a bunch of pusillanimous incompetents. Arrogance, Stanton reckoned. He thought he could do anything and he got careless. It was usually arrogance that undermined men like Apis in the end.

Looking at his watch he guessed that the meeting was in progress and that the conspirators would shortly send a postcard to the Black Hand chief in Bosnia Herzegovina to tell him that all was proceeding well. Another astonishingly stupid move in Stanton's view. The chief in question was currently hiding out in France and so could play absolutely no part in the planned hit on the following morning, so why the group compromised their security by bothering to keep him in the loop would remain for ever a mystery.

Stanton didn't know where the six plotters would be staying that night so he made no effort to track them. He knew they were in town, that was all. He would only be able to pick up their trail in the morning. Which was good. The later he intervened in events the less likely he was to prematurely adjust them.

As he went to bed that night, Stanton tried to feel some emotion about the immensity of what was about to happen. Brought here by the genius of a dead physicist, he was about to change the course of history. Prevent perhaps the single most renowned event of the twentieth century and so prevent its most disastrous war. He tried, but he couldn't. The brief surge of emotion he'd had about his mission on the train had left him. Maybe if Cassie had been there to talk to about it, or even the traitor McCluskey. Anyone. But there was no one. He was alone. He was always alone. He could never be truly intimate with anyone again because were he to share with them the central fact of his existence, the fact that he had arrived from the future, they would undoubtedly think him mad.

20

THE FOLLOWING MORNING Stanton rose early and assembled his equipment.

He'd given this a great deal of thought over the previous weeks, considering exactly what he would require.

In theory he didn't even need a gun. He needed nothing save his foreknowledge. He knew exactly what was going to happen throughout the day and he needed only to change one tiny thing about it to alter the course of an entire century.

All he had to do was to prevent Princip from getting a shot at the Archduke.

He knew where Princip would be standing and he knew what he'd be doing; he knew that Princip's window of opportunity had been agonizingly brief. Stanton simply had to stand in front of Princip at the moment at which his path was about to cross with the Duke's, and with any luck the killer would not even see his intended victim. He'd never even know he had missed his chance.

That was the theory, but things go wrong when theories are put into practice and Stanton needed to prepare for eventualities. His target was armed and, as history had shown, extremely happy to shoot. If anything went wrong, Stanton might have to shoot him. He therefore put his Glock pistol in the pocket of his Norfolk jacket, which was hanging over the dressing-table chair. He also reflected that the intervention, when it came, would occur within sight and earshot of a lot of heavily armed soldiers and policemen, all made nervous by the bomb attempt which Stanton knew would have occurred earlier in the day. It was possible that if Princip and he were involved in a firefight then others might join in. Stanton decided to take precautions against that also. He would wear body armour. It would be slightly restrictive but since Stanton was the only man alive with the specialist information to prevent global catastrophe he needed to make sure he *stayed* alive. It was for this reason that Chronos had supplied him with the armoured vest in the first place.

All of his equipment was, of course, the very best that twenty-first-century military technology could provide. Stanton knew the armour well; he'd worn similar kit many times. It consisted of a Gore-tex vest and groin flap fitted with polyethylene ballistic plates; these plates were capable of stopping the kind of armour-piercing ammunition which would not be developed for ninety years, and therefore offered 100 per cent protection from the small-arms technology of 1914.

Stanton was hopeful that he would need neither gun nor bullet-proof vest but it didn't hurt to be sure. He could remember his first staff sergeant in the Regiment pointing out that 'Better Safe Than Sorry' would have been a much more sensible motto for the SAS than 'Who Dares Wins'. Stanton smiled at the memory as he put on his protective vest. The staff sergeant had *hated* that motto.

'Who *dares* without proper preparation and training does not fucking win,' he used to say. 'He gets shot dead, and what's more the idiot probably takes good men with him.'

Stanton put on a shirt and tie over the vest and his Norfolk jacket over that.

Then, having prepared, he hoped, for any eventuality, he sat down to have one last study of the royal route, which he had up on his computer screen. On it he'd marked the places where all the assassins would be, the location of the first attempt and, of course, the last point, that infamous place where Princip was destined to murder the Archduke unless Stanton prevented him from doing so. Having satisfied himself that he could walk this route and find his marks without any map, he went downstairs and drank a cup of tea in the hotel dining room. Then when he judged the time right he set out to walk the short way to Sarajevo station. It was there that the royal party were scheduled to arrive and where this most important day of the century would really begin.

Guts versus the Black Hand.

'This is it, Cassie,' he found himself whispering under his breath as his fingers closed around the gun in his pocket. 'I'm going in.'

The crowd at the station was being kept at a good distance from the arrivals barrier by lines of police and soldiers but Stanton was tall and it was still possible for him to get a view. There were flags and bunting but not what Stanton would have called a festive spirit. The twenty-eighth of June was a Serbian holiday, the anniversary of a famous historic victory over the Turks. The decision to stage a royal visit on this day by a man who to many represented an occupying power was significant and provocative. Stanton sensed a great deal of anger in the deeply divided crowd.

The royal train arrived exactly as Stanton had known it would. Exactly as it had arrived in the previous loop in space–time. He had the timings and people present from the records of the subsequent trials and he was relieved to note that every detail was as it once had been.

He saw the six-car motorcade draw up. Just as he had known it would.

The local governor was standing stiffly with his entourage, as Stanton had seen him in those grainy photographs from another universe. He saw the mayor of Sarajevo and the police chief speaking together, heads bowed towards each other. He saw the flash powder pop as a photographer took a photo of them, a photo that Stanton had seen pinned to the wall of the Incident Room in the History faculty in Cambridge at Easter in 2025. The same photo that was contained in digital form in his computer at the hotel.

Stanton saw the Archduke's security detail standing slightly apart. Looking at the little team he felt a genuine sense of professional sympathy because he knew that those three

serious-looking men in bowler hats were about to face the protection officer's worst nightmare: losing contact with their charge.
And right at the start of the day too. Stanton knew that through
a ridiculous mix-up those officers would not ride with the royal
couple to their first engagement, which was a military inspection
at the local barracks, because three local officers had already
placed themselves in the seats reserved for them in the front car.
The protection squad would realize too late that there was no
room left for them, and the Archduke and his wife would be
driven off without their specialist team.

It would be the first little farce of a ridiculously farcical day.

The royal train arrived and Franz Ferdinand and the Duchess
Sophie descended from it on to the red carpet laid out on the
platform. They were a rather ordinary-looking couple who but for
the splendour of their dress would have turned no heads. Stanton
knew from surprisingly good photographs that Sophie had been a
beauty in her day but her looks were rather faded now by child-
bearing, care and worry. This was a very special day for her and
one she'd been looking forward to. It was one of the few public
occasions in her life when it was possible for her to be at
her husband's side and get the respect she craved and which her
husband considered her due. The problem was that Sophie was a
Czech, a noble one for sure but still a Czech, and so not considered a good enough match for the heir to the Austro-Hungarian
Empire. Franz Ferdinand had married for love. His uncle, the
Emperor, had been furious and had made it clear that Sophie
would remain a commoner and would never be allowed an
official rank at the Austrian court. What was even more wound-
ing was that the bitter old man had made his nephew swear an
oath that any children he had with Sophie could never inherit the
throne.

Stanton studied the woman's face, the face of a woman who
lived at the heart of one of richest and most powerful families in
Europe, but who every day experienced nothing but snobbery and
insult. The wife of the Crown Prince, the chosen consort of the

heir to a vast and ancient empire, who had less official status than the very lowliest Austrian lady at court. She was only with him on this day because he was visiting Sarajevo in a military capacity to inspect Imperial troops. Sophie, therefore, accompanied him not as a princess but as wife of the commander-in-chief and could therefore enjoy the rare treat of riding side-by-side with him through a crowd: a treat which in the previous loop of time had been her death warrant. Had the Black Hand chosen to strike at the Archduke on the majority of his public outings, Sophie would not have been present at all. At best she would have attended at a distance, kept in the background, sitting with a single maid in an antechamber and only allowed to see her husband when the grandeur and the pomp were over.

Stanton knew that both she and the Archduke had been aware that Sarajevo was a dangerous town for an Austrian royal to parade, but they preferred to accept that danger in order to get the chance to be publicly and proudly together.

They were prepared to risk their lives for love.

Watching her smiling shyly as she accepted the bows of the assembled officials, Stanton felt he understood the Duchess Sophie. She was on the outside. A loner. The victim of a bunch of upper-class snobs who had no better reason for their arrogance and pride than an accident of their over-privileged birth. Stanton knew a bit about that, and he was glad that because of him the much belittled Duchess would not die in agony in a few hours' time with a bullet in her stomach.

In fact, world wars aside, he was glad that he would save them both. They were in love; it was obvious even on this official occasion. Still in love despite enduring a life that consisted only of stifling formality and painful slights. He knew from history that their happiness and their sanctuary was contained entirely in their private love and the love of their children. After they had been shot on that same 28 June in another universe, both of them had continued to sit upright in their car, a single bullet lodged in each, dying together as they had lived. The Archduke had been heard begging his wife to live. 'Sophie, Sophie! Don't die!' he was recorded as saying. 'Live for our children.'

Stanton felt a strange surge of emotion. The man in the huge plumed helmet with the absurd braid on his shoulder was just like him. A lonely man who loved his wife and his children. Archduke Franz Ferdinand had set his face against his father and his inheritance for love, and he had died for love while thinking of his children.

And to cap it all he had even been a friend of the Serbs, the very people on whose supposed behalf he was about to be shot. Franz Ferdinand knew they had grievances and needed greater autonomy. Had he lived and become Emperor, the whole sorry history of the Balkans in the twentieth century would have been different. That, of course, was the very reason a xenophobic psychopath like Apis had wanted him killed, because he was taking the sting out of Serbian nationalism by being sympathetic to it.

Stanton liked the funny, stiff, shaven-headed old Archduke.

And he hated Apis for the cruel fanatic that he was.

The motorcade pulled away and the band stopped playing. Stanton could not help but smile at the looks on the faces of the three royal protection officers as they realized they'd lost the Duke and had better start looking for a cab. As a fellow soldier he felt their pain. They had *seriously* screwed up.

He turned away from the station and along with the rest of the crowd began to make his way towards the centre of the town. The royal route had been advertised in advance and everybody knew exactly where the motorcade would go after it had left the military inspection.

Stanton was liking the Archduke and his Czech duchess more and more. They knew they were in what was at least partially enemy territory and that the town was full of Serbian nationalists and yet they had elected to ride in an open car on a previously announced route. That was impressive behaviour. Stupid certainly. But brave and kind of noble. Like him, they had guts.

The virtual reconstruction of the fateful day that Stanton had in his computer told him that there would be three assassins waiting for the couple between the barracks and a reception that was to take place at the town hall. They would all fail in their appointed task, the first two with almost comical ineptitude.

Stanton spotted the first assassin, as he knew he would, in the centre of town in the garden of a cafe called the Mostar. This was Muhamed Mehmedbašić. He was one of the local guys, a carpenter from Herzegovina. Stanton stared long and hard, wondering whether he might have spotted the man in a crowd had he not previously studied his photograph on a wall in Cambridge and known him to be a terrorist.

For a moment he imagined himself in Afghanistan once more, surveying a group of workers as they assembled at the camp gate. Remembering the heat and the sand and studying the faces, looking for one who might have a bomb beneath his shirt, and missing the guy who shortly thereafter killed himself and three of Stanton's comrades. You really could never tell. People could look nervous and sweaty for any number of reasons. It didn't mean they had a bomb tied round their waist, and of course it didn't mean they didn't.

Stanton wondered where Muhamed Mehmedbašić was hiding his bomb. In his little shoulder bag, probably, although even there it couldn't be a very big one. Big enough no doubt if thrown accurately but Mehmedbašić wasn't going to throw it accurately. In fact, he wasn't going to throw it at all because he was going to totally lose his nerve.

Mehmedbašić had form. He was a serial failure. In Stanton's experience, the young men recruited by terrorist organizations usually were. Mehmedbašić was even the *son* of a failure; it was in his genes. His dad had been an impoverished noble. A fatal combination: failure and delusions of grandeur. Stanton could see it all over the young man as he shifted from foot to foot in the hot sun. The classic private bitterness of the public zealot. A man who wanted to take out his own inadequacy on other people.

And yet Apis had recruited him? How could he have *been* such an arsehole?

Didn't he profile his choices at all?

It wasn't as if Apis hadn't been warned. Mehmedbašić had failed as a terrorist before. At his last attempt at killing for the Black Hand he'd been tasked with hitting the Bosnian Governor, but sitting on the train on his way to the hit, Mehmedbašić had panicked when a cop happened to get on looking for a thief. He'd thrown his weapons out of the window.

A knife and a bottle of poison.

Once again Stanton wondered how these ridiculous comedy villains had ever managed to change the course of history. They were just so amateur.

The motorcade approached heading down the near empty street at a slow enough speed for a man with a steady nerve to throw a bomb. But Mehmedbašić did nothing. Stanton saw him twitch but that was all.

There was another Black Hand assassin close by. Vaso Čubrilović, a Serbian youth, this time armed with a bomb *and* a gun. He used neither, just stood there, frozen. The open-topped Gräf & Stift double phaeton in which the royal couple were riding passed by without incident.

Two stupid, useless boys, both carrying bombs, looked foolishly and sheepishly on. That was the foot-soldier of a terrorist organization for you.

The Archduke and his party were now heading down to the Miljacka river. Having studied the route they would take, Stanton knew that by cutting through some back streets he could arrive there before them, although it wouldn't really matter if he missed it. He was just an observer; his own part in the drama was yet to come.

Stanton arrived as expected in good time. There was a larger crowd gathered on this part of the route. Being down by the river, the area was more conducive to a day out and the crowd was in festive mood. Not everyone in Sarajevo was a radical Serb by any means and there were many who were loyal to the Austrian Crown. One onlooker, however, was intent on murder and he would prove to be the only member of the gang who would act decisively according to the original plan.

This man was Nedeljko Čabrinović. He was the firebrand of the group. He'd had many a falling-out with the others over his lax security and Stanton spotted him easily, standing straight, almost to attention, as if attempting to physically embody the nobility of his cause.

It was this moment that Stanton had agonized over. He knew that Čabrinović would throw his bomb and that it would bounce off the folded soft top of the royal car and explode underneath the following vehicle. Stanton also knew that this would cause severe injury to some twenty people in the immediate vicinity. Stanton had seen what bombs did to crowds and every instinct he possessed made him want to stop this bomb being thrown. He wanted to position himself behind Čabrinović and grasp his arms tight until the cars had passed.

But he didn't do it.

He couldn't. Because he knew that this failed attempt on the Archduke's life would be the cause of the royal party changing its plans after lunch. They would abandon their published itinerary in favour of visiting the hospital to comfort the wounded. It would be that decision that would lead them via a wrong turn and a stalled engine into the path of their killer. Stanton knew when that incident would take place and where. However, if he prevented Čabrinović from throwing his bomb, the entire history of the day would change completely and Stanton would be as helpless as the official security guys. Princip might get his chance in some other manner and Stanton would not be there to stop him.

And so he merely watched, sick to his stomach, as Čabrinović made his move. Franz Ferdinand and the Duchess were smiling broadly as the cars approached the river. They were clearly flattered and relieved at receiving such a positive reception. The crowds truly were cheering and Imperial flags fluttered in the hands of little children. Children whom Stanton must now see blown into the air and dashed upon the ground.

Čabrinović threw his bomb. It bounced off the royal car as Stanton had known it would and exploded as he expected. There was some satisfaction in that at least: the textbook-perfect occurrence of the bombing was proof that nothing of significance had so far changed in history. Stanton turned away from the mayhem; he'd seen too many bodies maimed to want to watch any more, but the fate of Čabrinović was of interest, if only because what happened next was so absurd that Stanton had strongly suspected historians of embellishing the truth.

As the angry crowd moved in on Čabrinović, he pulled something out of his pocket and put it in his mouth. Stanton knew that this was a cyanide pill, which had been supplied to the conspirators on the orders of Apis. However, as with so much of what the Black Hand attempted, it failed. It was too weak. Clutching his stomach, beginning to vomit and being pursued by the crowd, Čabrinović ran puking to the river and jumped in, hoping to drown himself instead. However, it was late June in what was famously one of the most gloriously hot and dry summers in years. The river was only thirteen centimetres deep.

Stanton watched as the police waded in up to their ankles and dragged the vomiting would-be national hero from the shallows. The cops then allowed the angry crowd to savagely beat him up before finally taking him into custody, still vomiting and with his shoes full of water.

The history books hadn't lied. It really was that stupid. Stanton thought about how thrilled McCluskey would have been to see it. He could imagine her crowing over it. 'Let's see the dialectical materialists claim *that* was a historical inevitability! You couldn't make it up.'

Stanton drove the memory of McCluskey from his mind. The associations were too painful. He should have torn the bitch's face off before he chucked her off that train.

Stanton walked away from the angry crowd. He knew that for

the time being Čabrinović's failed attempt would put paid to any further planned efforts by the Black Hand to kill their quarry. The Archduke's motorcade, its occupants now thoroughly alarmed, increased speed and hurtled past the remaining three conspirators, including Princip, whom the Black Hand had placed along the route. The royal car was now moving too fast for them to do anything, even if they'd had the nerve.

And there but for fate would have ended one of the most spectacularly inept attempts to assassinate a senior royal ever staged. Six agents, all armed with bombs or pistols, or both, and only one of them had even made an attempt at the hit. And he had missed.

But Stanton knew what would happen next. Or what had happened next on the last occasion space and time had passed this way together. Perhaps the most ill-starred encounter in all of history. An entirely accidental, completely coincidental and supremely improbable meeting that had changed the world.

21

'I MEAN, FOR *pity's sake*!' McCluskey exclaimed in outraged frustration. She was standing as ever in her favourite place in front of the fire. Despite the improvement in the weather, the evenings were still chilly and her fat, red hands were massaging vigorously at her overheated buttocks beneath the long khaki tail of her greatcoat.

'You could *not* make it up.'

It was the evening of Easter Sunday 2025. She and Stanton had spent the afternoon in Davies's Incident Room at the History faculty going over the details of the Sarajevo assassination. Now they were back in the Master's Lodge having just finished a cold supper and McCluskey was working herself up into a booze-fuelled frenzy of frustration over the whole thing.

'I *still* can scarcely credit it happened. If it wasn't true nobody would believe it in a million years. Six assassins!' she exclaimed, wiping a greasy hand across the bits of Cheddar that were stuck in her moustache. 'Six armed men! And every one of them was at some point within five metres of the target yet not one of them managed to kill him. So far, so brilliant! The plot's failed, *finito*. Done and dusted. Apis and his gang of psychos can bugger off back with their tails between their legs. They've spent months smuggling their gang of incompetent saddos into the country. Risked their whole underground railway to do it and all six of them have comprehensively screwed up.'

She splashed herself another glass of claret, depositing as much of the wine on the table as she managed to get into the glass, hacked another big lump of Cheddar from the cheese board, sandwiched it between two water biscuits and stuck it in her mouth beside her cigarette. 'The Duke's home and dry. He's survived the day,' she went on, spraying bits of cracker into the smoke-filled air in front of her face. 'Then what happens? The military governor of Bosnia, the *man responsible for the Archduke's security*, quite literally *causes* the assassination. What Apis and all his crazed, lunatic, craptaculously inept teenage zealots couldn't achieve, the Duke's own cop does for them. It's just *tonto*!'

Stanton could only agree with her. The more he studied the time-line of the Sarajevo killing, the more incredible the coincidences and the incompetence became.

'You're right, prof. It wasn't really Princip that killed the royal couple at all. It was General Oskar Potiorek.'

'*General* Oskar Potiorek,' McCluskey echoed with contempt. 'A general. He wasn't qualified to sweep the barrack-room floor. What a truly world-historical arsehole.'

Stanton reached into his file of briefing material and took out a photograph.

'The man who really started the Great War.'

They both stared at the old picture. If Hollywood had been casting an arrogant, blinkered, pig-headed, supercilious Austrian general of the old school, they could not have done better than used the real thing. Bullet head, shaven on the sides to three inches above the ears, forensically clipped moustache, chest full of medals, head tilted very slightly back, he fixed the camera with a stare of cold contempt, the faintest sneer playing on his lips.

'What's he got to sneer about?' McCluskey shouted, throwing her fag end into the fire and reaching unsteadily for more cheese and booze. 'I mean, seriously, what has this truly Olympic-class idiot got to sneer about? The man who decided to change the route of the motorcade for security reasons but *forgot to tell the royal driver*. He makes sure all the other drivers know but not the one driving the Duke! That's it! In a sentence. The reason the Black Hand got a *seventh* chance, which *amazingly* they didn't screw up, and the Great War started. I mean *blimey*!' McCluskey was actually pulling at her own hair in frustration. 'Princip's blown it. He *knows* he's blown it. In fact, he's given up assassinating for the day and wandered off for a sandwich. A *sandwich*! What *is* this? Laurel and Hardy? He mooches down to, where was it . . . ?'

'Schiller's Delicatessen.'

'That's it. *Schiller's Delicatessen*, sounds like Joe's Caff. Basically he's gone for the early-twentieth-century equivalent of a Big Mac and fries, no doubt wondering what he's going to say to Apis, who we know is the sort of bloke who shoots kings thirty times, dices up the corpses with a sabre then throws them out of the window—'

'Princip would never have met Apis, nor would he ever meet him,' Stanton interrupted. 'The Black Hand operated on a cellular model.'

'Well, whatever. It doesn't matter. The silly young bastard's blown his chance of being a hero of the Serbian people and he's gone off to take comfort in a cheese and pickle sarnie. Meanwhile, the Archduke's driver realizes he's lost the motorcade, because they know where they're going and he doesn't, and, in an effort to get back on track, chooses to turn into a street which, of all the flipping streets in Sarajevo, *happens* to be the one with Schiller's Deli in it! I mean, can you credit it? Can you *sodding* credit it? This is the start of the *Great War* we're talking about, and it comes down to a wrong turn and a cheese sandwich!'

For a moment McCluskey's outrage exhausted her. She reached into the pocket of her greatcoat and pulled out a golf-ball-sized wodge of tobacco. She then spent a moment trying to wrestle it into a cigarette paper before realizing that she was too drunk to manage it. She opted instead for the easier option of grabbing her pipe, which she kept stuck in the visor of a medieval helmet, and stuffing the tobacco into that.

'Don't forget the dodgy gear change,' Stanton reminded her.

He was enjoying her frustration; it reminded him of long past student afternoons. McCluskey had always been good value when properly outraged. They used to try to provoke her. On this occasion she needed no assistance.

'Oh, don't talk to me about the dodgy gear change. The bloody driver not *only* doesn't know where he's going, which I accept is not the silly arse's fault, but he can't handle a simple double declutch. History is holding its breath while yet another incompetent to add to the already crowded cast tries to put the royal car into reverse and *stalls* it. Stalls it! He is a *professional* chauffeur and he cannot reverse his car!' Her face was bright red now and the veins were standing out on her neck and forehead. 'At which point Princip walks out of the deli, lunch in hand, and finds himself *one and a half metres* from the very bloke he's supposed to kill. I mean, it's just unbelievable. The very man he and his hapless colleagues have spent all day trying to kill is sitting in front of him in a stalled motor in a confined street. What are the chances of that? It is just insane.'

Having been almost dancing with frustration on the carpet, McCluskey sank down into an armchair, exhausted. She took a swig of wine and a couple of big sucks on her pipe to restore herself but unfortunately managed to put the pipe back into her mouth upside down, thus depositing a great plug of burning tobacco into her lap. When she'd brushed that on to the rug and stamped on it she finally seemed calm.

'Haven't I always *said* history turns on individual folly and ineptitude!' she said. 'Come on, be honest, haven't I always said it?'

'Yes, you have, professor,' Stanton said, reaching for a bit of chocolate. 'History is made by people.'

'And the majority of people are arseholes.'

'Which is I suppose why the majority of history has been so disastrous.'

'But not this time!' McCluskey said, draining her glass and punching the air. 'Not this time! This time there's going to be another guy in town. And he won't be an incompetent idiot. He'll be a highly competent and highly trained British officer and he will save the world. Think of it, Hugh. You're going to save the world!' She reached for the decanter and took a chug direct from the flask. 'Happy Easter!'

22

STANTON HAD MADE his way down to the warren of streets by the Miljacka river and located Schiller's Delicatessen. However, since it was too early to enter he had carried on past, walking down on to the Latin Bridge.

Thinking about McCluskey and her Easter toast.

Waiting to save the world.

A flower seller approached him. A young woman of perhaps seventeen or eighteen with a basket of primroses in her hands. He didn't understand the words she was saying but their meaning was clear: she was hungry and she wanted him to buy a flower.

The girl was painfully thin. The evidence of want in her face and the hunger in her look gave her a slightly other-worldly quality, as if she were part spirit. Her cheekbones and her enormous eyes made her look like one of those Japanese cartoons of girl-women that had become so popular in the century from which he'd come.

For a moment Stanton was so struck by her that he merely stared. The girl turned away without a word, clearly having no time for men who wanted to stare at her but didn't buy a flower.

'Please. Wait . . .' Stanton called after her. He spoke in English but again the meaning was clear. The girl turned back to him, a question on her strangely ghostly face. 'I'm sorry,' he said, then, '*Es tut mir leid*,' in German.

The girl just smiled and held out her basket.

The smile was as enchanting as the face that framed it. Her

teeth were not good but somehow that added to her ghostly beauty. Her skin was pale but when Stanton smiled at her she blushed a little and her cheeks turned pink.

Stanton felt drawn to the girl, perhaps because she was all alone, like him. An outsider struggling in a cold and indifferent world.

He took out his wallet. He had nothing smaller than a two-krone note, which he knew was far too much, enough to have bought a dozen of her flowers at least. The girl reached into the purse at her belt and produced a handful of coins and began counting them out to see if she had sufficient change. Stanton smiled and waved a hand to make it clear that he didn't need any and that she could have the whole amount. Delighted, the girl took the money, gave him a flower and walked on.

Stanton watched her leave. He was glad he'd given her too much. The money had been supplied by the bastards who killed his family; why not make a hungry, delicate creature a little happier in a hard world?

He put the primrose in the buttonhole of his Norfolk jacket and turned once more to stare at the river. The Schiller Delicatessen was only around the corner and there were still a few minutes before the time would be right for him to enter it.

He looked over the railing of the Latin Bridge into the Miljacka river, thinking about the murky waters of the Bosphorus and that first morning, a month earlier. He no longer considered the possibility of jumping in. He believed absolutely in the importance of his mission. Besides which, he was learning to appreciate life again. Meeting the flower girl was a little part of that. Cassie was gone but there was still beauty in the world. Not for him perhaps, that part of his life was over. But it was beauty nonetheless and beauty was a wonderful thing.

Stanton checked his wristwatch. It was nearly time.

The watch had come with him from his old life. Quartz battery-powered and with more computing power than would exist anywhere else in the world for at least fifty years, and even when

168

such technological power did come to pass again it would take a machine the size of a small house to create it rather than that of a milk bottle top. Staring at his watch, Stanton wondered if perhaps after what he was about to do it would take longer than fifty years for the first proper computers to develop. After all, the majority of the great technological leaps of the twentieth century had been the result of military research. Perhaps, if he was able to bequeath the century a more peaceful beginning, those computers might never be developed. It occurred to him that this was another good reason for preventing the Great War. A few decades' delay in the development of smart phones and video games consoles would probably be a good thing.

Stanton watched from the bridge as a small, sad-eyed youth scarcely older than the flower girl and almost as hungry-looking approached, walking along the bank of the river and turning up the little street on which Schiller's Delicatessen was located. With a slight chill and a quickening of his pulse Stanton recognized that this was Gavrilo Princip. A young man whom he had travelled across space and time to meet. A man who was no longer about to make history.

Stanton continued to wait, checking his watch again as the seconds of the twentieth century progressed.

And then came the time to move. The Archduke's car was one minute away. Stanton could hear it approaching.

He walked off the bridge, up the tiny street and into Schiller's. His plan was simply to distract Princip's attention, place himself between the window of the shop and Princip, and play the bewildered foreigner, lost and waving a large and distracting map, speaking loudly in English and German, neither of which the young Serbian would understand. Hopefully this should be enough to prevent Princip even *seeing* the Archduke. After all, the sound of a car stalling in the street wasn't that uncommon even in 1914, and the driver would quickly restart his engine. If the distraction failed and Princip tried to leave the shop, then Stanton planned simply to physically restrain him.

That was the plan.

But when Stanton entered Schiller's Delicatessen to put his plan into practice, the plan changed.

Because history had changed. Gavrilo Princip wasn't there.

Stanton looked at his watch. There could be no mistake. Quartz timing didn't lie. Besides which, he could hear the Archduke's car turning into the street where it would stall outside the shop. It was just fifteen seconds away. At this point, if history were repeating itself, Princip would be leaving the shop, heading for his fateful encounter. But history wasn't repeating itself because Princip *wasn't there*. Something had changed history.

And the only person on the planet who could have done that was Stanton.

He heard the sound of the car stalling outside and rushed out of the shop. In the car just a metre and a half away from him sat the Archduke and his wife. Stanton was standing exactly where Princip *should* have been standing. Where Princip *had* stood the last time the universe passed this way.

So where was Princip?

Then Stanton saw him. And in that moment understood his own stupidity. Princip was across the street from him. On the other side of the car.

And he was with the flower girl.

Stanton had changed history. The indulgent tip he had given had altered the course of the girl's day. She had given up her work and gone instead to treat herself with her unexpected windfall. A windfall she had not received in the previous twentieth century.

Of course! What else would a hungry street girl given a little extra money for which she would not be liable to account do but make her way straight to the nearest food? The nearest food was Schiller's, and there she'd met Princip, whom she was not supposed to meet. And Princip was a teenage boy and she was a teenage girl. They had left the shop together, or perhaps he had followed her and approached her after she had made her purchases. Stanton could see that she had a paper bag in her hand.

All of this Stanton took in and understood in an instant. Just as he took in and understood that Princip wasn't looking at the girl any more. He was looking at the Archduke and realizing that, after all, his chance had come. Just as he had done in the previous near identical moment in time, except now he was on the other side of the car.

Because Stanton had put him there.

The girl was in front of Princip, between him and the Archduke, between him and Stanton. She was turning to look where Princip was looking, at the car and its illustrious occupants. And as she did so Stanton could see that behind her Princip's hand was moving towards his pocket. Stanton knew exactly what he had in that pocket.

Stanton's hand was also moving, down towards his own pocket where he had his Glock.

Princip's hand was emerging from his pocket now, holding something hard and grey which Stanton recognized from the many photos he'd seen of it. The gun that fired the first shot of the Great War and which, because of his carelessness, might be about to do so again.

Scarcely a second had passed but Stanton's own gun was in his hand now and he was assuming the firing position, levelling his weapon, straight-armed in front of his eye. But the girl was still between Princip and him. Only Princip's firing arm and part of his head were visible behind her. And that arm was also coming up to fire. The last time Princip had fired at the Archduke and his wife, he'd killed them both with just two shots. When studying the assassination, Stanton had been struck by how remarkable that was. Killing a person with a single shot is by no means a certainty even at point blank range. Certainly not with a 1910 Browning. Managing it twice in quick succession is even more unlikely. In their discussions on the murder both Stanton and Davies had wondered whether Princip had just been lucky or whether he had happened to be a natural shot. If it was the latter, then what he'd done in the previous dimension he could do again. Stanton couldn't take the risk that he could. He had to make absolutely sure of the Archduke's safety and he had to do it within the next half second before Princip had his own chance to fire. Stanton was a crack shot himself but Princip just wasn't presenting enough of a target from behind the girl for Stanton to be sure of taking him out singly.

There was only one way to be sure of hitting him.

'I'm so sorry,' he whispered, looking into the girl's big shocked eyes.

The Glock fired a bullet that could pierce armour plate. Passing through two bodies would scarcely even reduce its velocity. Princip was a small man, not much taller than the flower girl. His heart was directly behind hers.

One bullet passed through two hearts.

The girl died instantly. A micro second later Princip died instantly.

The Archduke and his beloved duchess scarcely knew what had happened.

There were policemen and soldiers running towards them. The same policemen and soldiers whom Stanton had studied in the famous photograph of Princip being arrested.

But this time Princip wasn't being arrested. He was dead and the Archduke was alive. Stanton had performed the first part of the mission tasked to him by the Companions of Chronos. He had saved Franz Ferdinand.

And he'd killed an innocent young girl.

23

STANTON RAN. Not back towards the river, which was where the police and soldiers were coming from, but up the lane towards Franz-Josef-Strasse, one of Sarajevo's main thoroughfares.

He had the advantage of the confusion behind him and only heard the first cry to halt as he reached the street. Fortunately it was busy, much easier to hide in a crowd than open country. He presumed he was being pursued but he didn't look back.

He'd killed the girl.

He'd caused her to change the course that fate had planned for her and when she crossed his path a second time he'd shot her.

He'd had to do it. He knew that. The mission counted more. The mission would save millions of innocent girls. The flower girl was just another unit of 'collateral damage'. Collateral that had got damaged because of him.

Because he was a stupid bastard.

What part of *leave no trace* did he not understand?

How did over-tipping hungry girls near crucial cafes only seconds before zero hour fit into it?

There was a tram ahead, stopped to take on passengers. He leapt on board and only when it pulled away did he allow himself to look back. There they were. The figures from the photographs, the ones who had been present in the immediate aftermath of the assassination. Stanton had their pictures in his computer. Pictures that had never been taken of an event that had never happened. Soldiers and police, some in Turkish uniform with pantaloons and fez, others Austrian-style with peaked cap and cutaway jacket. They were no longer leading away a teenage assassin, white-gloved hands clutching at the hilts of their swords to stop themselves tripping over them in their haste. Scurrying along in those famous images that had been flashed around a world that never was on a morning that had never been.

Now those officers would be captured in different images, some standing over the corpses of Princip and the girl, others ushering the shocked but relieved Archduke and Duchess into an alternative car. And others still, standing in the middle of Franz-Josef-Strasse staring angrily after a disappearing tram.

Stanton knew they wouldn't stare for long.

Soon they would be telephoning his description around the city. They hadn't seen his face but they knew his build and his height and what he was wearing.

And then there was the big question.

Did they know he was English?

If they did, their search was narrowed instantly by a factor of tens of thousands. Had anyone heard him speak?

Why had he spoken? It had been a stupid, *stupid* thing to do.

Three words. 'I'm so sorry.' Whispered to a girl whom he was a tenth of a second away from murdering.

Why? Why had he said it? What good could it do? None.

He'd said it to assuage his own conscience as he committed a terrible act. That poor girl had been a victim of nothing but his self-indulgence. He had been showing off when he gave her that two-krone note, getting a tiny thrill out of making a pretty girl smile. And now she was dead and he had potentially compromised his mission by placing a six-foot-tall gunman into the equation. A gunman whom the police must assume was a seventh conspirator. A gunman who fired bullets that no police forensics department would recognize. A gunman they might know was English.

Could he have made a bigger mess of things?

Because he still had the tougher part of his mission to perform. He had saved the Archduke and so prevented the immediate cause

174

of the Great War. But the underlying cause, the entrenched militarism of the Prussian elite and in particular the personality of the Emperor of Germany, remained. He still had to assassinate the Kaiser and he would be unable to do that if he was being questioned in a Sarajevo police cell as a suspected member of the Black Hand.

Looking out of the window of the tram he noted that he was heading east on Franz-Josef. His hotel was quite close.

The Europa was a first-class hotel, built by the Austrians. It was hardly the place the police would look first for a Serbian nationalist insurgent.

Unless they knew he was English.

Romantic English idealists were always getting involved in foreign nationalist causes. Lord Byron had started the trend a century before and such a man would likely be staying at a top-class hotel.

Everything hinged on whether they knew his nationality.

Had anyone heard him speak?

The Duchess had been closest to him when he fired his Glock. She was a cultured and educated aristocrat. If anyone in the group in and around the royal car would be capable of recognizing the English language over three whispered words, it was her.

He paid his fare to the conductor and got off the tram. There were two uniformed policemen in the street opposite but this was long before personal radios. They would not have his description yet. He calculated that he probably had another half hour before every policeman in the city would know to look out for a tall man in a tweed Norfolk jacket.

Five minutes later he was back at the Europa hotel.

Once in his room, Stanton tore off the clothes he was wearing and delved in his bag for as different an outfit as he could find. He'd bought a selection of things on his way back through London and he pulled out a pair of white cricket bags and a blue blazer with brass buttons. Hideous in Stanton's view, but a definite contrast to the sober, practical clothes he'd been wearing.

Then, having changed his clothes, he took up the tweed outfit, stuffed it into a pillow case and buried it deep in his bag for disposal later.

He knew he faced an immediate choice. Did he stay or did he run?

His first instinct was that he should run. Grab his stuff and get out before the police had time to start searching the hotels for Englishmen. But the fastest way out of town was by rail and by the time he got to the station there'd be police all over it.

He'd previously enquired about the town's one hire-car facility and knew that they had a machine available. But the paperwork would be complicated. Besides which, there were only two decent metalled roads out of town and the cops were bound to be setting up road blocks even now.

Immediate escape was too risky. He'd just have to sit tight and hope for the best. Hope that the Duchess Sophie's hearing was not as acute as he feared.

Experience had taught Stanton that if a man had to hide it was usually best to hide in plain sight. It tended to be the skulkers who drew attention to themselves. The best cover was a bold front, and if he was going to brazen it out, the sooner he began the better.

He went straight to the bar and ordered Scotch whisky in his loudest and most commanding English voice.

'To His Royal Highness the Archduke Ferdinand,' he said, raising his glass, 'and the Duchess Sophie. May God bless them both and damn to hell anyone who'd do them harm!'

'Hear hear, sir!' came an English voice from across the room, and a number of glasses were raised in agreement.

Stanton remained at the bar for the following two hours. Playing the part of a British tourist, a fervent monarchist, a true blue Imperialist and a complete idiot.

'Don't normally allow myself a snort till after luncheon,' he assured anyone who would listen, 'but when I heard about the royal couple's lucky escape I thought, dammit, the least a chap can do is drink their health. Cheers!'

The Archduke's two lucky escapes had made everybody talkative, and since there were plenty of English and Americans staying at the hotel, Stanton had no trouble in finding people to talk to. He didn't let on that he spoke German and French. The stupider he looked, the better.

'Astonishing good fortune.'

'Outrageous act of blackguardness.'

'Those Serbs have gone too far this time.'

'God bless the Archduke and Duchess Sophie!'

Stanton made much of the fact that he had seen action himself and had been often under fire – 'In Afghanistan mainly. Amongst the hill tribes' – which was true, of course, although it had occurred in another dimension of space and time.

He mentioned that he had been very close to the first bomb blast, swearing that it was a cowardly act to throw a bomb among innocent civilians.

'I did what I could, of course,' he said any number of times. 'Helped the ladies to their feet, gathered up a few youngsters and found their parents. But some of them were pretty cut up. Couldn't help much there, I'm not a medical man.'

As the seconds ticked by more information trickled in about the incidents. Mostly rumour and half truth, all of which ran around the chattering bar within a minute. Each story getting more and more embellished with each retelling.

'Apparently the assassin was in the act of drawing his gun when another man shot him dead.'

'No, the coward shot himself.'

'I heard it was a plain-clothes policeman.'

'Someone said it was soldiers. There was a fearful gun fight.'

'And a girl was involved too, apparently.'

'The brute shamelessly used her as a shield.'

'No, the girl was an assassin as well. These scoundrels are arming women now!'

There was talk of shadowy anarchists with cloaks and beards, sinister Ottomans and veiled femmes fatales. Conspiracy theories were quick to form too, the most popular being that the assassins were actually working for the Austrian Emperor, who was anxious to rid himself of an heir who'd made an impossible marriage. But to Stanton's huge relief there was no mention of an Englishman.

He was beginning to relax. If the Duchess had recognized the language in which he'd whispered those three foolish words, surely that would be part of the rumour mill by now.

The arrival of the first editions of the evening papers put the matter beyond doubt. Stanton was in the clear. He found a German language journal, which he read discreetly in a stall in the men's room. The article seemed well sourced and made sense. Describing the second attempt on the Archduke, the paper reported that there had been two would-be assassins, an unidentified man in a tweed jacket, and Gavrilo Princip, a nineteen-year-old Serb. It seemed that the unidentified man had tried to kill the Archduke but had missed and instead fatally wounded his own comrade, who was on the other side of the car in the act of drawing his own weapon. Tragically there had been a young flower girl standing between the two assassins who had died in the crossfire, macabrely killed by the same bullet that killed Princip. The article mentioned that Duchess Sophie, who was quite close to the man who fired the bullet, stated that he had whispered something before he fired, which she thought had been in Serbian, possibly 'God bless Serbia'.

Stanton made his excuses and left the bar. Once more his luck had held and he was in the clear. But he knew that the big grey eyes of the little flower seller would haunt him for ever.

24

STANTON LEFT SARAJEVO the following morning, departing from the same railway station at which he'd watched the arrival of the archducal party twenty-four hours earlier.

He bought a couple of newspapers at the station book stall, a local German one and *The New York Herald*. The date on the *Herald*'s masthead was Monday 29 June.

He had seen that *Herald* masthead before, with just that date displayed. In fact he had it with him, in digital form, scanned into the memory of his computer. The headline had been long and specific; they did things properly in 1914.

ARCHDUKE FRANCIS FERDINAND AND HIS CONSORT, THE DUCHESS OF HOHENBERG ARE ASSASSINATED WHILE DRIVING THROUGH STREETS OF SARAJEVO, BOSNIA.

The *Herald* had devoted its entire front page to the story, apart from a tiny paragraph in the bottom right-hand corner about a shipping accident. All the European papers had given the story similar prominence. Even in isolationist America, *The New York Times* had devoted a full half of its front page. Anyone with any sense of history at all had been able to see that nothing but terrible trouble could come from the murder of the heir to the Austro-Hungarian throne. Although few, if any, imagined how much.

And yet here he was with his bundle of newspapers in his hand, that fateful date upon them, and there was nothing of much significance at all. The headline beneath the *Herald* masthead was *THE CALIFORNIA GOES ASHORE NEAR TORY ISLAND* with the sub headline, *Bow of Anchor Liner Is Injured and Two Holds Are Full of Water*. This was the story that had been squeezed into a tiny corner of the edition locked in the hard drive of Stanton's computer. No one had been killed or even injured, the seas were calm, the accident had occurred quite close to Ireland, six British destroyers were attending the scene and it was reported that *should* an evacuation be thought necessary it was predicted that this could be effected easily and without any danger to crew or passengers.

That was the main story the morning after Archduke Ferdinand visited Sarajevo. A maritime accident with not a single loss of life. In this new twentieth century that Stanton had caused to come into being, Monday 29 June 1914 had been a *spectacularly* bad day for news.

It was surely only the still resonating loss of the *Titanic* two years before that made the story front-page news at all. That earth-shaking maritime disaster had been without doubt the biggest story of the century thus far. Even in Stanton's own century the *Titanic* story had resonated down the decades. Despite war and genocide without parallel, people had still felt the distant aftershocks of that strangely compelling disaster. Now, because of Stanton, there was every possibility that the story of that icy night and the loss of those fifteen hundred lives would *remain* the biggest story of the century. A benchmark for drama and tragedy that the remaining nine decades of the century would fail to match.

Because of him.

He was the reason that the journalists of the world were drumming their fingers on their desks that morning instead of struggling to report the scope of a killing that would cripple a century.

He felt proud of himself.

The death of the girl still cut him deeply but he knew in truth that it wasn't his fault. The simple fact was that he had been *there* and that he had *not* been there before. Tipping the girl or not tipping her, both would have caused *some kind* of an effect that had not occurred in the last version of the century. Whatever he did would have consequences he could never second-guess.

He had to move on.

And at least now he was relieved of the awful anxiety of the butterfly effect. History had taken a new course and he was as much in the dark about the future as anyone else.

He made his way along the train to the dining car and ordered coffee. He would have wine with lunch, Austrian wine. He wanted to celebrate. He wanted to tell someone. He wanted to shout out to the entire train, 'Yesterday I saved the world!'

Although, of course, he hadn't saved the world yet. There was the second part of his mission. The tough part. Assassinating the Kaiser. But there was nothing he could do about that for the moment. Not till he got to Berlin. All he could do was sit back, relax and watch the beautiful rugged countryside of Bosnia Herzegovina roll past the window.

The dining car was three seats wide with four-person tables on one side of the corridor and tables for two on the other. Stanton had chosen a single seat but the train wasn't full and there was nobody at the larger table opposite. He almost had the carriage to himself, until he heard from behind him the rustle of satin and caught a whiff of scent. A moment later a woman took a seat by the opposite window.

'Thank you,' she said to the accompanying porter in English. 'This'll be just grand.'

An Irish accent. Cork, he thought, though perhaps accents had changed so much since the future that he couldn't be sure.

'I'll take a cup of coffee certainly,' the woman went on, 'but nothing to eat for the time being, thanks all the same.'

Oi'l take a cup o' coffee.

T'anks all the same.

It was a nice voice. Some accents just sound friendly, always have, always will, it didn't matter what century you heard them in.

Stanton pretended to concentrate on his newspaper but stole a glance nonetheless. He was certain he could risk it unnoticed. He was, after all, trained in surveillance. If he could stake out fundamentalist insurgents he reckoned he could sneak a look at a pretty woman.

She had a book to read. In fact, she had several, plus notepads and pencils. She had pushed away the cutlery in order to make space for them.

Stanton wanted to talk to her.

For the first time since arriving in the twentieth century, in fact, for the first time since the death of his wife and family, he craved company. Female company. Perhaps it was the relief of having performed successfully the first half of his mission.

Or just possibly it was because she was rather beautiful.

Or if not beautiful, highly striking. Pretty would perhaps be a better word than beautiful. The hair was pale strawberry beneath her hat and she had classic Irish eyes, green with that tiniest downward turn at the outer edge. Smiling eyes they called them, although the same turn on a mouth would make a frown. There was a hint of freckles too. Her mouth was small, it certainly wouldn't have been considered a beautiful mouth in the decade Stanton had come from, a decade where for some reason women had taken to pumping up their lips to look like shapeless inner tubes. The teeth weren't quite perfect either, but then nobody's were in 1914. He liked it, it lent character.

And she had placed herself opposite him in a near empty carriage.

Stanton pulled his thoughts up short.

He stared hard at his newspaper.

She hadn't placed herself opposite, the waiter had. Doing that irritating thing that restaurant staff often did, clustering their customers together despite there being plenty of space.

Besides which, what did it matter where she sat?

What the hell was he thinking about?

This was the second time in less than a day that he'd been struck by feminine beauty and the first time had turned instantly to tragedy.

Still, he stole another glance.

She was in her late twenties or early thirties. Not much younger than he was. Travelling alone. Such a sweet face.

He poured himself another cup of coffee and, putting aside his *Tribune*, tried to focus on his German-language newspaper. He was on a mission, active service. He shouldn't be thinking about girls. Besides which, he was in mourning for his wife. He resolved not to look again.

Then the woman spoke.

'Well, what do you think?' she said, quite out of the blue.

Stanton looked up and glanced around, imagining that she was about to be joined by a companion.

'No, you,' she went on, looking squarely at Stanton. 'I was wondering what you thought.'

Oi was wondering what yez tort.

Such a lilting accent and quite pronounced. He wondered whether she didn't affect it a little, feeling that a smartly dressed woman who could afford to travel first class would in this age have been brought up to speak less colloquially.

'Excuse me?' Stanton said. 'Thought about what?'

'Me, of course,' the woman went on, 'or what else have you been thinking about since I sat down?'

'Well, I . . .' He was completely taken aback. Stanton was a handsome man and not unused to female attention but even in the twenty-first century he couldn't remember being called out in such a way. He expected it much less in a time when women most certainly didn't address strange men in public. 'I can assure you, miss . . .' he began.

'Oh, don't deny it and make me look a fool,' she said. 'Be a gentleman and admit it, why don't you?'

Stanton struggled to reply. She'd thrown him completely.

'I don't believe you caught me looking,' he said finally.

'So you *were* looking then?' she replied, affecting a semi-comical frown, like a prosecution barrister leaping on an inconsistency.

'I don't say that. I don't say that at all. I only say I don't believe you caught me looking. Be a lady and admit it, why don't you?'

She smiled and her eyes seemed almost to laugh.

'Ah,' she sighed, 'now, being a lady is never something I've been awfully good at.'

'So you admit you didn't catch me looking?'

'I never said I *had* caught you looking. I merely said that you *were* looking. And were you?'

He knew that denial was pointless.

'Well, perhaps a bit.'

'*So*, to get back to where we began. What did you think?'

Now he was really flustered.

'Well, I . . . how did you know I was looking at you if you didn't catch me?'

'Oh come on, Mr . . .'

'Stanton.'

'Mr Stanton, how much of an expert in human nature does a lone woman who's sitting opposite a lone man on a train have to be, to know that he'll steal a glance? I don't say you thought *much*, mind you. You might not have been interested at all. Or you might have thought, "Bother, wish she'd been blonde like those lovely Viennese girls." But you thought *something*.'

She looked at him with those very slightly hooded eyes, twinkling emeralds they were, framed beneath wild strawberry blonde tresses.

'All right,' he admitted. 'I have in fact been thinking about you since you sat down. And what I was thinking, I had no business to think, because I was thinking how very . . . nice, you looked.'

'Nice?'

'Yes. Very.'

'And why had you no business thinking that? I think it's a lovely thing to think.'

Oi t'ink it's a lovely t'ing to t'ink.

'Well, you know . . . a lady sitting alone and . . .'

'Oh yes, of *course*, because you didn't know I wasn't a lady, did you? Shall I tell you what *I* was thinking?'

'Uhm, yes, that'd be great.'

'Well. First of all, I thought you looked nice too. But on its own that wouldn't have made me speak to you. There's a lot more handsome men in the world than there are interesting ones, and to find one that's both is rarer still, and to come across one when you're sat alone on a train with hours and hours to go is a blessed miracle. I'm Bernadette Burdette, by the way.'

'Very pleased to meet you, Miss Burdette,' Stanton said. 'What made you think I might be interesting?'

Her nose wrinkled slightly in thought.

'Well, now. You have an interesting *face* but that can be deceptive. I suppose mainly the newspapers. Any man who is able to read the news in two languages and chooses to do so can't be a complete bore, can he? Particularly a soldier. Soldiers aren't usually the most sophisticated people in my experience. Certainly not my brother's comrades anyway. Or my brother for that matter.'

'How on earth did you know I was a soldier?'

'Oh, just your bearing, I suppose. And when I heard you order, you *sounded* like a soldier.'

'Heard me order? You mean, you . . .'

'Oh yes, I've been in the carriage for a little while. In a seat at the end. I had them move me to this one.'

Stanton tried to take stock. What was going on? Was she hitting on him? *Did* girls in 1914 hit on guys? For a mad moment he wondered whether in some way she was on to him. A mysterious female spy on a train who knew about his mission. But that simply wasn't possible. Perhaps she just wanted to talk to him.

And he knew that he wanted to talk to her.

'Might I join you?' he asked. 'Perhaps we could even have a bit of lunch together.'

'Well, I'm afraid that depends,' she replied. 'First you have to pass the test.'

'Test?'

'Where do you stand on female suffrage?'

He should have guessed it, of course. There was one issue and one only that dominated the thoughts of independently minded women in the early summer of 1914.

'I'm afraid I couldn't lunch with a man who didn't consider me of equal value as a member of society. It's a *very* strict rule.'

Stanton decided to lay it on thick.

'I think the fact that the women of the world are denied the vote—' he began.

'Except in glorious, wonderful New Zealand,' she interrupted.

'Except as you say, in New Zealand … is crazy, illogical, unjustifiable, imbecilic and deeply immoral. That is where I stand on the issue of female suffrage, Miss Burdette.'

'In that case, I think we must certainly have lunch,' she said. 'And I'd be obliged if you'd call me Bernadette.'

'After all,' Stanton added, 'women hold up half the sky.'

'Oh my goodness,' she said, gulping, 'that is one of the most beautiful things I've ever heard *anybody* say. Let alone a man. Call me Bernie.'

25

H E HAD KNOWN that he was properly flirting when he played the Chairman Mao quote. And sitting down opposite Bernie Burdette, he wondered to himself how he felt about that. He'd never imagined himself flirting again.

'Shall we order some more coffee?' she asked.

'You have some,' he replied. 'Bit coffee'd out, me.'

'Coffee'd out?' she repeated, looking puzzled.

'Ah, yes, army expression. It means I've had sufficient.'

'Oh. Well, I won't bother either then. We might have a cocktail, though, don't you think? Since we've nothing to do but sit. Cocktails are quite the thing these days, aren't they? Do you like cocktails?'

'Sure. What's not to like?'

As he said it he could hear the phrase clanging about in the wrong century like a great big throbbing verbal sore thumb. *Coffee'd out? What's not to like?* Why was he suddenly talking like a twenty-first-century teenager?

'What's not to like?' she asked looking puzzled.

She looked *so* pretty when she was puzzled. It made the middle bit of her brow wrinkle slightly, just above her nose.

'Sorry. Mess-room slang again,' he said. 'Certainly I like cocktails. As long as they're very dry.'

'I like sweet ones, with cherries and grenadine, or dark vermouth. Have you heard of a Manhattan? I've just discovered them.'

'Yes, I've heard of it. Although I'm a Martini man myself, if I'm mixing.'

'Well, I must say, that's better.'

'What's better?' Stanton asked.

'You smiling. You looked awfully serious before.'

'Did I?'

'Yes, with your newspaper. I noticed. You know, when you weren't watching me? I wasn't watching you, and you were frowning all the time. I thought you might be very fierce.'

'Oh, no, I'm not fierce at all. I suppose it's just that the newspaper was pretty dull and . . . well . . .'

'I'm not.'

'No. You're certainly not dull.'

He was smiling. He could feel it. The corners of his mouth exploring muscle shapes that had seen little use since he'd lost his family.

It occurred to Stanton that he was having fun.

When could he last have said that?

Not for a very long time. But quite suddenly, sitting on the Sarajevo to Zagreb express, a *steam*-powered express, opposite a captivating Suffragette, in her violet hobble skirt and straw boater with its matching ribbon, he was suddenly overcome by the intense *romance* of the situation. A steam train, and a pretty girl, on his way to Vienna, in *1914*. It was like some beautiful dream, and yet it was real.

Was it all right to have fun? Was it a betrayal?

'You're frowning again,' Bernadette said. 'Have I become dull already?'

'No!' he exclaimed, slightly too loudly. 'No way! I mean definitely not.'

'Good.'

What would Cassie think?

She wouldn't think anything; he loved her with all his heart but she had existed in another universe.

'So,' he said, 'you first. What's your story?'

188

'What's my story? What a nice expression. I don't think that one can be army. Do you mean from the beginning?'

'Well, yes, certainly. Although I actually meant why are you on your way to Zagreb?'

'Vienna,' Bernadette replied. 'I'm going through to Vienna.'

'Really? I'm going to Vienna too.'

'Then isn't it lucky we got chatting?'

For a moment her eyes met his.

'I'm on a bit of a tour really,' she went on. 'I came out to Hungary last year for the Seventh Congress of the International Women's Suffrage Alliance in Budapest. Perhaps you've heard of it.'

''Fraid not, sounds pretty heavy.'

'Heavy?'

'I mean fascinating.'

Stanton was acutely aware that this was the first conversation of any length he'd had since he'd uncovered McCluskey's betrayal a month earlier. He was out of practice. And in a different century.

'It must have been fascinating.'

'It was. Extremely. I stayed on in Budapest till last Easter.'

'Long congress. Lots to talk about, eh?'

'There was . . . uhm, a friend,' she said, reddening a little at the cheeks. 'Anyway I finally left last month and took a little holiday, wanted to get away, from myself as much as anything. I've been doing a bit of a tour of antiquity. I read classics at Trinity, you see.'

'Trinity? I went to Trinity.'

'Dublin?'

'No, Cambridge.'

'Thought so. Where of course they don't allow women. More fool them. Dublin has since 1904. I was one of the first. You wouldn't have thought Dublin would be more progressive than Cambridge, would you? It's 16 per cent women now. Pretty good progress, eh? Only 34 per cent to go. Anyway, I've been mooching about in Greece and Crete for the last two months or so and now I'm on my way back to rejoin the struggles.'

'Struggles in the plural?'

'Obviously. Votes for women and Independence for Ireland. What other struggles are there?'

'Ah yes. Of course.'

The two great dividing issues of British life that had been tearing the country apart for the last decade. What other struggles indeed? There were none. Not any more. Not now Archduke Franz Ferdinand was alive and well on 29 June. Britain could carry on fighting with itself.

'So you're a Fenian?' Stanton asked. 'I thought you said your brother was a soldier.'

'He is. We don't speak.'

'But you're speaking to me.'

'I'm not a bigot. I don't hate soldiers *per se*. I don't speak to my brother because he's with Carson and the Ulstermen. All my family are staunch Unionists, except me. I don't speak to any of them.'

'But you're Southern Irish, surely?'

'We're *colonial* Irish. We're not *of* it, we just *own* quite a lot of it. We're English and occupy a large part of County Wicklow. Have done since Cromwell. I was brought up there, though, so as far as I'm concerned I'm Irish.'

'Right down to the accent, eh?'

He said it to tease her. Because he wanted to see her blush again. He was pretty certain that Anglo-Irish landowners wouldn't have spoken with Irish accents, and whatever girls' school Bernadette Burdette had gone to would certainly have sweated it out of her if she had.

'Well, all right,' she admitted. 'I did put it on a bit at first. Just because it made the family so angry. But I'm used to it now. I do it without thinking. It suits me.'

'It certainly does.'

They talked for a while about the Irish Question. And more particularly Ulster. The issue that had brought Britain to the brink of civil war in the previous year and still threatened to. Bernadette, of course, felt passionate about it.

'They talk about loyalty to the Crown,' she said angrily, 'but when it comes to abiding by the Crown's laws then as far as Ulster's concerned loyalty can go to hell. You can't have democracy if people only agree to abide by the laws that suit them.'

'Well, what about the Suffragettes?' Stanton asked. 'And your campaign of civil disobedience and direct action? Isn't that the same thing? Taking arms against the law because you don't like it?'

'*Civil disobedience and direct action,*' she said, chewing over the words. 'Good phrase that. I shall write it down. You have a way with words, you know. And since you ask, no, it's not the same thing at all. We're not inciting the army to mutiny, are we? Civil disobedience, as you call it, is a very different thing to running in a hundred thousand rifles at dead of night and trying to start a civil war. But more importantly than that . . . I thought we were going to have a cocktail.'

Stanton laughed and called the waiter. He ordered a Manhattan and a gin Martini and asked to see the lunch menu.

'My treat,' he said. 'I insist.'

'You can insist all you like,' she replied, 'but I pay my own way with strange men. We'll ask him to split it and I shall sign for mine. You can do the tip if it makes you feel any more manly. My purse is in my luggage and I *never* carry coins in my pockets. It stretches the fabric and *ruins* the line.'

The waiter returned with the menus.

'For what it's worth,' Stanton said, 'I think you're going to win on women's rights. I really do.'

'It doesn't look that way at the moment,' Bernadette replied morosely. 'Half my friends are in prison on hunger strike and that swine Asquith doesn't seem to care at all. I think they're planning to wait us out until we're all either exhausted or dead.'

'Well, all I can say is I honestly think you're going to get the vote, and a lot more quickly than you think.'

'Really? You do?'

'Yes, I do, and I'll tell you another thing. There'll be a female MP within a decade and a female Prime Minister this century.'

She laughed, but he could see she was pleased he'd said it.

'And how would you know that, may I ask?'

He was about to make her gasp with his confident predictions of women taking their place alongside men in the industrial process, something which, in the previous version of the century, was set to occur within a mere *two* years, by which time women would be earning sexual equality and the vote with every rivet they hammered in and every aeroplane they produced.

But that would take a war. A massive war. The very war he was bent on preventing.

'Oh well,' he replied rather weakly. 'I just think it has to happen, that's all.'

'Well, we must make our dreams big, mustn't we?' she said. 'And I must powder my nose.'

While she was in the lavatory, Stanton reflected on the slightly unsettling thought that if his mission was a success, history would inevitably see much slower progress towards the emancipation of women. The Suffragettes had been taking direct action since 1905 and got absolutely nowhere. It was the Great War and the Great War alone that had been the game changer. Stanton doubted that Professor McCluskey had thought that one through.

The cocktails arrived and they ordered their food. The quality and taste of food, or at least expensive food, in 1914 was something that Stanton was still getting used to. It was so different and so much better than anything he'd ever experienced in his own century. Tougher sometimes but better, the tastes more alive. It was as if food had been in monochrome and had suddenly appeared for the first time in colour.

'Shall we have some wine?' Stanton asked.

'Of course,' Bernadette replied. 'Dutch courage.'

And she looked him in the eye again as she said it.

'So we've had enough about me for a moment,' she said,

taking a substantial swig at her Manhattan. 'What about you?'

Good question. What about him?

And the strange thing was, it took him by surprise. It shouldn't have, of course. She was bound to ask, but having gone four weeks without having had a proper conversation with a soul, he just wasn't ready for it. And before that, since Cassie's death, he'd scarcely spoken to anyone but McCluskey, and they'd rarely spoken on personal matters. He'd got so used to emotional isolation, explaining himself to no one, that he didn't know where to begin. He struggled to remember the back story Chronos had supplied him with.

'Well, I'm in from the colonies,' he began. 'Australia.'

'How interesting. Sydney or Melbourne?'

'Neither. The Western bit. Perth. They ignore it even over there.'

Chronos had decided on Perth for its isolation. Less chance of people knowing it or knowing anyone from it. And it explained his loner status. Perth, after all, was the loneliest city on earth.

'And I was in the army when I was younger,' he added. They'd also agreed he'd have some military background, going on the theory that a lie is always better if it contains elements of truth.

'Where have you served?' Bernadette asked.

'Pakistan, I mean, Northern India and a bit in Afghanistan.'

'Fascinating. The far-flung patches of red, eh?'

'Yes, that's it.'

'And your family?'

'Miners. Gold, actually, which is why I'm in a position to swan about the place in first-class carriages.'

'Sounds like quite an exciting life,' Bernadette commented. 'And why *are* you "swanning about"? What's an Australian miner doing on a train in Bosnia?'

What should he say? His back story had been planned for casual conversation. He'd presumed he'd never get into the more intimate kind, which was silly. He was only thirty-six, he was going to live a long time yet and he was bound to share confidences with *someone* sooner or later. And now it seemed that it had happened sooner. He was having a chat with an attractive woman over lunch. The sort of circumstance where commonly, if one liked the person enough, you generally got to know each other a little.

But what could he *say*? He couldn't tell her who he was or where he'd come from. But he didn't want to lie either. He liked her, he was enjoying his time with her, he *wanted* to share. He wanted to tell her something real about himself.

'Well,' he said, 'and please don't let this cast a downer . . . I mean, make us gloomy. But I suppose I should tell you that the most significant thing about me is that I was married with two children.'

'Oh, goodness,' Bernadette said. 'How do you mean "was"?'

'Well, I'm afraid I lost them. All three, a year ago in a motor accident.'

It felt good to tell her. It was the most significant thing about him. Not that he was a time traveller from another century, but that he had loved Cassie, Tessa and Bill and he had lost them.

'Oh my,' Bernadette said. 'I'm so very sorry.'

'Look . . . Bernie,' Stanton went on, 'I've been grieving for a year now. Consumed by a ferocious and *ravenous* grief that eats away at me day and night but never seems to finish me off. But they're gone and I'm here. And talking to you I was pretending for a minute that I wasn't the loneliest man in the world. Pretending that I could just chat for a while without, well, without all the emotional baggage, so to speak . . .'

Her eyes were wet with tears.

'Emotional baggage?' she whispered. 'Gosh, you really *do* have a way with words, don't you?'

'Anyway, what I'm saying is, would you mind if we carried on talking about you for a bit, because I was really loving that.'

'Well,' Bernadette said, dabbing at her eyes with her handkerchief, 'you've come to the right girl because I *love* talking about me.'

And she did. Through three courses and a bottle of wine. She told him about her childhood and her feminism and her trip to Greece. She skirted over her time in Budapest, when it was quite clear to Stanton she'd had her heart broken, so he changed the subject and turned the conversation to the previous day's events in Sarajevo.

'Thank goodness those Serbs didn't pull it off,' Bernadette said. 'God knows what sort of mess Europe would be in this morning if they had. It's obvious the Austrians are spoiling for an excuse to cut Serbia down to size and the Germans are egging them on.'

'You know your geopolitics,' Stanton said.

'Geopolitics?'

'Uhm . . . international affairs.'

'Well, it doesn't take a Bismarck to see how the cards are stacked at the moment. Russia would have come in for the Serbs, which would have brought in the French and that would have been that. We should consider ourselves very lucky the man that got away missed and killed his own comrade. If he'd been a better shot we might have been facing the real prospect of a European war this morning.'

'True enough.'

'Funny how the other man disappeared like that,' she mused. 'They got all the rest. Rounded up five of them besides the dead chap. What did it say in the papers? Big fellow. Over six feet? Moustache and sideburns. In his thirties. You'd have thought he'd stand out like a sore thumb. All the others were skinny pasty-faced kids. That Princip boy who got shot was only nineteen. You'd have thought a six-foot Serbian would be easy enough to spot.'

'Well, of course, he's only a Serbian when he opens his mouth. Otherwise he could be any big chap with whiskers. Could be me.'

'No. I don't think so.'

'Why not?'

'Something tells me you wouldn't have missed.'

195

The miles had rolled away as they chatted and quite soon their train was pulling into Zagreb station.

'Now then,' Bernadette said, getting up, 'we must both change trains for the Vienna Express but I don't want you to help me.'

'Really?'

'No. What's more I don't think we should travel together from now on.'

'Oh,' Stanton said and he didn't try to disguise his disappointment. 'I'd rather hoped we might.'

'You see, the thing is,' Bernadette went on, 'I don't want you to get bored with me. People do sometimes. I'm quite *intense*.'

'I don't think so.'

'We also have to consider the possibility that I might get bored of you.'

'Well, that's blunt.'

'Look, Hugh. We've just spent nearly five rather lovely hours together. There's ninety minutes to be spent in the waiting room at Zagreb then a further half a day on the train to Vienna, into which we get rather late. That would make almost twenty hours together, which is quite a lot for new acquaintances, and you see, I want us to have something left to talk about because . . .'

'Because what?'

She was blushing again, more deeply than ever. Her milk-white cheeks were crimson. She took a deep breath.

'All right. Here we go. It'll be past ten in the evening in Vienna and we'll both have to find a hotel and it seems to me that it would *cosier* and certainly more *economical* if we roomed together. There. I've said it. What do you think?'

Stanton didn't even reply. He was too taken aback. He'd known that things *might* drift that way. A man and a woman getting a little tipsy together over lunch always *might* end up in bed together. It was the bluntness that took him aback. It would have been bold even in 2024.

'To be frank,' Bernadette went on quickly, 'I've been thinking about it ever since you said that thing about women holding up

half the sky. I have never in my whole life heard anyone say anything remotely so lovely or so true. Quite honestly, I think I'd
want to sleep with any man who came up with it. Even if he
wasn't such a dish.'

Stanton had never before had cause to be grateful to the
memory of Chairman Mao Tse Tung. But he was now.

26

TRUE TO HER word Bernadette sat apart from Stanton in the waiting room at Zagreb and found a different carriage to him on the Vienna train. Even when they both sat for supper in the dining car she merely raised a glass to him from across the carriage.

Stanton was impressed.

She was right really. It had been obvious from almost the first moment of their conversation that there was a strong mutual attraction and this had been reinforced over a very long lunch. There had been a palpable electricity between them, an excitement that might perhaps have been difficult to maintain over a further eleven hours of close proximity. It would probably have been all right, but then again it could easily not have been. By arranging things as she had, Bernadette had certainly ensured that there would be a new and highly charged frisson to their encounter when they met in Vienna. She was, as his old army mates would have put it, a classy chick.

Eventually, as night fell across Europe, he drifted off to sleep in his seat and didn't wake up until the train was approaching Vienna.

When he got off the train he found that Bernadette, who had been in a more forward carriage, had already secured a porter and was waiting for him beyond the barrier.

'Share a taxi?' she said brightly. 'You can shove your stuff on top of mine if you like. Although you'd probably better handle the *emotional baggage* yourself. Wouldn't want anyone prying into that, would we?'

'Thanks. I'll hang on to my actual bags as well, in fact,' Stanton replied. 'Old habit.'

'Suit yourself. Had you thought about where you're staying?'

'Well, I'd heard the Hotel Sacher was very good. It's next to the Opera House, which sounds pretty grand, but when in Vienna, eh?'

'How extraordinary! That's where I'm staying myself.'

There wasn't much of a queue for cabs and soon they were on their way through the deserted streets.

'Not a soul about. Never is after dark,' Bernadette remarked. 'Lovely town in the day but dull as paint at night. The Viennese have to go to bed at ten, did you know? Or they get fined.'

'Come on, really? Fined?' Stanton replied. 'Can't quite believe that.'

'Well, as good as. They all live in apartment blocks, you see, and they have to pay a fee to the doorman if they're late so they all scurry home. Ridiculous, rushing their dinners for which they'll have paid twenty krone in order to save a handful of heller on the night doorman. Stupid, isn't it?'

'You seem to know a bit about the place, Bernie.'

'I spent a month here as companion to an aunt when I was eighteen. She loved her opera, which I don't much, but I loved Vienna and I still do. I was also here three years ago for a conference on Women's Health. It's the most relaxed capital I've ever been in. They go to bed early and rise late, and when they do get up, most of them seem to just sit in coffee houses and talk about theatre. You've no idea how many different ways of making coffee they have, one for nearly every hour of the day. I think the fact that it's such an old *old* capital and it used to be important but isn't much any more has made it more relaxed. I mean, if you go to London or Berlin everybody's so *busy*, what with us trying to stay ahead and the Germans trying to catch up. From what I've heard New York's more frantic still. Even Paris tries to look important in a superior kind of way. But Vienna, well, it's sort of *given up*, hasn't it? They know they've got a motley sort of half-baked empire and an ancient emperor who's more concerned with court etiquette than international politics. So they've stopped bothering, which gives the place a nice easy feel. Have you heard of Karl Kraus?'

Amazingly, he had. He'd studied the Austro-Hungarian Empire at university, under McCluskey in fact, and was aware of Vienna's famous satirist.

'Publishes a magazine, doesn't he? *The Torch*?'

'Well *done*. You really are the best informed soldier I've ever met. Anyway, he said, "In Berlin things are serious but not hopeless. In Vienna they're hopeless but not serious" – good one, don't you think?'

Bernadette continued to chat slightly frantically, pointing out buildings and parks as the Daimler taxi cab roared through the beautiful town, until quite suddenly they arrived at the Hotel Sacher.

'I suppose you think I've prattled on a bit,' she said, as Stanton settled the fare.

'Well, yes,' he conceded, 'but it's been interesting.'

'To tell you the truth, I'm a bit nervous. I expect you think I'm pretty fast but I don't normally do this sort of thing at all.'

'No, nor me.'

'It was the wine that started it. And that Manhattan. Still. We're in it now, eh?'

They went into the foyer of the hotel and approached reception.

'Can you do it?' Bernadette said. 'I know I'll go bright red.'

'Of course . . . you're sure you want to do this? I mean, just book one room?'

'Yes. I've crept along the occasional corridor in my time and I don't like it. You feel like a thief.'

'OK.'

'O-K?'

'American expression. I meant, fine.'

'Right. Well, off you go then.'

Stanton was surprised to discover as he approached reception that he felt quite nervous too, even a little embarrassed. It was a strange sensation. He was after all a mature man, a soldier. He had carried out clandestine operations in numerous countries and, even more impressively, in two separate dimensions of space and time. He was heavily armed, extremely wealthy and an impressive and commanding figure by any standards. James Bond himself would have been hard put to notch up any more cool points. So why was it that walking towards that reception desk he felt seventeen years old again?

Perhaps it was the man behind it. Tall, thin, grey-haired with a neat goatee beard. Like one of those old cartoons of Uncle Sam but without the benign twinkle. He looked like a schoolmaster who was about to tell Stanton off for having dirty pictures in his bag.

And it *was* a slightly sensitive situation, after all. Stanton knew enough about the period to be aware that no respectable hotel would allow an unmarried couple to share a room, and also that for foreign guests they would probably require some form of official identification on check-in. On the other hand, people must have had affairs in those days, as they have always done, and they must have had them somewhere.

'Good evening,' Stanton said loudly. 'Do you speak English? If not, perhaps you'd be kind enough to find me someone who does.'

He'd decided not to admit that he spoke German. If they wanted to try and argue with him, he'd make it as difficult for them as possible.

'I speak English, sir, of course,' Uncle Sam replied. 'Do you wish to secure a room?'

'Yes, my wife and I are just off the Zagreb train. Would have wired ahead but nobody at the Zagreb station telegraph office spoke English, if you can credit it. We want your best room, a bottle of hock, make sure it's good and chilled and something to eat. Cheese and cold cuts will be fine.'

'Of course, sir. If I might just see your papers.'

'Here's mine but my wife's are right at the bottom of her bag. I'm sure one will be sufficient . . .' He laid his Foreign Office letter down on the reception desk with its GR lion and unicorn stamp uppermost, placing underneath it a ten-krone note for good measure. 'Look here, somebody has left this money. You take it. Perhaps it won't be claimed.'

The receptionist took the money and Stanton took the key.

As he and Bernadette were escorted to the lift by the bellboy she whispered, 'I feel like I'm seventeen.'

'I was just thinking the same thing,' Stanton replied.

'Did you *really* bribe him?'

'Yes, and if that hadn't worked I was going to shoot him.'

Their room had a balcony and while the porter set out their bags they went and stood on it and looked out over the city, just as Stanton had done in Istanbul. Except that this time he was no longer alone. There was a near full moon and the whole of the venerable town was washed with silver.

Bernadette leant her shoulder against his.

'Is this the first time you've been alone with a woman,' she said, 'I mean, since . . .' She didn't finish her sentence.

'Yes, as a matter of fact it is,' Stanton admitted. 'If you mean, as in *alone* alone. I did spend a lot of this year as the guest of my old professor at Cambridge but she was very large and old and we only talked about history.'

'You had a *female* professor? At Cambridge? How did you manage that?'

'His wife, I mean. An old professor's wife. Took pity on me because . . . well, because I was on my own.'

Bernadette moved a little closer still.

'Well, it's very nice. For me, I mean – flattering. In a way. Or does that sound wrong?'

'No, it sounds fine.'

There was a knock at the door and their supper arrived. The waiter wanted to make a fuss of laying out the table with crisp cloth and silver service, but Stanton stuck a tip in his pocket and ushered him out of the room.

'Shall we have it on the balcony?' he said picking up the tray. 'It's a warm night.'

They settled themselves in the chairs and Bernadette smoked a cheroot.

'I took them up because my father said he couldn't bear to see a woman smoke. Now I can't do without them. Care for one?'

'No. I gave them up.'

'Goodness gracious. Why ever did you do that? I love it!'

'You should give up too,' he said. 'They're carcinogenic.'

'What?'

'They cause cancer, of the lungs.'

'Oh, that's all rot. My doctor says smoking actually wards *off* some infections. As does a nice glass of wine by the way.'

Stanton realized that he'd neglected to pour the wine and now found that in his eagerness to get rid of the waiter he hadn't allowed him to draw the cork.

'Be prepared's my motto,' he said, getting a multi-tool knife from his bag. 'Once a boy scout always a boy scout, eh?'

'Boy scout? What? Did you join when you were thirty? They only started six or seven years ago. My youngest brother was one of the first.'

'I just meant . . . oh, I don't know what I meant.'

'Useful bit of kit,' Bernadette remarked, eyeing his multi-tool.

'Yes . . . Australian. Cheers.'

He handed her a glass and they drank their wine in silence for a moment.

'Good hock,' Stanton said.

'Yes. I love German wine. Always sweeter than French.'

Stanton breathed in her smoke. It smelt delicious.

'And you?' he enquired. 'Any adventures since Budapest? I rather got the impression that you had a . . . thing in Budapest.'

'Yes, I did. I had a . . . a thing. And no. I haven't had a "thing" since. But then it has only been three months.'

'Did he break your heart?'

She looked thoughtful for a moment.

'Well, shall we say I got my heart broken . . .'

'Thought so.'

'But . . .'

'But?'

'All right,' she said, looking him in the eye. 'How about this? *She* wasn't a *he.*'

'Oh . . . right. So it was a woman who broke your heart.'

'Are you terribly shocked and disgusted?'

'Christ no! I mean, no. Why would I be?'

'Why *would* you be?' Bernadette was very surprised. 'Because that sort of thing is generally thought to be pretty shocking and disgusting, I should say.'

'Do you *want* me to be shocked and disgusted?'

'No. Certainly not.'

'Well, good. Because I'm not.'

'Really?'

Stanton wondered where to begin.

'Look, I know that society currently entertains a lot of prejudice when it comes to gay sex but—'

'Gay? What's the fact that it was gay got to do with it, and anyway it wasn't gay. It was desperate and strange and intense and . . . well, it certainly wasn't *gay.* In fact, it was really quite miserable, but I suppose that's what you get for developing a crush on an *extremely* serious Hungarian feminist.'

'Sorry, I didn't mean "gay" obviously. Wrong word entirely. Can't think why I said it. I was just saying that obviously I understand that same-sex love is frowned on at the moment . . .'

'*Frowned* on! At the *moment!*'

'Well, you know. I'm sure attitudes will change.'

'Really? I admire your optimism but I can't imagine why you'd think that. For me it was a bit of a dalliance, a surprise really, like a holiday romance. But I know quite a few people who choose to live that life exclusively and I can assure you that society makes things very hard for them indeed.'

'I'm sure it does,' Stanton replied. 'But personally I don't believe a person chooses their sexual preferences at all. To me, it's self-evident that they were born with them. And I feel very strongly that nobody should be discriminated against on the grounds of their sexuality.'

Bernadette leant across the table and took his hand.

'Hugh, that's . . . that's a *wonderful* thing to say. An *amazing* thing to say. Where *do* you come up with this stuff? *Nobody should be discriminated against on the grounds of their sexuality.* Hang on while I write it down.'

She went back into the room.

It seemed to take her rather a long time to write down a single sentence and when she returned she was in her underwear.

'Am I being awful?' she asked. 'It's just that you're so *interesting* I thought if we weren't careful we might end up sitting out here talking all night and never . . . well, never go inside.'

Even in the moonlight he could see that once more she was blushing deeply but the funny thing was Stanton couldn't actually see any more of her now than he had done before. Her underwear covered pretty much the same parts of her as had her ankle-length hobble skirt, apart from a slightly lower neckline and her bare arms. She was wearing a long white slip, gathered slightly at the waist and tapering in again towards the ankle. Curiously, despite the modesty of the garment Stanton found it incredibly erotic. Perhaps it was the moonlight on her bare white arms. When it came to the sensual power of glimpses of flesh, less could certainly be more. Something the lingerie designers of his century had long since forgotten.

He got up, took her hand and they went back inside the room together and turned out the lamps. Then with the moonlight streaming through the open balcony doors, he stepped towards her and lifted off her slip. The intensity of the moment was quite overpowering. Not only was it the first time he had been with anyone but Cassie in almost ten years but this woman was from *another* time.

1914. In the Vienna moonlight.

He stepped back from her while removing the stud from his starched collar.

She was completely naked save for her silk stockings which were secured above the knee not with suspenders but with garters.

That, however, was not what caught his attention. Nor was it her delightful bosom, larger than he expected but firm. Or the curve of her waist. Or the slight bulge of her belly. Deeply stirring though all those things were.

It was the pubic hair. There was just more of it than he'd expected. Sandy pale, full and curly. Even spreading a little beyond what would one day be known as the bikini line. He should have been expecting it. He *knew* about female pubic hair but he had never encountered it in its natural state. Cassie had waxed. All the girls he'd ever been with had either waxed or shaved, not necessarily the full Brazilian but certainly a *major* trim. He recalled the famous story of the poet Ruskin who it was said could not consummate his marriage because he was so shocked and disgusted by his wife's pubic hair.

Stanton wasn't shocked, he just wasn't used to it, that was all.

In fact, he thought it looked lovely.

'Well, are you going to take your shirt off or not?' Bernadette enquired. 'I'm beginning to feel a bit silly standing here.'

'Sorry . . . yes,' he said, beginning quickly to undress.

They collapsed together on the bed and began to make love.

For a few moments Stanton was consumed with a hungry passion as he gnawed and pawed at Bernadette's squirming body. It had been well over a year since he'd had sex and this sudden cessation of the drought had brought every nerve in his being to a state of urgent arousal. She too had abandoned herself to primal instinct and wriggled and writhed against him in his embrace, plunging a hand down to grasp away at him.

'Goodness,' she gasped. 'I have missed *these*.'

She was very different to Cassie, who had been more passive, happier to go with the flow. Like any couple who shared a bed exclusively with each other they'd fallen into habits together. Happily enough, but nonetheless he found the thrill of a new and unexplored body and a proactively different approach fiercely erotic.

And that nearly ruined the whole thing.

Thinking about Cassie.

Comparing Bernadette to her.

His wife. The undisputed love of his life and mother of his children. A surge of guilt swept over him. Almost as if Cassie were in the room and had caught him at it.

He could feel the passion dissipating even as Bernadette chewed hungrily at his mouth. That unwelcome thought. That distraction. A woman could fake it, ignore it till it went away, but with a man the evidence was on display.

In Bernadette's hand.

'Oh,' she said, 'did I do something wrong?'

This was absurd. He wanted this. He needed it. And he had every right to it. And the ridiculous thing was he knew Cassie would agree. Of course she would.

Cassie. *Cassie.* How could he get her to leave the room? To pop next door. Retire to the balcony.

He thought about Bernadette naked. About her revealing herself as she pulled her long slip up her body. Her shapely legs clad in white silk. He thought about her pubic hair. Lush and womanly. Strawberry blonde. Beautiful and actually – *appropriate.*

He put his hand down to touch her, it was so strange. He was used to things being smooth or stubbly depending on the level of maintenance. But this was soft. Warm and giving. *Luxuriant.* Fascinating. He wanted to plunge his whole being deep inside.

'That's better,' Bernadette gasped. '*Now* we're getting somewhere!'

Afterwards they lay together and finished off the wine and Bernadette smoked and snuggled in his arms.

'That was very nice,' she said, stretching a leg across his body.

'Yes, yes it was,' Stanton agreed.

'You didn't leave any . . . any *seed* in me, did you?' she asked. 'Bit late to ask really, but did you?'

'I don't think so. I tried to be careful,' he replied. 'I think it's all over your tummy and the sheets.'

'Good . . . better out than in, say I.'

Stanton thought how very strange an idea it would be if he *did* get a girl pregnant in this new version of the century. To have children in two separate dimensions of space and time was a mind-boggling thought. A thought which brought Tessa and Bill to mind, his children, who had been his whole life. Who were *still* his whole life.

Except that they were gone. And he was in bed with a woman who had died decades before they were born.

Bernadette must have sensed the progress of his thoughts.

'You don't feel guilty, do you?' she asked. 'About your wife, I mean . . . I'm sure she'd understand. Or is that presumptuous of me? Of course, I don't know what she'd think, obviously. But she would understand, wouldn't she? She wouldn't want you to be alone *all* the time.'

'Yes, I think she'd understand,' Stanton said, 'and no, I don't feel guilty.'

She put her head on his shoulder and kissed his neck. He put his arm around her and they lay together for a while. By craning his chin hard against his chest he could just see her face in the moonlight. It was such a sweet, sweet face.

But now the pretty upturned nose wrinkled a little. She was puzzled.

'Something up?' he asked.

'I thought your watch had stopped,' she said twisting her head so that she could look at it, 'but it hasn't, see, the second hand's spinning away. I can see the luminous hand.'

'So what?'

'Well, it isn't ticking. Your wristwatch doesn't *tick*,' she said. 'That's very strange.'

'Oh it does, just very quietly,' he assured her.

'No, it *doesn't*,' she insisted. 'I had it right against my ear and I have very good hearing and it doesn't tick.'

'It's a specialist piece. Very advanced mechanism. Swiss.'

'Hmm. *Seiko*. Doesn't *sound* very Swiss.'

'They're a very small firm. Very advanced. Years ahead of their time. I do sensitive work. I have to make sure I have the best equipment.'

'Which brings us to the point, actually. What *do* you do?' she asked, rolling on to her front, raising her head up and putting her chin on her hands. 'You are a strange and I must say rather intriguing man. You claim to be a soldier—'

'Claim? What do you mean, *claim*?'

'But you're also a gold-miner from the Australian wilderness. Yet you've not only heard of Karl Kraus but you can name his satirical magazine, which is published only in Vienna and which by the way you could read in German. You hold the most astonishingly enlightened views on women and on sex I have ever heard. And you have such a lovely turn of phrase that some of the things you say should be in a dictionary of quotations. You claim to have studied at Cambridge but didn't seem to remember that they don't have female students, let alone female professors. What's more you are as physically fit as any man I've ever met, fitter in fact. Your muscles are like iron, which is incidentally *most* attractive to embrace, and so far I've noted two scars on your person which I *think* may be bullet scars. You *never* let those two bags of yours out of your sight and you have a watch that *does not tick*. Not even the tiniest bit. Who are you, Hugh Stanton, and, honestly, what do you do?'

'Well . . . I *could* tell you,' he said, remembering an old line from his own century, 'but I'd have to kill you.'

She smiled.

'I *hope* you're joking. Are you a *spy* then?'

'I'm just a stranger on a train, Bernie. We both are.'

'*A stranger on a train,*' she repeated slowly. 'That does sound romantic.'

'It is romantic. For me anyway. I can't think of many things more romantic than bumping into a beautiful girl on the Sarajevo to Zagreb express and then spending a night with her in a moon-lit hotel room in Vienna.'

'Just a night?'

He didn't answer for a moment. Could he stay? For a little while? Have breakfast on their balcony and then stroll about the city all day and in the evening wine and dine and perhaps even dance. This was Imperial Vienna, after all. And then at the end of the evening return to this very room with Bernadette and . . .

But he had his mission and he had his secrets. So many secrets. And this woman was very clever and observant and inquisitive.

'I think perhaps just one night is for the best, don't you?' he answered.

'I suppose, perhaps,' she said, but very sadly. 'I think if we made it two I just might fall in love with you and I don't think I'm very good at love.'

'Anybody can be good at love. You just have to find the right person.'

'Did you love your wife a lot?'

'Yes. I loved her a lot.'

'I'm sure she deserved it.'

'She did.'

'So I just need to find the right person then?'

'Yes, that's all.'

'Not a Hungarian feminist.'

'Not by the sound of it.'

'Or a mysterious stranger on a train?' Her chin was still in her hands and she was looking at him. The moon was behind her, casting her into silhouette, but he could feel her eyes. 'Best to avoid them, too, you think?'

'All I know is that I don't really feel I have anything to offer anybody at the moment. And to be quite frank I rather doubt I ever will.'

'Emotional baggage?'

'Yes. Emotional baggage. Rather well-travelled baggage.'

'What will you do? In the morning, I mean, when I'm tossed aside like a soiled glove and left to skulk out of the hotel alone, forlornly trying to hide my shame?'

'I have an appointment, in Berlin.'

'You see! *Appointment in Berlin* – that sounds exactly like a spy novel.'

'Oh, it's nothing very exciting. Not as exciting as chaining yourself to the railings outside Buckingham Palace.'

'That's not exciting at all. It's embarrassing and terrifying and horribly uncomfortable. You've no idea the hatred we provoke. People jeer and spit, women too. And the police are *horrible*. It's as if they feel *threatened*. How can a woman chained to a railing be threatening?'

'You'll win in the end, you know. One day sex discrimination will actually be illegal.'

'Sex discrimination? *Wonderful* phrase. Let's hope you're a prophet. After all, women do hold up half the sky . . . Anyway, I think we should forget the future and concentrate on the present. If this is to be our only night together then I think we should make the most of it.'

And so they made love again and afterwards lay in the dark once more and Bernadette smoked another cigarette and Stanton wished he could share it with her. He didn't, though. He was having enough trouble keeping the tryst from being a ménage à trois as it was without giving Cassie an excuse to appear by the bedside table and tell him that Tessa had brought another leaflet home from school with a rotting lung on it.

'I envy you going to Berlin,' she said. 'I'd like to go one day. I want to meet Rosa Luxemburg more than anyone in the world. Have you heard of her? I doubt there's many Englishmen who have but you seem so terribly well informed in general.'

'I most certainly have heard of her. Marxist economist and *extreme* irritant to the German establishment,' Stanton replied. He was about to add, 'Eventually organized a German revolution and sadly ended up beaten to death in the street by a paramilitary murder squad,' before remembering that those things wouldn't happen for years yet. And hopefully now never would.

'You are *amazing*,' Bernadette said with delight. 'I cannot *believe* you. How many British soldiers have heard of Rosa Luxemburg? Only one, I bet, in the whole world and I've just made love to him!'

She kissed him hard and passionately.

Stanton smiled to himself. He'd always known his history degree would come in handy for something.

'She's a wonderful woman, you know,' Bernadette said thoughtfully. 'I can't think of anyone I admire so much. Very clever, very passionate, very brave and very important.'

Then, a little while after that, he fell asleep.

The first time in so very long that he had fallen asleep with a woman's heart beating nearby, and as he drifted into dreams he was astonished to realize that he was happy. Happy in that moment. Happy lying naked with Bernadette Burdette.

27

WHEN HE WOKE UP, perhaps an hour later, Bernadette wasn't in bed any more.

She had put her slip back on and was at the table in the sitting-room part of the room.

Where the porter had put Stanton's bags.

For a moment, as his consciousness surfaced, Stanton thought it was Cassie. He'd seen her sitting just that way so often, in the darkness, in her nightie. When she'd had some pressing work or study to do and had crept out of bed in the night to do it, and he'd awoken and seen her at the table across the room, her face a kind of monochrome grey silver, illuminated by the light from her computer.

But it wasn't Cassie.

It was Bernadette's face that was turned grey silver.

Illuminated by the light from a computer.

He was out of bed in a second but she was equally quick and he found that he was staring down the barrel of his own Glock semi-automatic.

It had been in his bag. Alongside the computer, which was concealed within a false book. The bag from which he'd got the multi-tool with the corkscrew to open the bottle of hock.

'For Christ's sake, what are you doing?' he said.

'I *beg* your pardon,' she replied, seeming genuinely surprised at what to her must have been an unfamiliar profanity.

'I said what are you doing? Put that down! Why did you look in my bag? Christ, Bernie, put that gun down!'

She didn't put it down but continued instead to point it with steady hand at his head.

'I got up in the night,' she said. 'And I wanted something to read, and your bag was open and I spotted a book in it. And I wondered what a strange man like you reads to amuse himself. I know it's wrong to pry but I'm a girl and I couldn't help it, and when I opened the book I found an even stranger thing.'

He hadn't locked his bag. The wine and the moonlight had got the better of him. He'd *meant* to relock it but then she'd started undressing and now a woman born in the 1880s had come into contact with a state-of-the-art twenty-first-century computer that would have looked like something out of science fiction in the *nineteen* eighties.

'Look, Bernie,' he began, 'that . . . that's a sort of light box . . . it's to do with photography . . . it's a kind of portable developing room . . . it's a secret invention . . . but nothing very mysterious, just small and compact, that's all.'

He took a step towards her.

'Don't move, Hugh!' she barked, levelling the gun in front of her eyes and taking aim between his.

'Bernie? What is this? You kind of guessed I was a spy. And you were right. I'm a sort of agent. I have equipment. Secret equipment—'

'I touched your "photographic light box",' she interrupted, 'and I don't understand it and I think it's very strange and quite frankly rather scary but not half as scary as the image that appeared on it.'

Stanton went cold. He remembered what had been on the screen the last time he had used his computer, in Sarajevo on the previous morning. Another imbecilic lapse of judgement. Why hadn't he quit out of the program? Why hadn't he shut down? 'Now look, Bernie,' he began.

'It was a map, Hugh. A map of Sarajevo. The Latin Bridge area

of Sarajevo on the north bank of the Miljacka. And the route of
the Archduke's motorcade was marked on it—'

'Bernie . . .'

'As were the positions of the would-be assassins. And of the
two assassination attempts.'

'I know but . . .'

'How did they describe the missing man, Hugh? Six feet tall
and a moustache. It could have been anyone. You said it on the
train, didn't you? It could have been *you*. Except that the man was
Serbian. But was he? Perhaps he was an Englishman who could
speak Serbian? Or even a Serbian who can speak wonderful,
intriguing English. What did it say in the papers about the gun,
Hugh? That the bullet that killed Princip came from an unknown
type?'

She waved the gun in front of his face.

'I'm a country girl. I've been around guns and pistols all my life
and I have never seen one like this before. And I've never heard of
Glock either. Quite frankly, I can't think what this thing is even
made of. More secret equipment? Perhaps secret *Serbian* equipment? You may be a spy, Hugh, but you're also an assassin and
the only thing that stopped you doing something that could have
destroyed Europe is that you killed the wrong man. Your own
man.'

There were tears in her eyes but despite that her hand was
steady and her expression resolved.

'Give me my gun back, Bernie,' Stanton said.

'Not likely. I'm arresting you, Hugh. I know it sounds
ridiculous considering how we've spent the last few hours but I'm
going to turn you in. I'm sorry but I have to do it because you are
a terribly dangerous man and if you resist I shall shoot. I may not
recognize the gun but I know a trigger when I see one.'

'You can't shoot a naked man, Bernie. It's not . . . it's not
cricket.'

'I damn well can and I will.'

'Not with the safety catch on, you can't.'

Her eyes flicked down and in that instant he strode forward and grabbed the gun from her with one hand while putting the other over her mouth just before it could let out a scream.

That same mouth which had so charmed him with its smile when they'd met on the train. The mouth which he had been kissing so ferociously just an hour before. And which had been kissing him. The pace of life in his new world was certainly picking up.

'Now listen to me very carefully because you've made a big mistake,' he said calmly. 'No, don't struggle! I very much don't want to hurt you because although I've only known you for a day I am already very fond of you so, please, stop wriggling about and listen to me. I didn't kill the wrong man, Bernie. I killed the *right* man. Remember what you said to me on the train? That you didn't think I was the sort of person who'd miss? Well, you're right. I'm not. I was in Sarajevo to *stop* an assassination, not commit one, and that's exactly what I did. I killed Gavrilo Princip before he could kill Franz Ferdinand. And, yes, I am a British soldier as I've told you but I've been seconded from the army for a very special mission. A highly *unofficial* mission. You see, some very influential people in Britain knew about the Serbian plans to attack the Austrian royal family but of course they couldn't send an agent to stop them. Not officially. Officially Britain has no spies and does not involve itself in espionage. A British citizen operating on behalf of his government in Bosnia would have been a serious breach of Austrian sovereignty, which could in fact have resulted in a crisis all of its own. So I was given leave from the army and sent in as a civilian to stop these people from carrying out their plan.' As he spoke, Stanton couldn't help reflect on the fact that every single word he was saying was entirely true, the only lie was one of omission in that he neglected to add that he'd been sent across a hundred and eleven years of time to do it. 'You see, my controllers in Britain could see *exactly* what you could see, what any sensible person could see. That if the heir to the Austro-Hungarian Empire was killed by Serbs there'd be a real possibility of European war. Global war, in fact. But it didn't happen, and it didn't happen because I shot Princip.'

She'd stopped wriggling and had been listening intently, her eyes growing wider with every word he said. Stanton tentatively removed his hand from her mouth. She didn't scream.

Then Stanton remembered that he was naked and felt rather stupid.

'If I just put my trousers on, can I trust you not to scream?' he said.

Bernadette nodded. But she clearly still had doubts.

'The British Government wouldn't have needed to send their own spy,' she said. 'If they knew about the plot, why didn't they just warn the Austrians and let them protect the Duke?'

Stanton could think of two very good reasons for that.

'Well, first of all it might easily not have worked. Britain is linked with Russia in the Triple Entente, remember, and Russia backs the Serbs. The Austrian military is paranoid about Russia and with good reason because only last year it turned out their own spy chief was a Russian mole.'

'Mole?'

'It means double agent. Did you ever read about the Alfred Redl scandal?'

Stanton had come across this catastrophe for Austrian intelligence during his preparatory research. The previous year, Redl, Austria's Chief of Military Intelligence, had been discovered selling his own country's entire battle plan to the Russians because he needed money to support his lover, who was a fellow officer.

'Yes. I read about it,' Bernadette admitted, 'pretty fruity stuff.'

'Well, because of Redl the Austrians have been fed misinformation by the Russians on a continuous basis since 1903, so they would very likely view information supplied by a Russian ally as deliberate misinformation.'

'It's a dark game, isn't it?' Bernadette admitted.

'You haven't heard the half of it. Consider this for dark. It's perfectly possible that even if the Austrians *had* believed a British warning about the Sarajevo plot, they might have let it go ahead anyway.'

'Go ahead? Let anarchists murder their own Crown Prince?'

'Think about it. This is a crown prince who married for love. Against the Emperor's violent objections. So violent, in fact, that he instructed the Austrian court to ostracize the woman and officially disinherited any children she had with Franz Ferdinand. Add to that the fact that most of the Austrian elite have been itching for an excuse to put Serbia in its place. In fact, Franz Ferdinand was one of the few doves; the Emperor was a hawk.'

Bernadette leant forward and squeezed his hand.

'Doves and hawks? God, I *love* the way you talk, Hugh.'

'So you believe me then?'

'Yes, yes, I blooming well do! But do you *really* think the old Emperor might actually have wanted his nephew *dead*? Because his wife wasn't posh enough?'

'Power is a dirty game, Bernie. A very dirty game.'

Stanton would have liked to show her how true this was. To tell her that in the previous history of the world, on hearing of his nephew's death the Emperor had actually expressed *relief* about it. That he was recorded as having said, '*A higher power has re-established the order which alas I could not preserve.*' That would have given her something to get wide-eyed about. The old man had thought God himself shot Franz Ferdinand to preserve the integrity of the Habsburg dynasty.

'So you see,' he went on, 'the only way to be absolutely sure the plot would fail was to prevent it ourselves. I was recruited to do the job by a group centred around Trinity College Cambridge, dedicated to preserving international peace. They call themselves the Companions of Chronos.'

'The God of Time?'

'Yes . . . because time was . . . running out to stop Europe from destroying itself.'

Bernadette was silent for a moment.

'Well, it certainly makes more sense than you being a

Pan-Serbian nationalist,' she said. 'Well done, by the way. I mean, on pulling it off.'

'I'd hoped to do it without having to kill Princip and particularly that poor girl he was with but he was in the act of pulling his gun when I arrived.'

'You had no choice.'

'No, I don't think I did.'

'Amazing that you were there at all. The papers said it was a mix-up and the car took the wrong turn. It's almost as if you *knew*.'

'One develops a nose for these things in my game.'

'A sort of sixth sense?'

'Something like that, yes.'

'Well, you did really really well.'

'Thanks.'

There was another pause during which Stanton took the opportunity to shut and stow his photographic 'light box'.

'Enough to make a girl swoon,' Bernadette went on.

'I find I often have that effect.'

'Are all spies as devilishly attractive as you?'

'Good God no. I'm far and away the sexiest.'

'Sexiest? Another rather splendid word. Where do you get them from?'

'It's a gift.'

Bernadette got up from the table and began once more to remove her slip.

28

THE FOLLOWING MORNING Bernadette and Stanton parted company and he continued his journey to Berlin, Imperial capital of the Second Reich and the place where he knew he must kill the Emperor.

Berlin was two cities.

That was the conclusion Stanton came to as he ate a dish of ice cream on the terrace of the Kranzler patisserie on Unter Den Linden.

One was nineteenth century and the other twentieth century.

The nineteenth-century one was about as nineteenth century a city as you could find, steeped in the Imperialist mind-set of the time. A fiercely militaristic town, capital of the garrison state of Prussia. No people since the Spartans had so gloried in martial ardour. No nation of the modern world, with the possible exception of the Zulus, ever idolized its army so completely. The army was far and away the most important and the most visible institution in the city after the monarchy, with which it was inextricably linked. The military were everywhere. Marching bands in every park. Grand parades on every Sunday (and any other day on the tiniest excuse). Officers strutting in the boulevards and lounging in the cafes in ornate dress uniforms which would have been entirely impractical for any other activity than raising a glass or bowing to a lady. Columns of troops marched about wherever there was space to march about. And there were sentries *everywhere*. Stanton had had no idea of the number of soldiers on the streets of pre-war Imperial Berlin. It was frankly a bit weird. No other city felt the need to place uniformed sentries outside every public building. Museums were guarded, national monuments, railway stations, public toilets. Anywhere that crown or municipal authority was extended there was a spike-headed soldier with rifle at his shoulder marching about, usually with the ubiquitous black-and-white sentry box behind him. To a military man like Stanton it was all quite fun; he enjoyed the sight of their impeccable turnout, their faultless drill and the shine on every boot. The Germans did military ceremony almost as well as the British and they did a lot more of it. The sort of show the Horse Guards put on outside Buckingham Palace once a day, the Reichsheer would mount at a sewage pumping station on the hour.

And where there could be no soldiers, then there were people trying to look like soldiers. Half the population of Berlin was in uniform, three-quarters if you counted waiters and hotel doormen. Every institution in the city seemed to have been moulded in the image of the military. Everyone from policemen to postmen to students to hotel concierges dressed like soldiers. Teachers wore uniforms.

And yet strangely Stanton found the overall effect was neither warlike nor threatening. Rather, it gave a slightly comical impression of benign and self-satisfied *permanence*. The postmen that looked like captains and the water board officials that looked like generals and the telegram delivery boys that looked like field marshals were just part of a happy pantomime. As if the whole city was the set of some Ruritanian comic opera and the people its chorus and principals.

Germany hadn't fought a real war since Bismarck had unified the country forty years before, and for all the martial music and stamping about, Stanton sensed no desire among the people of its capital city to fight one now.

A cake trolley passed by Stanton's table. They really liked their cakes, the Germans. Or, perhaps more to the point, they liked their cream. For as far as Stanton could see, cakes were really no more than whipped cream delivery systems, thin layers of sponge set between inch-thick layers of dairy fat. *Kaffee und Kuchen*, that was what they liked in Berlin. Stanton liked it too.

The whole place just felt so *contented*.

And of course that was because of the other Berlin. The twentieth-century Berlin.

The Berlin whose time had come.

Because, military pantomime aside, the place was *modern*. Even to a visitor from the twenty-first century it felt that way. It seemed to Stanton that there was scarcely a single building that was over fifty years old and many more appeared only to have been built the previous week. This was a city expanding more quickly and more dynamically than any other town in the world. There was a huge amount of motor traffic, far more so than Stanton had noticed in London, and everywhere there was evidence of power-house industry and cutting-edge technology. On the same streets where squads of soldiers marched there were banks of public telephones, automatic ticketing machines and the most efficient and well-organized trams in Europe. There were elevated railway lines and underground railways with stations on almost every corner. There was electricity everywhere; the whole town was wired, and more reliably than anywhere on the planet. When Stanton plugged in his personal computer using a customized transformer he'd found as steady a current as ever he'd had in the twenty-first century.

Berlin made *everything*. Most of the world's chemicals. The bulk of the world's electrical engineering. A large chunk of the world's steel. *All* the world's advanced cameras, telescopes and precision instruments. And above all it made incredible amounts of money. Even the great cities of the industrial USA looked enviously at Berlin.

Nutters aside, the last thing anybody in this city wanted was a war.

War would cost it everything. It *had* cost it everything.

The last time.

Stanton had *seen* the pictures. Pictures of this magnificent city in ruins. Hatred and slaughter stalking the town. He knew the history; every school kid from his time did, it was all they studied. How Germany had led the twentieth century to nightmarish ruin and in so doing had destroyed itself. How these plump, busy, prosperous people would in just a few years' time be shattered ghosts, disease-ridden and on the very brink of starvation, their world-beating economy destroyed and facing decades of nightmare, revolution, deprivation and oppression.

But it wasn't going to happen this time.

Because Stanton was going to stop it. He would save Berlin and he would save Germany. He would save its foolish, stamping toy soldiers and he would save its brilliant people, whom Stanton admired so much for their industry and their inventiveness, their crazy originality, their commerce, their science and their arts. He would save them from the terrible fate that awaited them.

He would save them from their kaiser.

Because outrage in Sarajevo or not, sooner or later Emperor Wilhelm, with his militaristic obsessions, his vanity and his raw wounded ego, would drag this young, dynamic nation into suicidal war.

A large picture of the Emperor hung on the wall opposite and to Stanton's mind that picture said it all. It was cartoonish in its vainglorious swagger, the great man viewed slightly from below as if surveying the whole world and intent on being its master. Dressed in a white uniform with steel breastplate like some angel of war, a colonnaded Roman background made his Imperial pretensions all the more clear.

And the left arm on his sword hilt, where it usually was, disguising the birth defect which many believed had shaped the psyche of the man. It was withered and fully six inches shorter than his right arm. Wilhelm had always bravely ignored the disability, taking part in every sport and military practice, but

226

nonetheless he had remained secretly prey to deep self-doubt and also a self-disgust.

Stanton asked for his bill and laid some Reichmarks on the saucer. And there was the Emperor again, on the notes and coins, Kaiser Bill. The man with the pointy-up moustache. The man for whom there was still only one Germany. The military one. Because it meant nothing to Wilhelm the Second that German industry was conquering the world. For him it had to be German arms that did the conquering, with him at the front in a helmet with a huge eagle on top.

Stanton looked at his watch. In less than twenty-four hours the Emperor would be dead.

He felt a pang of pity. Wilhelm was by no means all bad. But he was vain and cantankerous and pompous and unreasonable and emotionally unstable with a well-established small empire complex. Those were very dangerous characteristics in a person who was the undisputed war lord of the finest army on the planet.

He simply had to die.

29

STANTON LEFT THE cafe and walked out on to Unter Den Linden intent on one last reconnoitre of his chosen vantage point. It was a delightful morning and the sun was shining through the linden trees and the chestnuts, making a dappled pattern on the road. Cars, carriages and pedestrians hurried up and down and policemen waved their arms about.

When Stanton had arrived in Berlin, instead of checking into a hotel, he'd taken a short-let furnished apartment. He had no idea when a suitable opportunity to carry out his mission would arise and reckoned that he might be resident in the city for months waiting for the perfect hit to present itself. He certainly didn't intend to rush it. After all, he would very likely get only one chance. If he failed, there was a fair possibility he would be captured. Even if he got away, the Kaiser's security people would be so spooked that it might prove impossible ever to get another opportunity. He was painfully aware that unlike with the Sarajevo mission he had no benefit of hindsight this time, and that apart from having superior equipment, his chances were no better than any other assassin's would have been.

As it turned out he hadn't needed to wait very long at all because on only the third morning after he had arrived from Vienna a royal ceremony was announced to take place in Potsdamer Platz. A glance at the published arrangements was enough to convince Stanton that his chance had arrived.

He strolled along Unter den Linden and turned south into

Friedrichstrasse then on to Leipziger Strasse and into Leipziger Platz, from where he intended to take up his firing position.

Leipziger Platz was adjacent to Potsdamer Platz, the heart of Imperial Berlin. This was the great transport hub of the city, across which were laid numerous tram lines. The arrival of automobiles in large numbers had placed extra pressure on the *Platz* and extensive reorganization had been required. A new layout for the maze of tram tracks had been put in place and the Kaiser himself had been persuaded to journey in from his Potsdam Palace to declare it open.

This was considered a great coup for the municipal authorities who, unlike the army, found it very difficult to persuade the Emperor to interest himself in their activities. They had therefore made a great fuss over the arrangements for the ceremony, all of which were fully described in the papers.

Stanton had spent the days since the announcement had been made laying his plans. It was clear that he needed elevation to get a clear shot. The target would no doubt be on a podium but he was likely to be surrounded by staff and he certainly couldn't rely on the German security team being as unfathomably incompetent as the Austrian one had been in Sarajevo. Stanton only had to look at the difference in the state of the two nation's armies and economies to be clear that dealing with the Germans was going to be a very different thing from dealing with the Austro-Hungarians. Royal protection techniques and theory might have been less advanced than they were in Stanton's personal experience but it would nonetheless be a big mistake to underestimate the German police and Secret Service.

Fortunately for Stanton there existed an obvious platform from which to fire. Leipziger Platz was famous for its shops and restaurants, and most famous among these was the Wertheim department store. This was a truly massive structure at the end of Leipziger Strasse, facing on to Leipziger Platz: ninety metres of shop front towering over the plaza and offering an uninterrupted view of Potsdamer Platz beyond.

And the Wertheim had a roof garden.

A roof garden from which it was possible to gain access to the rest of the roof, and to which the only impediment to trespass was a sign on a small door informing the public that access was *Verboten*; a door through which Stanton had simply stepped on the three previous days and through which he stepped now.

These truly were more innocent times.

The roof area outside the fenced area of the cafe garden was much like the roofs of most large buildings, a maze of chimneys, pipes and ventilation shafts. Plenty of cover, making it possible to be completely concealed within a very few steps of leaving the cafe.

Having made his way to the position he had selected on the edge of the roof of the Wertheim store, Stanton looked out over Potsdamer Platz far below him. The great junction was criss-crossed with trams and cars and scuttling pedestrians. Tomorrow it would be filled with cheering crowds, marching bands and lines of policemen. And in the middle of it, his target. The vantage point simply could not have been more perfect. No sniper had ever been better served.

He crept back across the roof and made his way home.

That night, in his little apartment, Stanton got out his computer and attempted to write down his thoughts. The following day would be the last one when events in Europe would bear any resemblance to how they had unfolded in the previous twentieth century.

Preventing the Sarajevo assassination had merely put the catastrophe on hold. Europe remained a primed bomb with the Kaiser itching to light the fuse. It was still perfectly possible for the twentieth century to unfold in exactly the same disastrous manner that it had the last time. Tomorrow all that would change. He would eliminate the root cause of conflict and there would begin an entirely new history. One single bullet from another world would send the whole course of human events plunging into uncharted waters.

And with that his own mission, his purpose in this time and place, would be over. He would have done his duty.

And what then?

For the five weeks that he had been living in the past he had been able to avoid that question. The business of Chronos was too pressing, his work too important. But in just a few hours that would all be over. He wouldn't be a special agent from the future any more. Just a lonely man prone to strange and fantastical dreams about peoples and events that had never occurred nor would ever occur.

It would be time to face life in a century yet to unfold. Just like everybody else.

What would he do?

He stared at the blank document on the screen of his laptop.

The first word he typed was 'Cassie'.

He hadn't planned it but of course it was inevitable. Or was it?

He added a question mark.

Cassie?

Did she have a part to play?

Perhaps he really couldn't face a life without her.

He wrote: *Suicide?*

Then, almost at once, he pressed delete and watched the cursor gobble up that second word. It just wasn't an option. He was a soldier. He didn't run. Nobody was going to kill Guts Stanton, least of all himself. And the reason for that wasn't because of his old fear that there might be a heaven and hell.

It was because he *wanted* to live.

He could see that he had been given an opportunity more exciting and extraordinary than any man had ever been given in all the human story. A chance to live in a different and better age, before the world got small and boring, before man's horizon had been reduced to the parameters of a smart phone screen. He had a chance to be a part of a whole different course for humanity, to help shape it. Chronos had made him rich, he was uniquely trained, uniquely well informed and entirely without dependants or responsibilities.

It was actually a dream come true.

He pressed the delete button again. The cursor reversed backwards across the single word on his screen, erasing it one space at a time.

First the question mark. Then the 'e'. Then the 'i', the 's' . . . another 's', an 'a' and finally the capital 'C'. The whole word gone.

Cassie gone.

She would always be a part of his soul but she was no longer a part of his life. He was in another dimension of space and time, one in which she had never existed nor would ever exist. It was time to begin to live again.

The screen was empty once again. A blank page.

As was his life.

On a sudden thought he typed: Shackleton.

He could actually *join* him. A lifelong hero. The great New Zealander's Antarctic expedition wouldn't leave for another two months. With the money Stanton had and the skills he could offer, he was certain he could get a place on board. To join Shackleton on his quest to cross the Antarctic! For a man like Stanton that was Nirvana. To do it hard. The way the *real* heroes used to do it. In leather and oilskin. With ropes and dogs and ship's biscuit rations and only the stars and a compass for guidance. To do things the way men did them before the twentieth century ruined *everything*.

Shackleton.

He pressed underline. <u>Shackleton</u>. That was definitely an option. Any man in Stanton's old regiment would have given ten lifetimes for such an opportunity.

Next he wrote: *Everest?*

Could he climb it? He'd climbed some bloody tough peaks in his time. The Matterhorn, the Eiger. Why not Everest? He could be the first. The first to do it, forty years before it had been done in the last loop of time. And without oxygen. He could be the first human being on that summit, the first living thing to touch that pristine space. Before the rubbish, the discarded food packs and old equipment. The corpses and the frozen turds. To be there when it was *new*.

Next he wrote: *Fly the Atlantic?*

Lindbergh did in '27. Stanton would beat the anti-Semitic bastard. He had thirteen years. He'd start by learning to fly. In a *real* flying machine made of wire and canvas, not a pressurized metal tube full of duty free, in-flight catering and other people.

Perhaps he would somehow find a way to get back into the army. After all, he was a better trained soldier than any other man on the planet. Perhaps one day he would ride the Northwest Frontier! Or gallop across desert kingdoms with T. E. Lawrence.

Then Stanton surprised himself by typing another word.

Bernadette.

She'd been on his mind since the previous week in Vienna. He'd pushed the thought away through guilt about Cassie. About infidelity to a spirit. A memory. It was ridiculous. What the hell did he have to feel guilty about? He underlined the word.

Bernadette.

Then he closed his computer.

A handful of *Boy's Own* adventures and a beautiful girl with laughing Irish eyes. That was enough dreaming for one night.

He'd think about it all again the following evening. After he had finished his mission.

When the future was finally his to plan.

30

THE FOLLOWING MORNING Stanton rose early, turned on his little gas ring and made some coffee. He had no food in the flat apart from some chocolate but he wasn't hungry. He never was on the day of a mission. Some of the guys had sworn by a big breakfast before heading in country but Stanton always felt that hunger kept him sharp.

He began a final check of his equipment. Taking out his rifle, breaking it down, inspecting it, cleaning it one last time even though it didn't need it. Then packing it away again.

Next he put on his body armour underneath his jacket. He didn't *think* he'd need it. But then he hadn't thought he'd need his pistol in Sarajevo and if he hadn't had it in his pocket, Princip would undoubtedly have shot the Archduke and Europe would be only a couple of weeks away from war.

He put the Glock pistol in his pocket.

Then he took from the bigger of his bags a sheaf of printed leaflets. Leaflets he had brought all the way from the twenty-first century. Inflammatory leaflets coloured mainly bright red. He put the leaflets in the smaller of his two bags beside his rifle.

He was ready.

He left his apartment and took the U-Bahn, descending into the clean and efficiently run transport arteries of the city, riding the spanking new, punctual-to-the-second train and emerging at Potsdamer Platz.

The scheduled time for the royal appearance was still an hour

235

and a half away but already the presence of police and temporary barriers was attracting a crowd. A presentation platform had been erected above the great maze of new tram lines that had been laid, snaking silver tracks that weaved over and crisscrossed the venerable Potsdamer Platz looking like so much steel spaghetti. It was difficult to imagine how trams from all directions could navigate them without smashing together in the middle.

The platform was bedecked with flags and golden eagles, ancient symbols of military and Imperial power. They were in sharp contrast to the civic banner that hung among them proclaiming *Berlin! Weltstadt!*, announcing the municipal council's proud boast that their ultra-modern capital was the first world city.

Imperial and municipal. The two Berlins truly were meeting at Potsdamer Platz.

And in the middle of it, set at waist height, there was a purple ribbon stretched between two golden staffs.

That was where the Emperor would be standing. Scissors in hand.

Stanton turned away. There was nothing else to see at the moment. The troops had not yet arrived. Nor had any of the dignitaries who were to sit in the little grandstand that had been erected so the great and the good might watch the Kaiser perform his snip. Stanton stared back behind him, east across Leipziger Platz to the magnificent western end of the Wertheim department store. It really was a fantastic building. The façade was stern, angular and massively solid in grey granite. Four huge arches reached halfway up the rock face and above that stone pillars soared skyward to a steep, slate-tiled pelmet running around its entirety as if the building were wearing a steel helmet.

In Berlin even the department stores looked like soldiers.

That shop looked solid enough to stand for ever, as if nothing could dent its solidity and certitude. But Stanton knew different. He closed his eyes for a moment and conjured up the pictures he had seen of that very building in utter ruins. The gutted, burnt-out, half-smashed victim of war and revolution. That could happen. It *had* happened. But now it wouldn't. That shop would stand for centuries as its architect had intended, delighting generations of shoppers at the heart of a city too rich to fight.

Because of what he must do that day.

And it did seem as if fate was on his side this time. In fact, Stanton could scarcely believe his good fortune. Any gunman mounted on top of that steel grey precipice would have an angle of fire that would cover Potsdamer Platz in almost its entirety, certainly the part where the Kaiser would be cutting the ribbon. The three hundred metres or so between the store and the podium were open road and public plaza. There was literally nothing between where Stanton intended to place himself and his Imperial target.

He walked back towards the store, sweating beneath his protective vest. It was twelve noon and a shift of shop workers had just clocked off for lunch. The road was flooded with pretty girls all dressed in the Wertheim livery. Only a generation ago those girls would have been peasants as their mothers and grandmothers had been, but Berlin was growing at a frantic pace. It needed workers and it was prepared to pay. There were so many blonde heads, all bleached white gold by sun-drenched country childhoods. It was like walking through a field of daffodils.

He'd save them. He'd save those girls. They'd all have husbands and their children would have fathers because of him. Germany would survive. The better Germany, the Germany of fabulous department stores, expanding tram networks and bouquets of happy, pretty shop girls. The Kaiser would be gone but this time round he would not take Germany with him.

Wertheim's was simply enormous. It boasted eighty-three lifts. Eighty-three! In *1914*. Stanton had had no idea. If the year before anyone had asked him how many lifts the biggest shop in Berlin had before the Great War, he'd have guessed at perhaps six at the most. And Wertheim's wasn't even the biggest. There was Jandorf's and Tiet's and, largest and newest of all, the Kaufhaus des Westens. History had always taught Stanton to think of pre-war Berlin as a sort of urban military parade ground, but in fact it was basically all about the shopping, like a twenty-first-century airport. Crazy with success and awash with money. Such a lot to have thrown away to please an unbalanced ruler and a few vicious old generals.

Well, not this time around.

Stanton stepped beneath the great front arches and entered the famed atrium. Even though he'd reconnoitred it on each of the three previous afternoons it still took his breath away. It was like being inside a cathedral, a cathedral to commerce. A great glass-topped inner space reached up five storeys to the roof. In the centre was a huge statue of a noble-looking female peasant with a harvest basket in her arms, who no doubt represented some sort of pastoral ideal. The figure was framed by twin staircases, which curled around her and led up to five levels of smart internal arcades. Like the inside of a vast cream *Kuchen*, each layer stuffed with perfumes and chocolates, handbags and dresses, and all sorts of luxury items. Stuff which was about as far from the pastoral ideal as it would be possible to get.

Stanton headed for one of the eighty-three lifts. He passed the delicatessen and patisserie. More whipped cream, lots more. He wondered why they bothered with the cake bit at all.

He took the lift to the fifth floor and walked from there up to the roof garden. He wanted to be able to approach it discreetly at his own pace, not be ejected stage centre through the doors of a lift. He got out at household fittings and furniture: great heavy wooden cabinets and vast double-sprung cushioned settees. He wondered why they had decided to sell the largest, heaviest goods on the sixth floor.

Walking at a gentle pace, his gun bag firmly gripped in his right hand, Stanton took the short stairway up on to the roof garden. It was busy, just as it had been on his previous visits. Everywhere contented people were enjoying ices or ordering an early lunch. No *Kuchen* yet. They'd get into that in the early afternoon.

Stanton walked purposefully across the garden, a tall, impressive, commanding figure. A figure of authority. That was the way to avoid being challenged – look like you were in charge. Arriving at the door to the outer roof with its stern message of *Verboten* he paused and nodded with evident approval, as if finding everything in order. Then he took out a notebook and pen and strode through the door. He had done exactly that on his previous three visits. Had any of the busy and harassed waitresses thought to question him, which he thought extremely unlikely, he would have informed them that he was an inspector on a visit of inspection. One thing he knew about Berliners was that they respected authority, and if you displayed it, you had it.

As expected, he wasn't challenged. These were different times to those in which he had been brought up. Random mass terror was still a rare thing then and the concept of homeland security didn't really exist, as had been witnessed by the woeful security arrangements made for the Archduke in Sarajevo. In London the Prime Minister walked down Whitehall to Parliament from Downing Street every day, without a police escort. And that in a country which had the previous year been on the verge of civil war over Ireland.

This was an age where if a man had the small amount of balls required to walk through a *Verboten* sign, he could wander round pretty much on any roof he fancied. Even one that overlooked a place where the head of state was scheduled to present himself publicly.

Stanton looked at his watch. The Kaiser was scheduled to make his appearance in less than an hour.

The watch reminded him of Bernadette. '*It doesn't tick!*'

He really loved her voice.

He looked about himself. He was alone on the roof and completely unobserved. He began to make his way towards the eastern end of the building, moving from chimney to chimney, avoiding treading on air vents.

He was about halfway between the roof garden and the roof

ledge when he heard voices and before he had time to take cover two workmen appeared before him from behind an asphalt-covered ventilation shaft.

Fortunately they were more surprised to see somebody besides themselves on the roof than Stanton was, and he recovered first.

'Good morning,' he said loudly in German, moving to place the sun behind him. 'The staff in the coffee garden informed me that there were men on the roof. Kindly explain your purpose for being here.'

Again the natural presumption of authority was the key. Had he hesitated it was possible that the men might have challenged *him*, but he gave them no chance.

'We're works and maintenance,' one of the men replied.

'Please may I see your authorization,' Stanton went on.

Stanton could see that they were hesitating. No doubt they had performed maintenance work on the roof many times and never been challenged before. If he gave them time to think they might just decide it was them who should be asking the questions.

'His Imperial Highness is making an appearance in Potsdamer Platz this lunchtime. I'm sure you are aware of this. The surrounding area is therefore subject to inspection. Kindly show me your authorization *at once*.'

That did it. The men produced their time cards.

'Thank you,' Stanton said after a cursory glance, 'this is in order. Please inform me what the purpose of your work is here today.'

'A couple of the girls in cushions and soft furnishings were complaining about a fluttering and banging. They thought it was a bird, which sometimes do get caught in the air vents, but we can't find anything so either they imagined it or else it's got away.'

'Or it's dead,' his companion volunteered. 'They sometimes just die of panic. In which case the girls'll smell it in a day or two and we'll know to take the grid off and fish it out.'

'That's right,' the first man agreed.

'Good,' Stanton said, 'and your purpose here is finished?'

'Yes. We're done now. We was going on our break. We had thought about taking it here, sir. What with the sun and air, sir.'

Stanton noticed that the second man was carrying a vacuum flask and a small cloth-covered bundle, which he took to be their lunch.

'I'm afraid that will not be possible today. The roof must be cleared.'

The two men shrugged, touched their caps and left, exiting via a service hatch, which Stanton noted as a possible escape route should he need to make a hurried exit.

When the men had gone, Stanton pondered the encounter. He didn't *think* it would cause him problems. After all, he intended to be back in his apartment in Mitte before the police had even deduced that the shot might have come from the top of the Wertheim store. There was no doubt that his bullet, if successful, would make a pretty big mess of the Kaiser's skull and in the process punch the man clean off the podium. Working out an angle of trajectory from the corpse would be impossible so the cops would only ever be able to guess at the location of the gunman. He was a very long way away and the shot would be difficult using a gun made in 1914. It would therefore take them some time to include the Wertheim roof in their list of possibilities. If they ever did get around to interviewing the two workmen about the 'official' who had ordered them from the roof, the trail would be long cold.

It had been an unsettling moment, though, and he slipped off the safety catch of the Glock in his pocket just in case. If necessary he would kill anyone who attempted to confront him.

He was horribly aware that he only had one shot at saving the world.

Alone once more, Stanton made his way to the edge of the roof. There was a small ledge from which the slate-tiled 'helmet' of the building sloped steeply away for three metres or so, ending in a fringe of iron guttering that prevented him from seeing the colonnaded edifice beneath.

Stanton sat down, opened the bag he was carrying and took out the pieces of his rifle and sight. Having assembled the gun, he took off his jacket and bunched it up on the ledge as a cushion for a steady aim. Then he took stock of the scene that was now gathering in the Potsdamer Platz three hundred metres to the west.

Lines of troops had now assembled and the viewing stand was filling up. By looking through his telescopic sight Stanton could see the faces of the dignitaries and their wives quite clearly beneath their polished top hats and fancy confections of lace and flowers. The centre of the presentation podium was still empty but there were a number of people assembled at either end. Glancing further afield Stanton saw that a military band was playing, the sound of which was reaching him borne on the breeze. Between the band and the podium there was a space lined on either side with soldiers where it was clear the Emperor's car would cross the *Platz*.

He settled down to wait, hoping that the celebrated German efficiency would deliver the Emperor on time. In fact, he arrived a few minutes early, perhaps anxious to get such a boringly non-military function over with as soon as possible so that he could get back to his beloved parade grounds. There was a stirring in the crowd, and the rhythm of the distant music changed to what Stanton thought he recognized as 'God Save The King'. He was momentarily taken aback before recalling having read that the German Imperial anthem *Heil Dir Im Siegerkranz* used the same tune. The anthem signalled the arrival of the royal motorcade.

There was much cheering and waving of hats as the middle car drew up in front of the red carpet. The small crowd, which had been swollen by the host of golden daffodils on their lunch break from the department store, were clearly enjoying the occasion. A gaggle of dignitaries scurried forward to greet the monarch. Stanton couldn't see this part of the proceedings because the royal car was in the way. He could only imagine the great man trying to look interested while the details of the new tram-line pattern were explained to him.

A few moments passed and the party emerged from under the cover of the roof of the car and the Kaiser strode up the red carpet towards the podium. Stanton viewed the scene through his gun sight but there was no chance to get a clean shot. The monarch was leading the group and all Stanton could see through the crowd of top hats that followed him were the ostrich plumes of his ridiculous helmet. Wilhelm was, of course, in uniform. Only he would have felt it appropriate to dress up as an admiral of the fleet or a commander of the heavy cavalry in order to open a new tram junction.

The Kaiser mounted the platform. Stanton, who was already stretched out on his stomach behind the telescopic lens of his rifle, placed his finger against the trigger and took a view through the cross hairs. It was a fairly long range so the target bobbed about considerably in the circle of his lens but hopefully when it arrived at centre stage it would be still. But Stanton doubted that the Kaiser would remain still for long. The whole event was scheduled for only fifteen minutes and the Kaiser appeared to have brought no notes with him. Perhaps he would not speak at all and simply deliver the snip.

Stanton settled deeper into his firing position, the barrel of the gun resting on his folded jacket on the ledge.

The Kaiser took his position in front of the ribbon and nodded. It seemed he definitely did not intend to say anything as an officer approached him at once carrying a cushion on which was a pair of scissors. The Kaiser took up the scissors and reached forward to cut the ribbon.

Bang!

A shot was fired.

But it wasn't Stanton who fired it. Stanton felt a massive pain in his back, as if somebody had taken a clump hammer and brought it down with all their might on a space just to the right of his spine, just behind his heart.

He'd been shot at and but for the polyethylene ballistic plates in his Gore-tex vest he would have been dead already.

Stanton let go of his rifle and rolled over. Already the Glock semi-automatic was in his hand. All in an instant he saw a grey-clad figure with a shaven head standing ten metres or so away with a rifle at his shoulder. The figure must have managed to cock the bolt with inordinate speed because there was another crack and Stanton felt another horrendous blow to his chest, a ferocious steel punch from a tiny ballistic fist which left him gasping for breath. However, the body armour saved his life a second time and despite the twin blows he'd taken on the back and front of his body, Stanton was able to bring his handgun up into the firing position and return fire. He loosed off three rounds in scarcely more than a second. The first missed, but the second two hit the man in the arm and upper chest, knocking him backwards against the chimney in front of which he was standing.

Stanton didn't even watch his assailant fall fully to the ground. Even as the man slid down the chimney into a heap, Stanton had rolled back over on to his front. Gasping at the pain in his bruised chest, he took up his telescopic rifle once more. It had been in-credible misfortune that some sort of guard had happened upon him at that time. The Kaiser's people were clearly a massive step up from the Austrians, as indeed Stanton had feared they would be. They must have decided to sweep the roofs after all. Nonetheless as long as there weren't any more of them he might still have time to get his man.

Glancing down into the Potsdamer Platz he realized that the whole incident with the guard had only taken a matter of seconds. The Kaiser was still cutting the ribbon. It seemed to be proving troublesome and two officials had stepped forward to pull the thing tight to make it easier to cut.

Stanton thanked the heavens for the German public's appetite for military bands. Gun fights make a noise and while his own Glock was a relatively quiet piece the two rifle shots might easily have carried as far as the podium had a brass band not been play-ing. They had no doubt been heard in the roof garden but Stanton could only hope they had been ignored. There were plenty of motor cars in Berlin and cars from that time backfired a lot.

Putting all other thoughts from his mind, Stanton settled once more and, after a moment's searching through the magnified lens, picked up his target in the cross hairs. The Emperor was standing quite alone, behind the little ribbon at the front of the stage. The dignitaries had all gathered at the edges of the podium, apart from the two holding the ribbon. Stanton was glad to see that the Kaiserin was not present. He had no wish to shoot a man in front of his wife.

Now, with the Kaiser in his sights, he could see the man's face close up for the first time. It was shocking how familiar it was, even to a man born towards the end of the twentieth century. That moustache, so fierce and uncompromising, the waxed and carefully arranged glory of what had at that time been the most famous whiskers on the planet. The eyes, not unkind at all, but made deliberately fierce from years of assuming a look as stern as he could make it. Stanton knew that the Kaiser had been quite friendly and considerate as a schoolboy, but later as a guards officer and young ruler he had deliberately cultivated an abrupt and imperious manner. He'd thought it was expected of him.

Looking at the man, Stanton was also struck by his resemblance to the British royals, even the ones who had been born a hundred years after him. That was one strong gene pool. And powerful. *Incredibly* powerful. The British King, the German Kaiser, the Russian Tsar. All *first cousins*. How strange the world had once been.

Stanton raised the angle of his sighting by an infinitesimally small margin, bringing his cross hairs up to a point an inch above the space between the Emperor's eyes. The man was speaking now, perhaps complaining about the bluntness of the scissors, but keeping himself stiff and rigid as he did so.

Formal, proper.

Dead.

Stanton watched his target's head explode through the magnified lens. He had known he'd only get one shot and so had used ammunition that was designed to do the maximum damage.

And it had. As the man's body seemed to half float, half stagger backwards there was almost nothing left above its shoulders at all.

Stanton had completed his mission.

Archduke Franz Ferdinand was alive and the Kaiser was dead.

The Great War had been averted.

The world had been saved.

31

STANTON DISMANTLED HIS rifle and stowed it in his bag. He picked up the spent cartridge shell and stowed that also. Next he took a second empty rifle cartridge shell from his pocket. It was for a Mauser Gewehr 98, the German army rifle of the period. He put the empty shell on the ground where his firing position had been.

When the police discovered the shell they would presume they knew the make of the murder weapon. A German gun for a fictitious German killer. His own bullet would have disintegrated.

Now there was just one last element to the Chronos plan to be completed. An element Stanton found almost as distasteful as having been required to shoot an innocent man from a safe distance. This was to give the authorities someone to blame for the killing. Someone *German* so that the nation would look within itself for revenge and not abroad.

Stanton couldn't fault the logic. By 1914 Germany had the most developed and the most sophisticated left wing in the world. The pace and sophistication of Germany's economic revolution had led to a huge new class of educated men and women who were more than aware of their own exploitation. The Red Scare bogey-man was alive and well in pre-war Germany and hysterical reactionaries were ready to believe any slander against organized labour.

Stanton was about to give them a bigger stick to beat them with than they could have ever dreamt of. He didn't like doing it.

Blaming the Left for crimes they hadn't committed was an age-old establishment sport. But it had to be done.

Better a Germany fighting itself than fighting the rest of the world.

Stanton took one of the leaflets from his bag and placed it under the Mauser shell case. The leaflet was bright blood red in colour. It featured a stern and noble-looking working man who was bringing his mighty fist down on the head of a vicious little devil with the face of the Kaiser. The wording on the leaflet was very simple – *The Kaiser is dead! Workers rise up and take control!*

That was all, no detail. Nothing more specific.

'Let 'em sweat over it,' McCluskey had said. 'Let 'em *obsess* over it! Who killed Bill? The whole country will tie itself in knots.'

Having left his false evidence, Stanton put on his jacket ready to leave. He allowed himself one last glance down into Potsdamer Platz where, not surprisingly, absolute pandemonium had broken out. The crowd had surged forward and lines of soldiers, including the entire brass band, were struggling to keep them back while all the top-hatted gentlemen clustered together behind the podium where the ex-Emperor's body no doubt had landed.

Stanton knew that he was watching the epicentre of a storm. That moment when the pebble hits the pond. Already he could see many figures scurrying not towards the tragedy but away from it. Most of them would be police fanning out in an effort to find the perpetrator, but there would also be reporters, anxious to be the first to file the most astonishing and momentous story of the century. The undisputed ruler of the German Empire, virtual dictator of the most vibrant economy and fearsome military in Europe, had been murdered! Arguably the single most powerful man on earth was dead. Stories simply did not get any bigger.

So far the shock waves had scarcely reached the edge of Potsdamer Platz since they were still being propelled on foot. But let the first man reach a telephone or a telegraph office and the world would tremble at the astonishing news.

Stanton turned away. He had killed the Emperor less than ninety seconds before. The scene in the roof garden cafe would remain undisturbed for perhaps another two or three minutes. He wanted to be there when the news hit, not still out on the roof. He thought for a brief moment about checking on the guard he had shot. Possibly he was still alive and, if he was, there was an outside chance that the man could identify him later. Stanton decided to let it go. One cold-blooded murder was quite enough for one day. Besides, he needed to clear the scene of the crime quickly and distribute his leaflets.

Having sprinted back across the roof, Stanton paused for a moment outside the *Verboten* door to collect himself, then strode through, as ever looking confident, relaxed and in command. He doubted that anybody noticed him but if they did he was pretty sure the moment would not register. Why would it? The world was still the same as it had been for decades. A charmed, Edwardian world, ever steady and reassuringly unchanging.

That world would last about another minute.

Stanton exited from the roof garden by the same door he had entered it, walking down the flight of stairs to the fifth-floor furniture department. Then he strolled casually across the floor until he came to the top of the grand staircase which descended in gilded magnificence down five floors. Looking down, Stanton could see the top of the head of the female statue. It was also possible from where he was standing to imagine that one was squinting down inside her plaster blouse, a circumstance that had given a generation of schoolboys enormous comical pleasure. As Stanton passed the top banister he took from his jacket another sheaf of a hundred or so of the forged Socialist leaflets. Scarcely breaking his stride he balanced them on the top balustrade as he passed and then began to walk down the stairs.

He knew that they would not balance for long and, sure enough, before he had taken another five steps the pages came fluttering down the great stairwell of the atrium like large pieces of red confetti. Looking down as they fluttered past him Stanton could see that at the bottom of the fifth flight, down on the ground floor, clusters of people were gathering together and gesticulating; one woman had even swooned. Time seemed to slow down for a moment as Stanton watched the intense conversations begin to spread up the stairs as the leaflets descended to meet them.

People were grabbing at the red confetti now and as they did there were cries of anger and horror all around. Stanton kept walking down on to the ground floor where the shop was all of a sudden in complete uproar as everyone began to digest and protest the terrible news.

Stanton pushed his way through the excited throng, through the doors of the shop and out on to Leipziger Strasse.

Although it was a warm day there was a stiff breeze blowing east across the twin *Plätze* of Leipzig and Potsdam. Stanton turned west and as he did so he plunged his hand into his bag where the rest of his leaflets were hidden. In one confident movement he drew them out and dropped them to the pavement. Then he just kept walking, not looking back even once. He didn't need to. He knew that behind him the red leaflets would be gusting across the tram lines towards where the Kaiser's corpse no doubt still lay.

Stanton's mission was complete.

As the adrenalin rush of the previous hour began to subside, he had leisure to realize that he was finding breathing a little painful. Putting his hand to his chest he felt the rough quality of singed cloth and remembered for the first time since leaving the roof that he had been shot at twice. Glancing down he saw a black burn mark on his tweed jacket right in front of his heart. He knew there would be identical damage on the back of his jacket, again right in front of his heart. That guard had been a bloody good shot. It seemed German police training was as efficient as their army and their industry.

Stanton took off the jacket and folded it over his arm. Better to be out in shirt sleeves than displaying what might be recognized as bullet holes in your clothing.

Stanton probed gently at his chest and back as he walked, wincing when his fingers applied any pressure. He was badly bruised, there was no doubt about that, and would certainly be an ugly colour in the morning, but nothing was broken. So far his luck had held. If it changed now it didn't matter. He'd already saved the world.

32

STANTON TOOK A walk down Unter Den Linden and went for lunch in the Tiergarten. Bratwurst, mustard and a stein of beer. A typically German meal to celebrate the private knowledge that by what he had just done he had preserved a better Germany for the century to come. That Germany of contented, progressive people who were more fond of beer and sausage than conquest and murder. The Germany the previous twentieth century had corrupted.

The Tiergarten had been quiet and rather sedate when he had walked through it previously but now it was full and what would in another age be called 'buzzing'. The news of the Kaiser's death was crashing through the city like cannon fire, and as Stanton sat at his lunch it occurred to him that he was watching a city becoming collectively traumatized. All around him hundreds of identical conversations were occurring as the news was shared. Nannies with their charges, wide-eyed with shock, portly gentlemen waving their arms in horror, earnest students tight-lipped and grim. Each had been going about his or her business, strolling through the park, chatting to friends, pondering some private thought, only to overhear a comment or join a conversation and be suddenly transformed. Their faces turning in an instant to blank bewilderment and utter horror.

If it were possible for an entire city to go into shock, that was what was happening to Berlin.

Nobody in that city was ever going to forget what they were

doing when they heard the news that the Kaiser had been assassinated.

Stanton felt a little uncomfortable, almost like a voyeur spying on someone else's sorrows. That sensation brought to mind his own personal isolation and loneliness. He was still on the outside, still emotionally unconnected with the world in which he was living, in which he would always live now. Nonetheless that loneliness was tinged with elation. It came upon him in little waves. The world-historical task with which he had been entrusted was over and he had done his duty.

And he had done what a million British soldiers had dreamt of doing. He'd killed the Kaiser.

On that thought he decided to order another beer but discovered that he'd been lucky to get the first. On hearing the momentous news the owners had quickly concluded that serving beer and sausage wasn't an appropriate thing to do on such an afternoon. The waiters were at that moment closing the little entrance gate to their tea garden and telling the customers that they were shutting up indefinitely out of respect for the fallen Emperor.

Stanton decided to return to his apartment.

This wasn't his grief, his trauma. He might have caused it but he was not *of* it. His had been a clinical action, theirs was a guttural reaction. By dying the Kaiser had brought the whole city together far more completely than he had ever done in life. But Stanton wasn't part of it.

He had a bottle of raspberry-flavoured schnapps waiting in his room and some Liebfraumilch wine, keeping cool wrapped in a wet undershirt. He had laid these in in anticipation of not quite knowing what to do with himself after the event. So he decided to go home, get a little drunk and once more consider his future. A future that was finally his to consider.

On his way back to Mitte he noticed that it wasn't just the cafes in the Tiergarten that were closing their doors, the whole city was shutting down. Remembering that he had no food at all in his room he darted into a little grocer on a corner of the Alexanderplatz just before they closed their doors. He was lucky to get in, otherwise he would have had no supper and probably no breakfast either. He bought bread, cheese and ham, biscuits and some peaches, which would keep him going till the city opened up again. He knew the store, he'd shopped there before, and he recognized the young woman who was serving behind the till. On the previous day when he'd bought some summer fruits from her he had been rather charmed because she smiled so broadly and sang softly to herself while she measured out the strawberries. It had been a song about *Erdbeer* being sweet but not as sweet as love. Today, however, there were no smiles and no singing. The girl had been crying so hard she could barely count out his change.

'Our Kaiser is with God now,' she said, before adding, 'and may God curse whoever did this.'

She was cursing *him*. It was a strange feeling.

The grocer's girl wasn't the only one who was weeping and cursing. Leaders are always more popular in death and there were many on the streets unable to contain their emotions. Stanton saw one old woman beating her breast in despair. He'd never imagined anybody actually did that. He thought it was just some old-fashioned phrase from the days of melodrama, but this woman was actually pummelling at her chest in a kind of paroxysm of grief while another woman tried to comfort her. Those who weren't openly crying just looked drawn and grim as if they were forcing back tears. There wasn't a single person who was not obviously and deeply affected by what was clearly being seen as a national tragedy of previously undreamt of proportions. Stanton had expected as much, of course, but the intensity still took him by surprise.

He made his way back to his street and let himself into his building. The outer door opened into a little vestibule and stair-well where an old concierge sat. He was a taciturn man who had never said anything to Stanton beyond a brief *Morgen* or *Abend*. On this afternoon, however, the man felt moved to speak.

'Bastards,' he spat as Stanton greeted him. 'Those *swine*. Those vermin. Those *Untermensch*. We'll hang them all.'

'Who?' Stanton asked. 'Who will you hang?'

'The Socialists, of course,' he answered. 'And the Anarchists with them, those revolutionary scum.'

'Well, first the police have to catch them, don't they?' Stanton reminded the man.

'We know where they are,' the old concierge replied darkly. 'They can't hide.'

Stanton went up to his little room, laid out his food for later and opened his bottle of wine. He drank a glass straight down, toasting himself in the mirror above his wash bowl.

Now was the time to look again at the list he'd begun that morning. *Shackleton. Everest. Fly the Atlantic. Soldiering . . . Bernadette.*

Now at last he could move on.

But at that moment he found he couldn't even begin to move on. For some reason he felt no sense of completion whatsoever. He was as all at sea as he'd felt in those first moments when he had found himself apparently alone in the cellar in Istanbul, the taste of the half-naked Turkish girl's spearmint lip gloss still on his lips.

Drinking deep at his wine he tried to put this feeling of unease down to the fact that he had killed someone that day. That was a terrible thing to have to do, and any man who remained unmoved by such a thing should never be trusted with a gun. Stanton had killed before, of course, but not very often and he'd found that it never got any easier. But that was just the natural human horror at taking a life; he didn't *regret* it. Far from it, in fact. He was absolutely confident in his mind that he'd acted for the right reasons and done the right thing. If he had it to do again he would.

So why did he feel so unsettled?

Seeking comfort, he took a book from his bag. A book he had brought with him from the future and which also, because of him, would never now be written. It was the *Collected Poems of Wilfred Owen*. A favourite of Stanton's since he was a boy.

He'd read those poems many times since arriving in the past, because he could think of no better argument for his mission than those harrowing but infinitely moving chronicles of quiet heroism, appalling carnage and pointless sacrifice. Owen's heartfelt verse described more poignantly than any statistics ever could the nightmare that Stanton was preventing. It had given Stanton great strength to know that Owen would write different poems after his mission was complete. That instead of dying in a great and terrible war, Wilfred Owen would instead get his chance to live. And Brooke and Sassoon and millions of other brave young men whose lives were equally important, though their names had only ever been celebrated on neglected war memorials in town and village squares.

But that afternoon, with his wine and his schnapps and the great German warmonger dead, he found the poems didn't help. The troubled and uncomfortable feeling that had been growing in him since first he had emerged from the Wertheim store wasn't to do with him doubting the validity of his mission.

It was just that he felt – *uneasy*.

Things were getting noisier outside now. Stanton's window was open because of the warmth of the afternoon and it was beginning to sound as if the entire population of Berlin was spilling out on to the streets.

And if people were still weeping outside, then the sound of it was drowned out by other noises. Less peaceful ones. There were shouts and chanting and the occasional sound of breaking glass.

Also there were clanging bells, whistles and klaxons as the authorities spread their net hunting for a killer they would never find.

Sitting listening to it all in his apartment, the Liebfraumilch tasting bitter for all its sweetness, Stanton sensed madness in the air. He'd experienced something very similar before: in Kabul, when an American drone aircraft had gone out of control and crashed down on to a school, destroying it totally. The Afghan people had flooded on to the streets then just as they were doing in Berlin now. It had been a bad time to be an American, or indeed a Westerner of any kind. Stanton and his comrades had barricaded themselves into their compound and sat it out for days with their safety catches off.

It was Socialists whom the crowd was seeking this time but Stanton suspected that the hatred would be just as general and arbitrary. *Death to Socialists!* he could hear them chant through his open window. *Hang them all!*

That was the message: all of them. Not just the guilty ones, but all of them.

Leaning out of his window he saw people brandishing the early editions of the evening papers. He went downstairs and bought one himself. The grim, black-trimmed headline adhered to the elegantly verbose standards of the day. There was no KAISER DEAD, as would have been the case in Stanton's own age. Instead the headline ran: HIS IMPERIAL HIGHNESS IS ASSASSINATED IN BERLIN. *Socialist Conspiracy Is Suspected.*

Stanton felt a thrill at that. This was, after all, the first historic front page of a new and different twentieth century. He found himself thinking how one day the very headline he was looking at would be reproduced digitally in documentaries on the television in some other version of his own age.

But there was certainly going to be a price to pay. The mood in the street was getting angrier. Strangers were exchanging rumours that the police had uncovered a massive leftist conspiracy to over- throw the government. Stanton heard people speaking confidently about hundreds of 'Revolutionaries' and 'Anarchists' who had been poised to seize control.

Over and over again he heard the word 'revenge'.

33

RETURNING TO HIS room he drank a little more schnapps and read the first reports in the evening paper.

The police had proved every bit as efficient as he'd expected they would be and more. They had already discovered his firing position and the Mauser shell. Also there was a mention of a wounded man who'd been found nearby on the roof. The reporter presumed this person to have been a security guard. It seemed that the police were waiting to ascertain the extent of his injuries before trying to question him.

Stanton was glad he hadn't killed the guy, although he did wonder whether there was now a chance he could be identified. He decided that the risk of the guard having got a good enough look at him to give a description was pretty small. After all, as Stanton had spun around he'd been bringing up his gun in front of his face. All anyone could have seen with confidence was that he was tall and his hair was sandy blond. Plenty like that in the German capital. Besides which, the guard would probably die of his wounds anyway.

Despite the aching in his chest and back Stanton decided to take a walk. He drained his glass and went to the stairwell, then on an afterthought he returned to his room and took the Glock pistol from his damaged jacket and slipped it into his trouser pocket. It was an ugly night to be on the streets.

Stanton joined the milling throng which it seemed to him was gravitating towards the Brandenburg Gate. The gate had been erected by the Kaiser's father to commemorate Prussia's great victory over France and was therefore an obvious place to gather to remember a fallen German hero.

The mood outside was intensely emotional. Many wept as they walked, genuinely devastated by their collective loss. Others, however, had already transmuted their grief into fury and were shouting to the heavens for vengeance as they marched. Stanton was quite surprised at how quickly things were turning nasty. Of course he'd known that there'd be a massive public reaction and no doubt some random violence to go with it but he hadn't quite expected what seemed to be developing into a collective and self-perpetuating hysteria for instant retribution.

People were acting as if they'd lost a saint. A guiding star.

Of course it made sense. After all, he'd killed the Kaiser *before* the man had screwed up. The Emperor had died while he was still the leader of a country untainted by war and barbarism and whose principal features were a world-beating industrial economy, a global technological lead and a highly developed Social Democratic movement.

Watching the growing fury of the crowd Stanton was uncomfortably aware that for the German people in July 1914 their Kaiser represented nothing so much as progress, prosperity and peace. Yes, of all things – peace. The crowd didn't know what Stanton knew. As far as they were concerned, their King Emperor had been on the throne for twenty-six years and for all that time the nation had been at peace. And during that time Germany had grown into a premier world power with an industry to rival the United States, a navy that was threatening to one day equal Britain's and an army that had no rival at all.

Understandably those early-twentieth-century Berliners surging through the streets in angry despair saw the Kaiser as the most potent symbol of their growing power and prosperity and were fearful that with his death their good luck would end. Only Stanton among them knew that it was the Kaiser's *survival* that would have brought an end to their peaceful, comfortable world.

260

He wanted to shout it out: 'Hey, guys! It's OK! It's all good! The man was a warmonger.' He wanted to tell them that this apparent bastion of peace and stability had in fact led his country into suicidal conflict, and what was more had done it within *five weeks* of the current date. And that a mere four years after that, this man whom they were lamenting as the essential rock on which Germany's future depended would be skulking out of Berlin into shameful and ignominious exile in Holland.

But of course all that was history now, or more to the point it *wasn't* history. It never had been history and it never would be; it was just a strange dream in the mind of one single man on the planet. The new reality was that the mighty leader of the most successful ever period in German history was dead and his people were devastated.

And some of them were crazy angry.

Angry and getting dangerous.

Night had fallen and Stanton saw young men carrying clubs. Nobody carried a club unless they were looking for somebody to hit and these people really wanted to find somebody to hit. More sinister still were the gangs of students in their semi-military uniforms and caps, surging about in well-disciplined squads. They were carrying Imperial flags and the eagle banner and swearing that they would have vengeance or death.

But vengeance on whom?

Who should they hit with their clubs? Who should they march over with their banners? Who had done the deed? And who had put them up to it?

It was the Socialists that had done it. Nobody in Berlin was in any doubt about that. But which Socialists? And where were they? Where was their nest? Where were they hiding? The Chronos leaflet had been deliberately vague, leaving the mob with little to go on.

The later editions of evening papers changed all that. The journalists had had time to collect their thoughts and do some research and now began to name names. And while the newspapers couldn't actually name any *specific* conspirators, they could certainly name Socialists. And did so with great enthusiasm, in so doing pointing a finger of implied guilt.

'To the SPD Headquarters!' the cry went up. 'We'll flush the bastards out.'

And so the Brandenburg Gate was forgotten in favour of converging on the offices of the Social Democratic Party, a highly respectable parliamentary party which had attracted millions of votes at the last election, but a party which the newspapers were eager to remind their readers had until 1890 been known as the *Socialist* Workers Party.

Stanton hoped for their own sake that the leaders of the SPD were not at their constituency offices that night.

Or, more particularly, *one* leader. Because above the general din and shouts, Stanton noticed one name beginning to emerge as the principal figure of hate. One name whom the evening papers had taken particular care in advertising.

Rosa Luxemburg.

Bernadette's hero.

A famous Socialist who would one day set up the German Communist Party and die at the hands of a paramilitary death squad.

Or at least that had been Luxemburg's fate in the first loop of time.

Who could guess what her fate would be in the second?

But it didn't look good.

The very idea of Rosa Luxemburg seemed to infuriate the crowds. They hated her for a number of reasons. Because she was an uncompromising and highly vocal Socialist. Because she was a dirty foreigner, a Pollack no less, and only a naturalized German. Because she was a woman. And, most damning of all, because she was a Jew.

Stanton hadn't thought of that.

That the Jews would get the blame.

But why not? They got blamed for most things in Europe in

those days. And particularly for socialism. Ever since Karl Marx had first called on the workers of the world to unite, the Jews had been accused of being behind international socialism (while perversely also apparently being behind international capitalism). From time immemorial if there was any hating going on in Europe, the Jews copped it as a matter of course. It was therefore really no surprise that many in the crowd had already stopped blaming Luxemburg the Socialist for the death of their Emperor and had begun blaming Luxemburg the Jew.

Stanton *really* hadn't thought of that. He wondered if McCluskey and her fellow Chronations had done. Of if they'd cared.

The uneasy feeling Stanton had felt earlier had developed into a sick and leaden sensation in his stomach which, try as he might, he could not push away. He tried to argue with himself that this was just one night. That the crowds were shocked and upset. Certainly it looked as if things were going to be rougher than he'd hoped, but it would pass.

He allowed himself to be drawn along with the mob. And mob it was becoming, there could be no doubt about that. Stanton felt the weight of history on his shoulders. *New* history. History in the making.

He spotted a bonfire up ahead.

A bonfire in the street, not a big one, just a little brazier with red and yellow tongues licking hungrily at the air, but Stanton felt his stomach tighten further at the sight of it. Angry crowds making fires in the Berlin night. Flame-flickered shadows on the cobbles. Smoke in the air, drifting on the breeze towards the river Spree. He'd seen that before. Not personally but in countless documentaries and old news reels. Images that had been stamped on the collective memory of his twentieth century. Once recognized by hundreds of millions, now known only to him.

It was leaflets they were burning. He could see them, dancing orange hot in the night air. At first Stanton wondered if they were his own flyers, but that couldn't be. There had only been a few hundred of them, hours before and in another part of town. He caught one and pulled it down, black with soot and fringed with bright sparkle, but the smoky letters were still legible. It was a message from the Social Democrats. They'd guessed the way the rumour mill was working and had moved fast to declare their outrage and their loyalty to the Crown.

Fellow Berliners!

The leaflet read.

The murder of our beloved Prince is a crime against all Germans! We of the Social Democratic Party stand united with the nation in our condemnation of this heinous crime! Long live Kaiser Wilhelm the Third!

That final declaration of loyalty to the Kaiser's eldest son must have been hard for those sober-faced liberal parliamentarians to write. Young Willy was universally acknowledged to be a wastrel, a dilettante and a hopeless womanizer, his luxurious lifestyle being a particular irritation for those who, like the authors of the leaflet, yearned for social equality. Despite that, however, the SPD were anxious to tell the world that they stood behind the new Emperor. They must be pretty scared.

But the students on the street weren't interested. They didn't want to listen to mealy-mouthed Socialists offering weasel words of loyalty while in fear of their lives. They wanted vengeance and they weren't minded to let any little matter of their targets being innocent deprive them of it. So they burned the leaflets and surged onwards.

Soon the crowd with whom Stanton was moving came across a cloth-capped working man. He was distributing the leaflets the students had been burning. Stanton stood and watched as the unfortunate man was dragged from the pavement into the midst of the mob and beaten to the ground.

'It's your people who've done this,' the young men shouted as the boots went in. 'You Socialists and Jews.'

Stanton thought about intervening, even found his fingers closing round the gun in his pocket. But he did nothing. There was really nothing he could do. This madness would simply have to run its course.

By the time the crowd arrived at the Social Democrat head-quarters there were around three hundred of them, and there were at least as many again assembled outside the building already. The nervous Social Democrats had prepared for them by erecting a speaking platform beneath a hastily created banner that stated simply 'Loyalty to the German Crown'.

Stanton could see that they were terrified. Normally their banners demanded eight-hour working days, living wages and compensation for injury at work. Now they were anxious to assure the world they wanted nothing better than to be ruled by a drunken sex maniac.

There were various earnest-looking bearded men gathered on the platform, one of whom was attempting to speak. His gestures and body language appealed for calm but it would have been impossible for anybody even quite close to him to hear what he was saying above the boos and catcalls of the crowd. In front of the platform was a line of party supporters who had begun link-ing arms in an effort to protect their leaders. They were tough-looking men, working men with determined faces, but Stanton reckoned they'd be swept away in minutes if the crowd surged.

It occurred to him that he should actually be feeling satisfied at this sight. This was exactly what Chronos had planned, what he had been sent to achieve. A Germany turned against itself, no longer baying for foreign blood, but baying for its own. He could imagine the ruthless McCluskey standing at his shoulder, grinning at her own cleverness.

'You *see*! It's *people* who make history!' he could hear her chuckling. 'In this case, you, Hugh! The lone assassin who changed the world! One bullet and Germany heads down a completely different path. Can't see *this* lot having the time or inclination to invade Belgium any time soon. Too busy tearing each other's throats out.'

And Stanton *did* take satisfaction from the scene. There could be no doubt that in these early hours after his kill the Chronation plan was working like clockwork. Foreign wars were the last thing on any German's mind. They had scores to settle at home.

He had saved the British army. He'd saved all the young men of Europe and beyond. But for the time being at least it wasn't going to be pretty. Not in Berlin at any case.

'*Red Rosa! Red Rosa!*'

The crowd had begun an angry chant. They didn't want to listen to a bunch of anonymous identikit bearded leftie intellectuals. They wanted the star of the show, the bogeywoman, the revolutionary witch. The Polish whore. Rosa Luxemburg, revered by many, loathed by most. Still nominally a Social Democrat but notorious as a firebrand radical and passionate enemy of the Hohenzollern establishment.

She was who they wanted but Stanton didn't think they had a chance in hell of getting her. Rosa Luxemburg was a very bright woman and she'd have to be a suicidal lunatic to show her face to that crowd.

And then to Stanton's and indeed everyone's amazement that was exactly what she did. Emerging from the midst of the group which had gathered at the back of the platform. Limping forward on limbs damaged by illness at the age of five and resolutely taking centre stage.

She was a small woman, dressed soberly. Cream-coloured skirt, white blouse with black tie and a plain-looking hat which might have been some pastel colour but Stanton couldn't tell by the light of the street lamps. However, unlike the other people on the platform, she did not wear a black armband of mourning. Instead, she defiantly wore a red sash across her breast.

For a moment the crowd grew quiet, as astonished as Stanton

was to see her show herself when so many in the crowd had been baying for her blood. And in that moment of quiet she had a chance to make herself heard. There was no amplification, but she was used to public speaking and her voice was clear and audible at least to the front section of the crowd.

'My friends!' she shouted. 'I thank you all for joining us at this meeting and would beg your attention while I explain something to you. While it is true that I believed the late Emperor was a despot—'

She got no further.

Clearly the next sentence would have been a condemnation of that despot's murder but she didn't get a chance to say it. The crowd seemed almost to leap forward as one, like a beast hurling itself upon its prey. The thin line of party workers in front of the platform buckled instantly and the vanguard of students were on the platform before anyone had even a chance to run. The rioters then began at once to lay about themselves with their clubs, punching and smashing at the bewildered old men while loyal supporters tried to pull them to safety.

Bricks and stones were also being hurled at the building now and the sound of breaking glass filled the air. Stanton wondered where the police were. No doubt they felt they had better things to do that night than protect a bunch of Socialists from getting a hiding which, guilty or not, they richly deserved.

In the melee Stanton lost sight of Rosa Luxemburg and he hoped she'd got back inside the building. He admired her for her principles and also for her reckless bravery. He certainly didn't want to see her torn to bits by a savage mob. Besides, Bernadette thought she was one of the good guys. He really hoped she'd got away.

But then he saw her.

Captured. In the hands of he mob. Hoisted above their heads and being carried into the heart of the crowd. A tiny bundle. Helpless, like a mouse in the paws of a dozen cats.

And they were taking her towards a lamppost.

Surely they couldn't be planning to *lynch* her?

But they were. Not *planning*, of course. Just doing. The collective hysteria had become self-perpetuating. As was the way with mobs, they had their own momentum. Stanton knew that if he could have taken any of the individuals in that crowd aside and asked them quietly and calmly whether they really wanted to go through with what they were doing – to hang someone, without trial or evidence, to commit a cold-blooded murder in the street – most of those conservative young men would almost certainly have backed off. But together, sharing the madness and the joy of it, and of course the anonymity, they were beyond argument. Even if somebody had been able to find the voice to make one.

And their victim was such a perfect fit.

A Socialist had killed their Emperor and she was Berlin's most famous Socialist.

A woman. A foreigner. A revolutionary. And a Jew.

Who among the German *Junker* class really thought it mattered very much to hang a Jew? A hundred miles east they hung them for sport.

It was simply irresistible.

Stanton could hardly believe what he was watching. These ordered and contented streets he had been admiring earlier in the day, the electrified, tram-lined, motorized *Kaffee und Kuchen* delivery network that were the envy of the world, the arteries of the celebrated *Weldstadt*, the first global city, had become a jungle in a matter of hours.

The blood lust wasn't universal. There were some around Stanton who were looking about themselves in concern, shocked like him at the pace at which things were moving. But at the centre of the storm the mob had become a single many-headed monster. Stanton saw a rope thrown over the crossbar of the lamppost. An electric lamp, that bright symbol of an ordered and progressive nation, turned in an instant to a gibbet in the service of the basest and most primeval blood lust.

He caught a sight of the victim's face, flashing white then dark, white then dark as she twisted and turned beneath the harsh electric glow. Such a small face. Such a small woman. But a big one too. He'd read that when addressing a crowd she seemed to physically grow in stature, mesmerizing her listeners with a rich voice and biting wit. But all her famed intellect couldn't help her now. Stanton could see that her mouth was moving. Was she trying to argue with them? Trying to open their closed minds to the illogicality of their actions? More likely she was simply pleading for her life, which was an equally hopeless exercise.

There were so many hands on her now, pulling her, pushing her, *hoisting* her up towards the gallows. She had at most a minute of life left.

Stanton turned away. He didn't want to watch her die.

But then he heard a voice in his head. It was Bernadette. That sweet warm Irish brogue was at his inner ear. *She's a wonderful woman, you know. I can't think of anyone I admire so much. Very clever, very passionate, very brave and very important.*

That was what Bernadette had said to him on their night in Vienna. When her lips had been so close to his he had felt them brush against his skin as she spoke. And now in his mind she went on speaking: *What are you doing, Captain Stanton of the Special Air Service Regiment? Are you going to let this innocent and defenceless woman die? Is that what a British soldier does? Don't forget it's your fault they're lynching her! Do you have an ounce of honour in your whole damned body?*

She had a point.

And then Cassie was in his ear as well. Two women calling him to task.

He had her letter in his wallet – *I never minded being married to a soldier. Because I knew you believed in what you were risking your life for.*

That was the man she'd loved. A guy who did the right thing.

The girls were right. It was time to man up.

He turned again and began to push his way towards the centre of the mob. After all, what did he have to lose? His mission was done, history was unmade, his life was his own and his actions no more or less relevant than anyone else's. He was free to act as he chose and he chose to risk his life trying to prevent an innocent woman from being hanged in the street.

And if he joined her in her fate? It would be a good way to die. He didn't have much time.

Get a bloody move on! he heard Bernadette's voice in one ear.

Hurry, Hugh! Hurry! Cassie's voice urged him in the other. *They're going to kill her!*

He pushed and pulled and physically *chopped* a path through the people in his way, raining practised blows down on any who didn't move instantly in response to his barked command. He knew from experience that angry mobs, while dangerous, are also dull and stupid and a determined individual can do a great deal with them. People gave way to him instantly, no doubt thinking that he wished to be in at the kill, secretly pleased perhaps that others were doing the dirty work while they could enjoy the spectacle without taking any responsibility for it.

It took Stanton less than thirty seconds to get into the very heart of the disturbance and make his voice heard.

'Put her down and stand back!' he shouted in German. 'Every one of you! Leave the woman alone and stand back now!'

His voice was strong. Resonant. Authoritative. A voice that was used to giving commands and used to being obeyed. The wild-eyed young men with the struggling woman in their grip paused. Theirs was a group madness, an abdication of personal free will, a roller-coaster of hatred. Stanton's firm and focused intervention was like a stick shoved between the spokes of a spinning wheel.

He stepped forward again, forcing his way to the lamppost where Rosa Luxemburg was being held while her gallows was prepared.

He put a foot on the wider part at the base of the post and with one hand pulled himself up, thus gaining a little height.

'This woman is a member of a legal political party,' he shouted. 'There is no evidence whatsoever to connect her with the assassination of the Emperor and if anyone has any they should take it to a court of law!'

He almost had them on that. The word 'law' was like a blow. This was a generation of students whose professors could have them beaten for minor misdemeanours. Brought up within the Prussian military social culture, discipline and obedience were a religion to them. The ring of fury that was surrounding him and Luxemburg seemed to fall back a half pace or so, reacting instinctively to the presence of a natural leader.

Unfortunately there was one among the students who was also a leader of sorts and he wasn't in a mood to surrender.

A young man stepped forward and looked up at Stanton, his face illuminated in the lamplight from above. Cold, pale eyes beneath the peak of his little student cap. A pink schlager duelling scar on each cheek. This was a son of the aristocracy, a Prussian *Junker* to the toes of his jackboots. He, too, was used to being obeyed.

'And who the hell are you?' the student enquired imperiously.

Stanton stepped down from the post to reply. He still towered over the young student.

'I'm the man who's stopping you making a very serious mistake, *sonny*,' Stanton replied, bringing his face to within an inch of his adversary's.

It was a bold move and it didn't work. It would have done with a similar child of privilege in 2025, some arrogant, lazy-voiced posh boy being faced down for pissing in the street after an Oxbridge Ball. But the young man facing Stanton was of an aristocratic mind-set forged in the nineteenth century. He gave way only to others of his kind.

'She's a dirty Polish Socialist whore,' the young man shouted right back into Stanton's face. 'She killed the Kaiser and we intend to deal with her. If you attempt to stop us we'll deal with you too.'

Now there were two leaders and the mob preferred their own. Stanton sensed it about to leap forward once more. He had a split second in which to act. He reached forward, grabbed the leading student by the neck and in a practised and fluid movement threw him into a head lock. 'This man is under arrest for threatening an officer of the Crown,' he shouted. 'Anyone who comes to his aid will be arrested also.'

It really was a desperate shot. He had no uniform and his German was spoken in an accent that marked him as a foreigner. They had no reason to believe that he was a police officer other than the fact that he had aggressively claimed to be one.

He sensed the mood continuing to swing against him.

Stanton decided to produce his gun.

He hadn't wanted to. Experience had taught him that pulling a gun in a crowd was a very dangerous thing to do. It took everything to a whole new level. There would certainly be others in the crowd who had concealed weapons and they would very likely pull theirs too, leaving only the options of retreat or a firefight. Stanton believed that you should never produce a gun unless you were prepared to use it and he really didn't want to use his. Who could guess where gunfire would take an already appallingly volatile situation?

But it had to be done.

He pushed the *Junker* student to his knees and stepped in front of Luxemburg, holding his pistol high above his head.

'All of you, this is your last warning. Stand back in the name of the Emperor! If you continue to threaten either myself or this lady I shall shoot.'

If the surrounding students thought the little snub-nosed Glock was a rather strange-looking weapon, they didn't show it. They knew a gun when they saw it and the fact that Stanton had produced it convinced them he had the authority to do so.

Collectively they took a step back, leaving their leader isolated on his knees. The madness had not gripped them so totally that they were oblivious to the rule of law or the threat of being shot. Stanton didn't hesitate. Leaving the student he had 'arrested' on the ground, he took Luxemburg under his arm and pushed his way back to the platform.

'I must address the crowd,' she said. 'I must explain—'

'No more speeches,' he said. 'Get inside.'

While the various deputies gathered around their comrade and ushered her inside the building, Stanton jumped up on to the platform to address the crowd himself.

'Go home!' he shouted. 'This is no way to mourn the Emperor. Go home!'

The crowd probably would have dispersed anyway but the decision was made for them with the sound of clattering hooves on cobbles which heralded the tardy arrival of the police.

Stanton, having no wish to be arrested for impersonating an officer, stepped off the platform and, with no other exit options available to him, followed the Socialist deputies into the SPD building.

34

IMMEDIATELY INSIDE THE building was a large reception area hung with trade union banners featuring trades long forgotten in Stanton's century: wheel-tappers, lamp-lighters, panel-beaters, leather-tanners, boiler-makers, glass-blowers, riveters and wood-turners. On another occasion, Stanton would have liked to look at those beautiful murals, those heroic frescoes, embroidered in an age when worker solidarity had been a noble and inspiring crusade.

This particular evening, however, was rather too fraught for sightseeing.

In the middle of the room stood the group of bearded men who had been on the platform. They were fussing over Rosa Luxemburg, who appeared to be a great deal calmer than they were.

One of the men noticed Stanton and stepped forward to introduce himself. He was handsome if a bit frayed at the edges, with a high forehead, a thick shock of wiry black hair and a moustache that was badly in need of a trim. The eyes that shone behind his wire *pince-nez* were forceful but they were not unkind.

'Good evening, officer,' he said. 'My name is Karl Liebknecht.'

Stanton knew the name. It was one that was almost as familiar as Luxemburg's to any student of modern history. In the century now lost this man would be the only member of the entire Reichstag to vote against Germany going to war. And a few years later he would die alongside Rosa Luxemburg, beaten to death in a Berlin street.

'Hugh Stanton,' Stanton replied, 'and I'm afraid I'm not an officer. That was a ruse.'

'A ruse? How very surprising,' Liebknecht said. 'Although perhaps not entirely so. If you *had* been a policeman it would have been the first time they've ever done us a favour. I don't think you're even German.'

'No, I'm British. On holiday. Just thought I'd . . . well, lend a hand.'

'I must say that really is most extraordinary. You have done a very great and noble thing, sir.'

There was a chorus of agreement at this, half a dozen grey and heavily bearded heads nodding their approval.

'And how like an English gentleman,' a female voice interjected. 'You came to the aid of a damsel in distress.' Rosa Luxemburg came forward and took his hands. 'I rather think I owe you my life.'

She was even smaller than he'd thought; the top of her head came barely up to his ribs. But for all her diminutive size there was no doubt she had stature. Her face was so strong, with deep dark eyes and a long thin nose, the bridge perfectly straight, good skin and fullish lips. She was in her early forties and there were strands of grey in her hair but she still seemed youthful. For some reason Stanton found he liked her instantly.

'Just doing my duty, uhm, ma'am,' Stanton heard himself replying. He didn't know why he said it, although he supposed he had to say something.

'Your duty? Is it your duty to rescue Socialists? We could do with a few more of you about.'

'Well, you know. I think it's everybody's duty to come to the aid of people in trouble . . . besides, I was happy to do it because' – for some reason Stanton felt obliged to offer further explanation – 'I have a friend who admires you.'

'Really? Do I know him?'

'It's a she, an Irish Suffragette, and no, you don't know her, she just thinks you're important, that's all.'

'Well, when you see her please thank her for sending you to me. Will you take something? Tea, perhaps, as you're English.'

'Or we have whisky,' Liebknecht interjected eagerly. 'I could certainly do with one.'

'You could always do with a whisky,' Luxemburg replied with a smile. Stanton thought they seemed like quite a jolly bunch, despite the ordeal they'd just gone through. Interesting. If he ever imagined International Socialists at all, he probably thought of them as pretty grim. Maybe they went sour when they got into power; that seemed to be the way things usually went.

Stanton accepted a small whisky. He was a student of history, after all, and this was a pretty fascinating encounter: sipping Scotch right at the epicentre of radical politics at what was fast becoming its greatest crisis. It occurred to him that he might just be sharing drinks with the future rulers of Germany. Not a bad story to tell Bernadette!

He had definitely decided he would see Bernadette again.

The drinks were served in a small committee room. There were no servants. Liebknecht poured with enthusiasm and proposed a toast to 'the man who saved our Rosa'.

There was an enthusiastic 'Prost' and Stanton's back was slapped many times. Luxemburg herself, however, shook her head sadly.

'I'm grateful to you, Mr Stanton, of course,' she said, 'but I fear you may have merely provided me with a stay of execution. You won't be there the next time.'

'You think the mob will return?' Stanton asked.

'They may not be back tonight,' she said quietly, 'but I can assure you that they will return.'

'Well, yes, I admit it's probably going to be rough for a while and you lot will certainly need to watch your backs but surely it'll calm down in the end, won't it? I have a lot of respect for the German authorities. I'm sure they'll make sure order is restored.'

Luxemburg smiled at Stanton but it was a smile edged with fear and sadness.

'They don't *want* order restored, Mr Stanton,' Luxemburg replied quietly. 'They *did* this.'

Stanton was completely taken aback.

'What? Organized a mob to attack you?' he asked. 'I really don't think so. I was in among them and—'

'They didn't need to organize the mob,' she said. 'The mob organized itself after they killed the Kaiser.'

Stanton glanced at the circle of grim faces around him, some nodding in agreement, others with eyes cast down. He was astonished.

'You can't be serious?' he asked.

He was incredulous. He'd thought that crazy conspiracies were a symptom of the internet age, an age when any paranoid lunacy could gain credibility simply through instant mass distribution. He had plenty of experience of deeply serious-looking idiots assuring him that princesses had been murdered by their ex-husbands to stop them marrying Muslims, and presidents had been murdered by their own Secret Services. But he wasn't expecting that kind of deluded paranoia from Rosa Luxemburg, one of the most celebrated and sophisticated intellects of the century.

'Oh, come on,' he said, 'are you seriously suggesting that the German establishment *murdered* its own emperor? In order to get you lot? Come *on*. With respect, I don't think you're quite that important.'

'Don't you?' Luxemburg asked. 'I think perhaps they do. But it's of no matter, what will be will be. One thing I can tell you, sir, is that His Imperial Majesty was *not* killed by a Socialist. We have been organizing in this city for thirty years. We *know* our people.'

'Yes, but you don't know every lunatic, do you? It was probably a lone gunman . . . a mad man who *imagines* himself a Socialist.'

'With access to a printing press? Excuse me, but creating a leaflet of high quality which announces the death of the Emperor and calls for revolution is not something that one can have printed legitimately.' She produced from her pocket one of Stanton's own leaflets. 'Whoever created this had access to a secret press, not an item that lone mad men tend to have cluttering up their garret rooms. Printing presses are large and noisy things, Mr Stanton.'

Not the one that had created that leaflet, Stanton thought, while conceding to himself that Miss Luxemburg was not in a position to factor desktop laser printers into her equations.

'Look,' Luxemburg went on, 'I know it seems an incredible and rather appalling thought, but the only two groups who could possibly print something like this in secret are the revolutionaries, which is us, and the establishment. We know that none of our presses were used, so whose was?'

'Well, it might have been done abroad . . . or anything,' Stanton tried to protest.

'Really? Why would any foreign group of Socialists *possibly* want to do this? To kill the Kaiser virtually anonymously, and to leave a message that could only create a massive and brutal back-lash *against* Socialists. Why? The people who killed the Kaiser were sophisticated enough to produce this high quality leaflet and skilled enough to carry out a single-shot assassination at long range in a crowded city. And yet they left a message so utterly purposeless and vague that it could only have been designed to stir up trouble.'

'Yes, but . . . killing their own king?'

'Like you I find the cynical brutality of it quite incredible. I have lived all my life aghast at the complete moral vacuum that exists within the so-called Christian ruling class, and I *never* would have credited them with this. And yet I just can't think of a more likely explanation.'

Stanton didn't know what to say. Because she was right. In fact, what she was describing was exactly what *had* happened. A sophisticated group operating from within the elite establishment had killed the Kaiser and cynically framed the Left. The fact that the group had been formed in Cambridge in 2024 and not on the Wilhelmstrasse in 1914 was something Rosa Luxemburg could not possibly imagine. Apart from that, she was spot on.

'Clearly you can see my point,' she went on. 'It seems we must accept that some part of the military establishment has declared war on us, and that they are ruthless enough to sacrifice their own king to the cause. The times ahead are going to be truly terrible. There will be a repression which will be medieval in its brutality. The net will be thrown wide and all but the most ultra-conservative leaders and most obsequious and subservient peasantry will be considered fair game. The likes of us must go underground immediately or face arrest and disappearance. As I said, Mr Stanton, this is a war and there can be no doubt that we will lose all the early battles. But he who sows the wind may yet reap the whirlwind. They have raised the stakes. We must raise them too and fight fire with fire. Who can tell what the future may bring?'

Stanton looked around the group. The smiles had disappeared. They were all grim-faced and in deadly earnest. They were anticipating nothing less than civil war, followed by revolution if they had their way.

'And so, Mr Stanton,' Luxemburg went on, 'I suggest that perhaps it's time you left us to our troubles. I don't think you can defend us from the entire German state.'

35

T HE STREET OUTSIDE was almost empty. All that was left were a
few SPD volunteers guarding the doors of the building.

Stanton set off to walk back to his rented apartment. After his
conversation with Luxemburg and Liebknecht he was feeling
more uneasy than ever. He wanted a cigarette. Whisky always did
that to him. Scotch and a fag just went together so damn well.
Perhaps he could have one now?

Did he *really* have to keep his promise to Cassie? After all, he'd
never actually had the chance to make that promise. And even if
he had, there really was no chance of her catching him out.

Cassie and cigarettes led his mind on to Bernadette: the name at
the bottom of the list he'd made about his future. He decided that
very soon he'd go to Ireland. She wouldn't be hard to find. The
whole country was owned by a handful of families. He'd track
down the Burdettes of County Wicklow in an hour. Perhaps he'd
become a gentleman farmer in the lush pastures of the Emerald
Isle. He could certainly afford a decent spread.

For a moment he pictured himself with her, together in a big old
country house, dogs, horses, cows, corn . . . children?

He felt a pang in his heart. What was he thinking? He could
never replace Tessa and Bill. Besides which, he'd only known the
woman a night.

Perhaps it was the whisky that made him careless. Or the fact
that he'd recently faced down an angry mob and the adrenalin
was still pumping in his veins. Or else that there were two women

281

competing for space in his head. But for whatever reason, Stanton's usually finely tuned survival instincts were a little dulled and he did not recognize he was in danger almost until the threat was upon him.

A couple of footsteps, a shout and he was pinned.

A smell of schnapps and beer and cigars in his nose.

Angry voices in his ear.

Sneering, youthful faces all around. Precious, neatly clipped little moustaches above snarling lips. Peaked caps on shaven heads.

There were four of them that he was aware of. Two had held him by the arms and slammed him against a wall, while the other couple had already started laying in with their fists.

Shit. He was being beaten up.

Stanton was alert enough now. Sufficiently on his mettle even to have managed to tense his abs before the first punch went in. He was gratified to hear one of his assailants cry in pain as the man's fist made violent contact with a stomach sculpted in a twenty-first-century gym regime and rigorously maintained during his recent time in Scotland. Nobody, not even the very fit, worked out in 1914 in the way people were to work out a hundred years later – nobody had the time.

You couldn't tense your face, though, and now a fist smashed into his, seriously rattling his jaw. They were pummelling thick and fast and if he didn't gain release from the prone position they had him in he could easily and quickly be beaten to death.

They had his arms held tight, young strong hands gripping him fiercely. Release from that was not an option, so his best hope was his feet. Using the grip in which he was held as a convenient support, he kicked up his legs from his waist and then, pushing outwards from his shoulders, extended his body fully in mid-air, launching both feet firmly into the face of one of his attackers, breaking the man's nose and knocking him backwards to the ground. Then he let his feet drop back to the pavement but only in order to bounce off the ground and pop up again, extending himself fully from the shoulders once more and kicking out. The trick didn't work quite as well the second time because the other man dodged the kick, but Stanton was able to twist his body in mid-air and lock his legs around the man's neck instead. At this point he could feel the grip that held his arms loosening. He was in danger of being dropped on his head. However, he was able in time to grab on to the arms that were holding him and with another almighty twist of his body bring the four of them down on to the pavement together.

Stanton was the first on his feet.

'Come on, you bastards,' he snarled in English. 'Let's see how well you do when you're not attacking from behind.'

All four of the attackers got to their feet, although the one with the broken nose clearly had no intention of taking any further part in the battle. Stanton, on the other hand, was fired up. He hadn't had a proper fight in a long time and he was confident he could dispense with the three remaining assailants now that they no longer had the advantage of surprise.

Two of them came at him at once with the third hanging back, watching for a chance. Stanton floored the first two with single blows. It was that simple. Chop. Crunch. The young attackers had come along expecting a street brawl, an easy gang-beating of a helplessly outnumbered victim, and instead had encountered a highly focused expert in unarmed combat.

The young men seemed to be getting the message. They staggered back to their feet but showed no inclination to come at Stanton again.

'Run home, boys,' he said in German, 'because I warn you, if you try to jump me again, I'll break your necks.'

He turned to walk away but found himself confronted by a fifth man, the *Junker* student whom he'd faced off earlier. Clearly the man had found his shaming at Stanton's hands too much to bear and, having watched his tormentor disappear into the SPD head-quarters, had assembled his gang and hung around waiting for a chance to get his own back.

Now the young student was at a loss. His expected punishment beating had turned into a rout. Revenge had not been served.

'Go home, boy,' Stanton repeated. '*Geh' nach Hause, Junge* – you've got lectures in the morning.'

Maybe it was that that did it. The patronizing tone. The young man's face contorted with hatred and furious spite.

He drew a pistol.

Stanton didn't stand a chance. The student shot him in the stomach.

He collapsed to his knees, holding his abdomen.

He heard a voice from behind him, one of the other young thugs.

'Helmut! You've shot a cop! Are you crazy?'

'He's not a cop! You saw him go in with the Polish whore. He's one of them.'

'That's right – he spoke English,' another voice said. 'What cop talks in English?'

'We should clear out anyway,' the first voice from behind said. 'You got him in the guts. He's done for. It's murder, Helmut. We have to run.'

Stanton's vision was blurring now but he could see the man in front hesitate. He wondered whether Helmut was thinking about shooting him again. But instead he just ran past. Stanton heard the clatter of their boots as they ran away up the street.

He was alone now. Looking down at the rapidly growing mess of crimson on his stomach. An abdominal, that was very bad. Only the heart, the spine or the head could be worse, although none so painful.

He tried to collect his thoughts, which were swimming now.

He wondered if he could get back to his apartment.

Not a chance – he'd be dead from loss of blood before he got halfway.

Could he maybe make it back to Rosa Luxemburg? She certainly owed him.

Maybe. But even that was a few hundred metres and he was

losing a lot of blood very quickly. Any movement was going to increase the speed of that loss by a considerable margin.

Best to sit. Apply pressure to the wound and hope for help.

He heard a whistle. The gunshot must have alerted the police. Or perhaps somebody had heard it and called them.

He remembered his own gun. A Glock made in 2023. What were the laws on side arms, he wondered? Did they have to be licensed in Berlin in 1914? Either way a gun in his pocket was going to lead to questions. Particularly one of unknown make and revolutionary design.

He had another two in the larger bag in his apartment.

If he ever saw it again. If he survived the night.

There was a drain in the gutter between his feet. He pulled the Glock from his pocket and dropped it into the gridded darkness.

Then he lost consciousness.

The police found him shortly thereafter and took him to the Berliner Buch teaching hospital, where he was operated on immediately. He'd been lucky. It turned out that the bullet had not gone through his stomach but was lodged in the abdominal cavity. The student's pistol had been a pretty measly affair, probably normally only used on rats and rabbits. No vital organs had been perforated. Nonetheless it was a serious wound and removing the bullet required delicate surgery. This was successful but Stanton had already lost a huge amount of blood and was weak. His immune system couldn't cope. Almost inevitably for a time before antibiotics, the wound became infected.

At some point or other during the confusion of his delirious dreams Stanton heard a doctor say, 'He's dying.'

36

STANTON'S CONDITION CONTINUED to deteriorate over the next two weeks, during which he lay in his hospital bed either unconscious or delirious and on the edge of death. There were brief moments of lucidity when he was aware of doctors and nurses nearby. He knew that he was dying and he knew that he was being drugged to help with the pain. He had an idea that this was clouding his brain. It seemed to him that there was something he needed to tell those doctors about. Something he wanted them to fetch for him but he could not remember what it was.

It was during one of these moments of tormented dream-like consciousness that he opened his eyes and saw Bernadette Burdette.

She was talking to him. Talking and talking and talking. He loved listening to her voice even if he knew he was only dreaming it.

She said that she was sure he could pull through . . .

Oi'm sure yez'll pull troo.

And she said she would stay with him and keep talking to him until he did.

He felt overwhelmed with gratitude. He felt that he was weeping. Weeping in his dreams. He wondered where Cassie was. Why wasn't she sitting beside his bed too? Why was he only dreaming of Bernadette?

Perhaps it was just because she was so much more *talkative*.

'The whole awful thing where the mob tried to lynch Rosa

Luxemburg made it into the British papers,' he dreamt he heard her saying, 'and of course they were particularly interested in the story that a mysterious, tall, blond and fiendishly dishy Englishman had come to her aid, who had then paid the price for his chivalry by being shot in the street. Well, Hugh darling, you can imagine that my ears pricked up at that. After all, wasn't I thinking about my *own* mysterious Englishman in Berlin and whether I'd ever see him again? And of course it was you! They'd found your papers on you so they had your name and they even published photos. The one from your papers, and a grainy flash photo of you standing on the podium outside SDP headquarters. I couldn't believe it! You *do* get about, don't you?'

The story went on. He couldn't decide whether he'd heard it all at once or in bits. He certainly felt he'd heard it often, it seemed terribly familiar.

'They had all that information and yet it seemed no record could be found of you either in Berlin or in Britain! Well, there wouldn't be, would there? Bearing in mind your, ahem, what shall I say? *Profession.* The papers were appealing for anyone who knew you to come forward. Of course I don't really *know* you . . . except, well, only in a rather *intimate* manner that couldn't possibly be of any help in identifying you. And anyway I thought that perhaps they *wouldn't* identify you because, let's face it, you are a' – she dipped her voice to a hoarse whisper – '*spy*. And so I felt the best thing to do was to come to you and see if I could help. Maybe even get you home. But I'm afraid you're pretty ill, Hugh, and, well . . . they don't really think you should be moved. Oh dear, I've told you this story twenty times and now I suppose I shall have to tell you again because I feel sure that talking might help . . .'

Stanton didn't mind. He loved hearing her voice and hoped that she would keep talking until he died, when he could go to Cassie and tell her about his Irish friend, although of course he wouldn't tell her everything . . . And yet there was that *thing* he needed to tell *someone* . . . something that needed fetching . . . but he couldn't remember.

Once more his consciousness reconnected with Bernadette's voice; she was holding his hand now, telling him about Rosa Luxemburg.

'She came again this morning to see how you were,' Bernadette was saying. 'So brave of her, the streets really aren't safe for her just now. She has a gang of bodyguards who never leave her side. Hugh, I can't believe you told her about me! I nearly died when she said that you'd mentioned an Irish Suffragette who admired her! That was so sweet that you remembered. And telling her you saved her because of *me*. She actually thanked *me* for sending you to her in her hour of greatest need. *Rosa Luxemburg!* You can't believe what that means to a girl like me, Hugh. Rosa is the most important woman in politics, even more than Mrs P. She's overcome so much and inspired us all . . .'

Bernadette was squeezing his hand, probably too hard considering his rapidly fading strength, but somehow the firm touch of her skin on his seemed to give him a moment's clarity. He opened his eyes and saw her mouth moving, that small mouth that had fascinated him so . . . and the strands of strawberry hair framing her bright green eyes.

For a second he was back on the train to Zagreb, the first time he saw her. Should he offer her a Manhattan?

No. Get back. Get back to the present. With a huge effort he struggled to return his mind to the hospital. Something was telling him this wasn't a hallucination, that she really was beside him. If only he could remember what he wanted to tell her. Remember that thing he needed. There was *something* he needed.

'Bernie,' he whispered. 'Bernie!'

'Hugh!' she gasped. 'You're here!'

'No! No. Dying,' he whispered, struggling to master his fevered thoughts, 'dying. Listen to me, Bernie. You have to do *exactly* what I say because I shan't be able to say it again because I'm going to die. Go to my apartment. The key is in my jacket. Find my bags . . . remember my bags?'

For a moment he lost his focus as a vision rose before his eyes of Bernadette, her face illuminated by the ghostly luminosity of a computer screen, levelling his pistol at him in a Vienna hotel room. He struggled to push away the memory and stay on message but now he couldn't recall what he'd been saying.

'Yes, yes, Hugh, your bags,' she said. 'Tell me what you want from your bag.'

Her voice brought him back. That was it. He remembered what he needed.

'The smaller one. Open it. Again, key in jacket,' he said, struggling to form the words. 'In the bag there's a pouch marked with a red cross. In that pouch are boxes of little plastic needles.'

'Plastic? Sorry, what?'

'Like glass . . . clear tubes with needles . . . for injections . . . get them. Stick one in my guts and push the plunger every twelve hours. Hide it, don't show them . . . just do it, Bernie, do it.'

There he'd done it. He'd remembered . . . he could sleep now.

But she was still squeezing his hand.

'Hugh! Hugh!'

He heard her voice speaking urgently. Was it over? Was she back?

'Have you done it?' he asked, drifting away.

'No! No! Hugh . . . where is your apartment? You didn't say. Where is your damned apartment?'

'Mitte . . .' he whispered. 'Mitte.'

Then he was gone. Deep down into an unconsciousness where Bernadette could not follow. He left her far behind him in the light. He was in the dark now.

In a tunnel. *A bloody tunnel*. Who would have thought the old cliché was true? A dark tunnel with light ahead . . . and, yes, inevitably there was someone standing in the light at the end of it.

It was Cassie, of course. Cassie and the children waiting for him.

In the light at the end of the tunnel.

Why was he surprised? It was *just* like those people on morning TV shows who talked about near-death experiences said it was.

Cassie was saying something to him. He wanted to shout back that he had given up smoking. But Cassie had an Irish accent. She was speaking with Bernadette's voice. Why would that be? And what was she saying?

Mitte.

Why was Cassie saying Mitte? In Bernadette's voice?

'Mitte!' Bernadette was saying. 'Mitte! Have you any idea how many blooming apartment rental businesses there are in Mitte?'

He opened his eyes, experiencing suddenly a blessed and un-familiar clarity. He blinked and blinked again to master his blurred vision and focused on the sweet face hovering nearby. The slightly freckled nose, the slightly uneven teeth. She was talking to him.

'I visited fourteen before I found yours and each one I had to flutter my eyelids and pretend to be a poor helpless Irish colleen before they'd check their list of tenants. Still I got there in the end and I've been sneaking one of those funny things into your tummy ever since. I've had to tell them we're engaged so they let me sit. And I pay, of course, money always talks . . .'

The sensation of not being delirious was very strange.

'How long?' he whispered.

She actually physically jumped. 'My God!' she said. 'Is that you, Hugh? Are you back in the land of the living?'

'How long, Bernie?'

'Since you sent me to get your marvellous medicine?' she replied. 'Four days.'

He drifted away again for a little while and this time when he opened his eyes he felt that they would stay open. Bernadette had saved his life.

It took another week for him to get strong enough to leave and during that time Bernadette stayed with him through all of each day, leaving only in the evening. Of course, she was more intrigued about him than ever.

'Hugh. What *was* that stuff in the funny little needles?' she whispered many times. 'The doctors are just stunned; they'd presumed the blood poisoning would kill you. I haven't told them anything but it was damned hard shoving the things into you when they weren't looking. I do think you owe me an explanation.'

'It's a new medicine, Bernie,' he replied, 'in its very early stages. They call it antibiotics,' was all he could tell her.

But they had plenty else to talk about.

The situation in Germany was deteriorating by the day and as Stanton sat up in bed sipping soup and gathering strength, Bernadette brought him up to date on a country gone crazy.

'They imposed martial law on the morning after the assassination,' she explained, 'plus a month of official mourning, so it was actually incredibly hard for me even to get into the country. The borders are pretty much closed now, certainly to Germans trying to get out, and there have been *thousands* of arrests, I mean it, *tens* of thousands, in fact. It's pretty terrible. They're basically using the excuse to destroy the political opposition. The army's in control and thinks it's got a mandate to deal with absolutely everybody it hates, which is pretty much everyone except themselves. The SPD has been banned and all the trade unions have been raided and shut down. Loads of their people are being sent away to God knows where, some sort of prison camps, it seems. There are troops and police absolutely everywhere, the whole city's like an armed fortress. Also, for some reason they keep linking the Jews in with it all. The newspapers are convinced that socialism is a particularly Jewish idea, which I don't follow at all, but anyway there have been lots of attacks.'

'Official attacks?' Stanton asked.

'No, not *actually* official, just the mob, but I can't say as the police have been overzealous in intervening. The poor old Jews keep swearing undying loyalty to the Crown and trying to look even more conservative than the army but it's not doing them any good. Honestly, I thought pogroms were a Russian problem. I didn't think they could happen in a civilized country. And speaking of Russia, the Tsar seems to have gone completely mad too. He's announced *three months* of mourning for his "beloved cousin Willy". He's closed the Duma, arrested most of the deputies, *executed* some of them, and the Cossacks are thundering about the country sabring every Jew and Democrat they can find. Between Tsar Nicholas and Kaiser Willy the Third, half of Europe seems to be under the control of paranoid murderous lunatics.'

'Rosa Luxemburg predicted this,' Stanton said.

'Well, she was right.'

'She believes the assassination was a reactionary plot to deal with the Left once and for all.'

'Well, of course it is! Everybody with any sense at all has worked that out. What else could it possibly be?' Bernadette said vehemently. 'Why would any real Socialist have done this? This has got to be a plot. I'm not saying it was *official* but the army's behind this for sure. Kaiser Bill just wasn't war-like enough for them. It's no coincidence they did him in while he was opening some tram lines. They gain so much from this and the Left loses everything.'

It really *was* a credible theory. A bloody sight more credible than the truth.

Stanton thought about Apis and the Black Hand. They were army officers but that hadn't stopped them killing their own monarch for the greater good of Serbia. And of course military coups had been a major feature of his own twentieth century. History had almost lost count of the times army generals in RayBan sunglasses had bumped off legitimate heads of state.

'It'll calm down in the end,' Stanton said.

'I hope so.'

They were talking on the day Stanton was scheduled to leave hospital. His wound would still require care while it healed fully but the infection and blood poisoning had gone completely, to the utter astonishment of the doctors. From time to time they would put their heads round the door and shake them in disbelief.

'It's been wonderful of you to do all this, Bernie,' Stanton said. 'You know I would have died if you hadn't come.'

'Yes, I can see that,' she said. 'And if I hadn't gone and got whatever it is you made me get.'

'I can't believe that you just dropped your life and came to find me . . . it's very sweet.'

'Well, I don't know what life you think it is I've dropped, Hugh. I'm the original bored and pointless rich girl. Like most of my class, highly educated for absolutely nothing.'

'But the struggle? Women's rights? That's what you were going back for. When we parted, in Vienna.'

'I'm afraid that's all gone a bit by the wayside at the moment. The Ulster Crisis has just taken over *everything* and most women have forgotten about sex solidarity in order to take sides on that. You've no idea how violent things have—'

'Bernie,' Stanton interrupted, reaching over and taking her hand, 'when I was delirious and you were talking to me, you said a lot of stuff about yourself and your feelings . . .'

Suddenly he was aware that he didn't want to talk about politics at all. The subject had never interested him very much. He wanted to talk about her.

'Oh that,' she said, reddening into one of her delightful blushes. 'I was just sort of trying to keep you going really. Prattling away. It was probably a good thing you were delirious, otherwise you might have died of boredom before your little needles could get you better!'

He squeezed her hand a little more firmly.

'I *think* I remember you telling me that you had been thinking about me and that you wanted to see me again. Was that just prattling?'

For a moment she looked away, staring nervously at the coverlet. Playing with it with her free hand. Then she looked Stanton in the eye.

'Yes, well, perhaps I did say that but it's all rubbish, isn't it? What with all that emotional baggage you lug around inside that mysterious big locked bag of yours. And the way you shot off like a startled cat first thing in the morning in Vienna.'

Stanton tried to say something but she went on.

'No, no, I didn't mind. That was our agreement and you stuck to it and I had a lovely breakfast on our balcony before walking out with my head held high. So don't worry, Mr Stanton, I haven't come here expecting you to fall in love with me in exchange for playing nursemaid. To be honest I was happy just to be out of Ireland. It isn't much fun at all at the moment, or Britain in general for that matter. I mean, it's not like here, we're not arresting whole classes of people, but there are still plenty of troops on the streets.'

Stanton had wanted to continue talking about her. To tell her that she was wrong and that he had been thinking about her every day since Vienna. But this news took him back completely.

'Troops? On the streets? In *Britain*?'

'Goodness, of course you don't know, do you? We've been so busy talking about Germany I'd forgotten to say what's been going on at home. It's all happened in the last few days. Ever since Mr Churchill was killed.'

For a moment Stanton actually choked on his soup.

'Churchill?' he spluttered. 'Killed? In 1914?'

'Of course in 1914, what other year would it be? It was the most terrible thing. He was addressing a public meeting about Home Rule. His usual line, saying that it was treason for the Tories to threaten to support the army in resisting the law by force. Which, of course, it damn well would be. And then somebody shot him dead.'

'Somebody?'

'An Ulsterman, a Unionist. The man didn't try to hide. He was proud of it. Said it was Mr Churchill who was the traitor for trying to break up the United Kingdom and that he was a patriot defending the King's realm. You can imagine that the country's in uproar and not all on Mr Churchill's side either. I can tell you a lot of people are calling the murderer a hero. Meanwhile Ireland's gone berserk. Bombs. Riots. Armed Republicans openly on the streets in Dublin.'

Stanton felt cold. He actually felt tears welling up in his eyes.

'Hugh? Are you all right? You're shaking. I mean, I know it's dreadful news but there are plenty of people calling for calm too . . .'

Stanton lay back on his pillow and stared at the ceiling.

'Bernie, you don't understand. Churchill was *essential*. He saved us—'

'Saved us? From what? He'd got the fleet up to speed certainly, but fat lot of good that'll do anyone since everyone's far too busy tearing apart their own country to fight anybody else's. Look, I liked him myself, he was brave over Ireland and by no means the worst man in government on Suffrage, but he was just a Cabinet minister. What do you mean, he saved us?'

'It's nothing,' Stanton replied, pulling himself together. 'I just think he might have been destined for even greater things, that's all. Who knows, it may be that great things won't be required.'

'I'm afraid I think they will be. Everyone in the whole country is at each other's throats. Carson's men have taken control in Belfast with their hundred thousand rifles and the army's *refusing* to go in and sort them out. This isn't the men, mind, it's the generals! I think the way the military is acting here in Germany is giving them ideas. Some regiments have actually issued statements saying they won't enforce Irish Home Rule whatever the law says. It seems to be only the King's personal intervention that's stopped them marching on Westminster. So you can imagine that nobody's bothering much about women's votes at present. Quite frankly, it's beginning to look like there might not even *be* a parliament for women to vote *for*. So you see I was really quite happy to give it all up for a bit and come here and play Florence Nightingale. There's more to life than politics, eh? I mean, one does have to *have* a life, after all. Well, I do . . . but perhaps you don't want one. Or do you?'

'Yes, Bernie,' he said, now taking her hand in both of his. 'I do want to have a life. I want it very much.'

The following day Stanton settled his bill, thanked the doctors, who were still shaking their heads in wonder, and left the hospital. With Bernadette's help, he made his way down the massive steps of the hospital and into a taxi.

On entering his apartment he had expected to find empty bottles and rotten bread and cheese on the table where he had left his supper on the night of the Kaiser's death. Instead the place had been cleaned; fresh food had been put on the shelf and fresh flowers on the table. The bed had been made with clean sheets and the window opened to air.

'Surprise!' Bernadette said. '*Slightly* against my principles to clean up after a man but since you still have a bullet hole in your stomach I thought I'd make an exception.'

Glancing across the room Stanton noticed bags in the corner that weren't his. Bags he'd last seen in a hotel room in Vienna.

Those bags must have been empty because all of Bernadette's clothes were on hangers in the cupboard.

'Bit presumptuous?' she asked.

'No, not at all,' he assured her.

'Well, you're obviously going to need a nurse for a bit while that wound heals properly so I thought it might as well be me. But, honestly, I can pack up and go again just as easily if you—'

He turned to her, took her in his arms and kissed her.

'Come to bed,' he breathed through the kisses that she was returning.

'What about your stomach? The wound?' she gasped.

'I'll risk it.'

'For heaven's sake, don't burst your stitches. You just lie flat on your back and let me make all the effort.'

37

For the following week Stanton remained in the little apartment speedily regaining his strength. Bernadette shopped for him and cooked for him and cared for him and every night they made love.

And it was love. Stanton knew that. He was in love with another woman. Something he'd never imagined was possible.

Bernadette sensed his guilt.

'You feel like you've betrayed your wife, don't you?' she said in the small hours of one morning, sitting up in bed smoking her post-coital cigarette.

'I'm sorry,' he replied. 'Is it so obvious?'

'Only when you go quiet like this.' The window was open as the summer had remained glorious and moonlight flooded the room, falling on her pale skin so that she seemed almost luminous. 'You are allowed to have sex, you know. I mean, I don't think that's wrong. She's been gone quite a long time.'

'It's not the sex,' he replied. 'I don't think Cassie would mind me having sex with another woman. Particularly such a nice person as you.'

'Well, then, what would she mind?'

'I'm wondering if she'd mind me falling in love with you?'

Bernadette drew deeply on her cigarette. He watched her breasts rise as her chest expanded.

'Oh right, I see,' she said. '*Are* you falling in love with me, then?'

'Actually I think I already have done.'

'Well, that's a very good thing,' she replied, 'because I'm in love with you too.' She reached out and put her arms around him. 'And I *don't* think Cassie would mind that either because she loved you and you loved her, and if there's a heaven then she *knows* that she's dead and you're alive and must live your span, and that nothing that happens to you now in any way diminishes what you once had with her and will always have had with her.'

Stanton knew that he was at the second major emotional junction of his life.

The first had been meeting and marrying Cassie. Some people speak of finding love as 'completing' them. He'd seen films where the phrase 'You complete me' was offered as some great statement of romance. He'd never seen love that way, as some kind of minor adjunct to his own personality. The love he'd felt for Cassie hadn't completed him, it had *created* him. Before that, as far as he was concerned, there hadn't been much *to* complete. He could scarcely remember himself or his life prior to Cassie. He knew that his mum had died when he was a teenager. That he'd been to schools and found some sort of family in the cadets and joined the army, which had become his life. But you can't *just* be a soldier, you have to be a person too, a rounded human being who feels they have a place in the world, and Stanton had only begun to feel like such a person when he met Cassie. Her love for him had brought him into being.

And now had come the second junction. It hadn't occurred on the morning he arrived in 1914, massive in its significance though that moment had been. Significant to the *world*, but not to him. He had been the same person who had struggled with Professor McCluskey and the Turkish party girl moments earlier in another century. He had brought his grief and his emptiness with him across time and Cassie's absence had continued to define him every bit as much as her presence had done. But not now. Now quite suddenly he felt he could let go.

'Can I have one of those cigarettes?' he said.

Bernadette had just lit one for herself and so took it from her lips and put it between his. As she leant forward her breasts presented themselves inches before his face and he wanted more than anything to kiss them. So he took but one puff on the cigarette before leaving it smoking in the ashtray and once more they made love.

And afterwards they drank the bottle of strawberry schnapps that Stanton had opened on the night of the Kaiser's death. And they finished it and made drunken love, which fortunately didn't open Stanton's wound because it was now almost completely healed. Then afterwards Bernadette found that she had some brandy in her bag and they began on that and got very drunk and smoked more cigarettes and laughed and teased each other.

And Stanton realized that he wanted more than anything on earth to tell her who he was.

What he was.

He'd been so very alone with his secret and he was *still* alone. More so in a way because how could he pretend he shared a love if the person he loved knew *nothing* about him? How could they be as one if their relationship was so fatally imbalanced by deceit?

She'd know in the end. Not his secret, of course; it would take a wizard to guess that. But that he *had* a secret. A huge secret and one he was keeping from her. She'd know – girls *always* knew – and it would poison whatever love they had.

Then Bernadette spoke and he knew he was right.

She had been thinking the same thing.

'But if we do love each other,' she said, 'and we *do* love each other – I know you love me by the *way* you love me – but if we're to keep *on* loving each other, then –' she paused to take a sip of her brandy – 'you'll have to tell me.'

'Tell you what?' Stanton asked, although he knew the answer.

'The same question I asked you in Vienna. Who are you, Hugh? How is it that you've left no trace? You're a big, handsome, muscular, capable man. An *exceptional* man. I'm pretty sure most men would like you and I'm damn *certain* most women would want you. And yet you've *left no trace at all*. Your name and description were in all the papers appealing for relatives or friends and nobody but me came forward and you met me only weeks ago.'

'Anyone can assume a false name,' Stanton said.

'But the description? And the photos? All published in England, as I'm quite sure they were in Australia. And yet *no one* came forward. Not one good old honest gold-miner from the Australian outback ran to the local cops and said, "He's our mate! Telegraph Berlin!" Nobody, Hugh. You very nearly died, you lay in hospital for two weeks at death's door all alone, and *nobody cared but me*. Your wife may be dead and I believe that from the bottom of my heart. I've seen the pain on your face. But did your parents die too? Did hers? Did your whole family? School pals? Friends at work? Army comrades? Members of the local cricket club? Landlords? Old girlfriends? The chap who sold you your morning paper? The next-door neighbour? Are they all dead? Is *everyone* you have ever met in your life dead? Am I truly the only person on earth who knows you, Hugh?'

What could he tell her? What possible explanation could he offer for the question she was asking, which was, after all, so very fair?

That he'd been brought up by wolves?

There *was* no explanation but the truth.

Perhaps it was the booze. He'd had more of it than her and his tolerance would have been lowered through his recent abstinence.

Maybe there were still traces in his system of the drugs he'd been given at the hospital, making him a little delirious.

Perhaps it was simply the exhilaration of finally being able to love again.

Or maybe he was just sick to death of being the only person who knew.

Whatever it was, at that moment Stanton felt he had no choice. If he tried to lie, she'd know in an instant, and in that same instant their love would be destroyed. If he wanted to keep Bernadette Burdette, he would have to give her an answer. And since any lie that could possibly cover the situation would sound every bit as fantastical as the truth, there seemed to him to be no debate.

'Yes, Bernie,' he said, 'you are truly the *only* person on earth who knows me. And that's because . . . I have come from the future.'

She was silent for a minute.

'Darling,' she said finally, and it was the first time she'd ever called him that, 'that was very *slightly* funny. But only *very* slightly. And anyway it wouldn't matter how funny it was because I wouldn't laugh because this isn't a joke. I mean it. You have to tell me who you are or else who am I to imagine it is that says he loves me?'

'Bernie, it's true. I come from the future. From a different version of history. I came to *change* history.'

And he told her. The whole story. Beginning with the Christmas Eve on which he'd joined the Companions. He told her about his own century, or at least a little, a world of revolutions and genocide, of telephones in people's pockets and bubble-gum and environmental destruction. He told her about the history he'd come to change. About the death of the Archduke and the catastrophe of global war that followed. He told her about Isaac Newton's legacy and he told her about the plan that had been laid to change history.

She tried to stop him. She tried to shut him up, threatening that she'd leave him that very night if he insisted on such lies. But he begged her to listen. He poured more brandy and he drank his down in one and poured another. He locked the door and held tight to the key. He told her he loved her and that she had to understand.

And he told her that it was he who had assassinated the Kaiser.

And seeing her eyes go wide in horror he told her about the Great War and the carnage it wrought and how it had been the Kaiser's war and that he had to be stopped and that millions of lives had been saved. He told her how he was horrified at the way things were turning out in Berlin but he still believed from the bottom of his heart that he had done the right thing.

'I'll show you,' he said. 'I'll show you with the technology of the future. I'll show you pictures of what I've prevented. I'll read you heart-breaking poems that will never now need to be written.'

But as he went to get the smaller of his bags in which he kept the laptop hidden in a book, she stopped him.

'No, Hugh,' she said. 'I've seen inside that bag, remember? Show me what's in the bigger bag. If you love me, show me that.'

And so Stanton took his keys and opened the larger of his two bags and inside were a number of strange-looking guns and packages. And also, broken into three parts, were the unmistakable components of a telescopically sighted sniper's rifle.

Bernadette stared at the gun for a long time in silence.

'I believe you, Hugh,' she whispered, holding out her arms. 'Thank you. Thank you for telling me everything. You told me because you love me and I listened because I love you. And now I know. There's two of us now, Hugh. Two people in the world who truly know you.'

And he went to her and lay down on the bed in her arms.

'So shall we be together?' he asked. 'Will you help me begin again? Share your life with me? Help me build one for myself?'

'Yes,' she whispered. 'We'll begin tomorrow.'

'I have one last thing I need to do,' he told her. 'One last duty to the Companions of Chronos. I've decided I have to go back. Back to where I emerged into this century and leave a letter. A letter that describes the history I prevented. The Great War that I stopped. Because it's just possible that a hundred and eleven years from now another traveller will go to that cellar in Istanbul about to embark on a mission to adjust the history of this century. Maybe somehow in this loop of time the cellar will still be locked in 2025 and they'll find my warning, a warning of how much worse things could be. A warning to think twice before it's too late. It's a long shot but then everything in my life is . . . not least meeting you.'

'Shhh,' she said, 'shh. That's enough now. You've told me everything. It's time to sleep.'

Her voice was so musical. He loved it so.

He closed his eyes.

An immense burden lifted from his shoulders. He laid his head against her naked breasts and listened to her heart beat. He was no longer alone.

And in her arms he slept.

And she held him close and he drifted in and out of sleep and when he woke she held him closer and kissed him and she put her cigarette between his lips and he smiled and once more he slept. At peace for the first time since the day of the hit-and-run in Primrose Hill that took away his life.

A deep and contented sleep.

When he woke next it was dawn and there was light coming through the open window.

He felt cold.

And he was alone.

Bernadette was not in the bed.

38

S HE WAS NOT in the room.

His head ached. He glanced at the bottle on the bedside table. It was empty. They'd drunk it all. No. He'd drunk it all. He looked across at Bernadette's side of the bed. The glass he'd poured her, the one he'd filled as he had begun to tell his story, was scarcely touched.

He was out of bed in an instant.

He'd told her. He'd told her everything.

And she'd said she believed it.

And she had believed part of it. A very small part.

The part about him having killed the Kaiser.

Of *course* she hadn't believed the rest. Was he crazy? *How* could she have believed the rest? Would *he* have done? He'd doubted it even with the entire establishment of Cambridge University presenting the case. He *never* would have believed the story if she had been on his side of the bed and he on hers. Nobody would. Nobody ever could.

He was dressing now. And as he did so his eye ranged round the room. What should he take? What was essential? Nothing that wasn't already in his bags. For a moment he thought he'd left his wallet on the table but it was Bernadette's purse. She favoured mannish accessories; it was part of her political identity.

He looked at his bags. They were where they had been the night before. She hadn't touched them. If only he'd shown her his computer. The photographs, the history archive. Would she have believed him even then?

That he was a *time traveller*?

No, she would have thought he was a magician, an illusionist, or else had drugged her or hypnotized her.

But she would not have believed that he was *from the future* and that an entire alternative twentieth century, in which she herself had lived and died, had already happened.

He looked out of the window. It was early dawn and the street below was empty. Above him was a terraced rooftop which ran the length of the street. There was a pretty stout drainpipe offering a possible means of ascent.

He put on a leather jerkin he'd bought on his first day in Berlin, loading its pockets with the papers for the other identities Chronos had supplied him with. One German and one Austrian. If he had to run, which he was absolutely convinced he must, Hugh Stanton would no longer be of any use to him.

Next he took the larger of his two bags and emptied out the sniper's rifle, which was the heaviest item in it. It had served his purpose, and since Bernadette had seen it there was no point in further concealment. He also pulled out all but a single change of clothes and any books and other clutter he'd collected in the present century. Then he took the smaller of the bags, which contained his computer, his spare pistol, his smart phone with its precious photo album and his money, and emptied it all into the big bag. If he was truly on the run then one bag was definitely better than two.

One last glance around.

Now he was ready.

It was time to go.

Not that he cared whether he survived for himself. He felt at that moment that he'd be perfectly happy to die in a hail of police bullets. Chronos had drained the life from him. First it had taken away the love of his life and now in a way it was depriving him of a second chance to love. For he had loved Bernadette. He still loved her.

But he had a plan and he knew he must see it through. He still wanted to warn the new future about the old future. To leave an account of history as it had been before he changed it. He wanted to return to Constantinople.

He picked up his bag and took a step towards the door.

Before he could reach it the handle turned.

By the time it had revolved sufficiently for the door to be opened, Stanton was pointing his pistol at it.

The door opened and Bernadette entered.

Stanton smelt hot, freshly baked bread. There was a loaf under her arm.

'Goodness,' Bernadette said. 'Why are you pointing a gun?'

'You were gone,' he said quietly, from behind the pistol. 'It isn't yet five. Why were you gone?'

'I couldn't sleep,' she said. 'How would you expect me too? Lying beside a man from another world. It wasn't enough that you made me fall in love with you, then you had to turn out to be a time traveller?'

She was smiling as she said it. That beautiful smile he'd first loved on the train from Zagreb. But the smile was fading.

'You're still pointing that gun, Hugh. Why are you pointing a gun at me? Why are you dressed with a bag in your hand . . . you're leaving?'

He lowered his gun. Relief or at least the tentative hope of relief springing within him.

'I . . . I woke up and you weren't there. I thought . . .'

A shadow of sadness passed across her face.

'You thought I hadn't believed you?'

'You were gone, I . . .'

'And were you going too, Hugh? If I'd spent five more minutes in the queue for hot bread, would I have returned to find you gone?' She glanced at the table and at the bed they'd shared. 'And not a note? Not a bloody note to say goodbye? Is that what was going to happen? You were just going to simply *disappear*? You said you loved me!'

'I do . . . I do love you. I love you so much, Bernie. You were gone. I panicked . . . I'm sorry.'

He put down his bag.

Her face softened a little.

'I didn't want to wake you, that was all. I was shifting about and smoking myself silly and you are still healing and need your sleep and so I thought I'd go and buy some fresh hot bread and have it ready for you when you woke up. I don't think there's anything in the world nicer than bread straight out of the oven, don't you agree? We can have it with coffee and then stroll out later for a lovely late breakfast, or, better still, early lunch.'

Stanton smiled. Relief flooding over him. She could still be his. She *was* still his.

And yet he'd so nearly lost her. If he'd been just a little quicker dressing, if she'd been a little slower buying bread, he would never have seen her again.

'Shall we have a slice now?' she said, with a coy smile, 'or shall we hop back into bed for a bit first? It'll be just as nice in half an hour.'

He felt a rush of exhilaration, like he'd been drugged. She still loved him. She still wanted to make love to him.

'I vote hop back into bed,' Stanton said.

She began to unbutton her coat.

'Silly boy,' she said, taking off her coat, 'thinking I'd left you when I only popped out to buy you hot bread.'

Perhaps it was the repeat of the word 'buy'.

Was it that which made him remember?

Her purse was still on the table. Only a minute or two earlier he'd almost mistaken it for his own.

She was unbuttoning her blouse now, revealing her slip. He could see by the way the silk hung that she had no stays beneath it. Her breasts were free and unencumbered. He wanted to step forward and feel them. He wanted to kiss her. He loved her. He wanted her.

But her purse was still on the table.

'What did you use to buy the bread, Bernie?'

'Hmm?' The blouse was off now and she was unbuckling the thin patent-leather belt at her waist. Her skirt was fashionably short, ending just between the calf and the ankle, exposing the high buttoned boots of which he knew she was proud.

'Your purse is on the table. You must have gone out without it. I was just wondering what you used to buy the bread?'

She stopped her undressing for a moment.

'I had some coins in my pocket. Are we going to make love, Hugh, or are we to discuss the shopping?'

And so he knew she was lying. It broke his heart.

'Remember, Bernie,' he said, 'on the train? That first time we met? When you said you'd sign for your half of the meal?'

Did she remember? He did, every word. He remembered everything about that first meeting; it was precious to him.

'What are you getting at, Hugh?' she replied.

'You said that I could cover the tip if I liked because you never carry coins in your pockets. "It stretches the fabric and ruins the line." Her mouth was a little open now, revealing those sweet, slightly uneven teeth he loved so much. 'The police gave you that loaf, didn't they? So you'd have an excuse for having left if I was awake when you got back?'

If there had been any doubt left at all in his mind, the tiny hesitation on her face dismissed it. She was a strong woman. But she was clearly now the bait in an entrapment, a tense position to be in to say the least. She'd been caught in a lie and she was weighing her options. He saw all that in the tiniest flick of her beautiful green eyes.

And she knew he knew. The bluff was over. She didn't even try to protest.

'You're sick, Hugh,' she said, and now those enchanting emerald eyes were filled with tears. 'Deluded. You need to be . . . you should be in a . . . Hugh, you have to understand. You're insane.'

And Stanton discovered that there were yet greater depths of loneliness to sink to. He was sinking now.

'I'm not insane, Bernie, but I can see that you could never truly know that. What I've asked you to accept is too much to believe. I get that.'

I get that. Another phrase from another age. She used to find them so charming. Enlightening. Now all he saw in that lovely freckled face was fear. She was terrified of him.

'Hugh. You *killed the Emperor of Germany*. And you blamed innocent people and now they're being arrested in their *thousands*. You're a maniac. An evil maniac. A *homicidal* maniac. I loved you. I really loved you but you are sick and have to be put away.'

'Let me show you, Bernie,' he begged her. 'Let me show you the—'

'I don't want to look inside your magic photographic box! I don't care what tricks you have! I saw your little needles bring you back to life. I know that there's some sorcery about you. But you're also a murderer and I believe you tried to kill the Archduke too and . . .'

She dropped the bread and buried her face in her hands and wept.

He stepped forward. He tried to hold her but she recoiled as if his hands were made of red hot metal.

'Don't you touch me! Don't touch me, Hugh! I told you before. There's no love where there's lies and you're a liar. I don't know. Maybe you're not even mad at all, maybe this is some terrible British plot against Germany. Nothing would surprise me. All I know is that I hate you.'

He gave it up. There'd be time to deal with this new agony later, to place it alongside all the others.

What was he doing anyway? Pleading with her. Trying to hold her. The game was already up. She'd reported him to the police. The whole Berlin military complex would be electrified that the assassin was at last in their grasp. It was time to move on.

Pointing his gun at her once more he tried to compute his plan and his chances.

They hadn't come yet. They hadn't rushed straight back with Bernadette and smashed their way into the room, dragged him from the bed and pinned him to the floor with their boots. Instead they'd sent Bernadette back with bread and smiles and un-buttoned blouses to keep him where he was. Clearly they knew him to be a resourceful killer, heavily armed and desperate. Stanton deduced that they wanted him alive.

So what would they do? Take it calmly. Assemble a snatch team. Bide their time and grab him when he left the building.

We can stroll out later for a lovely late breakfast . . . or, better still, early lunch.

That was the plan. Take it at a leisurely pace. Clear the street. Get the arrest team in place. Make sure all the surrounding roads were blocked in case the first snatch failed.

Which meant that if he was careful, he might still have time to slip away.

To get to Constantinople and leave his warning.

Before finally jumping in the Bosphorus.

He went to the window and took a discreet glance out. Sure enough the street was no longer empty. He could see three male figures dotted along it. All in civvies: a bowler hat, a slouchy homburg and a boater. One with a newspaper, another a ciggie, the other just leaning. To an experienced observer like himself, they couldn't have been more obviously on stakeout if they'd set up a Gatling gun and pointed it at his front door.

'They know you're here, Hugh,' Bernadette said, sniffing back her tears. 'Please give up. I don't want to have to watch them shoot you.'

Stanton took a final glance. They were all watching the front door. None of them were looking up at his window. It was a large building, part of a long terrace of houses. There were a lot of windows. They probably didn't even know exactly which one was his.

He calculated that he had a decent chance of getting to the roof without being spotted. Then he sensed movement behind him.

313

Spinning round he was just in time to catch the raised arm bringing the cast-iron fire poker down towards his head.

Never underestimate the anger of a woman who's fallen out of love. Particularly an Irish redhead.

'Jesus,' he gasped, using Bernadette's own weight to turn her and putting her into a neck lock. 'You really are a wonderful woman, Bernie. God, I wish you could have believed me.'

'You're a murderer!' she shouted. 'A murdering lunatic—'

He clamped his hand over her mouth. They were five floors up but the window was half open and the last thing he needed was the police below being alerted by screams that their cover was blown.

'Ahh!' Now it was his turn to make a noise as he felt her teeth sink into his flesh. That same pinched little upper jaw with the ever so slightly over-sized front teeth wasn't quite so cute when the teeth were drawing blood.

He reached his other hand over the top of her head and, laying his palm on her forehead, stuck his fingers in her nostrils and pulled backwards. Her hair was in his face. He could smell the same scent on those crimson blonde strands that he'd smelt earlier when they made love.

Her jaw released him as her head went back but she kicked backwards at his shin with the heel of her high-buttoned boots and was able to twist her way out of his grip. He'd only been applying it at half strength. He was a big man and she was a slim woman, ninety kilos against less than fifty. He hadn't wanted to hurt her and now he was paying for his weakness with a bleeding hand and throbbing shin. She was facing him once more and he could see by the way she was drawing breath that she was just a half second away from screaming.

He did the only thing he could think to do. He punched her. An expert swing left to the temple that knocked her cold. It was the first time in his entire life he'd ever hit a woman. Let alone a woman he was in love with. He felt completely sick.

There were some scraps of paper on the table and a stub of

pencil. Bernie had used them to make little shopping lists during their week-long idyll. There was one there now.

Coffee. Rolls. Cheese. Fruit. Wine. Chocolate!!

Stanton swallowed hard. He'd been so happy.

He turned the note over and wrote: *I'm not the man you think I am. I'm the man I said I was. And as long as I live I will never forgive myself for striking you. I love you. Goodbye.*

It was pointless, he knew, and stupid. The last time he'd said sorry had been just before he shot the flower girl and that had nearly done for him. Unnecessary details make a man more traceable. But they had his handwriting from the forms he'd signed at the hospital anyway.

Next he stuffed Bernadette's loaf of warm bread into his bag. He'd been on the run before in hostile country and knew that it was best to grab food where you found it. Then he returned to the window.

The three stooges were still at their posts. A fourth had joined them. A senior figure for sure. Stanton watched as the new man, another bowler hat, went from the boater to the first bowler. He glanced up the road towards the U-Bahn station at the top. A uniformed policeman was standing with two workmen. He was pointing at one side of the street and then the other. He seemed to draw an imaginary line on the cobbles with his jackboot. They were discussing a road block. A small troop of soldiers appeared. By the way they moved, Stanton knew they'd been told to keep quiet. It was the first time he'd ever seen German soldiers out of step. Looking back down the street he could see a similar operation under way at the other end.

Now was his last chance. They were all occupied with preparing their trap. If he could just get clear of the apartment he had most of the morning to get a start on them. The police plan was for Bernadette to take him out for late breakfast. When would that be? Eleven? Perhaps ten but surely they wouldn't begin to get nervous before eleven. Twelve probably. They'd quite deliberately given themselves plenty of time to prepare their trap. It occurred to Stanton that they might also want to make sure of taking him without the possibility of the press or public seeing him or hearing anything he might have to say. After all, the police and the army were currently revelling in the *carte blanche* they had been given to crush the Unions and the Leftists. The revelation that the assassin had in fact been a lone English fantasist or spy would change the game utterly and put the cops in a pretty exposed position. Stanton was an inconvenience they'd want to handle pretty carefully. They were clearly planning to make their arrest away from prying eyes.

So he had time.

But not if Bernadette recovered consciousness, which she most likely would do quite quickly. He looked at her prostrate body. Stretched out on the floor. Her blouse still unbuttoned, her silk slip on display, one breast half exposed, a dome of flesh falling backwards towards her chin. It rose and fell evenly: that was good, her breathing wasn't disturbed. He didn't think she'd suffered much harm from the blow.

She moaned a little, she was stirring.

Reaching into his bag of equipment he drew out his medical kit, the one that Bernadette had brought to the hospital and thus saved his life. He took out a needle – not one of his antibiotics, a sedative. He knelt down beside her and, using his left hand as a tourniquet, found a vein and injected the sedative.

'Sorry,' he said again. It seemed to be becoming a habit. But he truly was, both for her and for himself.

He buttoned up her blouse and put a pillow under her head.

Then he shouldered the one bag he'd allowed himself, went to the window and climbed out. This was the moment of maximum danger. One of the police or soldiers five storeys below had only to look up and the chase would be on. But they were all pretty occupied and also trying to be discreet, his room was on the top floor, and the climb should take him less than a minute; he reckoned his chances were good. He got out on to the window ledge and reached up for the guttering. He was still stiff and weakened from convalescence but his wound had pretty much healed and he'd been diligent in doing his stretches and physio since leaving hospital. He hoisted himself up over the gutter without too much pain and scrambled on to the tiled roof from where he was able to traverse the whole length of the street and descend beyond the barricade.

He'd escaped the trap. But he'd had to assault and drug Bernadette to do it. The thought filled him with despair.

Having returned to street level he walked briskly out of Mitte towards the Lehrter Bahnhof. He stopped at the first decent hotel he could find and took a room, readily accepting the stern warning that since the hour was early and the maids had not yet begun their work he must pay for the previous night. Stanton was, in fact, counting on the earliness of the hour as the principal factor in enabling him to assemble a disguise. He was aware that Bernadette would be able to describe his clothes and so he hoped to find replacements among the returned overnight laundry. He expected that by now it would have been left outside the rooms but that the occupants would not yet have opened their doors to collect it.

He was in luck, and as he made his way along the corridor towards his room he was able discreetly to collect a whole gentleman's wardrobe. Once he was in his room he laid the clothes out on the bed and set about changing his personal appearance as best he could. He took his shaving kit and his multi-tool knife (which contained scissors) from his bag and, pouring water into the wash bowl, began shaving his head. It's not an easy thing to do oneself, and Stanton was anxious not to draw attention with a skull covered in cuts and scabs so he forced himself not to rush. Fortunately the mirror, which stood on the dresser behind the wash bowl, had two hinged side flaps, and so by twisting a bit he was able to get sight of most of his head. He shaved all his hair save for a patch on top, which he fashioned into a very short crew cut, German military style. In Stanton's view probably the ugliest male hairstyle ever devised.

Once he'd finished with his head, he shaved his face. During his time in hospital his beard had grown. He hadn't shaved it off because Bernadette had liked it. 'Every Suffragette secretly wants a caveman to drag her about,' she'd said dryly, 'or so the *hilarious* cartoons in the papers tell us.' Now he shaved himself fully leaving only a small moustache, which he trimmed down into a neat military style. The German identity that Chronos had supplied him with was made out in the name of Ludwig Drechsler, a German *Junker* brought up in East Africa. When creating the character McCluskey and her team of forgers had decided that, just as with the Australian back story they had given him, a colonial past would mitigate any strangeness in his accent and his language.

When he'd finished shaving, Stanton took the water bowl, which was full of hair and whiskers, to the communal bathroom at the end of the corridor and carefully disposed of it in the lavatory. He didn't want them looking for a shaven-headed man. Then he packed up his bag and left the bedroom. It was barely thirty minutes after he'd entered it. He locked the door behind him and put out the 'Do Not Disturb' sign. Then, avoiding reception, he left the hotel via a back entrance and walked directly to the station, which was just five minutes away on foot. He bought a ticket to Prague, which was the first southbound train available. Stanton only managed to catch it by running along the platform and jumping on as the train pulled away.

As he sat down in his seat, he glanced at his watch. It was less than seventy-five minutes since Bernadette had returned to their apartment with the bread.

By the time the police decided to break into the apartment and found her unconscious body on the floor, he was already halfway to the German border.

Two days later he was back in Constantinople.

39

STANTON'S CAB CLIP-CLOPPED through the darkened streets from the Pera Palace Hotel and headed down to the dockside area.

The last time Stanton had made the journey he'd been in a Mercedes limousine with McCluskey beside him. The memory seemed already strange and distant. He was becoming an early-twentieth-century man.

The cabby spoke a little English and a little German and was inclined to chat, particularly when he heard the address that Stanton was heading for. It seemed that the hospital had only recently been the venue of a terrible double murder. There had been a break-in and a doctor and a night nurse had been killed.

Stanton was a little unnerved. Break-ins happened from time to time of course and they sometimes turned violent. But that one should have occurred in this *specific house*, Newton's house, seemed somehow *ominous*.

He asked the cab driver if he could recall the date.

'A couple of months ago,' came the reply. 'The end of May or the beginning of June . . . yes, that's it. The morning of the first of June. I remember it was my wife's name day.'

Stanton swallowed hard.

The break-in had happened on the morning of his arrival.

He had been there. Just shortly after midnight. The house had been so peaceful and but for the gramophone record so quiet.

Yet now it seemed that had Newton's coordinates been timed to

319

occur only a little later, Stanton would have stepped from the future into the middle of a violent crime.

His mind went back to the nurse he'd seen, bent over her desk as he'd crept past her half-open door. Had she been a victim? Almost certainly, she had been the only person up. He recalled thinking that she was the first human being he had seen in his new world. Now it seemed that he was also the last person who saw her alive. Except for her killer. Stanton remembered the bearded man he'd surprised at the front door as he dragged the semi-conscious McCluskey out of the house. Not long after that encounter the man must have become the killer's other victim.

Stanton felt cold. Was it him? Had he brought death with him?

To a doctor and a nurse in Constantinople?

To the Jews of the Russian Steppes? The Socialists of Germany?

The flower girl in Sarajevo? To Churchill? The man so crucial to the salvation of the previous twentieth century but already dead in this one?

Somewhere a bell was chiming. It was 2 a.m.

What passing bells for these who die as cattle?

The opening line of Wilfred Owen's 'Anthem For Doomed Youth'.

Stanton whispered it under his breath. A reminder of why he had done the things he'd done. Yes, many were dying now, but their numbers were as nothing compared to those who had died before. A whole generation would not now 'die as cattle' as Wilfred Owen's had done. And Stanton would leave his warning in Newton's cellar lest any future Chronations act in haste to change another century. Stanton wished he had brought the Owen anthology with him to leave in the cellar beside his letter. No document could better demonstrate the appalling human capacity for self-inflicted disaster or show how bad things could really get.

He paid off his cab and walked up the same street that he'd escorted McCluskey along two months earlier. Approaching the same door from which he'd emerged into the early twentieth century.

The house looked completely quiet. Just the same as when he'd left it, apart from the fact that the windows were now barred. He hoped very much they hadn't added bolts to the door. His skeleton keys wouldn't help him if they had.

But the door opened and he slipped inside.

He crept along the familiar corridor and past the half-open door. Glancing in he saw that a nurse was sitting at the table as before, but this one was older and grey-haired.

He looked away. He had never been a remotely superstitious man but nonetheless he couldn't help wondering whether it had been his evil eye that marked that other nurse for death. Fate avenging itself against the efforts of Chronos to cheat it?

He told himself he was being a fool.

Fate? Evil eyes? Ridiculous?

But no more ridiculous than a man breaking into a house in order to visit its cellar in the hope that a hundred and eleven years hence somebody might read the history of a century that never happened.

Stanton crept to the cellar stairs door, unlocked it and made his way down. He moved the wardrobe, unlocked the second door and slipped back inside Newton's cellar.

It was pitch black but he'd brought his torch and in its bright LED light he could see the footprints he and McCluskey had left, and the mark in the middle of the room where she had lain at his feet. He flashed his torch about; he was looking for the not yet broken chair and the table. His idea was to put his letter on it.

But as he walked further into the cellar, something caught his eye on the edge of his torch beam.

Something dark a little way across the floor.

A line of marks in the dust.

Playing his torch on them Stanton recognized them for what they were. Another set of footprints. Footprints that most definitely had not been there before. Somebody had been in this cellar since Stanton had last been here.

For a moment a sort of panic gripped him as if he'd seen a

ghost. It was an unusual sensation for Stanton and he mastered it only with difficulty. His heart had begun to beat furiously; he gulped for breath. He struggled to get a grip of his thoughts. There had to be a logical explanation, and of course there was one.

Those marks must have been made by the intruder. The man who broke into the hospital and had killed the doctor and the nurse. No ghost, just a house breaker.

But why had he come down here?

What was he hoping to find?

Stanton played his torch along this other line of prints. They seemed to lead nowhere. They began at the door and then . . . stopped. As if the man had entered the cellar, explored it for a few steps and then . . . disappeared.

Stanton took a step towards the prints, his free hand closing round the handle of the pistol in his pocket. Was the intruder still in the cellar? How could that be? The break-in had happened two months ago.

But if the man wasn't still there, why did his footprints stop in the middle of the room? Where had he gone? He couldn't have just evaporated. It occurred to Stanton that billions of people had done exactly that in the century from which he had come. Evaporated into thin air. But those billions had taken their world *with* them. They had left no footprints.

Where was the man who had left these?

Stanton's body tensed, as if expecting some furious killer to leap from the darkness as he stared down at the line of marks in the dust.

And then he realized.

Heel – sole – heel – sole.

The footsteps weren't leading from the door into the middle of the cellar.

They were leading from the middle of the cellar to the door.

The intruder hadn't made them and then disappeared.

He had *appeared* and then made them.

40

IT WAS JUST after 7.30 in the morning on what the pre-Liberation calendar had referred to as Christmas Eve.

The year was One Hundred and Three.

Or 2024 in Old World Years.

The dawn was bitter cold. There was a thick mist on the road and the People's Revolutionary Army road marshals were out in force waving their reflective paddles and their luminous batons.

The PRA was in the process of shifting the whereabouts of its South Eastern Mobile Missile Defence Shield and the frozen morning air of what had once been called Cambridgeshire was thunderous with the roar of diesel engines. The massive missile carriers lumbering across the county took up the majority of the width of the road and the marshals were nervous and aggressive. The tarmac was thick with ice and they didn't want one of those bad boys skidding off into a ditch.

Stuck between two of the enormous transports, trying to weave a way through, was a Mercedes van which displayed the markings of the Department of Internal Security. Every paddle-wielding squaddie on the road jumped to attention and delivered a flurry of salutes as it passed by. Nobody dissed the Department of Internal Security. Failure to show sufficient respect to any Department of State, let alone the DIS, was considered a failure to show respect to the Party Secretary. And they put you in a camp for life for disrespecting the Party Secretary. If you were lucky.

Inside the van there were four female security officers and one manacled prisoner in the uniform of the Stornoway Gulag. Stornoway was the most notoriously brutal re-education facility in the British Precinct of the USSR. Its uniform was a thick coarse blue overall incongruously trimmed at the wrists and pockets with tartan.

The prisoner was female also, manacled at her hands and feet, her ID number tattooed on the dome of her shaven head. None of the guards spoke. Each of them seemed to be cowering in their respective corners of the van, as if they were trying to get as far away from the prisoner as possible.

Which they were.

Who knew what she could achieve? Even manacled as she was.

She'd throttled guards with her own chains in the past.

She'd killed three of her own babies. Some said she ate one.

She should be killed herself, of course. That was the opinion of the guards.

Shot through her bald tattooed head and dumped in a Hebridean peat bog.

But the Party didn't kill people. Not at least until it had bent them to its will.

And KT503b678 was still a long way from bending.

Besides, even if they did shoot her through the head, she'd probably just get up again. That's what people said about KT503b678. That she was immortal. Or perhaps a ghost already. The stories of her numerous escapes were legion. After her last she'd survived in the wild for months. She'd killed a road cop and fed off his body for two weeks. When they found her they had to first deal with a pack of wild dogs she'd tamed. The dogs were all found to have rabies. Maybe she had rabies too. It would explain her madness and her violence.

She had been slated for a full lobotomy after that. All the Stornoway guards had applied for seats to observe the process, but then there had come a surprise stay of mental execution.

The Party wanted her. Or at least some high-up Party guys did. The State Research and Education Facility had requested she be delivered to them for observation. It seemed that the comrade professors had decided to have a look at her.

Why was that, the Stornoway guards had asked themselves as they caged KT503b678 up for transportation. Maybe to find out what could make a person fight so hard. To find out how a conscious brain could continue to resist all the indoctrination and the torture. How it was that a person could survive as an *individual* against the entire might of the state.

Or maybe they were going to try and clone her. There'd been a lot of rumours about a new army of super-strong cancer-resistant storm-troopers going to occupy the American nuclear rubble. Maybe KT503b678 was the blueprint.

That would make sense.

You wouldn't want to meet two of KT503b678. Let alone an army.

The Department of Internal Security van finally peeled away from the missile convoy it had got caught up in and headed off towards the State Research and Education Facility which prior to the Glorious Liberation had been known as Cambridge University.

There the four DIS guards gratefully passed their charge into the hands of the Comrade Master of College, who was waiting with his own Security Team.

'Bind her securely,' the Master instructed, 'and take her to the inner cage.'

KT503b678's limbs were already chained together and now her whole body was wound around with nylon cable lock-ties. She was then carried bodily through the ancient gateway. They carried her past the old porter's lodge with its machinegun-toting occupant and across the concrete parade ground in the middle of which was a broken waterfall. A crumbling symbol of wasteful bourgeois decadence.

The security detail then made its way into the great stone building that had once been the college chapel. Now, stripped of its turrets, its leaded windows and all its decorative symbolism, it served as the Party meeting room for the Political Purification Committee.

The Comrade Master and three other comrade professors, all dressed in their Party overalls, followed the security team and their struggling prisoner into the hall. Inside, the ancient vaulted space had also been stripped of all previous decoration and was hung instead with red flags and images of the Party leaders.

Rosa Luxemburg and Karl Liebknecht, the revered fallen heroes of the First Revolution.

Otto Strasser, the original Great Navigator and leader of the Second Revolution.

And his fourth-generation descendant Kurt Strasser, the current Great Navigator.

A large cage stood in the centre of the bare concrete floor.

KT503b678 was deposited into this and the cage securely locked. Then, working through the bars with wire clippers, the guards snipped off her cable ties thus allowing her some freedom of movement. Her limbs, however, remained chained.

The guards were dismissed, leaving KT503b678 alone with the Comrade Master and his colleagues.

'Comrade KT503b678,' the Master barked harshly, 'as a girl you were a Model Communist Pioneer and later the highest-ranking graduate of the People's Military Academy. You joined the elite Special Forces and served heroically in the battle for New York. Yet you threw all this away to become criminal vermin. Why?'

The prisoner did not reply, merely massaging the raw bloody sores where the manacles had torn at her wrists.

'I know the answer,' the Master went on. 'I never ask a question to which I don't know the answer. You betrayed the revolution for love. For Petty. Bourgeois. Trivial. Private. Love. Not for the love of the Great Navigator, which is your duty. But the love of one ordinary man. You knew full well that private love is proscribed and yet instead of purging yourself through work and self-denial you embraced this decadent emotion. What is more, you loved an enemy. An American soldier. A capitalist pig. That is why you were sent to a gulag and why when his brat emerged from your womb you were forced to drown it.'

The prisoner spoke for the first time.

'They drowned my child,' she said slowly. 'Not me.'

'They put it in the sink and held your hands upon it. The flesh that touched it as its half-minute of life came to an end was yours. It was still tied to your body by its cord. You drowned it. Just as you drowned your other babies. The babies of the rapes.'

'Yes. I drowned those.'

'Because they were from the seed of your violators?'

'No. Because I had learnt by then that children of the gulags are better off dead. We are all better off dead and the younger the death the less painful the life that precedes it.'

'Why then don't you kill yourself, KT503b678?'

The prisoner sighed. An exhalation of utter sadness that seemed to drift over the high, thick, defensive walls of her ferocious anger. She turned her face upwards. Towards the shadows of the great vaulted ceiling that once had resonated to the music of divine choirs.

'Death is the only friend I have and I long for its embrace,' she said, 'but I will not kill myself.' Her anger was returning. 'I will make the Party kill me.'

'The Party doesn't kill, KT503b678. It is kind and compassionate. The Great Navigator cares for all his children, even those who have lost their way. The Party doesn't kill. It educates.'

'By rape and torture. By killing babies.'

'Yes. By killing babies,' and now it was the Comrade Master's turn to sigh. 'How can that be?' His voice was suddenly suffused with sadness. 'Infanticide as a tool of government? How did we arrive at such a desperate state of affairs?'

He drew up a chair quite close to the cage and sat down on it. His three companions gathered round him as if forming a guard. There was fear on all their faces. Desperate fear. But also a desperate sort of hope.

'KT503b678, I should like to discuss history with you,' the Comrade Master said.

'And I only wish to kill you,' KT503b678 replied.

'No, no, you mustn't kill me,' the Master went on. 'We are the same, you and I.'

'We're not the same, Comrade Master. I hate the Party from my very soul and you are its creature.'

'Don't make the mistake of thinking that just because a man serves something he is its creature. I take a practical view. Since the only way to survive and to live in some modicum of comfort in this world that the Party made is to *serve* the Party, then of course I serve it. But I am not its creature. I despise it every bit as much as you do. Like you, I hate it from my soul.'

'Did it murder your babies?'

'Yes, it did, as a matter of fact. Although my babies were never flesh and blood,' he replied. 'My babies were art and culture. Learning. Literature. Paintings and poetry. The many parts of beauty, which is a tender and delicate infant, and the Party killed it before I was even born.'

KT503b678 wasn't listening any more. She had been subjected to so many and so varied forms of interrogation in the past that she had long since ceased to wonder why the functionaries of the Party asked or said the things they did. Double-think was second nature to them. Besides, she'd spied something at her feet, a screw lost during the construction of her cage. Perhaps she could use it to pick the locks. Perhaps then she could stick it into this Comrade Master of College's eye and press it through to the brain with her thumb. Then perhaps finally they'd have to kill her and she'd be released. To sleep at last like the man she loved and their baby.

'But I have seen that infant's many ghosts,' the Comrade Master continued. 'We keep them hidden here. Forbidden manuscripts and pictures, ancient texts and forgotten learning. Secreted deep in shadowy vaults. Squirrelled away in long-forgotten wall cavities. Buried in cobwebbed tombs – I have seen something of what has been lost.'

She had the screw now. Between her toes; she had only to continue to clench them until the point when they freed her arms and then she would have a tool and a weapon. In the past she'd killed and killed again with less resource than that.

'And so, KT503b678, I would like to ask you a question.'

She didn't reply.

'Please,' the Master went on, 'answer my question and I promise I shall let you keep that piece of sharp metal that you have clenched between your toes.'

KT503b678 looked at him in surprise. Most Party people were idiots. So caught up in their own self-importance and self-preservation that they noticed nothing. You could trick them and fool them and they never knew. This one was different.

She nodded. 'All right. Ask me your question, Comrade Master of College.'

The Master sat silent for a moment. He took from the pocket of his dungarees an ancient yellow parchment and looked down at it, seeming to draw inspiration from its contents.

'If you could change *one* thing in history,' he asked, 'if you had the opportunity to go back into the past, just once, to one place and one time and change one thing, where would you go? What would you do?'

41

'I WOULD CHANGE NOTHING, Sir Isaac,' Master Bentley said firmly, while refilling the wine glasses. 'I would leave both well and ill alone.'

'Yes, Mr Bentley,' Newton replied, nodding sadly and looking, if it were possible, even older than his eighty-four years. 'So would I.'

They had been debating Newton's question, considering the mistakes of history and the current condition of humanity, asking themselves whether some change to the former might improve the latter, and they had been forced to conclude that, deeply unsatisfactory though Britain in 1727 was, pox-ridden, semi-bankrupt, riven with religious and dynastic strife and in constant danger of a Jacobite revolution from the Scots, nonetheless it was developing along sufficiently satisfactory lines to make any idea of tinkering with its history too big a risk to contemplate.

'Any hypothetical change,' Bentley observed, 'no matter how minor, would immediately open up the possibility of an infinite number of unknowable variables. We might make matters worse.'

'Exactly. We might very well make matters worse,' Newton agreed, staring out of the window, against which a heavy rain was rattling, 'and I have wrestled with the horror of that possibility these thirty years past. It has tormented my days and haunted my nights. It has made my life a misery.'

'But why, Sir Isaac?' Bentley replied with an indulgent smile. 'After all, it's just a game. We cannot *actually* alter the past.'

'No, sir, we cannot.'

'Well, then. Put away these angry thoughts and enjoy the wine.'

'But three hundred years from now an opportunity will arise whereby others can.'

'Alter the past? Surely you're not serious?'

'Deadly so, Master Bentley. It may be that those people of the future discover this possibility themselves, in which case my conscience is clear. But if they don't? Should I guide them to it? That is the question which makes my every waking moment a torture and every dream a nightmare.'

Master Bentley tried not to laugh. It was clear to him that Newton's great age had enfeebled his mind.

'Well,' he replied, in the tone that people are apt to use towards the very old when asking if they enjoyed their supper or if they want their cushions plumped, 'perhaps best not to worry about it, eh? Three hundred years is, after all, a long time away.'

Newton frowned angrily and shifted impatiently in his seat. The nostrils of his famous long nose flared.

'A long time, Master Bentley? You think so?' he asked. 'By what measure is it a long time?'

'By any reasonable measure, sir, I should say a *very* long time.'

'So by *reasonable* measure, we are in fact talking about *your* measure.'

'Because I am, I hope, a reasonable man.'

Newton's anger flashed. 'You may hope it, sir, but on present evidence I would dispute it. What seems a long time to you would be but an instant if you were a planet and even less so if you were a star.'

Bentley gave a gentle laugh, maintaining his patronizing manner, making it clear that the Master of Trinity College was not to be goaded even by Trinity's greatest son.

'It might *seem* different, Sir Isaac, but it would still be the *same amount of time*. Just as a day seems long to a bored schoolboy and short to a busy adult but it remains the same length of day.'

The Master took a delicate sip at his claret, clearly pleased to have delivered such an elegant and telling argument and confident that Newton must concede his point.

His confidence was misplaced.

'Remains the same?' Newton demanded angrily. 'Does it? How so?'

'Well, of course it does!'

Newton banged the table with his fist, upsetting his wine for the second time that afternoon. 'What do you mean, "of course it does"?' he shouted. 'What sort of argument is that? You're a teacher! Or so you claim to be! You must know that it is not enough simply to *assert* a point. You must make some demonstration, offer up some *reasoning*, some *proof*.'

Finally Bentley's smug reserve deserted him.

'Proof? What proof can I give beyond the fact that logic requires it?' he said, his voice rising. 'Time is time. It ticks away from the beginning until the end.'

'But it doesn't, you damned fool!' Newton exclaimed. 'Am I really the only person on earth to have grasped this fact? Time is not linear. It does not go along on a steady course like a road from London to York. It does not *have* a beginning and it does not have an end, nor is it the same to one person as it is to another, nor to two planets or a million stars. It is different in *all circumstances*. Because it is *relative*.'

'Sir Isaac, I beg you calm yourself!' Bentley implored, alarmed at Newton's passion and regretting having allowed himself to be drawn into it. He did not want the most famous scientist in the world dying in his sitting room. 'No man on earth is more sensible of your genius than I, but what is *relative* about it? Time is time. Listen to the clock, you hear it ticking? Each second recorded, the same to all men. Seconds that were once in the future and now lie in the past. Seconds which progress, one after another, be they noted or ignored, here, there and everywhere. Tick tock – another gone! In this room. On the sun. Amongst the stars. In heaven and in hell. Tick then tock. And so God's Universe moves on second by second from Creation until Judgement Day.'

'Tick tock tick tock! What are you *talking* about, you imbecile!' Newton shouted, actually staggering to his feet and shaking his fist. 'The thing your clock records, Mr Bentley, and which announces itself with its tick and its tock, is quite obviously an *invention of man*. An essential convenience to give order to his day. It lends an *imagined* shape to the *experience* of time within the *vicinity* of the clock. Surely that must be blindingly obvious, even to you! Your solid and unchanging second is in fact nothing of the sort. It is a mysterious and flexible thing. It is different everywhere it exists. Because it is *relative*.'

'So you keep saying, Sir Isaac!' Bentley snapped, rising to his feet also, once more giving way to his own irritation. 'But relative to what?'

'To the conditions in which the person who is experiencing it finds himself. *Where* he is. Whether he is in *motion*. How *fast* he is going. If he is travelling *towards* something or *away* from it. Whether that thing is *also* in motion. And beyond all that you must factor in the position and parameters of every other atom in the universe because every single one of them is *relative* to absolutely every other one.'

The two men were face to face now, Newton's spilled wine on the rug between them, his great nose almost touching Bentley's chin.

'Please, Sir Isaac,' the Master said finally. 'Can we not debate this in a civilized manner?'

'There is nothing to debate,' Newton replied, collapsing back into his chair, old and tired once more. 'I understand what I am talking about and you do not. You are to be forgiven. None understand it but I, and I curse a cruel fate which has given me the insight to do so. I have discovered how to change the future. Only God should be able to do that. And yet God has given me the key. I cannot ignore what I know, what *God* has revealed to me. Even if it drives me mad. And so, Master Bentley, I bequeath to you and your successors these letters and this sealed box.'

42

STANTON STARED AT the footprints for a long time.

He examined each one with his torch. Almost pleading with his eyes to see a different story than the one that lay before him. But there could be no doubt about it. The footprints started in the middle of the room and headed for the door.

Just as his and McCluskey's did.

His mind simply reeled at the dawning realization of what this must mean.

Someone had followed him through time.

But that couldn't *be*. He'd seen the equations. Professor Sengupta had been quite specific. The timing was absolute, the junction in time lasted less than a second. The Chronation traveller must leave at midnight on the night of 31 May 2025 and arrive at fifteen minutes after midnight on 1 June 1914. There was no chance to sneak through afterwards. No next bus that would be along in a minute.

He turned off his torch for a moment and allowed the darkness to envelop him, concentrating on computing all known facts. What Sengupta had explained. What he had experienced. The new evidence on the dusty floor before him. The truth was hurtling towards his consciousness like a battering ram at an already half-smashed door.

The next bus hadn't come along in a minute.

It had taken one hundred and eleven years.

More than a century had passed since he and McCluskey had first left their footprints in the cellar.

That was the awesome truth.

And now *that* century had been consigned to oblivion just as his own had been. The loop had been rebooted for a second time. This was now the *third* version of the century, not the second. Another agent had come visiting from another future, from the future *Stanton had created*.

That agent had come to change the past.

The past *Stanton had created*.

And through which he had lived.

His mission had failed. Whatever had happened during the century that had unfolded after he had saved the Archduke and killed the Kaiser must have been terrible. Perhaps not as terrible as his own but terrible enough for another generation of Chronations to gather in a different 2025 and seek to use Newton's calculations to change history.

Stanton wasn't making history any more. He was just part of the history another agent of Chronos had come to make.

Stanton sank to his knees in the dust. His torch falling from his hand.

He had lived a *whole second life*. And yet he knew nothing about it because he and the whole world had been rebooted. From the moment this second Chronation arrived in 1914, Stanton's second life had disappeared from history just as his first had disappeared at the moment of his own arrival.

What had *happened* to him?

Had he found Bernie again? Had he had children? How long had he lived? How had he died?

Perhaps it had been no life at all. Perhaps the last time he had passed this way he had dropped off his envelope on the little wooden table, gone down to the Galata Bridge and thrown himself into the Bosphorus.

None of it mattered because none of it had happened. History had begun again not for a second, but for a *third* time.

His *life* was now beginning for a third time, in a third version of the twentieth century. And Cassie had only been in the first of them.

Yet in his mind she'd been dead less than a year.

He picked up his torch and looked once more at the new set of footprints. They were smaller than his by several sizes but the boot was a tough, heavy-treaded working shoe with what he thought might have been steel heel and toe caps. There was no way a man wearing those boots could have got along the corridor upstairs without making a noise, no matter how loud the gramophone had been. Small wonder then that he'd disturbed the doctor and nurse and had had to take them out.

Pretty poor fieldcraft.

Studying the prints once more, it crossed Stanton's mind that the second man had 'landed' in a different place to the point where he himself had arrived.

That was wrong, surely? Newton's coordinates were so specific and his sentry box so small that the second arrival should have arrived at the same place as his own. His footsteps should be on top of Stanton's own.

In fact, *he* should have been on top of Stanton. Surely this new Chronation, using the same coordinates that Newton had passed down, would have arrived in the same place and at the same time as he had done?

Stanton bit his knuckle in an effort to concentrate. Sengupta had talked of time as a disobliging Slinky, and that was how Stanton's mind felt, trying to disentangle its crisscrossed coils.

He thought back to Christmas Eve 2024. To Sengupta's lecture in the Great Hall at Trinity, seven months before. *Two* universes before. He heard once more the sing-song Anglo-Indian voice, explaining that the movement of time was like the movement of the planets, not quite symmetrical.

As each loop of space and time progresses, space and time are gained, just as in the case of leap years. And so although the two moments of departure and arrival are simultaneous, our time traveller will in effect arrive fifteen minutes after he leaves.

Space had slipped a little and so Newton's coordinates had been in a slightly different place this time. A little further from the arches where the old wine still lay and the shadows were so deep even his torch could scarcely penetrate them.

And time had slipped too.

It had 'leapt' a quarter of an hour. In this version of the century, Stanton and McCluskey had been followed. After they had stumbled out of the cellar, past the nurse in the corridor and the doctor at the front door, another Chronation traveller had arrived minutes later and blundered after them, alarming the house and killing the nurse and the doctor.

Stanton tried to imagine the man who had made those other footprints. What was he like? What future had he come from?

What had he come back to change?

The century in which this other Chronation had lived had begun with a world in which the Archduke had survived but the Kaiser had died . . .

The Kaiser had died.

Assassinated in what was without doubt the most stunning event of the new century so far. Any future Chronations looking back on this time and presented with a chance to change it must surely choose the Kaiser's assassination as the most influential moment. The point when things started to go wrong. Just as McCluskey and her crew had chosen the death of the Archduke.

It would be *that* they'd want to prevent.

The very thing *he'd* been sent from the past to do.

Those new footprints came to undo what he had done.

Stanton's mind went back to the moment on the roof of Wertheim's department store, the moment before he shot the Emperor. Remembering the impact of a bullet slamming into his body armour. Remembering spinning round and seeing a grey-clad figure.

Then the second shot hitting him above the heart, both shots supremely accurate. Only his armour saved him.

The truth was clear.

His attacker that morning hadn't been a guard at all. He'd been a traveller from the future.

Stanton shone his torch once more on the footprints in the dusk. The man who'd made those was the man who'd tried to kill him in Berlin. But he'd reckoned without Stanton's body armour. The second Chronation plot had failed. Stanton had assassinated the Kaiser for the second time and this time he'd also shot the man who'd been sent to stop him doing it.

What had happened to the man afterwards?

He cast his mind back to the evening of the assassination.

Going downstairs from his apartment and buying the paper . . . the first editions that bore the earth-shattering news. They had mentioned a man 'thought' to be a guard. The article had said that the extent of his injuries wasn't known. That the police were waiting to question him.

Was his Brother in Time alive?

Stanton got up. He couldn't stay in the cellar of the hospital all night.

By the light of his flashlight he found the ancient table and placed his written account on it. His account of his own century.

Which he must have done *before*.

He must have laid that same account on that same table in the previous loop in time. He wondered if this second generation of Chronations had found it. Had it survived in the cellar? Had they read it?

He hoped not with all his heart, because if they had, then *still* elected to try to change history, it could only mean that the history he'd created had been even worse than the one he'd been trying to fix.

He needed to know.

He needed to find the man from the roof of the store.

43

STANTON DETERMINED THAT he would book a ticket on the following morning's train to Berlin.

It would be risky. Clearly the police would still be hunting him and they had photographs, from his ID papers and also from the confrontation outside the SDP headquarters. And no doubt a detailed description from Bernadette.

On the other hand, he wasn't entirely sure how much the German authorities *wanted* to catch him. He'd noted that there had been absolutely no mention of beautiful Irish girls or lone British assassins in the papers, so clearly the police were keeping this part of their investigation secret. In the meantime, the ongoing repression of the German Liberals, Socialists and Trade Unionists continued unabated. The police and the army were clearly still using the pretext of an investigation to settle old scores, and the emergence of an actual culprit, particularly a lone foreigner, would spoil all the fun. Stanton calculated that even if the police did find him they would keep quiet about it.

But he didn't intend that they would find him. He had a pretty decent cover identity; he'd travelled incognito in tougher circumstances than this. At least in Berlin he wouldn't have to worry about racial profiling as he had in the mountains between Pakistan and Afghanistan.

He'd been in the clothes he'd stolen from the hotel since leaving Berlin and so he spent the day in Constantinople buying a suitable wardrobe for his Ludwig Drechsler identity. Civilian but in military style, blazers and tight cavalry-cut trousers. He also bought a clear glass monocle, which for some reason were highly fashionable among German officers at the time. He calculated that even were he to bump into the British officers he'd encountered on his first morning in 1914, they'd be unlikely to recognize him behind his Prussian façade. He took care to speak only German.

That evening he sat once again in the Orient Bar of the Hotel Pera Palace. On this occasion he drank schnapps and accepted the cigarettes the barman offered him. If the man noticed any resemblance between this chain-smoking German *Junker* and the ex-British officer who had sat in the same seat two months earlier, he didn't say.

The following morning Stanton journeyed once more to the Sirkeci terminal and took a train for Berlin.

For a moment, as the train pulled away from the station, he wondered whether he actually missed McCluskey. She'd been so full of glee when they'd made this trip together, sorting through the various sweets and cigarettes she'd bought, looking forward to the greatest adventure of hers or any life. But no. He didn't miss her. He wished she'd left him alone in his happiness and let him disappear from time with Cassie, Tessa and Bill. If she had been with him now, he'd chuck her out of the train all over again.

The journey dragged.

He was restless and disturbed. He no longer marvelled at the strangeness of it all, the smell and the noise and shaking of steam transport, the pantomime costumes that at first had made him feel as if he was an extra in some elaborate historical movie. It was all becoming ordinary and familiar. He'd finally lost the habit of checking constantly in his pocket for a mobile phone, which he had at last accepted would never ring again. He knew now to remember to buy books and papers at the station as there would most certainly be no other form of distraction available on the train . . .

Unless of course you got talking to a fascinating woman who would end up breaking your heart.

The thought of Bernadette was intensely painful, particularly since his journey took him through Vienna. But strangely, Stanton found comfort in the pain. It was proof to him that his heart *could* be broken again. That contrary to what he had presumed after Cassie's death, he still had a living soul. He was capable of love. And he still loved Bernadette.

On his arrival in Berlin, Stanton decided to stay in a hotel rather than rent another apartment. His policy was, as ever, to hide in plain sight, and so he took rooms at the Kempinski, one of the finest and most frequented hotels in the city, playing the part of the rich and arrogant German colonel, home with his fortune and happy to let the world know it.

'I am Kapitan Ludwig Drechsler, ex of the Imperial African Schutztruppe,' he barked out as he marched up to reception, his tone and swagger exhibiting the impenetrable self-confidence of a white man used to lording it over native troops. The receptionist began to murmur obsequious words of welcome but Stanton slapped his German army papers and leather gloves down on the desk with a loud smack and barged rudely on. 'I require a two-bedroom suite with a bath and water closet. The very best rooms in your establishment, mind. If you don't have rooms to fit my specifications and of the *highest* possible standard, please direct me to somewhere that does.'

No one would suspect this gauche ex-Africa man trying to impress hotel staff in the big smoke of being an English imposter on the run for murdering the Emperor.

Having deposited his bags in his room, Stanton returned to the ground floor and set about his business right away. It had been almost a month since his rooftop firefight with his fellow time traveller and the trail was going cold.

He took a cab straight from the Kempinski to the central city library where he intended to begin his search by scouring the previous month's newspapers for news of the wounded gunman. Old school research; eight weeks earlier he'd have been cursing the lack of internet, but he no longer even noted its absence. He was an early-twentieth-century man now. He ought to be used to it. It was his second time round.

The library archive was well run and well indexed and he soon got on the trail of his target, finding various small articles mentioning the mystery figure who had been found on the roof of Wertheim's and been shot in the course of an apparent attempt to save the Kaiser. There wasn't a great deal of information in the articles beyond the fact that the person had not been a guard of any sort, which he'd already guessed, of course. He did learn one thing, however, which he hadn't been expecting at all. The reporter who had filed the original report had made the presumption that the wounded figure was a man. Subsequent reports revealed that she was in fact a woman. This other generation of Companions had chosen to send a female agent back to the past. Why should he be surprised? Back in Stanton's own twenty-first century he'd known plenty of highly capable women in the military. Yet he'd just presumed the other footprints had been left by a guy with small feet. Perhaps he'd already become so steeped in the post-Edwardian mind-set that the idea of a female Special Forces operative hadn't even occurred to him.

Bernadette would have been thrilled at the very thought of such a thing.

She kept dropping into his mind unbidden.

He missed her horribly. He didn't resent her for having betrayed him. He knew she had had no choice. How could she possibly have believed his story? How could he have been so *stupid* as to tell her? Drunk and in love was how, of course, a combination calculated to cloud any man's judgement. But he really should have known better. Nobody on earth could believe his story.

Except that now there was one person who would. Another woman.

The newspapers reported that the police believed the woman to be unbalanced and possibly a member of some sort of strange cult, although it didn't explain why. Apart from that, Stanton gleaned that she had survived his attempt to kill her, had been wounded and that she remained very ill.

After that, the story dropped out of the papers altogether.

The last mention of the woman had been in the *Berliner Tageblatt*. Stanton jotted down the by-line of the journalist who had written the article and enquired at the library reception for the address of the newspaper.

'I can give you the address,' the librarian told him, 'but there's nobody there. The police have closed it.'

She gave the information brusquely as if she didn't want to discuss it further. Stanton understood. The *Tageblatt* was a Liberal-leaning paper; he recalled Bernadette saying it was the only mainstream publication that was even halfway principled. Clearly it had now fallen victim to the current army purge. The librarian was a classic 'new woman', as they were known. Hair in a severe bun, tortoiseshell glasses, neat blouse fastened with a neck tie, a Suffragette for sure and probably a reader of the *Tageblatt*. In Stanton's current disguise she would certainly take him for a reactionary German militarist and no doubt blame him personally for the loss of her newspaper.

'That's a shame,' he replied. 'I very much wish to speak to one of their writers. Could you show me to the telephone directories, please.'

The woman gave a perfunctory nod towards a table on which several copies of the Berlin phone book were lying. These were the days when libraries were the repositories not just of literature but of all civic information.

Stanton leafed through the Fs, looking for Anton Fiedler, the author of the *Tageblatt* article. He was hoping that a journalist sufficiently senior to justify his own billing would be on the phone, and he was in luck. Herr Fiedler himself answered the phone and was happy to provide his address. Stanton thanked the librarian and grabbed a cab.

Stanton didn't explain to Fiedler why he wanted to find the woman who had been shot on the roof, and Fiedler didn't ask.

The man was out of work, one of the many thousands of victims of the increasingly violent and vindictive post-assassination crackdown. All Fiedler wanted in exchange for information was money, and Stanton made it clear that he was prepared to pay.

'It's a damned good story,' Fiedler said, having allowed Stanton to take him to a local bar and order drinks. The man lodged in the Wedding district of the city, an area associated with working people and radical politics. 'But the cops wouldn't let me run with it even before they closed the paper. What's wrong with them? It's crazy. It's like they think anybody who isn't actually a Prussian general is a revolutionary. The *Tageblatt* was about as radical as sausage and potatoes, but they're acting like we were putting the Communist Manifesto on the front page.'

Stanton steered Fiedler back to the topic in hand.

'The story,' he asked, 'what was so damned good about it?'

'I'll tell you what was so damned good,' he said, leaning in a little closer, wiping the beer foam from his mouth then depositing it in the lock of greasy hair that hung across his forehead. 'The woman's a witch, that's what's so good. I saw her in her cell before the police had got round to shutting everything down. Almost bald, her head covered in stubble and you could see a number tattooed on it. More tattoos down her arms and legs too. Horrible amateur scribbles, probably done with a knife and ink. Must have hurt like hell. Still, perhaps she likes a bit of pain. I've got an informant in the central lock-up who says she's got scars all over her body. And plenty more tattoos too – on her *mushi*, for God's sake. A *woman*. A *white* woman with a tattoo on her *cunt*. Pretty shocking, eh?'

Stanton did find it shocking, although not for the reasons Fiedler imagined. He had known many tattooed women; most of the tougher girls in the army had acquired some ink but they weren't *covered* in it. And amateur tatts? Knife and ink jobs? And scars? It seemed to Stanton that those other Companions of Chronos had made a peculiar choice of agent if they were hoping to find someone who could blend easily into the world of 1914.

It made him wonder even more just what sort of world this woman had come from.

Fiedler ordered another beer and filled his shot glass from the bottle that Stanton had put in front of him. His greasy fingertips left prints on the glass. Stanton noted that his shirt collar was quite soiled. This was a man who only a few weeks before had had his own by-line in a major daily and rented a telephone. Now he was clearly skimping on hot water for both his person and his laundry. These were cruel times. Stanton reckoned that Fiedler was about a month away from destitution. He was certainly drinking as if he was.

'Apparently the woman's a foreigner of some sort,' Fiedler went on, anxious to maintain access to the bottle. 'Probably English, although she spoke German as well. A strange shorthand sort of German, my man told me, with quite a few Russian words in it. All most peculiar.'

'Do you know where they're keeping her?' Stanton enquired.

'Well, not at the lock-up any more. She was wounded, remember. And I know that she got sick, blood-poisoning I imagine. So often it's not the actual bullet that does the killing . . . I suppose I *could* ask around. But fieldwork is expensive.'

'The sooner you find out,' Stanton said, 'the better I'll pay. In fact, if you tell me now I'll give you another hundred marks on the spot.'

Stanton had guessed that Fiedler was holding out on him, trying to drag out another pay day. He'd clearly already pursued the story as far as he could.

Fiedler smiled. 'You're a good reader of men, Kapitan Drechsler, you should be a journalist.'

'Sadly it seems to be a shrinking market.'

'Yes,' Fiedler agreed grimly. 'Pretty soon the only information left in this city will come direct from the Wilhelmstrasse. Anyway, the police have put her in a hospital, hoping she'll pull through and they might get something more out of her. She's guarded, though. They won't let her talk to you.'

Fiedler wrote the address down on a beer mat.

The Berliner Buch. Stanton's own place of recuperation. Good, he knew it a little already and it was the last place the police would ever expect the Kaiser's assassin to return to.

Stanton left Fiedler with his money and the bottle and went looking for a cab. If this woman was wounded and still in hospital, then it was almost certain that her wounds were infected. He needed to hurry. She might quite easily already be dead.

44

STANTON WAS PRETTY sure he could spring the woman, if she were still alive. Hospitals were never secure, no matter what efforts were made to make them so. Too many people coming and going, too many gowns and facemasks, too many emergency cases scurrying about. Hospitals hadn't been secure in the twenty-first century and Stanton was confident that they would be considerably less so a hundred and eleven years earlier.

But getting her out was just the first problem. Next, she would have to be concealed while she recovered. Hiding a sick, possibly unconscious woman who had been sprung from protective custody while also providing her with the care she'd need would require preparation.

He'd known from the start that if he could find his target at all they would probably be very sick, which was why he had secured a double-room suite at the hotel, just as he had been forced to do for McCluskey on their first night in Constantinople. He hadn't realized, of course, that this new charge would also be a woman. A fact which would require an explanation if he didn't want to arouse the interest of the hotel detective. He imagined she'd be too young to pass for his mother, as McCluskey had done. A sibling was called for.

'My sister will be joining me from Dar-es-Salaam,' he announced at reception, having returned to his hotel after questioning the journalist Fiedler. 'Her health is delicate and she has been ill, a hunting wound sustained in the bush. We have come home to the Fatherland for her hospital treatment and now she must convalesce. She is to occupy the second room in my suite. I trust your hotel can offer every comfort in such a situation?'

The hotel manager (to whom Stanton had insisted on speaking) assured him that they could, and to Stanton's relief did not ask for a second set of papers. The sister of a German officer wasn't required to submit any. Stanton's ID would cover them both.

Next Stanton hired an automobile, a beautiful maroon-coloured Mercedes Benz four-cylinder town car. He absolutely loved it. Squatting down in front of the radiator grille and turning the crank handle to start the engine, he forgot the intensity and emotional turmoil of his situation and allowed himself a moment of sheer joy. No electric starting motor for this baby. If a man wanted to start it he had to pump the crank.

As the great machine shuddered into life, throbbing violently, he climbed in behind the wheel and sat back on the hard-sprung leather seat. Running his hands over the polished mahogany instrument panel, he could scarcely believe that this was the first time he'd been behind the wheel of a car since leaving the twenty-first century. In happier circumstances, classic wheels would have been the first thing he'd have treated himself to. To drive a vintage car when it *wasn't* vintage at all but cutting-edge technology was about as good as it got for Stanton. And to drive it on near empty roads, with motor roaring, leather, brass, rubber and steel rattling. A huge primitive Neanderthal machine with its own unique personality. And *difficult* to drive. No power anything, no synchromesh, just man against metal.

Experimenting with the gears and clutch as he guided the car out into traffic, Stanton swore that if ever he got off the time-warp roller-coaster he was on he'd buy half a dozen. Never mind women, he'd have cars! And bikes too. British bikes. He'd tour the country on a state-of-the-art 1914 Enfield. He'd take a Norton to the Isle of Man and win the next TT Race.

Maybe take a Triumph round Ireland and drop in on . . .

But he couldn't think about that now. Bernadette must wait. There was a new woman in his life. A time traveller from the future.

He'd come to 1914 imagining that with the death of the Kaiser his business with Chronos would be over. But with the arrival of a second agent of Chronos and the realization that perhaps he hadn't 'fixed' the century after all, he knew that he could not retire from active service yet.

He was still a soldier and he was still on duty.

Stanton drove his Mercedes through Berlin. A map on his knee, searching out a medical supply store that he'd located from the phone book at the hotel. He found that he was smiling. Just the sensation of driving a car made him feel better, like he was finally back in control and getting on with things. Playing with the clunky, chunky controls and feeling the throaty thunder of the hand-made engine as it vibrated under the huge shining bonnet gave Stanton his first moments of pleasure since he'd fallen asleep in Bernadette's arms.

And once again she was on his mind. It seemed to happen every few minutes.

He wondered if he had sought her out in the century that had now disappeared from time, the one where the death of the Kaiser truly had signalled the end of his mission. He felt sure he must have done. Never mind Shackleton and Everest and all the bloody cars in Birmingham. He wanted Bernadette. He wanted her now and he knew that he'd have wanted her the last time the world had passed this way. Perhaps he had won her back, somehow getting her to Cambridge and showing her Newton's box, which even now must lie in the attic of the Master's Lodge. That would convince her, surely. It was perhaps the only proof that would, and it was currently in the care of the Master of Trinity . . . He'd have only to break in and . . .

Had he done that once already? In that now lost century and life? Had he tracked her down, taken her to Cambridge and produced in triumph the evidence that would make her love him once again? Make her *make* love to him again? It was a confusing and extremely frustrating thought.

He bought a surgeon's gown and mask at the medical supply store and then drove on to Leipziger Platz, across which his epoch-changing bullet had sped on its journey into the Emperor's brain. He parked directly outside Wertheim's. The place had been teeming with shoppers and jammed with traffic the last time he had been there but it was almost empty now. Two uniformed doormen leapt forward eagerly and guided him in to a parking place. Their help wasn't needed; there were no other cars trying to park.

This previously bustling monument to Berlin's economic miracle was a very different place to when last he'd exited it, scattering forged Socialist pamphlets behind him. It was sombre and quiet now. The great female statue in the centre of the atrium had been draped in black as if in penance for the store's unwitting role in the national tragedy. Black banners hung where previously there had been coloured silks and chandeliers. Every member of staff had on a wide black armband. But no amount of ostentatious mourning was going to turn round the fortunes of Wertheim's department store now. It was a ghost shop, forever tainted by its grim association with the Empire's darkest day. The massive deductions and almost desperate promotions being offered were shunned by even the most committed bargain-hunters. Stanton reckoned he was one of only half a dozen shoppers in a store that had previously served thousands by the hour.

Three members of staff approached him at once.

'I need a lady's nightdress and cap. Loose, plain and simple – my wife is an invalid. Also a day dress and items of undergarment.'

He was led to the second floor where the ladies' clothing department was located, the centre of a small crowd of overly attentive staff. He was at once asked the most obvious question.

'And what size is Madam?'

Stanton cast his mind back to the footprints in the cellar . . . those working boots would have been perhaps a UK size six.

Glancing at the female staff lined up in front of him, he selected one on shoe size.

'Perhaps like you, miss,' he said.

After making his purchases he drove back to the Kempinski and hung the lady's day dress in the closet of the spare room, placing the underwear in a chest of drawers. Then he put the surgeon's mask and gown and the nightdress and cap into his bag and slipped some sedatives and his gun into his pocket.

On his way out of the hotel he approached reception.

'I hope to be bringing my sister from hospital this afternoon,' he explained brusquely. 'You will oblige me by having a wheel-chair waiting at my disposal.'

He drove his hired car to the Berliner Buch hospital, the place where Bernadette had sat her vigil over his unconscious and poisoned body. There were some parking places available in an area reserved for senior staff and ambulances and Stanton took one. Towing and clamping were blights of the future. He'd be happy to pay a fine.

He walked up the great stone steps of the building, through the colonnaded entrance and into the hospital. Once inside he ducked into the first lavatory he found and put on his surgeon's gown. Then, unchallenged, he wandered further into the hospital and found a porter. He enquired about the whereabouts of the female police prisoner, explaining that he'd heard she was something of a circus freak and he wanted to get a peek.

The porter was happy to oblige, giving directions and saying that he didn't think the Herr Doktor would be disappointed.

Stanton made his way to the correct floor, picking up a wheel-chair on the way. He left the chair at the entrance to the lift and sought out the correct room. The door was guarded by two uniformed men whom Stanton approached without breaking his stride.

'I must check the patient's pupil dilation for signs of diaspora,' he said, making up a condition as he spoke. 'The process will take only a few seconds. Kindly accompany me into the room so you may witness that the inspection has been performed and that the patient remained secure in your care at all times.'

There was hesitation on the faces of the officers. Stanton pressed on before they could articulate it.

'If you allow me to be in the presence of your charge unsupervised I shall be forced to report you to your superiors,' he snapped. 'The police have entrusted this hospital with this woman's care and I shall not allow myself to be placed in a position which compromises your own security protocol. I insist that you secure your charge while I am required to lay my hands upon her.'

The bullshit worked. Once more the prevailing German predisposition to obey authority stood him in good stead. The two guards dutifully followed Stanton into the room, where he swiftly immobilized them, spinning round and hitting the first man in the temple with his left, followed by a right upper cut to the second man's jaw. Both went down and Stanton administered the same sedative he'd been forced to give Bernadette a week earlier.

Then he turned to the figure lying on the bed, feeling quite suddenly almost overcome by the momentous nature of the meeting.

Two time travellers from different versions of the universe meeting in a third.

She was unconscious, as he'd expected her to be. Her wounded arm and shoulder were heavily bandaged and looked badly swollen. Her blood was poisoned just as his had been and without twenty-first-century medicine she would surely slowly die.

He put his hands on the coverlet.

There was no time to dwell any further on the incredible nature of the encounter. That he was about to touch the skin of a being from another age. After all, he was just such a being himself.

He pulled back the coverlet. She was dressed in the usual hospital standard open-backed nightshirt. He produced his pocket multi-tool, cut the straps and pulled the garment off her.

He gulped and almost looked away. He'd never seen such

damage done to a body. He'd seen bullet scars before, he had a couple himself. And whip scars and knife scars and the faded marks of bone-splitting bludgeons, but never *all on the same body.*

The tattoos were also unnerving, a tangled mass of poorly executed and extremely violent imagery in a naïve, amateur style that reminded Stanton of Russian prison tattoos. The disfiguring scribbles were punctuated with official-looking numberings and what appeared to be some form of medical record, listed under the woman's right breast. There was also a series of messy Caesarean scars at the bottom of her stomach.

He took the nightdress from his bag and leant forward to lift the woman's shoulders from the pillow and put the gown over her head.

Then, quite suddenly, the woman's left hand shot upwards and took hold of his throat in a vice-like grip, a grip Stanton recognized as practised and one that would collapse his larynx in seconds. He resisted the instinctive urge to grab at the wrist of the attacking arm, fully aware that in a tug of war the advantage lay with her. She had her grip established and he had only seconds left.

Her eyes were open.

He was sure she'd been unconscious. She was deeply fevered and her body was wasting away and yet some primeval survival instinct had jerked her from unconsciousness at the feel of an alien touch and lent her incredible strength.

'Nobody rapes me,' she snarled in English.

The pain in Stanton's throat was intense. He could feel the various cartilages in his larynx collapsing; his voicebox was about to be forced into his trachea. He'd never known a grip like it, and this was a woman, and a sick one at that.

He had no choice. His hands had been on her shoulders. He let go, drew both his hands back and then chopped them into either side of her neck.

The grip didn't slacken at all. Not a millimetre.

It was incredible.

He'd held back on the blow certainly, but only very slightly, because he didn't want to actually kill her. She was now very close to killing him.

He double-chopped her again. And again. Her neck was like steel cable. It was as if he was karate-chopping a lamppost.

His head was swimming. He was starting to black out. This was ridiculous. Impossible. Ten seconds earlier he had been about to remove a helpless woman from her hospital bed. Now the same woman was squeezing the last breath of life out of him.

He remembered the multi-tool with which he'd cut the straps on her gown. He'd put it on the cabinet beside her bed. He flailed an arm towards where he thought it would be and found it. The scissor function was still extended. He swung it round and plunged it deep into the woman's extended arm.

It gave him less than a second. He felt a momentary slackening. She hadn't let go but there was the tiniest fall in pressure. Her eyes had widened too. He did not believe that she was fully conscious but the stab in her arm had brought her a little closer to the surface.

He hit her again.

The eyes flamed for a moment. Then they closed.

She slipped back into unconsciousness.

And as she did so, slowly the vice opened.

Stanton had no time to dwell either on the agony in his throat or the appalling shock of this woman's savagery. She had nearly killed him, from a prone position on a hospital bed, weakened by infection and with one arm completely disabled. Tattoos or not, it seemed perhaps that those other Companions knew what they were doing when they chose her after all.

She seemed genuinely unconscious now but nonetheless Stanton was wary. He thought about administering a sedative but not knowing what drugs were already in her body decided he couldn't risk it. But he kept a needle ready just in case. He tore a length of sheet and bandaged the scissor wound he'd made, then he wrestled the nightdress on to her naked body and finally placed a lady's bed cap on her head.

It was a strange moment because with the cap on her head and the white ruff at her collar, this snarling savage was transformed into a picture of innocence and calm. Apart from one or two small scars, her face was unmarked and seeing it framed in white linen was a revelation. She looked *gentle*. Stanton could hardly recall the skinny, sinewy, scarred and disfigured warrior's body that lay beneath her gown.

He gathered her up in his arms and, stepping over the prostrate guards, crossed to the door and took a look outside. The corridor was empty. That was all the luck he needed. As long as he could get from this room unseen he felt confident he could brazen out the rest. He marched out of the room and towards the lift. He looked neither right nor left and held his head high. A nurse appeared in front of him. Instantly he barked an order.

'This patient is dehydrated and has fallen into a faint. Fortunately I was on an inspection round or she would be prostrate on the floor right now. But we will speak about that later. For the moment there is a wheelchair by the lift. Bring it immediately.'

It was agony for him to speak after the damage that the woman had done to his larynx. Perhaps his rasping voice was even more intimidating because the nurse jumped to attention and almost saluted. It wasn't her job to enforce security or to ask questions. Quite the opposite. Her job, which had been drummed into her since first she began her training, was to obey doctors. She scurried off at once, although in fact Stanton was walking so purposefully that despite her panicky desire to please they arrived at the wheelchair at the same time.

'Thank you, nurse, that will be all,' he said, gently lowering the woman into the chair.

While in the lift, he pulled off the surgeon's gown and stuffed it into a cavity under the seat of the wheelchair. Now he was a fond husband collecting his wife from hospital. When the lift doors opened on the ground floor he wheeled the chair confidently towards the front doors.

'Soon have you home, my dear,' he said as he passed the reception area.

Then straight through the front doors and out into the open air. There was a wheelchair ramp to the left of the stone stairs and moments later Stanton was putting his fellow Chronation into the Mercedes.

45

THE WOMAN'S WOUNDS had been nothing like as life-threatening as Stanton's own had been. He had been shot in the stomach; she had been shot in the arm and the upper chest, towards the shoulder, missing the heart and the lungs. Nonetheless, blood infection is equally serious whatever the size of wound that causes it, and Stanton's new roommate's arm was horribly swollen. He could only hope that it hadn't taken too deep a hold and would respond to antibiotics. The idea of performing an amputation in a hotel room was pretty daunting, even one which had such a new-fangled convenience as an en-suite bathroom.

To his relief, the woman responded to treatment, and once Stanton had cleaned her wounds and begun a course of antibiotics, she very quickly started to show signs of recovery. By the end of the first night her fever had begun to subside and her sleep was less disturbed.

He bathed her, attended to her bodily needs and fed her as best he could, spooning tiny amounts of thin soup into her mouth when her consciousness seemed closest to the surface. He wondered about trying to set up some kind of intravenous drip of sugar solution. He felt he had the skills to jerry-rig one but decided against it as it would have looked very strange to the maids and waiting staff who visited the room. Hotels don't like people dying on their premises and Stanton did not want to alert the management to how serious his 'sister's' condition had been when he brought her in.

He tended her for four whole days before she regained her consciousness and her strength began to return. In that time he could only speculate on the character and nature of this other version of himself and on the cosmic strangeness of their mutual situation.

And it was *cosmically* strange.

The chain of events that Isaac Newton had set in motion two (and three) centuries earlier had resulted in this incredible junction of beings from two separate worlds meeting in a third. In a hotel room.

As he sat watching her in the long hours of the night, measuring her pulse and listening to her breathing, Stanton had a constant sensation of being out of body. As if all the various versions of himself he now knew to have existed were somehow separate to *him*. His first life, which had ended with the spearmint kiss of a stranger in a cellar in Istanbul. His second, which was a mystery to him except for the knowledge that he had lived it in the century into which the woman sleeping near him had been born. And born long after he must have died. And now this third life, which began when his scarred and tattooed patient had first made her imprint in the dust on the cellar floor in Constantinople, and so rebooted the loop, thus sending Stanton and the whole world back around it once again.

And who was she? What terrible things had been done to her? And why? What world had these other Chronations been seeking to fix?

Having washed and cleaned her each day, he knew her scars by now as well as she must have known them herself. Better, in fact, particularly the crazed white spaghetti of healed lacerations that covered her back and buttocks and the backs of her legs.

These were marks of a cruel and terrifying abuse. She had suffered under a thick lash. A cat o' nine tails. Thin canes and heavy batons. She'd been stabbed with a stiletto dagger, slashed with knives and bitten by men and animals. She'd been shot and she had been burned. Stanton felt naked fury welling up inside him to see evidence of such abuse.

How had she even survived it?

The same way that she was currently surviving her near fatal encounter with septicaemia. Because she was clearly the toughest individual he had ever encountered, male or female. Not as strong as him, certainly, but immeasurably tougher.

Nonetheless, even a superwoman should have been dead with the kind of punishment and cruelty this woman had sustained. Clearly whoever had tormented her had also prevented her from dying. It seemed to Stanton that they had been trying to break her, and had refused to allow her release until they had done so. They had tortured her and beaten her but each time they had stitched her wounds and set her broken bones, the obvious conclusion being that they had done this in order that she would get well enough for them to attack her again.

Who did that? Who cared so much about controlling another person, bending them to their will? Subduing the spirit of a single individual?

He stared at the sleeping woman.

She didn't look so tough now.

Asleep on her pillow, her face framed by the white nightcap, the snowy sheets against her chin, her breath gentle and even. What dreams were diverting her subconscious, he wondered.

She had a fine face. Sharp and angular but noble. The nose had been broken and was bent, but not disfiguringly so. Stanton found himself wondering if she might even be beautiful.

He would know when he could see her eyes. He'd seen them once but only for a moment and then wild with fire and from a faraway place. He didn't know what colour they were.

Speculating on the colour of her eyes brought his thoughts almost inevitably to Bernadette. Those green and sparkling Irish eyes. Smiling eyes as the old song had it. Not smiling, though, the last time they'd met his. Then they'd been wet with anger and pain. Would he ever see them smile again?

He felt his own eyes closing. He was tired; he had tended the woman for days, getting very little sleep. His head nodded in his chair.

Almost asleep now. His breathing falling into a rhythm with that of his strange and mysterious charge. His comrade. In many ways a sort of sister.

But as he drifted he sensed the movement.

Of course he'd known he should have manacled her, secured her to the bed. But somehow he hadn't been able to bring himself to. Her wrists and ankles showed the marks of having been bound so many times, sore, permanently bruised and scarred. He just couldn't add to that. And she'd seemed so peaceful.

She wasn't peaceful any more.

His eyes snapped open to be confronted by a vision of death. An avenging angel, clad in voluminous white, descending on him like a snow eagle swooping down on a rabbit.

He saw her eyes now as she fell towards him, burning embers in a face of ice.

There had been a fountain pen and paper by her bed, with which Stanton had been keeping a diary of her symptoms. The pen was in her fist now. An inky dagger. She must have been aware of it for a while. Lying in bed, feigning unconsciousness, awaiting her chance.

There is always a weapon available if you care to find it.

That's what his SAS fight instructor had told him. Clearly she'd been taught the same lesson.

The pen was descending fast, its nib closing on his right eye, the ball of which it would pop before travelling on into his brain.

Stanton turned his head in time. The nib tore into the top of his earlobe and crumpled against his skull. The trajectory of her dive completed, the woman crashed down on top of him, her whole body against his, toe to toe, head to head, together in the easy chair.

This was Stanton's chance, an opportunity to use his greater weight. He rolled her, and even in this moment of extremis he was clear-headed enough to try not to land her on her injured arm. He wanted her well enough so that he could persuade her to stop trying to kill him.

The two of them rolled out of the chair, tipping it over on top of them as they hit the carpet. This time Stanton was on top, an advantage which he put to immediate use by pinning her.

'Stop this!' he spat in English, the language she had used to him. 'I'm your friend. I saved you.'

'You shot me!' she snarled. It was the first time he'd heard her speak since the moment in the hospital when she'd imagined in her delirium that he was trying to rape her. Did she sound Scottish?

'You shot *me*!' Stanton heard himself protesting.

'Because you were about to kill the fucking Kaiser, you fuck!'

'Because of Chronos,' he grunted, struggling to keep her pinned. 'I'm a Companion of Chronos. I *know* what you are. I know about Chronos. I'm from Chronos too.'

To Stanton's astonishment she actually smiled, stopped struggling and smiled.

Except it wasn't a smile of pleasure or fun, it was bitter and cold, really more of a sneer.

'I know. Asshole,' she said. 'I know you're from Chronos.'

'You *know*?'

Stanton was so astonished he momentarily relaxed his grip. Fortunately she didn't detect the half second of weakness, or if she did she decided not to exploit it.

'How do you know?' he asked.

'We read your letter.'

It was the last thing he'd expected. In fact, with all the distraction of discovering that he was not the only visitor from the future and of then establishing contact with his counterpart, he'd forgotten all about his letter. It had only ever been the longest of long shots that it would survive. A desperate throw of the dice, a nod towards history.

'My God,' he said. 'It was still there?'

'Yes, it was there. We found it on the night we entered the cellar. On the night I journeyed back in time.'

Now it was her body that relaxed. She no longer seemed predisposed to fight.

'So . . . can we talk?' Stanton asked. 'If I release you from this pin-down will you go back to bed, let me check you haven't done yourself any harm trying to kill me and let me order some tea so we can talk?'

She thought for a moment, then nodded.

Warily he released her and got to his feet. Reaching down he offered her a hand. He could see the thought process in her mind. This was a woman who clearly viewed every moment and every gesture with maximum suspicion. But she was still weak and her violent strike at him had tired her.

She took his hand and he drew her to her feet. She sat down on the bed but didn't get in.

'So, talk,' she said.

There was so much to discuss. Stanton decided to start with the most recent astonishing revelation.

'You actually read my letter? It was still there? After *a hundred and eleven years*?'

'Yes, it was still there. In the time that I come from Istanbul had been a dead town for nearly a century.'

'Dead?'

'It was cleared in the great starvations of the 1930s. All the cities of Eastern Europe and Asia Minor were. Prague, Warsaw, Budapest, Sarajevo, Zagreb, Istanbul. The Party couldn't feed them so instead they drove the people out into the country to make war on the peasants for what could be found. They died of starvation in their tens of millions, which of course was what was intended. Those that survived tried to fight back and the Party responded using chemical warfare. They poisoned everything south of the Danube. When the Master and I entered Newton's cellar, no one had been near the place in eighty years. The cellar was still locked.'

Stanton's mind was reeling. Chemical warfare? Mass starvation? Cities dead for decades? What sort of world had this woman come from?

He tried to focus his questions. Start with the most immediate. Like in all good fieldwork, deal with the most pressing issue first.

'Why did you try to kill me just then?' he asked. 'Surely you can see I've tried to help you?'

'It's my mission to kill you,' she replied.

'Yes, but you failed. Your mission was to kill me before I killed the Kaiser. Why bother now?'

She looked at him and suddenly the fire reignited in her eyes.

'Because you ruined my fucking century, you stupid fucking *cunt*!'

She lifted her nightdress, all the way to above her breasts revealing the length of her tortured body. '*You* did this to me. You did it to millions and millions of people. *Billions*. You killed my children!!'

And suddenly the rage was on her again. As she dropped the nightdress hem he saw her abdominals tense into rigid corrugated iron. One foot was moving backwards, preparing to anchor a second spring at him.

'Stop!' he said. 'Don't do it! I'll win and you know it. Maybe not on your day but this isn't your day. You're weak. You've been bedridden for a month and lost whatever weight you had. You can't beat me, so stop. You're just not well enough to fight me yet.'

She paused and looked at him hard.

'You're right. I'm not well yet,' she conceded. 'But soon I will be.'

She sat back on the bed and Stanton went into the vestibule where the internal telephone was situated. He ordered some tea and coffee and food.

'What's your name?' he asked when he returned.

'They call me Katie.'

'Short for Katherine?'

'No. K-T. Short for KT503b678.'

'I'm Hugh Stanton.'

'I know your name.'

'From my letter?'

'No. I've known it since I was six years old. All young pioneers learn it. You're in the history books.'

That certainly took him aback.

'Really?'

'Of course you are. We all learn of the unbalanced bourgeois British zealot who unwittingly lit the spark of revolution by trying to frame honest Socialists. How you were sheltered by the Irish whore Burdette, but that you betrayed her and ran like a coward, leaving her to the Fascist Monarchist police.'

Stanton swallowed hard.

'Well,' he said, trying not to think of Bernadette or what might have happened to her after the police realized she'd let him go. 'You know now that I'm not a zealot and I'm not unbalanced. I am just like you. I was brought to Cambridge in 2024. I presume you were brought to Cambridge too?'

'I heard the Master use that name,' Katie conceded. 'It's a bourgeois name. The place has a number now.'

'I was brought there by the Companions of Chronos.'

'I know,' she said. 'I've told you, we read your letter.'

'Well, then you know something about the terrible events of my own century,' Stanton said. 'You know that I killed the Kaiser to prevent the most terrible war in history. A war that marked the beginning of a terrible century. A century in which humanity learned to murder on an industrial scale. Whole populations died in the 1930s and 1940s, the Jews, the Gypsies, the Poles, the Ukrainians, all slaughtered. All slaughtered by Russian Soviet Communism.'

Now she really did smile. A broad wide smile that stretched fully across her face. And yet still a smile with not a single gram of joy in it.

The smile of a corpse.

'I know,' she repeated. 'I read your letter. I know about your "terrible" war, your "Great" War, which began with the killing of an archduke at Sarajevo . . . Tell me, Hugh Stanton, how long did it last? This war that so corrupted and cursed the century into which you were born?'

'Eleven years,' Stanton replied. '1914 to 1925. The Great War lasted eleven years.'

'Oh, *eleven years*,' Katie replied with bitter sarcasm. 'And tell me, Captain Stanton, how long did the *Second* World War last?'

Stanton was confused.

There had been no Second World War in the century from which Hugh Stanton had come.

The century which McCluskey had sought to correct.

In Stanton and McCluskey's century there had been only one world war. The Great War.

'One was enough,' Stanton asserted. 'More than a decade of deadlocked butchery. A butchery that ruined all the great nations of Europe utterly. Britain, France, Germany, Austria, Russia.'

'But not America,' Katie sneered. 'They didn't fight in this *terrible* war, did they? This war which you call Great?'

'No, they kept out of it. That was why it went on so long. Woodrow Wilson would have brought them in but he was shot on the steps of Congress by Isolationists. So the war dragged on in deadlock until in the end both Germany and Russia had Communist revolutions. Germany's under Luxemburg; Russia's under Stalin. You know what happened then from the letter I wrote. Stalin was stronger. He betrayed Luxemburg. He had her and Liebknecht murdered in the streets. The Russians spread their 'revolution' west, through the Ukraine and Poland, through Germany and into France and on to Spain. By 1930 only Britain remained free, holding out under Winston Churchill. Isolated, alone, with the Russians on the Channel. The rest of Europe and all of Asia was enslaved under Stalin's paranoid genocidal regime . . . a regime which murdered millions and millions of people, right up until 1951 when the Americans produced their bomb and destroyed Stalin's Soviet Empire in a single day. All those decades of misery for half the globe stemmed from the terrible Great War. The war I stopped.'

'Yes, you stopped it all right,' Katie agreed. 'Because of you, in my century there was no war in 1914. Germany was *not* destroyed. So Rosa Luxemburg didn't have her revolution in 1925 in a nation exhausted by a great war; instead she had her revolution in 1916. As a reaction to the brutal police state *you* brought about by killing the Kaiser. Her revolution didn't begin in a nation blighted by poverty and starvation and war exhaustion, like in your century. It began in the richest, most developed country on earth with the biggest army and the most advanced technology. In my century, the Russians weren't the top Communists, the Germans were. The German USSR that Luxemburg established in 1916 was a global colossus. So when the vermin Strasser had her killed and made himself German Soviet dictator, he was the most powerful man in the world. A red kaiser. The revolution spread to Russia and was unstoppable. *Then* Strasser began his war and along with his Russian servant Stalin he took over all of Europe, *including* Britain. There was no "Churchill", whoever the fuck *he* was, to "stand alone". Britain wasn't fit to fight anyone; it and its Empire had been fatally weakened and divided by the Civil War over Ireland. Strasser's "revolution" spread to China, India, South America. Soon only America remained outside German Soviet control. But they didn't save the world. Because when the atomic bomb was finally developed, it was Germany not America that had it. Berlin ordered a nuclear strike. I was one of the soldiers that occupied the rubble of New York. The globe was conquered! You think *you* lived in a shit century? With your *one* war, a bit of genocide and a half-arsed little nuclear strike. And after that nothing to worry about but something called *global fucking warming*, whatever that is. Try living in a century where the *entire planet* is ruled by a fourth-generation Communist lunatic. Where the *entire planet* is one vast network of prison camps. Where love is treason and they make you drown your own babies and every person in the world is an ant, a drone, a robot. Beaten, murdered. Dying in the mines, starving in the fields. Or doing mass synchronized dances in the Red Squares of Berlin, London, Moscow and Washington. Thousands prancing about with red ribbons in their hands while the Party fossils stand on their platforms and gloat. A world where there is no freedom. No individuality. No joy of any kind. *That's* the world you bequeathed us, when you shot the Kaiser and sparked a revolution. You stupid bastard. You stupid *stupid* bastard. Your century was paradise! Why didn't you leave well alone?'

She burst into tears.

Stanton was completely taken aback. In the short time he'd known Katie he'd come to presume that her heart and soul were constructed out of the same stuff as her body. He'd never imagined she could cry.

He tried in vain to justify what he'd done. To explain why the Companions of Chronos of his world had tasked him to do what he had done.

'Katie, you read my history. The Russian USSR killed tens of millions before it was beaten.'

'But they *were* beaten! In the end they were stopped. How could you have thrown away a century where the killing *actually stopped* and what's more had been stopped for *seventy years*?'

Stanton could not meet her eye. The dawning realization that his whole mission, the mission which had begun with the murder of his own family, had actually resulted in the enslavement of the whole world was too much to bear.

46

IT TOOK KATIE another week to fully recover, during which time she and Stanton agreed an uneasy truce and formed an equally uneasy alliance. Sitting together in their suite at the Kempinski, they made a plan.

Clearly the century in which they were both now living was heading for utter disaster. Katie had failed to stop Stanton killing the Kaiser and so history was developing as it had done in her century, hurtling towards a global totalitarian misery without end.

If nothing else was changed, the whole dreadful sequence of events that would lead to four generations of psychopathic dictators ruling the earth would play out exactly as before.

Both Stanton and Katie could see that it was imperative for them to try to influence the shape of this third loop in time using their unique knowledge of the previous two. They had to try to find a way to prevent things from taking the course that they had in the second loop, and perhaps beginning a history which was preferable to even the one in the first loop, the one Stanton had been born into. And which he had helped throw away.

This last thought was still a very sore and sensitive subject for Katie. She still could not begin to understand how the Chronations of Stanton's time could have imagined that a century in which global totalitarianism had been defeated could ever be improved on.

'I suppose we wanted a century in which it had never existed at all,' Stanton tried to explain, 'and also, after that we wanted a world where the applications of human ingenuity didn't develop on such crass and environmentally disastrous lines.'

But the more he heard about the world from which Katie had come, the more he understood how utterly and criminally deluded McCluskey and her crew of smug geriatrics had been. How deluded *he* had been. People made history and people screwed it up, that was what McCluskey had always maintained, and she sure had been right about that. Incredibly, she had ended up proving her own thesis. *She* screwed up.

If only Newton hadn't been so damn clever.

But all that was in several pasts now. There was only one present, the here and now, and they had to make a plan.

Sitting up together late at night, Katie ravenously devouring every delicacy she could find to be delivered to their suite, they decided what they must do.

They would kill Rosa Luxemburg.

At first Katie had wanted to kill Strasser. He, after all, had been the one to hijack and corrupt Luxemburg's revolution. He had fathered the hellish dynasty that spawned generations of homicidal demi-gods to lord it over a global population of synchronized puppets.

But Stanton disagreed.

'Strasser was a thug,' he argued. 'He stole something noble, even beautiful, and debased it. Anybody could do what Strasser did, and if we take him out of the equation somebody else will take his place. Stalin or one of the other members of Strasser's Central Committee.'

Katie had by this time explained her history in detail and Stanton recognized many of the names included in it from his own century: Goebbels, Röhm, Zinoviev. Others he had never heard of: Beria, Kamenev, Hess. Adolf Hitler.

'Anyone can destroy something,' Stanton went on, 'but to *create* it takes talent and I'd suggest that to make a successful revolution takes genius. Luxemburg is a uniquely talented in-dividual, a political visionary and a truly great communicator. I know, I've met her. She's more special than any of the dull bullies who followed her. And without her there'd have been nothing for them *to* follow. We need to remove the shovel, not the shit.'

Stanton didn't like the idea. In fact, the plan he was advocating pained him deeply. He knew Luxemburg. She was a good woman. A kind woman . . . and Bernadette loved her. But he also could see that taking her out of the German equation was his best shot at putting right the wrong he'd done. At preventing the German revolution from happening and hence preventing its disastrous corruption followed by its world domination.

'So we kill Luxemburg,' Katie said, tearing at steak and sausage with her fingers.

'Yes.'

'And then I'll kill Strasser.'

'That's your choice. Right now he's only twenty-two years old.'

'I don't care if he's only twenty-two months, twenty-two days. I'll tear him to pieces with my bare hands and eat his heart while it's still beating. Then I'll kill the rest of his committee,' she said, 'even the ones who are only children now. Then I'll find the parents of the ones that haven't yet even been born and I'll kill them too. And I'll kill them horribly. In revenge for the crimes that will now never be committed.'

Katie drank deep at water from the jug. She took no alcohol, explaining that remaining in control while others did not had proved useful to her in the past.

'And maybe,' she went on, wiping her mouth with her sinewy, ink-blackened arm and looking hard at Stanton, 'maybe I'll kill you as well because the truth is that all of this, *all* of this, is your fault.'

Stanton stared back, meeting the challenge of her eyes. He hadn't asked for any of this. And he'd lost his children too.

'Maybe you're right, Katie,' he said quietly. 'Although I think you'll find I'm not so easy to kill. What I and the people of my time set in motion was disastrous, that's pretty clear. But I stayed with the mission when I saw how it had gone wrong. I could have walked away but I didn't. I found you and I saved you. And because of that we have a chance to pool our knowledge and try again. There's a phrase from my century, *third time lucky*. Do you know it?'

'There was no luck in my time, Hugh Stanton. The word and the very *idea* were banned. The Great Navigator directed all things for the peace and harmony of all. Luck is a bourgeois notion.'

'Well, we're directing things now. And we're going to get it right this time. And for that reason, before we begin our plan we have to go back to Constantinople one more time. To the cellar from which we were both born.'

'Why?'

'Because we're going to make a better century and, when we've done it, we want it to be left that way. So we must place your warning next to mine.'

47

TRAVELLING WITH KATIE was complex. The Chronations of her
time had not had the resources or the technological sophistication to supply her with papers or currencies. In fact, there had
been very few early-twentieth-century documents left for them to
forge. All evidence of the petit bourgeois past had been destroyed
in successive 'cultural' revolutions and purges. Great buildings,
museums, pictures and books. Virtually nothing remained of
the time before the Dynasty of Great Navigators had taken the
helm.

It had been as much as the Chronations of Katie's world had
been able to do to smuggle her to the ghost town once known as
Istanbul and place her in the cellar in the dockland area at the
appointed time. Katie had arrived in 1914 with not much more
than a couple of guns and a few bits of gold which had been
supplied by a senior Party dentist. The only aids the Master of the
State Research and Education Facility had been able to give her
were a compass, a map of Europe, a piece of paper with the
location and time of the assassination of the Kaiser and a suit of
rough male clothing and boots. She had lived by her wits as she
made her way across Turkey and the Balkans, stealing and killing
to get whatever she needed.

'I've been on the run for most of my adult life,' she explained.
'That's why they chose me. But if you want my opinion anybody
could survive in this world. The fields and woods are full of food,
the peasants are trusting and the border guards shout out a

warning before they shoot, which is very foolish of them since it allows me to shoot them first.'

Stanton and Katie travelled by train across Europe. Katie maintained her guise as a man wearing a suit of clothes that Stanton bought her. She refused point blank to wear the women's clothing of the time, maintaining not unreasonably that it was ridiculous and would severely restrict her fighting ability.

Due to her lack of papers they were not able to cross borders by train but instead got out at the last stop before each one and hiked out into the country to find a suitable point to cross. By such a manner the two Chronations crossed Europe north to south and returned once more to the city where both their adventures had begun.

Once more Stanton took rooms at the Pera Palace Hotel and that evening in the dark of night, for the final time, he made his way to the house that Isaac Newton had bought when first the business of Chronos began.

'I wanted to ask you,' he said to Katie as they reconnoitred the street, 'was it really necessary to kill the doctor and the nurse when you came out of the cellar?'

'The woman in the room in the corridor heard my footsteps,' Katie answered. 'My boots were too heavy, and steel shod.'

'Didn't you think to come in rubber soles?'

Katie stopped in the darkened street and turned to Stanton.

'Those boots were donated by a soldier who probably paid with his life for losing them. Without them I would have come to this time either barefoot or at best in canvas moccasins. You have no comprehension of the utter poverty of the world you created, Hugh Stanton.'

Stanton kept silent after that. Together they broke into the hospital building using Stanton's skeleton keys and crept down into the cellar.

It was just as Stanton had left it, with the two sets of footprints and the chair and the table on which lay the letter to the future that Stanton had left.

'Your history,' Katie said. 'The one I found.'

'No,' Stanton corrected. 'The one you found was left at the beginning of the century in which you were born, the century I created which disappeared the moment you entered the past and rebooted history all over again. This letter was left in the new version of the twentieth century, the one that you are creating. The one in which you'll die. That letter is the same letter as the one you found down to its last molecule but it exists in a different version of time.'

'Well, let us hope there's only ever one version of mine,' she said.

Katie approached the table and put a second envelope beside Stanton's. The history of her own twentieth century. A catalogue of utter misery, written out during the long hours they had spent travelling on the train.

Two different versions of the future lying side by side. Both terrible but one vastly more terrible than the other.

'So, it's done,' she said. 'Now if another traveller passes this way at least there's a chance they'll know all that we know.'

'But if we succeed in our mission,' Stanton replied, 'if we're able to prevent the German revolution, perhaps there won't be another traveller.'

'Perhaps,' Katie said.

Stanton turned his torch beam from the table where Katie was standing to the shadowy arches where the ancient dusty bottles were laid down.

There were the footprints he had left, halfway between Katie's and the arches. Stanton played his torchlight into the darkness of the vault.

A thought occurred to him.

One which made his soul shiver with dread.

He stepped towards the darkness.

'Where are you going?' Katie asked.

'Towards the past,' he said. 'Your footsteps are ahead of mine. I came here to change history and I did. A century passed and then you came for the same reason, but time had slipped a little and the sentry box had moved. Just like Sengupta said, *As each loop of space and time progresses, space and time are gained.*'

'Sentry box?' Katie asked. 'Sengupta? What are you talking about?'

Stanton didn't reply. He was under the first arch now.

He turned his torch to the floor. Were there marks? He thought perhaps there were but the dust was so thick he couldn't be sure. He shone his light once more on the bottles, sooty black upon their shelves.

'Perhaps I wasn't the first,' he said. 'After all, why should I have been?'

And then he saw it.

Wedged in among the rows of bottles.

An envelope.

He reached out and took it from its place.

Then he walked a little further into the catacomb. McCluskey had said it stretched back away under the street and the next house along.

After a few more steps Stanton found another envelope.

Then another.

And another.

Five, six.

Nine, ten.

'What are you doing?' He heard Katie's voice behind him. 'If we've done what we came to do we need to clear out.'

Stanton returned to where she was standing. He was carrying the brittle, yellowing papers in his hands. He had twelve, perhaps there were more; the cellar went further back and deeper than he had gone.

'It's what I feared,' he said quietly. 'I wasn't the first. There have been many.'

He put the bundle of papers down on the table beside his and Katie's own.

They sat together on the floor and by the light of their torches began to read.

The stories of a dozen centuries. A dozen *twentieth* centuries.

The same hundred and eleven years repeated over and over again beginning each time in 1914. Sometimes the authors came back to save or to kill the Archduke. Others to save or kill the Kaiser. Others came with their sights set on some different figure altogether, monsters in the making, too young as yet to have committed the crimes they were destined to commit if left to live. But each time the result had been the same. A nightmare catalogue of human brutality and human misery. War and genocide. Bigotry and fear.

Some versions, like Stanton's own century, had resulted in some kind of human progress, although never it seemed enough to persuade the Chronations of those times to leave well alone. Others, like Katie's, were simply unmitigated nightmares descending ever further into a hellish darkness, the type of which only humanity is capable of inventing.

Sitting together in the beams of their torchlight, Stanton and Katie read of dictators and secret policemen. Of terrible science and murderous disease. They read of Communism corrupted over and over again. And also of something called Fascism, of which neither of them had heard but which had sometimes gained the upper hand, although the result was just the same.

The name Hitler came up in four separate histories.

Stanton didn't know him at all; the Austrian fanatic had played no part in his century, but Katie knew him as one of Strasser's henchmen.

In other centuries, however, it seemed this terrible man had been able to make himself the boss, a monster the equal of Stalin and Strasser. Harnessing Germany's might to conquer half the world and murder half the people in it. Two previous Chronations had come back specifically to kill him while he was still a penniless dosser, painting his watercolours in Vienna.

Hours passed. Time was moving on. Soon the hospital above

them would be up and bustling. Stanton laid the papers back on the table all together.

'I think perhaps we're the first Chronations to meet,' he said. 'Those who came before us simply rebooted the previous one's creation and the loop went round again. You were supposed to kill me but instead we met.'

Katie nodded, still staring moist-eyed at the papers she'd been reading.

'So many other women forced to kill their babies,' she whispered.

'This can't go on,' Stanton said firmly. 'The twentieth century can't spin in time for ever, a howl of pain ringing across the universe into eternity. Same century following same century, a planet and a race lost in loop, destined to suffer alternative versions of the same nightmare for ever.'

'No,' Katie said quietly, tears glistening on her cheeks now. 'It can't go on.'

'So, after we've killed Rosa Luxemburg,' Stanton went on, 'and done what best we can to give this new century a chance, we have to go to Cambridge.'

'Yes,' Katie said, 'and destroy Newton's box. There can be no more Chronations. I must be the last.'

48

KT503B678 NEVER GOT the chance to go to Cambridge and close the loop in time, but she died ensuring that Stanton might.

The Turkish police were waiting for them when they tried to leave the house. They'd lingered too long reading ancient histories in the cellar and been overheard by the night nurse on duty.

As they opened the front door of the building, car headlamps were turned on and a warning shouted. The street was full of police, crouching behind cars and wagons.

Katie made her decision without hesitation.

'I will engage these people,' she said. 'You find another way out.'

'But—' Stanton began to protest but Katie stopped him.

'You can survive much better in this civilized world than me,' she said, 'and besides, it's time for me to die. I always swore that I'd never take my own life, that the Party would have to kill me, that I'd die fighting them. Well, this way I will. Because if my death helps you escape, then perhaps the Party will never even exist. Besides, it's time. Time for me to join my babies.' Her eyes were bright and far away. 'Go. Do what you can for this last twentieth century. Then go to Cambridge. You *have* to go to Cambridge, Hugh. Make it so that finally history can move on.'

'I will,' Stanton replied.

Then he leant forward and kissed her on the cheek.

To his surprise she reached out and put her arms round him. Drawing him to her in an embrace. It was the first physical contact of any sort that they had had since she had leapt from her sick bed at the Kempinski hotel in an effort to kill him.

The hug lasted only a few seconds but it seemed to Stanton that in those seconds there was a world of sorrow. Her body quivered as she gripped him tight and laid her head on his shoulder.

When she stepped away, her eyes were glistening with tears.

She produced a gun from each of her pockets.

'Goodbye,' she said.

'Goodbye.'

Stanton turned away and made his way back through the house. There were doctors, nurses and patients peeking out of doors but he ignored them and they didn't try to stop him.

Once more he was heading for a rooftop escape and he realized that for the second time he was leaving behind him a woman about whom he had come to care deeply.

He made his way up the various flights of stairs. The sound of rapid fire behind told him that Katie had engaged the police. He knew that she would make sure he had enough grace to make his escape. It wouldn't be their choice when to kill her but hers when to die.

He found a skylight in the attic of the building and made his way out into the night.

Alone once more.

He was never to return to the house of Chronos in Constantinople.

Instead he made his final trip to Berlin.

He knew where to find Rosa Luxemburg. The history of her time of struggle and the glorious revolution that followed had been holy writ to Katie and her fellow Communist pioneers. During their time together travelling across Europe she had been able to give Stanton the address of the safehouse in which Luxemburg and Liebknecht had gone underground during the months of persecution. That house had become a shrine in Katie's century, a place of pilgrimage for high Party officials. Stanton intended to ensure that in this century it would be remembered only as the place where a briefly notorious Social Democrat had been shot by an unknown assassin.

And then . . . then?

Stanton knew what then. He had thought of nothing else during his final train journey from Istanbul.

He would find Bernadette Burdette. Whether she was in custody in Berlin or home in Ireland or somewhere else altogether, he'd find her. He would make her travel with him to Cambridge, at gunpoint if necessary. Then, he would take her to the Master's Lodge at Trinity and somehow he would show her Newton's box. Then once she had seen it and knew that he had not lied, he would destroy it, closing the loop in time for ever.

And then he and Bernadette could face the last ever twentieth century together. Her riding pillion on his 1914 Enfield.

That was Stanton's plan. It was Guts Versus Newton.

End game.

And so from his hotel room at the Kempinski Stanton equipped himself for another assassination. He had no body armour this time, having left it in the apartment he had shared with Bernadette, but he had one of his Glock pistols, which he checked and loaded carefully, although he knew he would require only one bullet.

He made his way to the secret Socialist safehouse and lay in wait, hiding in the car he had hired for the job. Katie had told him that Rosa Luxemburg was known to emerge each day, heavily disguised, ready to go about her business of agitation and revolution.

As expected she emerged from the house. Liebknecht wasn't with her but she was flanked by two bodyguards. Stanton hoped he would not have to kill them also. He doubted it would be necessary; he had a clean shot.

Sitting in the driver's seat, he wound down the window and, resting his pistol on his arm, took aim. He didn't need a rifle; the range was close enough and the Glock an accurate weapon.

Then he heard a noise behind him. Turning he saw that a man was leaning in through the passenger window, which was open thanks to the late summer warmth. The man was pointing a gun at Stanton. A gun Stanton recognized as a type not known in 1914, and which, like his own weapon, was made of polymer, a substance not yet invented.

And Stanton understood.

Another century had passed.

A century in which he'd killed Rosa Luxemburg but must then have died himself because he had not been able to destroy Newton's box.

For here was another visitor from the future.

A man come to prevent the assassination of Rosa Luxemburg.

Stanton thought all this in the moment his eyes met his brother Chronation.

And he wanted to cry out: 'Kill me if you must but for God's sake go to Cambridge and destroy the box.'

But thought is quicker than speech.

He never said a word.

And at that moment in space and time, Hugh Stanton was taken out of the loop.

49

ISAAC NEWTON STARED at the spinning wheel.

It was nearly midnight and he was utterly exhausted, having spent many hours in a coach returning from his trip to Cambridge.

Now he was home in his niece's house and she had prepared him hot milk because he professed himself too preoccupied to sleep. And so they sat together, she spinning thread on her wheel and Newton staring into it. Round and round it went, returning after each revolution to the place it started and then spinning around again.

Newton saw space and time in that wheel. He saw it spinning round and round but never progressing. In constant motion but also stationary. Never moving beyond its fixed course.

Was he right to have arranged to pass on the benefits of his insight? Was it *always* better to know? That had been the guiding principle of his life. Better to know. To shed light on the mysteries of the universe.

But this time? To offer men yet unborn the chance to cheat fate? To shape a different destiny to the one God had created for them?

Isaac Newton was a Christian man. He had spent a lifetime trying to understand God but he had never desired to *be* God.

He decided that he had made a mistake. Sometimes it was better to simply leave well alone.

Time was not the spinning wheel.

Time was the thread it made.

In the morning he would go back to Cambridge and demand that Master Bentley return his box. Having made the decision, Newton felt that he would sleep more easily.

And he did, for when his niece shook him gently to usher him to bed she discovered that the old man was dead.

Ben Elton is one of Britain's most provocative and entertaining writers. From celebrity to climate change, from the First World War to the end of the world, his books give his unique perspective on some of the most controversial topics of our time.

He has written fourteen major bestsellers, including *Stark*, *Popcorn*, *Inconceivable* (filmed as *Maybe Baby*, which he also directed), *Dead Famous*, *High Society*, *The First Casualty* and *Two Brothers*.

Elton's multi-award winning TV credits include *The Young Ones*, *Blackadder* and *The Thin Blue Line*. His stage hits include the Olivier Award winner *Popcorn* and the global phenomenon *We Will Rock You*.

Loved the book?

Join thousands of other readers online at

AUSTRALIAN READERS:

randomhouse.com.au/talk

NEW ZEALAND READERS:

randomhouse.co.nz/talk